12/1£

Praise for the delightful Hannah and Kiki mysteries . . .

Love and the Single Corpse

"There's never a dull moment in Griffin's latest Hannah and Kiki romp . . . The engaging, mature characters who populate the pages will be enormously appealing to older audiences."
—*Publishers Weekly*

"These two weave their way through this delightful story while taking pot shots at each other and anyone else who gets in the way. Full of humor, this 'frolicking' mystery leads us on a merry chase."
—*Rendezvous*

"Readers will have lots of fun with Kiki and Hannah, and though there's a lot of good-natured humor here, this book also takes a hard look at some of today's current medical practices."
—*Romantic Times*

"This lighthearted look at the elite and their foibles is delightful."
—*Old Book Barn Gazette*

Date with the Perfect Dead Man

"You will snicker, chuckle, and finally laugh out loud at all the funny mannerisms and antics of the characters. The trip from page one to the end is a quick and hilarious one."

—*Rendezvous*

"A hilarious amateur sleuth tale. The protagonists are extremely funny yet likable even when tension is at its peak. Annie Griffin shows her talent by pulling off the difficult task of putting a mystery inside a mystery and making it seem easy to accomplish."

—Harriet Klasner

A Very Eligible Corpse

"A humorous and diverting new series."

—*Library Journal*

"This delightful mystery is full of twists and turns. Annie Griffin delivers a first rate whodunit that will keep readers guessing until the last page. It's a fast-paced page turner that's wickedly funny."

—*Affaire de Coeur*

"Will leave readers laughing from start to finish. Annie Griffin has scribed a winning opening gambit in what is hoped to be a long-running series."

—*Midwest Book Review*

"It's such a treat to see people in ther sixties presented as individuals, not stereotypes . . . *A Very Eligible Corpse* is told well and the plot is all too believable, with a cast of characters that will ably carry on a series."

—*Mystery Review*

Tall, Dead, and Handsome

ANNIE GRIFFIN

BERKLEY PRIME CRIME, NEW YORK

This is a work of fiction. Names, characters, places, and incidents either are the product of the author's imagination or are used fictitiously, and any resemblance to actual persons, living or dead, business establishments, events, or locales is entirely coincidental.

TALL, DEAD, AND HANDSOME

A Berkley Prime Crime Book / published by arrangement with the author

PRINTING HISTORY
Berkley Prime Crime mass-market edition / November 2001

All rights reserved.
Copyright © 2001 by Sally Chapman Osbon.
Cover art by Mary Ann Lashen.
Cover design by George Long.

This book, or parts thereof, may not be reproduced in any form without permission.
For information address: The Berkley Publishing Group,
a division of Penguin Putnam Inc.,
375 Hudson Street, New York, New York 10014.

Visit our website at
www.penguinputnam.com

ISBN: 0-425-18223-1

Berkley Prime Crime Books are published
by The Berkley Publishing Group,
a division of Penguin Putnam Inc.,
375 Hudson Street, New York, New York 10014.
The name BERKLEY PRIME CRIME and the BERKLEY PRIME CRIME
design are trademarks belonging to Penguin Putnam Inc.

PRINTED IN THE UNITED STATES OF AMERICA

10 9 8 7 6 5 4 3 2 1

ONE

It was lust that propelled Kiki Goldstein down the sidewalk that sparkling April morning—pure, bodice-ripping, lip-smacking, unadulterated physical and emotional greed that saturated every cell, from each frothy strand of her bottle-blonde hair down to the tiny hearts glued to her "Kiss Me" peach toenails.

She would have called it by another name. A romantic hunger. A passionate yearning. A ringing of the whoopee bells in the temple of her love. She had spent a lifetime applying absurdly romantic interpretations to the carnality that, from the age of thirteen, had driven her with the power of nuclear fusion. When the truth was all so simple. Kiki Goldstein loved men. And it was for this and this alone that she chugged down the pavement, breasts bouncing, high heels clicking, in hot pursuit of her more practical sister, Hannah Malloy.

With an exaggerated exhale of frustration, Kiki hustled as fast as her frame (plumpish), age (sixtyish), and stiletto heels (foolish) allowed. Which kept Hannah many paces ahead. Kiki detested physical exertion outside of Macys annual lingerie sale or the bedroom. The tight clothes and high heels she always wore weren't suited to it, and such vigorous activity wreaked havoc on her undergarments, which were exotic and of complex engineering. But each step Hannah took brought her that much closer to the Hill Creek town hall and the total annihilation of what Kiki considered the only hope for her currently barren love life.

"Don't you do it, Hannah!" she shouted, one fist punched into her hip, the other wildly swinging her fake fur handbag. "You'll ruin my life. I need a man, dang it, and I'm going to do whatever it takes to get one."

Never taking her sister's melodramatics seriously, Hannah smiled and playfully cupped her hand against her ear. "Ah, spring is in the air. It's mating season, and we hear the familiar cry of the brightly plumed California Crested Mancatcher, identified by its peculiar squawking noise."

"Go ahead, make fun if you want," Kiki called out as she stomped along, her breathing labored. "But I'm telling you, this time I'm really desperate."

Hannah chuckled. Kiki had been desperate since puberty. Brisk in mind and body, Hannah moved her tall, slim form determinedly down the tree-lined sidewalk, skillfully dodging a Rollerblading grandfather and a young woman pushing a baby stroller at max speed. But after a moment, the frantic snapping of Kiki's high heels and the knowledge of Kiki's bad knees softened Hannah's heart. She stopped and waited for her sister.

Confronted once again with Kiki's outfit, Hannah wrinkled her nose. Courtesy of the Sausalito thrift shop, Kiki resembled a senior citizen hooker, her short, stout body packed into a leopard-print spandex skirt topped with a fringed black motorcycle jacket. Her chunky feet were squeezed into silver open-toed heels a size too small, resulting in a bulging at the front of the foot Kiki called toe cleavage. To complete the fashion disaster, Kiki's hair swept upwards into something akin to a smashed cabbage, her eyes were laden with the usual fuzzy false eyelashes, and her Tahiti Pink lipstick lay on her lips as thick as fudge.

Watching Kiki trudge up the sidewalk with the stooped posture and tight geisha steps enforced by her skirt and high heels, Hannah wondered why menopause drove some women into such bizarre fashion excesses. Was there something about decreased estrogen that made them obsess with animal print clothing, exaggerated jewelry, and ludicrous shoes? But Kiki's fashion philosophy was, if you've got it, flaunt it, and if you ain't got it, cover it up with something flashy. In contrast, Hannah was known for the simple elegance of her clothing. Her primary submission to vanity was her shoulder-length hair, which Lady Clairol kept a youthful auburn.

Huffing and puffing, Kiki at last caught up at the foot of the walkway leading to town hall. The quaint brown stone building was of pseudo-Spanish design, surrounded by politically sensitive, California-native, drought-resistant shrubbery. There the sisters paused, Kiki for oxygen, Hannah for courage.

Turning around, Hannah fixed her keen eyes on the town.

Hill Creek, a small suburban village in Marin County just north of San Francisco, was a special place, part magic and part mundane, a town of professionals, of eccentrics and professional eccentrics, where dogs had therapists and the locals took care of their karma with evangelistic fervor. What Hannah loved most about Hill Creek was its woodland beauty and small town atmosphere, its feeling of being an oasis in the middle of the techno-fueled, traffic-jammed Bay Area metropolis.

Hannah inhaled the cool air, ripe with the scent of last night's rain, and drank in the sight of Mt. Tamalpais towering majestically behind the town, its lush green slopes veiled in fog. She admired the town's tree-lined main street, the quaint ivy-covered shops, and the flower-filled planters dotting the sidewalks. The charming sight reminded her of the town's uniqueness, of what she was trying to save. Over the years the influx of high-paid professionals had lured in the hip chain stores, designer coffee bars, and boutiques with dresses that cost more than Hannah's monthly pension. But although the town had changed, it had not been ruined. Hannah straightened her shoulders and curled her hands into fists. At least not yet.

She pivoted to the town hall entrance. *Be bold*, she told herself. *Be decisive and fearless*, she commanded silently, then, feeling a gnawing anxiety, checked her watch and wondered if it would be better to put it off until after lunch. It would be so much easier to save the town from ruin on a full stomach.

"Please, Hannah, I'm begging you. Don't do it," Kiki whined, pulling her sister's hand to the abundant silicone of her chest. "It will be the end of all my dreams."

"Really?" Hannah raised an eyebrow. "From the stories you tell over breakfast, your dreams usually involve oiled-up lifeguards and leather thongs."

Kiki narrowed her eyes into what she hoped would be a look of belittling contempt, but these things never worked for her, and she succeeded only in dislodging one of her eyelashes. "I can't help my dream life," she said, contorting her face as she pressed the eyelash back on with her finger. "It's my id or psyche or whatever, and it's not my fault if it's X-rated. And you know what I mean. If you run against Alex Portman for mayor, he'll see both of us as enemies, and he'll never ask me out."

"This isn't war. It's just a small town election for mayor. The truth is, I don't think you're Alex's type. I'm sure he finds you very attractive," Hannah fibbed, to protect her sister's feelings, "but with all the female attention he gets from his seminars, he's probably interested in much younger women." That was the kindest way of putting it she could think of. The reality was this: Alex Portman would never give Kiki or any woman in her early sixties a second glance, in spite of being close to that age himself. A preening, egotistical, barnyard rooster, he would more likely be interested in twenty-year-old twins who had posed for *Penthouse*.

"You're wrong about that," Kiki replied with the irrational confidence wired into her at birth. "I have loads of assets no younger woman can compete with."

"I doubt he's interested in your IRA."

Kiki emitted an exasperated whoosh of air. "Just spit it out, Hannah. You don't think I have a chance with him, do you?"

Hannah thought that was exactly what she had been saying. When it came to men, sometimes you just had to hit Kiki smack between the eyes with the ugly truth. "You have a better chance of a beagle flying down from the sky and kissing you on the lips." Hannah's forehead corrugated when she saw her sister's pained expression. Hannah's barbs only masked the soft spot she had felt for Kiki from the time they were toddlers. "I'm sorry, but I don't want you to get hurt, especially by a man like Alex. He's a self-obsessed braggart who's made his reputation off some brainless seminars."

"They're not brainless. They taught me to explore new spiritual dimensions," Kiki said. "Before his seminar I had no idea I had these paranoxes in my inner life."

"The word is 'paradox.' "

Kiki waggled a hand. "Whatever. You should try one, Hannah. His seminars would open up your emotional channels."

Hannah let out a dismissive "pfft" that communicated more than words. She hadn't taken Alex's seminar, and didn't plan to, even though she was just about the only one in town who hadn't. Bravado renewed, Hannah charged up the walkway.

Being mayor of Hill Creek was far from a high-stress position and left plenty of time for Alex Portman to run his popular seminars, "Busting Your Love Barriers." The one-day seminars had earned him the informal title of Dr. Love. It was true that Hill Creek residents had bewildering difficulty in maintaining love relationships, but Hannah felt certain this was because of a rampant disease called self-obsessionitis, and not subconscious negative images as Alex assured everyone. Granted, Alex had a gift for turning complex psychological issues into mass-marketable pabulum. His cure for emotional upsets was an absurdly simple process he called Holistic Floral Visualization. Whenever you felt yourself coming up against one of your love barriers, you closed your eyes, pressed your fingers together in front of your face and visualized a certain flower that supposedly represented the special love deep inside you. Kiki's flower was a daisy. The very idea of it made Hannah want to puke up her wholegrain breakfast muffins, but everyone else in town seemed enamored with it, their brains filled with daisies and dahlias to the point of hay fever.

"It's so like you, Hannah. Always different from the rest," Kiki said, waddling behind. "If everybody's going upstream, you've got to go downstream. If they're to the right, you're to the left. And you're wrong about Alex and me. That second time I took Busting Your Love Barriers I went up to him afterwards. I asked him about that date I had with Bernie, and if he thought Bernie had backed off because he feared my sexuality."

"Iraqi commandos would fear your sexuality," Hannah tossed over her shoulder.

Kiki ignored the comment. "And when Alex spoke to me I could tell he understood my deepest, innermost, truest self. He had this intense look on his face—"

"Gas pains," Hannah muttered.

"And I think we really connected."

They reached the town hall steps, where Hannah stopped to organize her thoughts. The last thing she wanted was to hinder Kiki's love life, but Kiki's love objects changed as often as her hairdo, and usually turned out just as badly.

Kiki dug into her handbag and pulled out her checkbook, opening it and pointing to the little calendar on the back of the check ledger.

"See this? I've been keeping track of my romantic encounters. I mark the days where I've had physical contact with a man by circling them in red."

"Are you counting your chiropractor?"

"Not funny. Take a look."

Hannah peered more closely at it, which was difficult without her reading glasses. "I don't see any marks."

"My point exactly." Kiki shoved the checkbook back in her purse.

Hannah affectionately took her sister's hands in hers. "Kiki, try to understand that I have to take some action. As of this morning, Alex has canceled four meetings with me. If he isn't going to listen to my concerns about Signatech moving to town, then I have no choice but to become the mayor myself and take charge of things. Or at least try."

Hannah said this with more confidence than she felt. She was the type who kept to herself and was more interested in poetry and gardening than public office. The idea of running for mayor and putting herself in front of the whole town was radically contrary to her nature. But Alex was pushing the town council to allow Signatech, a growing software company, to move to a Hill Creek site only a few blocks from town center, and Hannah mightily opposed it.

Years ago, as a hippie in Haight-Ashbury, Hannah had protested against the Vietnam War, poverty, and oil tank spills. She had marched for women's rights, burned her bra, ripped up other people's draft cards, and sang "Blowin' in the Wind" as the police pushed her into a paddy wagon. It all seemed so long ago, and she realized with dismay that over the years she had grown increasingly staid. She supposed she had been too busy working as an executive secretary for much of anything else, but now that she was sixty-two and retired, it was time to get the old fight back.

"But Hannah, you've already talked to every council member and didn't change their minds. Hardly anyone signed your petition, and the newspaper didn't print your editorial. And those flyers you handed out. People were using them as pooper-scoopers."

"That was my fault," Hannah admitted, wincing at the memory. "I shouldn't have handed them out at the dog park."

"I hate to put a damper on your civic-mindedness, but the bottom line is, most people in town want Signatech to move here."

"That's because they're confusing change with progress. Change isn't always good. When I'm mayor, they'll listen to me and see that I'm right."

Signatech was a reputable software company and in an obviously clean industry, but it wasn't that kind of pollution Hannah was worried about. Hill Creek's villagy atmosphere lessened a bit with each passing year. If Signatech moved in, it would be gone forever. Hannah felt certain the town's narrow streets couldn't handle the increased traffic or parking, and she couldn't find where anyone in the town government had studied the issue at all. Everyone was so fixated on business and money, they weren't interested in assessing the potential negative impact. She had lived in the town most of her life, and in her well-formed opinion, Signatech would be the ruin of it.

In a last ditch effort to save her nonexistent love affair, Kiki hustled up the steps and threw her back against the double entry doors, her arms flung dramatically outward.

The sisters eyed each other like two gunfighters. Hannah knew she could easily move her sister from the door. Unsteadily perched on those high heels, Kiki could have been toppled with a toothpick. Being the nonviolent sort, Hannah opted for the dangling-of-the-carrot approach.

"The truth is, by running for mayor I'll be providing you with so many opportunities to be thrown together with Alex," Hannah said craftily. "The election's only three weeks away, and there will be town meetings, debates, political coffees. He'll be at all of them." Kiki didn't look convinced, so she went for the clincher. "And as my campaign manager, you'll be there, too, ready to spar with him over issues."

Kiki's eyes flickered as her erratic mental circuitry processed this titillating data. The truth was that when she had attended Alex's seminar she had been only one more moisturized, Estée Lauдered face in a sea of love-starved women. As a campaign manager at a political meeting she would stand out, and she felt certain that once Alex got to know her he would quickly be captivated, especially if the lighting was dim and the alcohol flowed freely.

"What would a campaign manager wear?" Kiki asked, knowing that stuffy business suits wouldn't show off her assets.

The edges of Hannah's mouth curled upward. "Something daring, as a metaphor for our aggressive platform."

Kiki's shoulders drew back. "A plunging neckline to correspond with unemployment figures?"

Hannah frowned, but then reminded herself that the good of the town was at stake. "And high hemlines to correlate with the rising local economy."

Kiki squinted as she tried to think of a political metaphor to justify her new Bosom Buddy pushup bra with Expando-Lift maxi-fill padding. Something about raised spirits in the community was crystallizing when Hannah loudly cleared her throat.

"Ms. Campaign Manager, may I pass?"

Kiki clutched her hands in front of her chest. "Thank you, thank you! This has real possibilities. Alex and I are so right for each other, and I'm sure he'll realize it when he gets to know me. Oh, Hannah, I want love, I want romance, I want deep kisses, champagne, and chocolate. Just like our Lauren's going to get from that cute Detective Morgan."

It occurred to Hannah that their twenty-nine-year-old niece Lauren was a long way from any chocolate or champagne when it came to Larry Morgan. To date, the good-looking but shy young man had only given Lauren a trail map and a snack bag of granola for their nature walk the previous week on Mt. Tamalpais. He did occasionally look at Lauren with a lovesick expression, which was encouraging, but as far as Hannah could tell, their relationship remained oddly platonic, even though Lauren was, as Kiki described it, hotter to trot than a bug on a fan belt.

Hannah smoothed her hair more firmly into its sleek low ponytail, and straightened the hem of her taupe jacket. She had no time to ponder either Lauren's or Kiki's love life. The longer she waited to file for the mayor's race, the harder it would be to work up the nerve.

Hannah swept the air with her hand. "Please, Kiki, step away. The future of Hill Creek must be protected."

Now taking a self-serving view of her sister's political aspirations, Kiki hopped aside. Hannah took in a long anxious breath, pulled the door handle, and marched inside.

After making sure no one was looking, Kiki grinned devilishly, then gave her breasts a nudge upward, emitting a gratified "ooh" at the resulting increase in cleavage. She may have been sixty, but her breasts, a gift from her dead husband Cecil, were only a perky twenty-one, and she wanted to make certain Alex Portman got a gander at them if he happened to cross her path. Mammary glands locked and loaded, she hurried into the scent-free, politically correct, and heightened consciousness of the Hill Creek town hall.

Kiki found Hannah just inside the doorway, where her sister

had paused to work up another burst of chutzpah, the previous one having already wilted. Hannah faced a bulletin board that sported dozens of brightly colored flyers advertising personal growth classes, the type eagerly gorged upon by the town's spiritually hip population. Hannah found herself amazed at the variety—Dialogues of Non-dualism, Chi-kung, Sacred Gurdjieff Movements, Kali Puja Worship, Releasing Your Inner Goddess, and Freeing Your Orgasm via the Internet. Hannah didn't understand any of them, and she yearned for her old hippie days when in order to be spiritually attuned, all you had to know was that it was the Age of Aquarius.

"Don't waste your time with those classes, Hannah," Kiki told her. "All you need is a day of busting your love barriers so you can open up your love flows."

"My love with John is flowing quite nicely, thank you," Hannah replied, referring to her boyfriend John Perez. She looked down the hallway at the sign that read "Town Clerk." "I can't put it off any longer."

Hannah hoisted her handbag farther up her shoulder and again took off, her sensible crepe-soled shoes squeaking against the linoleum as Kiki's high heels clattered behind. As Hannah headed down the dull brown corridor she noticed several large color photographs on the walls, all of Alex Portman posing with minor celebrities who had passed through town. Before Alex's reign as mayor the walls had been hung with old black-and-white photos of Hill Creek in the 1920s when the town was just a few buildings and a railroad station, but Alex had replaced them with these publicity shots of himself. *What hubris,* Hannah thought.

Hannah and Kiki were a familiar sight around town, and several people gave them a cheery hello. The sisters had grown up in Hill Creek. They had moved away during their marriages, but Hannah returned after her husband died, and Kiki had moved in with her after Cecil's death. And although the sisters were as different as two women could possibly be, they adored each other and would each secretly admit that they enjoyed living with each other more than they had with any man.

When Hannah reached the town clerk's office, she paused, her hand firmly on the knob, summoning up one last surge of rationale-defying pluck.

"Wait!"

Hannah jumped, startled at the shout, and saw their next-door neighbor Naomi swooping down the hall, her bright blue tunic flapping behind her, like some huge mutant insect on the attack. Naomi's tunic was her usual daily wear, but today she had a strange addition. A clump of long brown feathers sat on top of her head, positioned with a hair clip so they hung forward in her face. She wore matching feathers around her wrists.

"You scared us half to death," Hannah said, her hand pressed against her chest.

Naomi grabbed Hannah's shoulders. "Don't do it! Don't run for mayor!"

Kiki's mouth dropped open. "You want to date Alex, too?"

"Don't be silly, dear," Naomi replied in a suddenly matter-of-fact tone, then her chest swelled dramatically. "Red Moon has given me a sign." She made this last statement in a theatrical whisper, her eyes rolled upward.

At the mention of Red Moon, Hannah's concern drained away. Naomi made her living as a psychic and spiritual advisor, channeling the spirit of Red Moon, a supposed five hundred-year-old Hopi snake shaman. For fifty bucks an hour, cash preferred, Naomi would fall into a trance, allowing Red Moon's spirit to take a temporary sublet of her body, a feat that Hannah felt must have been hard work, since Naomi's body was on the largish side. Once in the trance, Naomi à la Red Moon dispensed life advice in strange Hopi metaphors.

Hannah gave the air a sniff. "What's that odd smell?"

"Herbs and bacon fat," Naomi said, pointing to the small burlap pouch hanging on a narrow leather strap around her neck. "My own recipe."

"New diet?" Hannah asked with a wry smile.

"It's my sacred healing talisman. I'm cleansing evil spirits. And I wouldn't be sarcastic. I'm wearing it for you."

"Red Moon's predicted something?" Kiki asked, her face contorted with angst. Kiki believed wholeheartedly in everything Red Moon said, although she, like everyone else, had no clue what the hell he was saying. Ask about your love life, Red Moon talked about running buffaloes; pose a question about moral issues, and you got ten minutes on coyotes hunting in the golden grass.

Naomi's head bobbed, causing her feathers to tremble. "I was meditating just an hour ago, and at the end, you know, the part when I enter my otherworldly bliss state, well, I got this image of you, Hannah, in the backyard this morning saying you were going to file for the mayor's race. And I distinctly heard Red Moon's voice say something so distressing."

Kiki pressed her palms to her cheek. "My God, what was it?"

Naomi glanced around to make sure they were alone, then pulled Hannah and Kiki closer. "I don't want anyone else to hear."

"Why, was it dirty?" Hannah asked.

"This is serious. Red Moon said—" Naomi bit her lip with astral misery. For a moment she couldn't speak, but at last she inhaled deeply and held up a hand, palm outward. "Red Moon said, 'So ey yat tey, so ey yat te.'"

Hannah and Kiki joined each other in an extended moment of mental blankness. "He speaks Yiddish?" Kiki finally asked, remembering the curse words Cecil used to shout when he got the credit card bills each month. It was what finally killed him.

"No, silly, it's Hopi. So ey yat tey," Naomi repeated with irritation. "It's part of the chant Hopis do when they're speaking to the dead."

"I don't see your point," Hannah said.

"Do I have to spell it out? There's an obvious connection between you running for mayor and death. That's why I'm wearing my sacral turkey feather headdress, to ward off evil." Naomi shook her feathered wrists in Hannah's face then again grabbed her shoulders. "Please, don't run for mayor."

Her hands clutching her throat, Kiki emitted a terrified squeak, her brief political enthusiasm now obliterated. "Listen to her, Hannah, please listen to her. Red Moon's always right."

"He's always right because he's so vague you can't pin him down," Hannah said stoutly, when in truth, Naomi's warning had produced a disturbing tingle at the back of her neck. She would never say it aloud, but deep down she believed in Red Moon. So many of his predictions had been so eerily accurate that she couldn't dismiss them. She was on the verge of asking Naomi to tell her more when they all jumped at a loud scraping noise followed by a fearful yelp.

"Oh, my God, was that Red Moon?" Kiki shrieked.

"Only if he's working in the town clerk's office," Hannah told her. Afraid that someone had been hurt, she shoved open the door, and she, Kiki, and Naomi stumbled inside together.

Everything looked normal. The town clerk's office included a ten-by-fifteen-foot waiting area with metal chairs lining the wall, and beyond that a long counter stacked with trays filled with various forms. Behind the counter was a large room of filing cabinets, stacks of paper, and several battered-looking desktop computers, the white walls scattered with framed pronouncements of various laws protecting workers' rights. A vase of primroses sitting on the counter brightened the drab surroundings.

"Step right in, and welcome!" a deep and powerful male voice announced cheerfully from somewhere above their heads, as if God were hovering over them sporting a plateful of barbecued wieners and an apron that said Kiss the Cook. "I'm Alex Portman, mayor of Hill Creek, and I want to personally invite you to join us in our communal oneness. We're a town focused on expansion of our spiritual dimensions as well as managed business development."

"Hah," Hannah said, crossing her arms with vexation.

"Alex? Are you here?" Patting her hair, Kiki's eyes darted around the room expectantly.

"It's a recording," Hannah said. "The man's ego knows no bounds."

"Alex had it put in a few weeks ago," Frannie said from behind the counter. Frannie, about fifty, with dyed red hair she wore in girlish waves, had worked in the town clerk's office since she was twelve, or at least it seemed that way. "Isn't it great? I just love that communal oneness stuff."

"We heard someone cry out," Hannah said. "Is everything okay?"

Leaning over the counter, Frannie pointed to the door that led to the back office. Hannah looked down and saw Althea Lamont crouching next to a file cabinet, her wrist chained to one of the drawer handles.

"Behind on those parking fines?" Hannah asked.

"I'm protesting Signatech's planned annihilation of the Yellow-bellied Bush Cricket. But every time Frannie opens the door she hits me! Look, I have a red mark," Althea said, pointing to an invisible injury on her shin. She wore khaki walking shorts covered in pockets, kneesocks, and hiking boots, her long graying hair braided and twisted in a knot. It was her standard garb, but today she had supplemented it with a sweatshirt that read "Portman Is A Prick." "I demand police protection!"

"Well, you're not getting it, you loony," Frannie told her. With her index finger pointed at her own skull and gyrating in a little circle, Frannie looked meaningfully at Hannah, tilting her head in Althea's direction.

Althea was famous in town for irrational exuberance when it came to social causes, especially after she threw herself in front of a bulldozer to protest the widening of a freeway. The bulldozer wasn't moving at the time and had no driver, but this wasn't apparent in the photo that ran on the front page of the *Marin Sun*, and from that point on, Althea's reputation was fixed. In the past few months she had turned her self-righteous zeal upon the insect world, becoming unusually sensitized to their physical and emotional needs. Most people attributed this to the recent death of her husband, whose face had resembled a praying mantis.

Just then Frannie's assistant Donna, a small thin girl with wire-rimmed glasses, whizzed past Frannie and opened the door to the left of the counter, hitting Althea on the shin.

"Ouch! Brutality! I'm being oppressed! You're all witnesses!" Althea shouted, rubbing her leg.

"I didn't mean to do it, but you're right there in the way," Donna said in a frail voice, clutching a file folder to her chest.

"You did it on purpose. You're trying to deny me my civil rights." In her excitement, Althea jerked on her chain and the entire cabinet scraped along the floor a few inches.

Frannie glared at her. "Stop that, Althea, or I'll call the police. You're defacing public property. Vandal!"

"Lackey running dog of the plutocracy," Althea shot back.

Frannie pressed her hands against the counter and leaned menacingly forward. "Did I hear you use a curse word?"

"Now everyone calm down," Hannah said.

"Butt out, honey," Frannie said with no particular malice. "This is official town business."

"Oh, please, girls, listen to Hannah," Naomi said, fretfully waving her hands. "There's very negative energy in this room. Very negative. I have a vial of sacred shaman water that came from a Cheyenne medicine man in North Dakota. A little sprinkling might neutralize the evil."

"Oh, could you try it, please?" Frannie asked. "Althea rattling on about those silly crickets is getting my chakras clogged up."

Frannie was one of Naomi's long-standing channeling clients, especially grateful for Naomi getting her in touch with her past life as an eighteenth-century French courtesan. Frannie's life had, save the current situation, been dull as a dirt sandwich, and it brought her such joy to think she had once kicked up her heels, even if it was almost three hundred years ago.

Hannah noticed that Donna, still by the file cabinet, had closed her eyes and pressed her hand against her head.

"Someone's wearing scented products," she said, her rail-thin body beginning to sway. She pointed a quivering finger at a hand-printed sign on the wall that read, "Please don't wear scented products, including perfumes and deodorants." "The chemicals are very potent," Donna said. "I think I'm going to faint." She dropped her file folder, the papers flying across the floor, and rummaged frantically through her pocket. Eyes still closed, she pulled out a white surgical mask and slipped it over her nose and mouth.

Althea gave the air a few exploratory sniffs before directing an accusing nose at Kiki, wiggling it like a rabbit's. "It's her. She's a walking chemical factory."

Donna, Frannie, and Althea all looked at Kiki as if they had just found out her underwear was stuffed with nuclear waste. Jaw dropped in indignation, Kiki put her hands on her waist. "So I like a little perfume. It's Madness."

"It's not madness, I'm just hypersensitive," Donna said, her voice muffled by the mask as she stooped to pick up the papers.

"She means that her perfume is called Madness," Hannah explained.

While doing little hops, Naomi flapped her hands in the air. "The negative frequency's building to destructive levels. Let's all take a deep cleansing breath, then I really think I should do a sacral sprinkling."

"You can sprinkle later," Hannah said. "First, I want to know what's going on here. Althea, I understand that you're protesting, but why chain yourself to the file cabinet?"

"As a metaphor. Neither I nor the Yellow-bellied Bush Cricket will stand to be moved," Althea said with a haughty lift of her chin. "Portman is going to let that company build on a vacant field near Cypress Avenue, which is the native home of the Yellow-bellied."

"The town owns the land and can do whatever it wants with

it. Besides, it's just a silly old insect," Frannie said, now leaning one elbow against the countertop, her chin resting in her hand.

Althea's face puckered. "It's endangered."

"You're going to be endangered if you keep blocking that door. It's a fire exit," Frannie warned. "I don't know what you're complaining about anyway. We're going to have that rummage sale and use the proceeds to move the silly crickets to a new location."

"That's just a smokescreen," Althea replied. "No one knows if the Yellow-bellied can be moved. And how would you like it if someone came and moved you from your native habitat?"

"My native habitat was Iowa and I didn't mind moving one bit," Frannie said.

"Well I refuse to move from *this* spot until Portman agrees to meet with me."

Shaking her head, Frannie turned her attention to Hannah. "Why are you here, hon? Are you finally going to build that deck you've been dreaming about?"

Hannah steeled herself. "I'm here to enter the mayor's race."

A foreboding silence fell across the room as its various occupants absorbed this startling information. Naomi dropped to her knees, took two rocks out of her velvet backpack, and began clapping them together as she chanted.

"Against Alex?" Frannie asked, dumbfounded. Donna let out what would have been a shocked yelp, but the mask made it sound more like a suffocating gerbil. She scurried out of the room, her papers clutched to her chest.

"Power to the people!" Althea shouted. When she tried to raise her fist the filing cabinet scraped against the floor. "Sorry," she mumbled, then raised the other fist. "I'll back you a hundred percent. Good old Hannah, striking a blow for the Yellow-bellied Bush Cricket!"

"I'm not running for mayor to save the cricket, Althea," Hannah told her, noticing that Naomi had gotten out her vial of sacred shaman water and was flicking it around the room with her fingers. "I have nothing against crickets, of course."

"It's garden slugs she hates," Kiki chimed in.

"The reason I want to run against Alex is that I don't think that a big company like Signatech will be good for the town. I've done some research on the Internet and the company's growing at an annual rate of thirty percent. Even if the town could handle the traffic when the company first moves in, what will happen in a couple of years?"

"You're wasting your energy, Hannah. Everybody else in town, except for Althea, is thrilled about it," Frannie said. "Think of the business it will bring to the local shops. You can't stop progress."

"People will stop coming to the shops because there won't be any place to park. Signatech employees will be taking those spots because the Cypress Avenue site isn't large enough for ample parking. And a company the size of Signatech will clog up the streets, and the town doesn't have the easements to widen the roads," Hannah quickly continued. "If that company moves in, ten years from now we'll all be shaking our heads and wondering what happened to the town's charm."

"You tell it, girl," Althea cried. "We can't let ourselves be raped by corporate America!"

Frannie clucked and shook her head. "You're fighting a losing battle."

"Her favorite kind, the poor dear," Naomi said, flicking Hannah with water.

"You just don't understand that Alex has the best interests of Hill Creek at heart," Frannie said. She gave Hannah a questioning look. "Have you taken his seminar?"

"No, she hasn't," Kiki said.

Frannie crossed her arms and looked at Hannah with pity. "That explains it." She lifted the scarf draped across her neck and displayed her yellow "I've Been Busted" button. "You have barriers, Hannah. You're full of repressed love flows."

"I most certainly am not," Hannah replied with mounting irritation. "Where's the form? I'm running for mayor."

"If you insist on humiliating yourself, I guess I'll go dig one up." Frannie disappeared around a corner. Naomi stopped flicking water, and tilted her head.

"What's wrong?" Hannah asked her. "You have the strangest look on your face."

"I sense malice in this room. I'm serious," Naomi said. She turned in a slow circle, her eyes closed. Kiki looked on with anguish. "The sacred water wasn't enough," Naomi said, opening her eyes. "We need a more thorough spiritual cleansing ASAP. I'm telling you, Hannah, something terrible's going to happen."

Kiki grabbed Naomi's sacred water, sprinkled some on her head, whimpered with fear, and then drank it straight from the vial.

"You're being so ridiculous," Hannah said with a forced chuckle, ignoring that first ember of apprehension that usually preceded an inferno. She turned up her palms and lifted her shoulders. "What could possibly happen? There's nothing more dull than local politics."

TWO

HANNAH STOOD MOTIONLESS ON A sidewalk on Hill Creek's main drag, her face inches from the trunk of a leafy sycamore growing in front of the Book Stop café. Round tortoiseshell reading glasses perched on the end of her patrician nose, she scrutinized the fuzzy black-and-white photo staring back at her, not sure of what she was seeing. She had personally designed the bright yellow flyer promoting herself as mayor, and tied one to each of Center Avenue's tall trees where everyone would be sure to see them. Getting her face out before the public had seemed like a great idea, but now, confronted with this particular one, she realized she had exposed herself to mischief.

Hannah's lips puckered with concentration, leaving her unaware of the town humming around her. People bustled down the pavement carrying canvas bags filled with organic groceries, and children on silver microscooters whizzed by, giddily shouting to each other in celebration of Saturday and their release from school.

Hannah had never liked looking at pictures of herself, but this photo was especially unnerving. Finally realizing what she was seeing, she laughed out loud. The badly drawn balloons with dots in the middle were breasts. Someone, most likely an errant teenager suffering from too many self-esteem classes and overly permissive parents, had drawn them with a black marker beneath Hannah's neck.

There was a loud, juicy snort, and it didn't come from Hannah. "My sentiments exactly," she said, leaning down to give her pet pig Sylvia Plath a pat on the head. "I prefer something more natural looking." Hannah had just dropped off her dog Teresa S. Eliot at the vet for her booster shots. Sylvia also had a vet appointment for a much-needed toenail clipping, but not until eleven o'clock, so Hannah decided to take the black Vietnamese pot-bellied pig for a constitutional around town. It was Sylvia's curse that everything she ate went straight to her hips, and she needed the exercise.

Hannah gave the picture another look. It was bad enough that the cartoon breasts obscured the slogan, "A Vote for Hannah Malloy Is a Vote for Hill Creek's Future," but to draw breasts on her was completely inaccurate since she had no breasts at all. A cancer survivor, she had undergone a double mastectomy eight years earlier, and had decided against reconstructive surgery. Her chest was now a smooth landscape covered with a rambling tattoo of ivy and flowers. It would have been more realistic to draw a bouquet of petunias beneath her neck, but this aspiring Picasso couldn't have known. Hannah noticed that at the top of the flyer someone—Althea, most likely—had scrawled "Protector of the Yellow-bellied Bush Cricket."

Since Hannah had filed for the mayor's race a week earlier, she had tied her campaign flyers to trees, tacked them on shop bulletin boards, and personally handed them out in front of the Hill Creek Grocery, stopping shoppers on their way to the parking lot to outline the key points of her platform. Although she began the campaign with jangling nerves, she constantly reminded herself that there was no reason for such qualms. Wasn't she a long-term and well-respected member of the community? Didn't she have intelligence, long work experience, and a commitment to the good of the town? Every day that week, while she spread alfalfa pellets around the base of her roses, she repeated confidence-building affirmations and assured herself, ad nauseum, that there was no reason why she couldn't beat the suede Birkenstocks off Alex Portman.

Yet with each flyer Hannah delivered and each hand she shook, she got the impression that the townspeople considered her campaign an amusing idea but nothing to be taken seriously. They smiled, they nodded, they slapped her on the back and said, "Go get 'em, girl." But half of them wore "I've Been Busted" buttons, and when they walked away she caught a couple of people closing their eyes and pressing their fingers together in front of their faces while they visualized their flowers. She had seen Kiki do it a hundred times. It was disturbingly obvious that most of them had no intention of voting for anyone except their adored Dr. Love.

After ripping down the old flyer and tying up a fresh one,

Hannah checked her watch, then hurried across the street, Sylvia snorting with irritation at having to trot at such an imprudent speed. Between an elegant boutique and the holistic herb shop, Hannah paused at the threshold of One Hand Clapping, the salon previously named Lady Nails, and still called that by all its long-time patrons. After tying Sylvia's leash to a cedar-covered re-cycling bin, she did a quick check of the sidewalk to make sure there were no half-eaten candy bars Sylvia could gobble, then opened the shop door.

Lady Nails was the town's informal supercomputer, the place where town data was input, processed, and regurgitated into a highly enhanced, user-friendly form. Hannah didn't normally go in for gossip, not that she would admit to it, anyway, but she felt certain that with some pumping she would get a more ac-curate status of where her campaign stood amongst the towns-people. This was the secret reason why she had earlier offered to drive Kiki home from the salon, even though Kiki needed exercise as much as Sylvia, having the same addiction to sweets.

Once inside, Hannah inhaled the heady scents of aromather-apy oils, nail polish, and perfume, and ran her eyes along the salon's symphony of pinks—pink floor, pink walls, and pink vinyl-covered chairs, the monochromatic theme broken up by numerous fluffy green ferns that hung from the ceiling. She expected to be greeted by the usual buzz of chatter and music, and was astonished when she instead heard enthusiastic shout-ing. A cotton ball hit her in the face.

As Hannah swatted it away she saw Kiki lumbering down the long narrow salon, balanced on her heels, tufts of cotton sprout-ing between her pedicured toes. Kiki's arms wildly pumped and her fingers fanned so as not to muss a fresh coat of "Kiss Me Pink," the visual effect being that of some unfortunate dancer having an epileptic seizure in mid-Macarena.

A dozen women in various states of manicures and pedicures cheered and hurled cotton balls as Kiki clumped along to the far end of the salon. When she reached a small table against the wall, she stooped, knees creaking, in front of a plate of glazed donuts, picked up one with her teeth, then waddled back as fast as she could, her eyes wide, teeth bared behind the donut.

Ellie, the salon's owner, clicked a stopwatch. "Twenty-two seconds!" she announced to applause. "That beats Bertha."

Kiki did a small victory hop, her own version of the end zone dance, then plopped breathlessly into a chair. Shiloh, Ellie's twenty-something assistant, helped Kiki eat the donut without destroying her still tacky nails.

Noticing her sister, Kiki waved. "Oh, hi, Hannah. Did you see me?" she said through a mouth of dough and sugar. "I won the pool, the whole thirteen dollars."

"It wasn't fair," Bertha Malone complained from her perch in a high pedicure chair. "I ate Chinese last night and I'm retaining water like a blowfish. I'm always at a disadvantage."

"Like you didn't pick up fifteen bucks from Twister last week," said Gladys, a local librarian, whose disgruntled tone told of a grudge harbored from that competition.

"And people worry about the idle minds of youth," Hannah joked.

Ellie and Hannah exchanged a smile. "Things have been a little slow lately," Ellie said, and they both knew she wasn't talking about business. Gossipmongering was the salon's raison d'être, and lately there had been precious little gossip to monger. This lack of mental nutrients had at first produced a listlessness among their group, and then gave rise to a rash of games and bets that grew in silliness every day. It started off with a simple bet on Marilyn Monroe's dress size, progressed to the correct lyrics of the *Petticoat Junction* theme song, and had since degenerated into that day's donut-retrieval-while-pedicured-and-manicured relay. Hannah worried that unless some decent gossip fell their way, and fast, somebody was going to break a hip.

Hannah had done her part. Her running for mayor, along with Naomi's predictions of death and destruction, had provided some top quality chin-wagging until the women realized that Hannah had a better chance of buying a taco on Mars than she had of beating Alex Portman. Of course, no one told Hannah this, for fear of hurting her feelings. At least, no one had told her yet.

"I didn't expect you here so soon," Kiki said, then raised a plump foot, its toes lacquered a frosted peach. "What do you think?"

"Gorgeous," Hannah told her, spying their niece Lauren sitting in a manicure chair at the end of the row, thumbing idly through a magazine. "Lauren, I don't see you in here very often."

"She's getting a leg wax and a manicure," Kiki said with a

sly wiggling of her eyebrows. "She's going out with our cute
Detective Morgan tonight. I think she should do her fingernails
blood red."

Lauren turned pink, and she pushed her shoulder-length
brown hair behind her ears. "Oh, no. Just a nice clear polish.
Red would be too much. Way too much."

"I could pierce your belly button. Men like that." This came
from Shiloh, the human pincushion. Lauren blushed again.

"Grab a magazine, Hannah," said Ellie. "Kiki'll be done as
soon as I put on her clear coat."

"Thanks. I'll just wait over here."

There wasn't a free chair next to Lauren, so Hannah chose
one adjacent to Wanda Backus, who was in the middle of a foot
treatment, her feet drenched in minty-smelling green slime and
covered in plastic bags.

Wanda gave Hannah a pitying look. "How are you holding
up with your campaign?" she said loud enough for all to hear,
her voice having the same falsely pathetic tone she would have
used to inquire after somebody's sick parakeet. Wanda, who had
more plastic in her than a Honda, had recently had fresh fat-
injections in her lips, and now, puckered with sympathy and
coated with chic beige lipstick, her mouth looked like reclining
buttocks. Behind her manufactured compassion her eyes remained shrewd. Hannah knew that Wanda's competitive streak
had her sick with jealousy over Hannah's mayoral campaign and
kicking herself for not thinking of it first. Even though Wanda
felt certain that Hannah didn't have a snowball's chance, it still
had gotten Hannah a lot of attention, and attention was Wanda's
oxygen.

"Things are going well," Hannah fibbed. "I think I'm making
progress." Hannah saw everyone in the salon staring at her with
sympathy.

Wanda reached over and gave Hannah's shoulder a squeeze.
"You just keep up that positive attitude, dear. It's so emotionally
healthy." It was then that Hannah noticed Wanda's "I've Been
Busted" button pinned to her white Donna Karan pullover.

"Aunt Hannah's attitude is always positive," Lauren said, giving her aunt an encouraging smile.

Looking around the salon, Hannah forced a smile as the dis-
mal truth sunk into her. Her friends all knew that she was going
to lose to Alex Portman. Wanda wouldn't have hit her with such

saccharin comments if Hannah weren't an object of salon pity.
Things were worse than Hannah had ever suspected. She slid
down in her chair.

"Wanda meant that Hannah's attitude is even more positive
than usual," Kiki said, shooting Wanda a look. "Didn't you,
Wanda?"

"Of course that's what I meant," Wanda said with cloying
sweetness. "Thank you for clarifying it, Kiki."

Kiki beamed. "Any time, Wanda."

"Love your toes, Kiki," Wanda said with a singsong lilt. "That
color suits you."

Kiki stretched her lips into a stingy smile. "You're so sweet
to say so."

A low collective groan rumbled through the salon. Since Kiki
and Wanda had attended the Love Barriers seminar three months
earlier they had called a truce in their years of petty disputes.
But rather than ending their silly feud they had only covered it
up with a cloying superficial friendliness, like pouring syrup on
a turd, and everyone longed for the old days when Kiki and
Wanda had been at each other's throats. Then they could count
on some intermittent excitement—barbs thrown, insults hurled,
the occasional handbag dumped, and that titillating incident with
the chicken manure at the Urban Farmer Nursery. All this drippy
sweetness was not only irritating, it was deadly dull. And it
wasn't as if the women's hostilities ever lasted long. Kiki and
Wanda always made up just so they could have the fun of fighting again.

Pleasantness and contentment had its place in life, but too
much of it could turn a person comatose. Hill Creek's inhabitants benefited from high incomes, low crime rates, and an eye-
candy environment of trees, hills, and ocean. Everyone knew
their luck in having what others didn't, and to assuage the guilt,
they fretted over rain forests and genetically modified tomatoes,
and donated generously to charity. The truth was, all their easy
living would quickly lapse into stupefying boredom except for
their absorption in the fascinating minutia of each other's lives.
And lately, when it came to juicy tidbits, life had been dryer
than old toast, and the whole town was in desperate need of
some human folly, some brazen indiscretion they could hash
over.

"Yes, Hannah, we all think you're being very brave, consid-

ering your predicament." The comment came from Bertha, former Twister winner, whose toenails were being painted a frosty
gold by Ellie. Bertha was a long, heavy-set woman with all the
seductive femininity of Ernest Borgnine, and her dainty polish
looked as out of place as on the toes of a moose. Her main role
in life was serving as Wanda's best friend, "serving" being the
operative word. A transplant from chic Santa Fe, Bertha adver-
tised this social resume by wearing cowboy boots, denim outfits,
and pounds of turquoise jewelry. "To stand up for what you
believe in when all the odds are against you."

"The odds being against her don't mean a thing. Hannah can
beat the odds," Kiki said, leaning forward so that Shiloh had to
grab her foot to keep it still. Not wanting to stir up any of the
trouble predicted by Red Moon, Kiki had done zero as Hannah's
campaign manager, but that didn't mean she would tolerate crit-
icism of her sister.

Wanda chuckled derisively. "Hannah's making a laudable
public statement, but even she can't think she'll win."

Hannah felt a pang and considered quietly exiting out the
backdoor.

Kiki's mouth tensed. "And why can't she?"

"Because Alex Portman is, well, he's Alex," Wanda replied,
starting to sound just a wee bit testy. The other women's ears
pricked up. "He's handsome, brilliant. He's a star."

Only in the sense that he's a gaseous body, Hannah thought,
but didn't say.

"And he's a wonderful mayor."

Hannah gaped at Wanda. "A wonderful mayor? Give me an
example of something he's accomplished."

"Well, let's see," Bertha said, eager to get into the fray. She
thought a second then raised a turquoise-ringed finger. "He put
that new statue in the park."

"The statue is of him," Hannah said.

"He expanded the town hall by adding the assembly room,"
Wanda offered.

"He's using the space for his seminars," Hannah replied. Irritated, she bolted out of her chair. "That's the point. He's all
self-absorbed spin and no action, and the town council isn't
much better these days. They follow him like lovesick sheep.
Hill Creek needs a mayor who'll tackle some issues." Hannah
paced the pink linoleum, her fist raised, her political fire stoked.

"A mayor who cares more about the town's welfare than photo ops. Alex looks great, says all the right things, but accomplishes nothing."

Ellie looked up from Bertha's toes. "He's bringing Signatech to town."

"Which is even worse. At least before he wasn't having any effect on the town one way or another. Now he's doing damage." Halting, Hannah directed the only non-manicured finger in the room at Wanda. "A point I'll be bringing up during tomorrow night's debate."

Hannah retracted her finger and stuck her hand in her pocket, the very mention of the debate bringing a queasiness to her usually rock solid stomach. She told herself she couldn't remember the last time she had been so nervous, but then quickly realized that she *did* remember, remembered every second of it in Technicolor, Dolby Sound detail. And it was this memory that pained her with every step she took closer to the debate. She caught Kiki's eye, saw her sister's compassionate expression, and knew that she was remembering the same humiliating event.

Hannah knew it was absurd to let an event from eons back still bother her, especially something so silly. She had been in high school, running for president of the junior class. Just before the vote there had been a class assembly for the three candidates to give campaign speeches. Hannah had labored over her speech for days, rewritten it a dozen times, practiced it again and again in front of her mirror. When it was time for the assembly she was ready to take on the world, but a few minutes before the start she had gone to the girls' restroom with Kiki, then a sophomore. When they opened the door, Gladys Wanamaker had just gone into a stall. At the time Kiki had been in competition with Gladys for the attentions of Billy Boseman, a first-string football player. Hannah warned Kiki not to start anything, and Kiki assured her she wouldn't. Then, in hopes of getting some dishable dirt, Kiki stood on the toilet seat so she could see over the stall partition and determine if Gladys wore a girdle. Kiki slipped and her loafered-foot plunged into the toilet, wedging itself there. It took Hannah five minutes to free her shrieking sister. Panicked that she was late, Hannah had quickly used the toilet for the purpose for which God had intended, then ran to the assembly room.

The laughter began as soon she rushed onto the stage, the horrible sound growing into a roar. It was old Mrs. Hannibal who pulled the long train of toilet paper from the back of Hannah's pleated skirt. To Hannah's credit, she didn't run away, although she desperately wanted to. She made her speech, each painful word uttered through humiliation as the entire junior class stared at her with ridiculing grins.

Her thoughts returning to the present, Hannah shook off the image. No point in rehashing an ancient mortification when such a fresh one was at hand.

"Hannah's going to knock 'em dead at the debate tomorrow," Kiki said, in hopes of irking Wanda. "She's really been practicing that speech. But don't make Alex look too bad, okay, Hannah?"

Wanda and Bertha cackled. "As if she could," Wanda said. "The man's practically a god in this town."

"She could make him look bad if she wanted," Kiki replied, a distinct edge in her voice.

Wanda aimed narrowed eyes at Kiki, and the salon hushed, everyone eager for a rekindling of the feud. But just as Wanda started to lob her first stink bomb, the Buddhist prayer chimes jingled. Every well-moisturized neck craned toward the opening door where they saw the handsome, charisma-drenched presence of Alex Portman.

Even in jogging shorts and a sweaty T-shirt, Alex did look a bit god-like, Hannah had to admit. At fifty-nine, he was still gorgeous, his chin strong and his nose Grecian, his tanned body sculpted with muscles, his clipped gray hair boyishly ruffled from his jog. His face beaded with sweat, he raised a plastic jogger's bottle to his lips and took a gulp. The red bottle bore the words "I've Been Busted."

"I see you girls are busy creating spiritual harmony, making yourselves as beautiful on the outside as you are on the inside," he said with his trademark smoothness. "But it's your inner light that I see shining through with such radiance." He raised his hands and lifted his eyes to the ceiling. *Just like those plastic Jesus figures people stick on their dashboards*, Hannah thought. He returned his gaze to the women, his smile widening into a playful grin. "Your inner light's so bright, a guy needs sunglasses."

All the women twittered, while Hannah said a silent "ugh."

So typical, she mused. Alex always smooth as silk, saying what everyone wanted to hear. The town had problems that needed to be dealt with, but Alex never took action on anything controversial. Not until Signatech. Hannah looked hard at him as he bent down in front of Bertha, flirting with her. The idea crept into Hannah's head that it was very strange that he would choose that particular issue on which to take a stand. There had to be a reason.

Alex strutted deeper into the salon, displaying a jaunty confidence that lesser men couldn't have mustered in that womb of femininity. Yet when he came across Hannah, he faltered slightly. She thought for sure she saw some fleeting trepidation in his eyes. Was he worried about her as an opponent? The expression quickly disappeared. Hannah shifted in her seat. She must have been mistaken. He casually leaned an arm on the shelf that held the Princess Diana altar, no woman complaining that he had his sweaty arm against the memorial photo, his elbow violating the Princess's left nostril. If any other man had done it the women would have pelted him with cuticle pushers.

"I want to make sure we're all nurturing our life force," Alex said. Putting his bottle on the shelf, he pressed his palms together in front of his chest. "Have we all been participating fully in the day's life experience? Have we been visualizing our flowers when we feel love channel blockage?"

Hannah was feeling some blockage, but it wasn't in her love channel. She rolled her eyes as the other women giggled and nodded. Why couldn't they see what a sham he was? As he struck a pose, Hannah studied his profile and decided he had definitely undergone plastic surgery. His jawline was too firm, and his eyes had the slight but telltale protruding that meant he had undergone a couple of eyelifts. Hannah remembered the old saying that in your twenties you got the face you were born with and in your forties the face you deserve. In Hill Creek, when you hit your fifties you got the face you could pay for.

"I felt some negative flows this morning, but I just visualized my daisy and reclaimed my love dynamic," Kiki told him, batting her eyelashes so hard her eyeballs were close to lift off. She daintily crossed her legs, wiggling her bare foot in his direction. It didn't seem to Hannah that toe waggling was the way to a man's heart, but Kiki felt that toes were the last part of a woman's body to age, so she exposed them as much as possible.

Dr. Love glowed with approval. "Good work, Kiki. You've made such progress."

"Considering where she started," Wanda said, sucking in her cheeks.

"What do you mean by that?" Kiki asked, her love channel hiccuping.

Wanda smiled sweetly. "Just that you were such a hard little nut." She put an unpleasant emphasis on the last word.

Her face screwing itself up, Kiki opened her mouth to eject a sharp retort. Every woman in the salon inched forward, their expressions hopeful. Hannah thought she noticed a look of amused contempt on Alex's face, and knew he was looking forward to a squabble as well. Hannah wanted the truce over as much as anyone, but she didn't think it wise to finish it in front of the mayor. Kiki would be so embarrassed later.

"Are you ready for the debate tomorrow night?" Hannah quickly asked Alex. The room's tension deflated. He slid his eyes her way.

"Haven't had much time to think about it." He took another sip from the bottle, then smiled. "Are you planning to give me a hard time?"

"No more than you deserve," Hannah replied good-naturedly. She couldn't help being sucked in by his charm just a little.

"I like a bit of competition," he told her, and Hannah felt her heart sink. The casual way he said "a bit of competition" told her exactly how insignificant a threat he considered her. A born politician and gifted public speaker, he was going to thrash her in the debate and in the election as well. She'd be lucky if she got five votes, and she had gotten six in the high school election. Hannah sighed, wondering if she should just move to another state. "And I think you'll give me more of a challenge than Charlie."

Charlie Wright, a local garage owner and town council member, was the only other person in town with the gumption or foolishness to go up against Alex, but it wasn't because of Signatech. Charlie had jumped eagerly on that bandwagon. He seemed to have entered the race more out of personal dislike for Alex than for policy reasons, his annoyance with the mayor in town council meetings well known.

Alex took another sip from the bottle. "To show there aren't any hard feelings, I'm having a lunch party tomorrow, and—"

"Before the debate?" Hannah interrupted. "Won't you be busy practicing your speech and preparing for questions?"

Alex grinned, displaying his expensive dentistry and complete disdain. "I prefer to be relaxed. It's my birthday, and I'd like to have you there. It'll be a small, quiet party. Charlie's coming too. It'll give all of us candidates a chance to loosen up before the debate. I mean, we're all in this together, aren't we?"

Hannah tried not to return his dazzling smile but found her lips curling up before she could stop them, the way she couldn't help smiling at a good dirty joke. *Bad lips, down boys.* The man's charisma oozed all over you. No one stood a chance against him. "I suppose," she said.

"Good, then I'll see you there. Tomorrow at one-ish."

"Can I come too?" Kiki asked, bouncing in her seat, "I'm her campaign manager."

"Uh, yes, of course," Alex said quickly, after a hesitation that only Kiki failed to notice. He moved his eyes back to Hannah and stepped close to her. "You know, I sense a lot of tension in you. I think you have some barriers that need to be broken through." He touched her cheek with his finger.

"Oh, she's loaded with barriers," Kiki said loudly, trying to get his attention. "She's a walking Hoover Dam."

"Yes, I'm seeing that," he said. It occurred to Hannah that he was flirting with her, and she couldn't imagine why, unless it was to be patronizing. Hannah's face paled. Did he consider her some kind of joke, a lapdog to be patted then ignored? Is that what everyone thought of her candidacy?

"You're an interesting woman," Alex continued. "I'd like to create a safe space for you to explore your authentic self. Maybe we could do a one-on-one love barrier breakdown session. Would you like that?"

The other women gasped. A one-on-one love barrier breakdown session was what they all dreamed of.

"Uh, I don't think so," Hannah replied, stiffening.

"That's a shame." He gave her a lingering look before turning to the other women. "Well, bye for now, ladies. Remember, think communal oneness, and if you feel a love barrier, just bust right through it." With a two-fingered salute, he exited the salon, breaking into a jog as soon as he was outside.

For a moment, the women sat spellbound, captivated by the lusty scent of eau de Portman still lingering in the air. Bertha and Gladys rose from their seats and watched through the window as he dashed across the street barely hesitating for traffic; he simply held up his hand, feeling certain any car would stop. The traffic moved so slowly on Center Avenue there wasn't too much danger of being run over. Still, Hannah figured you could light up Las Vegas with the power from his ego.

"What conceit," Hannah said. "What hubris."

Kiki looked wistfully after him. "What a personality."

"What a butt," Ellie added.

Kiki's mouth curled into a wicked smile. "That too. And at his age." She turned to Wanda. "The party will be an opportunity for me to get to know him so much better."

Wanda's lips twisted, the idea of Kiki cozying up to Alex like a punch in the spleen. Kiki was an unlikely candidate for his affections, but you could never count her out. What Kiki lacked in youth and attraction she made up for with blind aggression. "He was only being polite because he knows Hannah doesn't have a chance against him."

"You're wrong about that, Wanda," Kiki said, the words coming out with venom. "My sister will beat the poop out of Alex. Just you wait."

"Of course she will," Lauren chimed in.

Hannah was touched by their loyalty, but the ugly truth was that she had put herself in a hole. She was going to lose, not that it was that important. She could live with that kind of defeat. The worst part was that Signatech would take over the town. She felt depression creeping over her, along with the desire to eat something jam-packed with calories. She cast a longing eye on the plate of doughnuts.

"She doesn't have a snowball's chance in hell," Wanda spat. "And everybody knows it."

Hannah opened her mouth to agree with Wanda and put an end to the spat, but Kiki interrupted.

"I think you better visualize your flower, Wanda," Kiki said. "What was it? Oh yes, a snapdragon."

Wanda inhaled sharply and gave Kiki a frigid look that meant that war, or a least a major skirmish, was on the horizon. The other women sighed with relief. At last something was going to disturb the calm waters, only at the time they didn't realize exactly how much.

$\mathcal{T}$HREE

$\mathcal{I}$F ANYONE EVER WRITES THE global, all-encompassing history of lingerie and its impact on contemporary society, Kiki Goldstein will surely be mentioned as one of the most intrepid adventurers in that wilderness of elastic and lace.

Throughout her lifetime she had explored every bra and girdle, experimented with the pad and pushup, boldly forged into uncharted waters in the use of household objects to augment lingerie science's limited vision. Sure, she had stuffed socks in her bras like everyone else, but her imagination hadn't stopped there. Over the years, Kiki had used masking tape to lift her derriere and Elmer's Glue to maximize her cleavage. Her frenzied inspiration had blossomed in her teens when, in an attempt at tactile realism as well as size, she padded her bra with canned biscuit dough, enjoying an unexpected bonus when her body heat caused a rising effect.

It wasn't only vanity that fueled this creativity, but a quest for the lithe yet buxom body Madame Fate had, surely by clerical error, denied her. The miracle of silicone had finally given her the breasts she had prayed for, but the rest of her body was unfashionably plump and globular, drifting ever southward with the effects of age and gravity. Nevertheless, a warrior in makeup and lace, she continued to fight the good fight against time and DNA, always courageous, always innovative, using whatever implements happened to be handy.

"Oh piddle, my bra's coming loose," Kiki said, flipping down the visor, then scooching up on the seat to see herself in the mirror, impeded by the ends of her pink scarf blowing up and obscuring her face. She had put the scarf on at the last minute to protect her hair when the Cadillac's cantankerous convertible top refused to close. "Do you think I should just take it off and go braless?"

Turning north up High Valley Drive, Hannah glanced at her

sister with mock enthusiasm. "Good idea. It'll pull the wrinkles out of your face."

"This is serious. My paper clips are coming loose." Returning her attention to the mirror, she swiveled her shoulders, studying the effect with a critical eye. "Everything's sliding sideways."

Hannah kept her eyes on the road as the Cadillac climbed up Escondido Drive, the car expressing its reluctance with coughs and sputters. The road was twisting and narrow, suited for sleek BMWs and Porsches, not a 1972 gold Cadillac Eldorado convertible the size of a barge.

Hill Creek's narrow streets curved around the base of Mount Tamalpais, with some, like Escondido, snaking all the way up the mountain. Alex's section of the road lay midway up the incline, with costly homes tucked away on either side behind high-priced landscaping. It was Sunday and the street was quiet, with only a couple of Hispanic workers hauling plant debris from a two-story Mediterranean where someone, probably named Mitzi, decided she just couldn't stand those frightful oleanders another single second. It was twelve-thirty, and in a lower rent neighborhood you might have seen families coming back from church, but in this area people weren't the church-going type. They worshipped their inner child and their Reiki masters, and they prayed at the altar of the Nasdaq.

"I'm missing something. Why are you talking about paper clips?" Hannah asked.

Kiki gave her the look that said, *You're so incredibly dense.* "I didn't have the right bra for this dress. It's cut nice and deep around the shoulders, which is really sexy." Kiki twisted toward her sister, giving her shoulders a shimmy. Running late, Hannah had barely given Kiki a look when they walked out the door. Now she took in Kiki's hot pink dress with foreboding. Kiki had been beamed down straight from the Planet Zsa Zsa. The top clung to Kiki's ample figure as if she had been sprayed down with a garden hose, its deeply cut armholes exposing her pudgy arms and shoulders as well as a chunk of leopard print bra. In contrast, its skirt was a fluffy confection, which, along with Kiki's curled and swept up hair, made her look fabulously ridiculous, like a pudgy poodle stuffed into a pink tutu.

"I'm going for a look that says I'm mature, but still frisky," Kiki said, checking her lipstick in her compact mirror.

Hannah thought the look was more like manure and real risky, but didn't say it, since it was too late to go back home and change. They were already half an hour late due to Kiki's beauty preparations and Hannah practicing her speech for that night's debate. Stopping at a stop sign, Hannah took a better look at her sister. Kiki's self-tanning cream—bought on sale and applied liberally—had begun taking full effect, turning Kiki's face radioactive orange.

"You see, my bra straps showed," Kiki explained, since the perplexed look on Hannah's face indicated that the woman just wasn't getting it. "So I got this great idea, and I hooked paper clips to the straps, then put a rubber band between them. The rubber band pulls my bra straps together so they don't show. And you say I'm not good with mechanical things. But, darn it, I'm getting slippage."

"The pressure is probably stretching the rubber band," Hannah said, wanting to add that the pressure of holding Kiki's chest together would have strained steel cabling. "I know you're doing this to snag Alex, but I have to warn you. Bertha told me this morning at the grocery store that she heard he's involved with someone."

"I can overcome that."

"Does it involve a felony?"

"I'm not telling you any more. A girl needs her privacy."

"I don't want to hear, anyway. Just be on your best behavior."

"I'm only going to flirt with him a little."

"Remember, there's flirting and there's molestation. You need to know the difference. Now help me find Alex's house. It's number twenty-five. I see a lot of cars up there, so we must be close."

The Cadillac creeping along, they spotted Alex's address. A gray two-story Cape Cod, it had a curving drive of dark gray pavers, and a velvety lawn a shade of green Hannah always imagined she would see in Ireland. The house looked shiny new, though it was probably a remodel, the same as almost every house on the street. People in Marin seldom knocked down old houses. They preferred to expand and remodel them beyond recognition, and Hannah always considered this a reflection of the way Marinites often remodeled themselves. The local inhabitants were usually transplants from Nebraska or Mississippi or some other state they felt too small-minded to suit their big-time aspirations. They moved to the physical and intellectual

limit of the continent, changed their faces with surgery, their
bodies with personal trainers, and their brains with psychother-
apy until they were new and improved, barely recognizable ver-
sions of their former selves. But Hannah suspected that the
Marinites' old selves lay just beneath the glossy surface. Look
hard enough and you would find the old original beams and
joists.

Cars filled the street in front of Alex's house and Hannah had
to drive a block up the hill before she found a space at the curb
big enough for the Cadillac. She curbed the wheels, turned off
the engine, and checked her hair in the rearview mirror, while
Kiki pulled a bottle of perfume from her handbag, the heavy
flowery stuff Hannah referred to as "Eau de Lech," and gave
herself a blast on her neck, elbows, bosom, and knees. Hannah
jumped out of the car before the vapors could damage her lungs.
The remains of that morning's fog cooled the air, and Hannah
shivered. The cold didn't bother Kiki because she ran a few
degrees hotter than her sister.

"I'm so glad you changed your mind and decided to come to
the party," Kiki said, falling in step with Hannah as they walked
down the hill, Kiki holding onto Hannah's arm so she wouldn't
topple forward on her ankle-strap high heels. "It's going to give
him a chance to see me in a social setting. That's where I do
my best work."

"I'm going to this party for two reasons. First, if I don't,
everyone in town will think I'm a coward," Hannah said, reaching up to check one of the dangly beaded earrings that Perez
had given her. She decided that if she had to walk into Alex's
party a loser, at least election-wise, then she was going to be a
good-looking, well-dressed loser. She had worn her favorite
dress, a calf-length purple silk sheath, and pulled her hair back
into a sleek chignon. She had even worn makeup, including
mascara and blusher, along with her usual red lipstick.

Kiki frowned. "Why would people think you were a coward?"

"Because he's going to pummel me in this election. I don't
know anyone who's voting for me except you, John, Lauren,
and Naomi." She paused. "And I'm not so sure about you. But
at least I've raised the Signatech issue, and that's the main reason I'm here. I'm going to have a quiet talk with Alex and voice
my concerns to him directly. Who knows? Maybe I can change
his mind."

They started up a brick walkway lined with tufts of lavender that in a couple of months would bloom into a streak of breath-taking purple. Wide curving flowerbeds fronted the house, planted with a variety of salvias, verbena, and Mexican sage. A few dwarf cherry trees dotted the landscaping, the branches exploding with pale pink flowers. It all looked perfect, not a dead leaf on the ground. They were a few yards from the door when they heard their names called. They looked around but saw no one.

"Yoo hoo! Over here!"

Hannah turned and saw Althea sitting on the grass beneath a cherry tree near the corner of the house. Next to her stood a shakily printed placard that read "Save the Endangered Yellow-bellied Bush Cricket" and between her knees, a tall, narrow, primitive-looking drum.

"What are you doing?" Hannah asked as she and Kiki walked over.

"Exercising my civil rights." Althea proudly held up her wrist to show that she was chained and handcuffed to the tree. "He thinks he can placate me with that asinine rummage sale. Naomi loaned me the drum. Don't you love it? Every time Alex hears it he'll know I'm here, a living reminder of his treachery." She picked up a long mallet and gave the drum an ear-throbbing whack. After savoring the sound a moment, she gave Hannah a disapproving glare. "And what are you doing here? Succumbed to the devil's charms, eh?" Her eyes darted to Kiki. "Your bra strap's showing. Yes, Ms. Malloy," Althea said, returning her attention to Hannah, "traitor to the cause. You're going to suck up his cheese balls, gulp down his liquor, chat up his shallow, cricket-killing comrades. For shame." Althea said all this with a dramatic glissando, giving the drum a couple of thumps for emphasis.

"It's nothing of the sort, and you know it," Hannah said with more tartness than she intended, but Althea's remark stung. "If I can't beat the system, I have to try and change it."

"Oh, of course. Try to work from inside the system," Althea said with sarcasm. "That's what all revolutionaries say when they go soft."

Hannah lifted her chin. "I haven't gone soft."

"Prove it. I have an extra pair of handcuffs," Althea offered. "Together we could really show him a thing or two."

Kiki saw the contemplative glisten in Hannah's eye and gave her sister a poke. "Listen, Hannah, two women in their twenties chained to a tree is a hip political statement. Two women in their sixties doing it means they've both had strokes."

Hannah frowned. "It would get attention."

"So would running down the street naked tooting like a choo choo." Kiki pushed Hannah up the walkway. "You want to have a discussion with Alex, don't forget that. You can't do much persuading if you're chained to a tree like a German shepherd."

Hannah saw the logic. They stopped at the double, single-paned French doors with shiny brass handles, and just as Hannah started to ring the doorbell, she turned back to Althea. "Can I bring you some water?"

"No, thanks. It makes me have to wee, and I've already had to use his bathroom once," Althea said regretfully, reflecting on the tougher aspects of environmental consciousness. Then her eyes flickered as an idea struck her. "On the other hand it would make an emphatic political metaphor if I dropped my shorts right here and—"

"Don't even think of it," Hannah warned. "How about something to munch on?"

"It insults me that you would ask. I refuse to eat any of his food even if it means I waste away into a pile of bones right here," Althea replied. With a shrug, Hannah rang the doorbell. It chimed Bach. Cute.

Maggie, a friend from the Rose Club, opened the door. When Maggie wasn't growing gorgeous hybrid teas she worked at Alex's cleaning house and cooking. She was an interesting bird and Hannah had always liked her. Maggie had the ears and eyes of an eagle, and always knew the inside skinny on what was going on around town. And she was one of the few women Hannah knew who had eased into late middle age without trying to thwart it, even though Mr. Gravity hadn't been kind. Maggie's face was deeply lined and she didn't try to hide it, wearing no makeup and leaving her short-cropped hair a silvery gray.

"Hannah, Kiki, come on in," Maggie said with a welcoming smile, opening the door wide. "It'll be so good to have someone here I know. Most of these people I've never seen before. Where did they come from?" Maggie stepped out onto the porch. "Althea, hon, you want some more of those little vegetarian rumakis? Charlie said you loved that last batch he brought you."

Hannah gave Althea a look.

"Maybe just a few," Althea said quickly, avoiding Hannah's gaze, "to keep my strength up. Pounding the drum is so draining, I need the nutrients."

"I'll have them in a jiffy," Maggie told her. "Now get in here, girls," she said to Hannah and Kiki, nudging them inside. "I made all the food myself, including some killer pink daiquiris. And I've got juice I bought just for you, Hannah. Cranberry-grapefruit."

Hannah thanked her, always grateful when people remembered she was a teetotaler, reformed after decades of wine guzzling.

They entered Alex's house to the pounding of Althea's drum, and as soon as they stepped into the entryway, Hannah's heart sank. She had zero chance of any private chat with Alex. What he had called a quiet little lunch was in reality a boisterous party with close to fifty people in the living room alone, all of them shoulder to shoulder, chatting and laughing. A woman in a black dress and pearls played soft jazz on a black baby grand. Placed strategically around the room were large crystal vases with sprays of some exotic flower Hannah couldn't identify. Over a carved stone fireplace hung a yellow fabric banner that had "Vote For Portman" printed in big red letters. It's a campaign party for his supporters, Hannah realized with irritation. And he had the nerve to invite her.

While Hannah regretted ever walking in the door, Kiki radiated delight. She rushed forward to check out who was there.

With Kiki occupied, Maggie sidled close to Hannah. "I'm voting for you," she whispered. "I know other people who are, too, but they just don't say it out loud."

"Am I the political equivalent of hemorrhoids?" Hannah said good-naturedly. "Is voting for me that much of an embarrassment?"

"Of course not, but, well, Alex is the politically correct candidate, if you know what I mean. He hosted the book reception for the Dalai Lama last year, and then with his seminars."

"Yes, those seminars," Hannah said, unable to hide her scorn.

"Maybe on one level they seem foolish, but they've helped some people, they really have. The truth is, Hannah, and I mean this as a compliment, most people, when they think of you, think of your poems in the *Marin Sun* or your prize-winning roses.

They don't understand how sharp you are and what good ideas you have. But believe me, Hannah, there are people in this town dead set against Signatech, even if they don't broadcast it. I'm one of them, but you know I can't say anything publicly." Alex's voice rose above the loud conversation, followed by his raucous laugh. Maggie worriedly glanced his way, then back at Hannah. "He'd throw a fit if he knew."

Just then Althea's drumbeat grew louder and more rapid. "Oh, Althea wants her rumakis. I better scoot." Maggie took off before Hannah had a chance to thank her for the supportive words.

"This party looks scrumptious," Kiki said, back at Hannah's side. "So many good-looking men."

"This whole event is an Alex Portman love fest. Why did I come?" Hannah muttered.

"I would have died if I'd missed it." Kiki smacked her lips. "I've got to get one of those pink daiquiris."

"Don't overdo it. Best behavior, remember? It's possible that I have potential voters in here," Hannah said, considering what Maggie had just told her.

Kiki made a face. "Dreamer. No offense, but we might as well relax and enjoy ourselves. Most of these people have never laid eyes on you, and half of them are wearing 'I've Been Busted' buttons. There are only a couple of people I even recognize. I see Charlie Wright, and there's Mary talking to Alex. Hmmm. Sexy outfit."

Across the room, Hannah spotted Frannie in a blue cocktail dress standing next to Alex and Mary Katowski, a town council member. Mary was in her forties and had the figure of a twenty-five year old, which she had packaged nicely that day in slinky black slacks topped with a red blouse. Alex looked elegant in casual pants and a pale blue sweater.

Kiki's mouth bunched into a scowl. "Why there's Wanda! How did she get in here?" Kiki shot off to investigate. The pianist started playing a tune by Gershwin. Hannah moved to the dining room, where a long Biedermeier-style table was set with appetizers and drinks. She poured herself a cranberry-grapefruit juice, then wandered back to the living room and over to the fireplace for some intensive people watching.

The fashionable crowd looked well past their second cocktail, everyone juiced up and chummy. Hannah sipped her cranberry-grapefruit and checked out the particulars. Everyone was upper-crust Marin, a social strata well out of Hannah's league, with lots of bleached teeth, fake tans, and taut jaw lines. They dressed in dark fabrics accentuated by hefty jewelry and expensive haircuts, the women mostly blondes and redheads with curiously plump lips and straight noses. The men had tiny cellphones clipped to their Armani belts, ready for calls from their brokers even on a Sunday. They all looked giddy, high on stock options and Prozac.

Hannah noticed only one person in the room who didn't look like he was having any fun. Charlie Wright stood sulkily at the far end of the room, leaning against the arm of a suede sofa, not talking to anyone. Hannah guessed that he had realized he had been duped into coming, and unlike her, he didn't appear to be going with the flow. But then Charlie was the gloomy type who always seemed to be alone and not liking it. Not that he was an unattractive man. Any straight, halfway breathing adult male in the Bay Area was considered attractive by the female population. But Charlie's thinning hair never looked quite clean and his clothes were always haphazard. His party finery consisted of a green tweed jacket that was probably the height of fashion if you lived in the far reaches of Scotland and hung out with sheep, but was woefully dowdy at this chic gathering. Hannah found his lack of fashion sense charming, but most people wouldn't.

Hannah started in his direction, determined to cheer him up, but he took off, disappearing into the crowd before she could catch him.

Naturally nosy, she was interested in seeing Alex's house and managed to get the general layout through the mass of people. The living room bore a rustic elegance, a kind of intellectual country chic with original oil paintings on pale taupe walls, old ceiling beams, and a polished, distressed wooden floor covered with aged oriental rugs. She went up to the built-in bookshelves that covered an entire wall. The books were philosophy, classic fiction, and tall, glossy art books, the rows occasionally broken up by some small, artsy statue. The books looked color coordinated, and Hannah suspected with amusement that a decorator had bought them en masse.

She looked around for Kiki and found her flitting about, breezing along from man to woman then back to man again, always keeping one eye on the prize, which was Alex. He leaned against the piano, talking nonstop. From the rapt looks on the women surrounding him, Hannah figured he was outlining his cure for cancer or his new scientific discovery that reverses the aging process. Hannah saw Kiki ooze her way into the little group, but the women protected their turf, not letting Kiki get within grabbing distance of the man.

Cranberry-grapefruit not being her favorite juice or even one she especially liked, Hannah navigated through the crowd looking for the kitchen and a glass of water.

Following the delicious smells from the oven, Hannah found the kitchen at the back of the house. Though it was small compared to the other rooms' spaciousness, Hannah would have killed for it. She fell in love with the paned windows that opened to the garden, the gleaming granite countertops, and rich walnut cabinets.

Maggie had just taken out a tray of meatballs from the oven. Hannah asked where she could find a glass, and Maggie pointed an oven-mitted hand to a cabinet near the sink. There was a window by the sink and another larger one on the left wall over a built-in winerack. Hannah happened to glance that way while she filled her glass from the tap, and a rosebush outside that large window caught her eye.

It was too early in the season for full flowering, yet this rosebush already had two gorgeous buds, the petals white, tinged on the outside with deep red. Normally Hannah could name any rose with just one look, but this one stumped her. Alex had joined the Rose Club a year earlier, and Hannah suspected he had done it just to drum up business for his seminars. She considered that maybe she had been wrong about him, because the mysterious rosebush looked well shaped and cared for, and out the other window she saw more roses on the perimeter of the garden. Dying for a closer look at the spectacular rose, she moved toward the winerack, but a small crowd had gathered there, asking Maggie for meatballs. The things were selling like hotcakes, and the meatball-mad group stayed by the winerack waiting for Maggie to get the fresh batch onto a platter. Hannah was never to be thwarted when it came to a rose. Seeing the large greenhouse-style conservatory on the other side of the kitchen, Hannah headed for it. She thought the room would provide a decent view of that side of the garden.

About ten tables had been set up for lunch in the conservatory, each set with a white cloth, good china, gleaming silver, and a vase of flowers. The conservatory's glass walls provided a perfect view of the garden, so Hannah made her way through the tables to the far end where she thought she might get a better look. Maybe it was an antique rose, possibly a French bourbon.

"A bouquet for you, my lovely."

Hannah inhaled a cloud of spicy men's cologne and found Walter Backus, Wanda's husband, in the middle of it. Nattily dressed in a sharp blue blazer with a red silk handkerchief spilling out the top front pocket, Walter gripped a short glass of clear liquid that Hannah guessed was either gin or vodka, which was what Walter drank instead of water. In his other hand, he held a vase of flowers from one of the tables.

"May I say you look marvelous, as usual?" he said, his words slightly slurred, confirming Hannah's guess as to the contents of his glass. He moved his face close to hers and pushed out his lips like a dying flounder to kiss her, but she moved her head away just in time, and he kissed air.

"Give me that," hissed a voice sounding somewhere between a cat in heat and screeching tires. Wanda grabbed the drink from Walter's hand and whacked it down on the table next to him. Walter watched with sorrow as the sorely needed anesthetizing liquid sloshed over the glass's edge.

Wanda, who had the lithe figure of someone who had been dead a few weeks, wore tight black pants and a black cashmere sweater that perfectly coordinated with the dark glower she was giving her husband. Hannah couldn't decide who looked the most ticked off—Wanda, Walter, or Kiki, who stood fuming a few feet away. After getting a good look at Kiki's face, the award went to her.

"Stop running away from me. I want to know how you finagled an invitation to this party," Kiki said to Wanda through gritted teeth, a wineglass half-filled with pink daiquiri in her hand.

Giving Walter a temporary reprieve, Wanda pivoted to Kiki. "I told you, he called and invited me."

"After she made a big donation to his campaign," Walter said, obviously after revenge. He slid his hand on the table, inching his fingers toward his drink. Wanda's eyes turned glacial.

"You gave money to Alex?" Hannah said, her tone hurt. She

couldn't help feeling betrayed. She had known Wanda a long time.

"I'm going to make a donation to your campaign, too, Hannah," Wanda said sweetly.

Holding her wineglass with two fingers, Kiki waggled her pinky. "Liar."

The word "liar" was a gauntlet thrown. Wanda's eyes narrowed into little slits suitable for the ejection of laser death rays, and Kiki stared back with that brand of in-your-face bravado that comes from a snootful of spirits. Hannah noticed people spilling into the conservatory, and she knew she had to calm things down before Kiki and Wanda started throwing things.

Mary Katowski stepped into their circle and saved Hannah the trouble. "How are you folks doing?" she asked, appearing as concerned as Hannah about a potential catfight. "It looks like you're about to have a fistfight." Mary's cheeks were flushed, probably from the daiquiris, and the color heightened her quiet loveliness. She was one of those women who was pleasant-looking at first glance, beautiful if you took a longer look. Yet Hannah always thought that behind Mary's beauty was the sadness of someone whose life hadn't lived up to expectations, the same expression on those women in the *Oprah* audience who stand up and say how strong they've grown just as the tears start gushing. Hannah's heart always went out to them. She had been there herself.

"We're fine," Hannah told Mary. "I promise we won't start a brawl. At least not inside."

"I love the flowers," Mary said, looking at the tall vase still in Walter's hand. The flowers were a deep blue, small and cowl-shaped, a dozen of them hanging in vertical rows off long green stalks. Each vase held seven or eight stems along with a cluster of greenery. "Is it larkspur?"

Hannah nodded. "That or monkshood."

"That Alex," Walter said, his tone mocking. "Such excellent taste." As he spoke, his fingers wrapped around his drink, but Wanda slapped it away.

Hannah examined the flowers more closely, running her finger along the soft petals. "I think this is monkshood. You never see it at the florist. I wonder where it came from?"

"From Alex's garden," Mary answered. "Maggie told me she cut them herself late yesterday. She wanted to get the house set up in advance, so today she could concentrate on the food."

"She cut them yesterday?" Wanda said. "They don't look the tiniest bit wilted."

"Maggie has a secret for making them last," Mary said.

"A secret she'll share?" Hannah asked.

Mary laughed. "Maggie shares everything. She uses lemon-lime soda. It sounds crazy, but she adds a little to the water and swears it makes the flowers last twice as long."

"Soda? You know, I'm very thirsty," Walter said, giving Wanda a nasty look. He pulled out the flowers halfway and put the vase to his lips. Hannah took hold of his wrist.

"I wouldn't drink that," Hannah told him. "Those flowers are highly toxic and the water is probably toxic as well. Besides, Walter," she said, her smile turning wry. "You prefer other poisons."

"True, but I don't get them as often as I'd like," he replied moodily.

Listening to this exchange, Wanda got that kink in her upper lip that meant she was about to verbally bludgeon her husband, but Alex's arrival thwarted the attack. It was politically incorrect to browbeat your husband in front of Dr. Love.

"I'm so glad all of you could come. I feel so supported, so whole," Alex said, giving everyone his beaming I'm-the-Buddha-and-You're-Not smile. All other conversation in the conservatory halted, everyone's attention riveted to him.

He was in his rightful place, Hannah thought. Centerstage, all eyes upon him. She envied his confidence; she wished she had it herself. Alex bestowed more smiles and platitudes, sprinkling them on everyone like fairy dust. Mary and Wanda looked at him like he was Jesus and Brad Pitt wrapped up in one. Kiki looked at him the same way she would look at a fat slice of fudge cake. Walter just kept looking at his drink, still out of reach.

"I feel such a caring connection in this room," Alex said. "A feeling of such love and conscious living."

Of gastrointestinal distress, Hannah thought, wondering if this was when they were all supposed to kiss his ring. It was social situations like these when she missed liquor the most. Reformed drunks knew the hardest place to be sober was a party. She sipped her water and tried to pretend it was Walter's vodka.

Sometimes if she concentrated really hard she could almost feel a little relaxing buzz. Not this time.

"Alex, I'd like to discuss some issues—" Hannah started, but was interrupted by Kiki, who pushed past Hannah to get next to him.

"You're so right, Alex. I really feel a connection," Kiki gushed, giving her chest a jiggle.

"And almost everyone here is a Love Barrier graduate," Alex said. "Except you, Hannah. Now how are we going to get you into a seminar?"

"By tying me down and giving me sedatives," Hannah joked. Walter giggled, but everyone else gave her a cool stare, so she decided to soften the sarcasm. She was, after all, running for office. "Maybe one day I'll be talked into it." *When cows fly.* "But what's more important right now, Alex, is that you and I get a chance to talk about Signatech. If we could just find a private place."

As soon as she said it Alex stepped close to her and whispered in her ear, "You just don't give up, do you?" Hannah felt his hand rest on her behind. Her mouth opened slightly and she fell into a sort of stupor that lasted a good three seconds before she jumped away.

Not liking the whispering, Kiki inserted herself in the now wide gap between Alex and Hannah, pressing herself against him. "Alex, I was wondering—" she said, but before she could attempt her infamous pouty look and simultaneous thigh grab maneuver, Charlie Wright wrapped his hand around Alex's bicep.

"I want to talk to you," Charlie said, his tone gruff. He took a fortifying gulp of daiquiri. "In private."

The smile Alex gave him looked strained, but Alex excused himself from the group and the men walked just outside the conservatory's glass door, Alex closing it behind them.

Kiki glared at Charlie, ticked to the hilt at him for taking away her love object just when she had gotten things to the body contact stage.

"Grannie sucking eggs," Kiki muttered to Hannah, but Hannah wasn't listening, being way too busy trying to figure out what Alex had meant by that strange comment. If he thought she was going to drop out of the race, he would soon find out he was wrong. But even more puzzling was the rude way he had touched her. He did it as if she had invited it.

"Poor Kiki," Wanda said, the words drawing back Hannah's attention. "Always panicked for a man and never able to have one." Bombs away, direct hit. Kiki's face turned the color of her pink dress. Hannah shot Wanda a warning look, but she ignored it. "Everyday I thank God for my dear Walter. We couldn't live without each other. We have such a close, spiritual connection."

Wanda loved to wax on ad nauseum about the strength of her marriage. Whenever she started in on the topic, Walter always wore a morose look on his face, the same one Hannah's dog Teresa wore when she ate a lot of grass. Feeling sorry for him, Hannah casually put her hand on the table and, with one finger, pushed his drink within grasping distance. With a grateful nod, Walter took hold of it and downed the whole thing before Wanda could wrench it away.

"To our love," he said, his empty glass raised high.

Kiki was still red-faced and chewing her lip. Mary leaned close to her. "Your bra strap is showing," she whispered.

Kiki glanced at her shoulder and frowned. "Oh, darn." She reached one hand inside her top and began fiddling with the straps.

"You don't think I can beat you, is that it?" Charlie said to Alex, his voice tinged with rancor, his raised volume easily heard through the glass door. Everyone in the conservatory turned to look. The two men stood close together, Charlie pulling himself up to his full five feet, eight inches, his chest puffed and his finger jabbing at Alex's chest. Next to Alex's imposing height and good looks, poor Charlie, all nose and no chin, seemed a lesser species, a lone duck quacking at a magnificent swan.

Alex held up his hands, palms out, his Dr. Love smile firmly on his face. "Listen, Charlie, we're going to sit down to lunch in a few minutes. Take the seat next to me and we'll talk."

"Don't try to placate me. I'm not one of your little groupies."

"All I said was that I'd be surprised if you beat me," Alex told him. "I wish you the best of luck in the race, but the truth is, the town supports me. I've been a good mayor."

"You've been a popular mayor," Charlie replied. "Not a good one. And you know it."

Alex's smile faded. Hannah suspected he was experiencing some serious love channel blockage.

Mary let out a mew of disapproval then opened the door. "What are you talking about, Charlie?"

Charlie looked at her with pained eyes, then he turned back to Alex, his expression again flint hard. "Alex can explain it."

"Now, Charlie," Alex said, clasping Charlie's shoulder, "let's reconnect here. I think we should do a visualization together. Come on, Charlie, share this moment with me."

There was definitely a moment, but not the kind Alex was talking about, Charlie looking like he would rather connect his finger to an electrical outlet than connect anything with Alex. Hannah watched Charlie stiffening, his face reddening with anger. Worried that Charlie might actually throw a punch, Hannah was about to step toward them and try her best to defuse the situation, when Kiki's errant breasts, so often having a life of their own, saved her the trouble. At that moment a small projectile whizzed out of Kiki's top.

Wanda slapped her cheek and yelled. "Ouch! What hit me?"

Kiki's mouth rounded into a horrified "oh." Everyone, including Alex and Charlie, looked around the conservatory to determine what had been thrown and who had thrown it, but Hannah guessed the truth. Kiki's paper clip and rubber band contraption had exploded, her leopard print bra straps dropping down onto her arms, her breasts flopping to each side. One wrong move and they might escape the dress altogether. Kiki bolted from the room, clutching her dress top with one hand and dragging her sister with the other. She shoved through the people, then down a long hallway.

"You have to help me," she said to Hannah through clenched teeth.

"I can't. I've got to go back there and say something to Charlie. He looked so upset."

"He'll get over it. My situation's desperate."

The first open door was Alex's office. Kiki pulled Hannah inside, shut the door behind them, and locked it. It was a wealthy man's lair, painted a deep green with wood-framed engravings on the wall and a small bronze copy of a Degas ballerina on a credenza. Hannah noticed a photo of Alex shaking hands with the governor. A large legal-style oak desk sat near the back of the room, and behind it a comfy leather chair.

"Shouldn't we be in the bathroom?" Hannah asked.

"No, I've got to find another paper clip. I'll go through his drawers." Kiki began opening the desk drawers and rummaging through them. "Darn, wouldn't you know he'd be the neat type? Where would he keep paper clips?"

Hannah looked on with distaste. "You shouldn't be going through his things. It's an invasion of privacy."

Kiki stooped down and searched the desk's deep side drawers. "This is an emergency. They're going to sit down to lunch soon, and if I don't get out there quick I'll miss the chance to sit next to him. But I can't go back with my boobs loose."

Hannah tried to stifle a laugh but couldn't. "Maybe you should call the fire department."

"Keep the tacky comments to yourself." Kiki dropped to her hands and knees to search the floor. "The faster we find a paper clip, the faster we get out of here. So if I were you, I'd move my tushie."

Hannah knew it would be faster to give in than to protest. "I'll go through the trash. There might be a paper clip in there, though what I think you really need is an industrial crane." She knelt down and sorted through a wicker basket of mostly used envelopes with cellophane windows, the type that couldn't be recycled. She saw a few yellow sticky notes, some wadded tissues, an empty aspirin bottle, but no paper clips. Hearing laughter from the party and Kiki's repeated curses, she was about to give up and return to the party when one of the yellow notes stuck to her finger. As she pulled it off she noticed something scribbled on it, something that grabbed her attention. She read it, confused at first, and then with a creeping clarity that made her sick at heart.

FOUR

"WHY ARE YOU STARING INTO Alex's trashcan?" Kiki asked. "Is there something interesting in there of a personal nature?" A prodigious snooper, Kiki trotted over and peered down into the wicker basket, hoping wildly for crumpled love letters addressed to her, or revealing drug prescriptions.

"Not the kind of personal you're thinking of," Hannah replied.

"Then why waste time on it? Look, I found a paper clip, a nice big sturdy one." Kiki held up the object that for others would be an office product but for her was lingerie. "It'll only take a minute for me to get fixed up if you'll help me."

The information Hannah had just confronted had given her the jitters. She tucked the yellow note into her small velvet drawstring purse and helped Kiki attach the paper clip to her bra strap and then the rubber band. Her breasts safely harnessed, Kiki fluffed her skirt and checked her lipstick.

"Okay, I'm ready," she said, pasting a big smile on her face, but it wafted away. "What's wrong?"

For a few seconds Hannah battled over whether or not to confide in Kiki, but it was the kind of thing she just couldn't keep to herself. She pulled the yellow note from her purse. "I found this in Alex's trash. I think he's got something going on with Signatech."

"What are you talking about?" Kiki grabbed the note and stared at it in confusion.

"The letters 'STCH' are written in capital letters, and below that is the number five thousand followed by 'opt' and then the number six with a dollar sign." Hannah pointed at the last line. "And there's this long number with the dash in the middle."

"So?"

"The capital letters are the stock market symbol for Signatech. I know because I came across it several times when I was researching the company. And that last long number with the dash, it has to be an account number. It's similar to the ones for our IRA account. 'Opt' is probably an abbreviation for options, with six dollars as the option price."

"What do you mean by option?"

"An option is when a company gives you the right to buy stock at a certain price, usually a price lower than the stock's market value. So you buy the stock option at, say, a dollar, but the stock could be worth ten dollars. So you've just a made a nine-dollar profit without lifting a finger."

"How do you know this stuff?"

"Before I retired I spent at least a month out of every year typing up figures for annual reports and employee stock plans. I used to tell you about it, but you weren't interested."

Kiki's eyes scrunched as she struggled to get some of the data to register, but she wasn't having any luck. "I don't understand what it all means."

"It means that Alex Portman shouldn't be owning Signatech stock options when he's making decisions about the company moving to Hill Creek. His decisions should be based on what's best for the town, not what's best for his pocketbook. Signatech stock is currently running at about twenty-eight dollars a share. Five thousand options at six bucks each means over a hundred thousand dollars. Stock options come directly from the company itself. What's Signatech doing giving stock options to Alex?"

Kiki dismissively flapped her hand. "Oh, Hannah, you're always getting so riled up about things. It can't be what you think."

Hannah moved next to Alex's oak desk, running her eyes over the top. There were several piles of neatly stacked papers and a tray of unopened mail just begging to be scrutinized. "I'm going to find out one way or the other. You go back to the party. If someone asks for me, tell them I'm making a phone call." She flipped through the papers on the desk, not sure what she was looking for, then she locked in on Alex's black IBM laptop. If he was doing something unethical, any emails or files regarding it would be on his home computer and not his computer at work. Her hand moved toward it.

"Don't touch that!" Kiki slapped Hannah's hand.

Hannah wondered why her sister looked so rattled. "Why do you care?"

"Well," Kiki said, then paused, grappling for words. "Because it's an invasion of privacy."

"Kiki, you look in people's medicine cabinets when you use their bathroom. You go through men's underwear drawers to see if they wear boxers or tightie whities." Hannah's eyebrow lifted. "You go through women's purses when they leave the table to see if they're taking Oriental herbs that might have improved their skin."

"I looked in Wanda's purse that one time," Kiki said. She tried to toss it out casually, but she oozed panic. Hannah's Kiki radar detected a disturbing blip, and if she hadn't been so concerned over Alex and Signatech, she would have put the sisterly squeeze on Kiki until she spilled the goods. But just then Hannah had more important issues on her mind.

"Go back to the party. Jump in Alex's lap, have a fainting fit, hump his leg, anything to keep him occupied. Just don't let him come back here."

Kiki stood there, chewing her thumbnail while Hannah riffled through another stack of papers, and then she bolted out of the small office, closing the door behind her.

Hannah moved fast. She thumbed through every pile of papers on Alex's desk, and searched every drawer, finding nothing connected to Signatech. She lifted the top of the laptop, hearing with glee a soft whirring sound as the screen came to life. Using the mouse, Hannah clicked on an icon and opened his email system. Alex, like Hannah, had set the operating system to save his email password. That way he didn't have to retype it each time. It also allowed Hannah to go directly into his email with no trouble.

As soon as the first menu popped up in front of her, the guilt set in. It was wrong to invade Alex's privacy, and illegal for all she knew. She started to close the computer, but as soon as she touched it, her alter ego, the one that wasn't such a stickler on ethical issues, spoke with a tantalizing frankness. If Alex was doing something to hurt Hill Creek it was her duty to uncover it. Why should she be so skittish? What had happened to the old spirited Hannah, the brave, never-back-down Hannah, the one who had marched against the war and for women's rights, who had run bare-breasted into the police barricade at that pro-abortion rally in 1972? So what if she broke a few rules? With a bold and defiant index finger, she stabbed at a button and opened his inbox.

With all that buildup she had expected some marching music and waving banners, but all she got were a few emails that, from their subject headings, looked disappointingly benign. She clicked on the icon for deleted emails, knowing that people normally only cleared their deleted emails every few months, if they knew to clear them at all. She had worked for multiple presidents of the same corporation and one of them had gotten fired because he didn't know that deleted emails stayed in a special file until you disposed of them. The ones he had forgotten about had been quite incriminating.

Hannah hit pay dirt. She found at least a hundred emails that Alex had deleted but hadn't cleared. She scrolled through them, stopping when she heard footsteps coming down the hall. The steps passed and she assumed it was someone wanting the bathroom. Hurrying, she found several emails that had the subject heading "Stock." She clicked on one and opened it. It was from Alex's broker discussing some stock the guy felt sure would double over the next month. Nothing to do with Signatech. Hannah kept clicking on emails until she found the one she needed. The message was dated two months earlier from a Signatech vice president named Haynes and outlined an agreement giving Alex Signatech stock options that would vest once the company got town approval for the move. Dr. Love had taken a bribe.

She considered printing it, but was afraid that whoever had gone to the bathroom would hear the printer on his or her way back down the hall. She slid lower in the chair, her heart heavy. This potential dirt didn't bring her an ounce of joy. How could Alex have taken a bribe when so many people in town trusted him? All that bull about communal oneness. She reminded herself that maybe she was wrong. Maybe Alex had a perfectly reasonable explanation. And maybe the tooth fairy would pop in and give her a quarter. Still, she would ask him about it in private. If he had an explanation, fine. If he didn't, she would demand that he make the stock options public, and if he wouldn't do it, she would do it for him.

Hannah closed the email and scrolled through the rest of the screen. She saw a message showing her own electronic address as the sender, which was odd, since she didn't remember ever sending Alex any emails. Possibly he was on her distribution list for the Rose Club newsletter, but she had mailed that out the previous month, and the email she was looking at was dated from only a week before. She was about to open it, but her hand froze when she again heard footsteps and voices coming down the hall. She sat motionless. The voices sounded male and female, so she doubted they were heading for the bathroom. She closed the laptop, shutting it with a soft click. The footsteps halted in front of the office door, and along with them Hannah's heartbeat. She should have locked the door after Kiki. Too late now. She ducked beneath the desk, rolling the chair in as close to her as possible. The large desk had a solid front, so if someone opened the door to peek inside she wouldn't be seen.

Despair filtered through her as she heard the click of the knob and the sound of the door brushing against carpet. She closed her eyes and mouthed a curse.

"Everyone's about to sit down to lunch," a woman's voice whispered. "We can't do this."

"It's okay," said a male voice Hannah recognized as Alex. She heard the door close, followed by the lock. "We won't take long. We're used to offices by now. We've been making love in them for months."

The woman giggled. "Are you sure we should do this?" Hannah covered her eyes with her hands and mouthed, "Please, God, no, please, no."

Apparently God had a cute sense of humor. "I'm sure," Alex said. "Just relax. You know you want it."

The woman giggled again. Hannah burned to know her identity but not as much as she wanted to avoid being discovered hiding under the desk, so she stayed crouched in the small space, her knees aching, not daring to peek. *Please go away*, she silently begged. *Do it in the bedroom, the bathroom, on the kitchen counter.*

But the frisky couple had definite plans about staying. The desk bumped against Hannah's head, and she said a silent "ouch." Every corpuscle in her body groaned with foreboding as she heard the unmistakable sounds of heavy kissing.

A red silk blouse dropped on the floor by Hannah's foot. She wracked her brain to remember who had worn it, but couldn't, not with her mental wiring in its current stressed state. The noises got hotter and heavier. The desk started shaking and Hannah buried her face in her hands. How had this happened? It was one of those moments when a woman realizes she needs to reevaluate her decision-making processes, take stock of her life, consider taking up croquet or needlepoint, develop gout, anything to keep her safely at home and out of disasters like this one. These things never happened to anyone else she knew, except Kiki. Hannah wondered if it was genetic. If Alex found her, he would think she was some crazed pervert. What if he told people? Her reputation would be shot.

She instructed herself to remain calm. She took a very deep, very silent breath. All she had to do was stay where she was and be perfectly quiet. She checked her watch. It was a little after one. Maggie had to serve lunch soon, and Alex seemed like the self-centered slam, bam type, so it would all soon be over, and then she would go to her grave without ever telling a soul about this humiliating incident.

With a jolt, Hannah noticed that the blouse lay dangerously close to her feet. From the noises above, she felt certain the lovers were too busy to notice, so she gently pushed the pile of silk to a safe distance as the above-desk activity accelerated. Hannah kept her eyes on her watch. The happy couple managed to share some communal oneness, integrate physically, and bust through their love barriers in only three minutes. Hannah admired their efficiency. She personally had never made love on top of a desk, although that one boss of hers had, which was why he had been fired. If you're going to do those things at the office you shouldn't describe them over email.

"I love you," the woman whispered.

Hannah heard a zipper being zipped then felt another big bump against the desk.

"Damn it, Mary, I told you not to talk like that."

Hannah's mouth dropped open. Alex was sleeping with a city council member? Wasn't fishing off the company pier like that unethical?

"Listen, I know now's not the best time to tell you," Alex said. "But I feel a need to be totally honest with you. We can't see each other anymore, not like this."

"What do you mean?"

Hannah turned up her palms and mouthed, "What do you think?"

"I mean from now on our relationship needs to be strictly professional."

"So you fuck me and then break up with me?"

Hannah heard the beginnings of tears in Mary's voice.

"I'm afraid someone's going to find out about us."

"Why does it matter?" Mary said. "Don't you want to tell people about us?"

Alex's long silence answered Mary more profoundly than words. Hannah thought she could actually hear Mary's heart breaking.

"Listen, Mary, I don't want this to continue. We're not going to screw around anymore and that's the final word."

"Is that what you call it? Screwing around? You said our relationship was long-term. You made promises. You told me you loved me."

"I tell everyone I love them. I teach love seminars."

Hannah scowled. She felt like jumping out from under the desk and punching the son of a bitch.

"You're a sham," Mary said, her voice breaking, now in the middle of a full-blown crying jag. Hannah felt awful for her. "I always knew it, but wouldn't admit it. You're a moneygrubbing fake."

"Keep you voice down, for chrissakes." Alex sounded hard and cold, totally unlike his usual silky smooth self. *This was the real Alex*, Hannah thought, *the remodeled house with the old rotten floor boards finally exposed*. "Go upstairs and take one of my sedatives. I don't need a scene. I've got important people out there."

"You bastard," Mary whispered fiercely. Hannah nodded, mouthing an "Amen." A shaking hand reached down and grabbed the red blouse. "You fucking bastard," Mary repeated several times, keeping her voice low. Hannah heard light foot-steps followed by the door opening and closing. The she heard Alex buckle his belt and straighten up his clothes before he, too, made an exit.

That walking pile of shit, Hannah thought, still under the desk. Taking bribes was bad enough, but doing what he just did to Mary. That was unforgivable.

Burning with anger, Hannah got out from under the desk and straightened her clothes. It would have been so easy for Alex to have let Mary down easily. He could have told her in private, anyplace where she didn't have to go face a room of people immediately afterwards. The worst part was that he had sex with her first, then dumped her. That was cold, calculated, and designed to inflict maximum pain. It was unforgivable.

Hannah had an urge to walk out into the party, give him a swift kick in his Dr. Love command central, and tell everyone what a miserable scum he was. But that was Mary's prerogative, not hers. And Alex Portman would get his just desserts at the debate that night when she asked him in front of a hundred people and the local newspapers about those stock options from Signatech. Dr. Love would find out what it felt like to receive some unanticipated, unwelcome, and jolting news.

$\mathcal{F}$IVE

$\mathcal{W}$ANDA LICKED HER PINKIE THEN used it to smooth her pencil-thin eyebrow. "Politics. Such a scummy business. Full of deceit and lies and dirty dealing." The edges of her mouth curled up as she watched the crowd moving into the town hall assembly room for the mayoral debate. "Don't you just love it?"

Looking at Wanda's face, Hannah felt increasingly uncomfortable. Wanda lived off gossip and intrigue, and she currently exhibited the keen-eyed anticipation of a starving vulture circling over something wounded. Hannah had a sinking feeling it was her.

"You're wrong," Hannah said. "The mayoral candidates are behaving with decency and integrity." Other than a little bribe taking by the mayor, and Charlie almost socking the mayor in the nose that day at the party. But what was perfect?

"You look awfully stressed right now, Hannah," Wanda said, her concern sincere. "Are you okay?"

"Me?" Hannah asked, pressing her hand to her chest. "I'm fine. Really enjoying myself." *Just like I enjoyed that root canal last year.* Hannah gave Wanda a brave smile, not wanting to give her the satisfaction of knowing that her insides were liquefying into mush. She hadn't had anything to eat except for the two bites of salmon she managed to choke down at Alex's party. By the time she sat down to lunch, she was far too upset to eat, especially with Alex laughing and chatting as if nothing had happened, and Mary noticeably absent.

Hannah and Wanda stood in the back of the room near a double doorway that led to the lobby. Wanda still had on her black outfit from the party. Hannah had changed into a conservative dark blue dress, one she had bought a few years back for a funeral.

The assembly room had been added to the town hall the year

before. The project had been Alex's idea, and he had worked for weeks with the architects in getting the right design. It wasn't until later that Alex announced he planned to rent the room—for a low fee, of course—to hold his Love Barrier seminars. Big enough for two hundred love-starved people, the room was lined with stained wood, which, along with a matching vaulted ceiling, gave the place a rustic charm. Up front was a low stage extending to a peaked glass wall. The glass overlooked a wooded lot, so the stage enjoyed a pretty backdrop of trees. Hannah guessed that Alex thought all those green leaves would bring out the color of his eyes.

For the debate, chairs had been set up in even rows on each side of a center aisle. A banner that read "Don't Forget to Vote" hung over the glass above the stage, and red, white, and blue crepe paper draped the walls. So Dr. Love's words would blare out with crystal clarity, Alex had overseen the installation of a state-of-the-art sound system, and at that moment John Lennon crooned "Imagine" through top-quality German speakers. Lennon would have approved.

Her fist pressed against her mouth, Hannah stared with dread at all the people moving past her to find seats. Several friends waved and said hello as they went by, and Hannah returned their greetings with a forced cheerfulness and the clenched-teeth grin of someone whose bowels hadn't moved in weeks.

The crowd was mostly female, and at first it gratified Hannah to think the local women were so interested in town issues. She hadn't seen this many Hill Creek women in one place since the Macys lingerie blowout a few months earlier. But as she watched them scuttle by, their makeup fresh and their perfume thicker than industrial pollution, the truth hit her. These women weren't interested in civic topics. It was Alex they had come to see, to ogle and pay homage to their love-busting hero. And she planned to stand before this Alex-cult and confront their idol with the fact that he was a political cheat. It occurred to her that these women could turn vicious when they wanted, a fact she had learned the hard way over a fifty percent-off silk camisole at that Macys sale.

Three lecterns stood on stage, with Hannah's name hand-printed in black on a sign fastened to the lectern on the left. The sight of it tightened her gut, the scene looking remarkably similar to her high school campaign debacle. For the tenth time, she reached behind and made sure there was no toilet paper hanging out of the back of her dress.

"I won't mince words," Wanda said. She ran her palm over her sleek cap of hair. "You look very, very nervous, and there's no reason to be. Yes, Alex is going to eat you alive tonight, gnaw the flesh right off your bones. But, dear, try to feel the love that's behind it." Wanda crossed her arms and squinted at her friend. "You know, you've been acting jumpy ever since Alex's lunch today. You poor thing. There's no reason to get so down on yourself. Remember, there have to be some losers in this world in order for there to be winners."

Hannah wished she had one of those rifle-sized squirt guns. She felt an elbow in her ribs and found her sister attached to it.

"We've got a problem," Kiki said. Wanda brightened. "Lauren won't come out of the ladies room. She's locked herself in a stall, and she's on one of those weeping jags."

"She didn't rent *Terms of Endearment* again, did she?" Hannah asked. "I thought the video store agreed not to let her have it anymore."

"It's worse than that," Kiki replied. Her surgically sculpted nostrils flaring, Wanda stepped in closer so as not to miss a syllable. "Our cute Detective Morgan is here with another woman." Kiki gave the last two words the same husky inflection she would have used for "Nazi spy." Hannah flinched. This was not good.

Lauren was an intelligent, kind-hearted girl, but socially slow to the point of being in reverse. Hannah blamed it on the death of Lauren's mother ten years before, which Lauren had taken hard. Hannah and Kiki stepped into her mother's shoes, and on the whole Lauren thrived, except when it came to her social life. As far as Hannah could tell, Lauren had never had an actual relationship with a man.

Kiki went on. "As soon as Lauren saw Morgan walk in here with that tramp—"

"Don't call her a tramp," Hannah reprimanded. "We don't even know her, and it's not right in any case."

"Okay, as soon as Detective Morgan walked in with his little piece of gutter fluff, Lauren ran for the restroom. She says she's staying in there until she hits menopause. You've got to help."

"I can't. I'm supposed to be on stage in two minutes," Hannah told her, the old high school trauma too vivid for her to go anywhere near a ladies room with Kiki just then.

"I thought she and Morgan had a big date awhile ago," Wanda said. "Didn't things progress?"

Kiki shook her head with the gravity of a surgeon telling the family that the patient had just died. "She thought they were going to a movie. Turned out to be a film on camping safety at the fire department."

"Poor, poor thing." Wanda opened her Gucci clutch and pulled out something. "Give her this." She pressed some tiny tablets into Kiki's hand. "It's Valium."

Hannah's brow furrowed. "I didn't know you took tranquilizers."

"I don't. I'm completely soul-enriched and peaceful. They're Zeno's."

Hannah's brow furrowed more deeply. Zeno was Wanda's nasty little dog. No one loved animals more than Hannah, but even she had trouble warming up to this detestable canine, who snarled constantly and enjoyed peeing on people's shoes.

"He's been under stress, you know, with Saturn being in retrograde, and him being a Libra. Then there's his flea problem. His tranquilizers are perfectly safe for humans. Walter takes them all the time."

Hannah found it interesting that everyone who lived with Wanda, including the dog, needed to be sedated. Her tropical fish were probably on Quaaludes. "I don't think Lauren is at the point of needing medication."

"But close as a nose hair. I'll keep them handy," Kiki said, and dropped them in her purse. She turned back to her sister. "Okay, I'll try and talk Lauren out, but if you ask me, her problem is that she dresses like a spinster schoolteacher. She's got to branch out with her wardrobe. Strut her stuff. Shake her bootie." To demonstrate, Kiki pumped her arms and shimmied her hips. "If you're going to catch a fish you need to jiggle the bait a little so the fish knows it's alive. I should give her a Kiki Beauty Blitz."

Hannah considered taking the tranquilizers herself.

Kiki took off, with Wanda right behind. Hannah was looking around for Perez when she saw Mary, who was the debate moderator, walking briskly up the aisle toward her. Mary wore a blue pantsuit, pearls, and the visible suffering of the recently dumped. It occurred to Hannah that Mary and Lauren should get together for a couple of margaritas and some verbal man bashing, but then she realized there wasn't much similarity in the two situations. Lauren had received a blow, but the damage was surface only. You could tell by Mary's face that her wound had reached bone.

"It's time to go up, Hannah. We'll be starting in three minutes, and I want all the candidates in their seats," Mary said, her voice flat. Hannah saw a deadness in her eyes. She felt sorry for Mary having to face Alex only hours after his brutal treatment of her. Hannah wanted to console her, but she couldn't let on what she knew.

Hannah said that she would be right up, and Mary walked down the aisle toward the stage. Hannah was about to follow when she saw Perez come in through a side door. She waved, and he headed her way. She noticed that he had dressed up for the occasion, with a sport coat and slacks, his receding gray hair carefully combed. Knowing he was getting favorably assessed, he gave her his best grin, the type that crinkled up his eyes and always melted her. Perez was a rare combination of hard edges and softness. Before he had retired he had been a Marin police chief, a good one, good enough for the local departments to still call him when anything big came up. He had been tough and relentless at his job, but now he had mellowed into a doting grandfather, an enthusiast of dogs and hiking, and the tender lover of Hannah. She couldn't believe her luck.

"You made it," she said as soon as he reached her.

Like an embarrassed fifth grader, he checked to see if anyone was looking before brushing his lips against her hair. "Knock 'em dead tonight." He stepped back, studied her, then clasped her hand. "Are you okay?"

"Just nervous."

"You've got lots of people here for you."

"Kiki says that if I get too tense during my speech, I should imagine everyone in the audience naked."

"But try to imagine me a little thinner," Perez joked.

Hannah heard the clicking of high heels and saw Kiki rushing through the lobby.

"Lauren's coming out, thank God," Kiki said. "Wanda's helping her fix her makeup. I wanted to get out here quick because there's something I need to tell you, and I wouldn't want Lauren to hear it, not in her situation."

"What is it?" Hannah asked.

"Just that my love life is taking off like the space shuttle. Alex is meeting me for a drink after the debate. I knew that pink dress would do the trick."

Hannah looked incredulous. "When did this happen?"

"Just now. Today at the party I told him I wanted to meet him after the debate tonight for a drink to discuss campaign issues. He didn't answer then, but I just checked our voicemail and he said he'd meet me."

"Kiki, it's not right for you to be discussing my campaign with him."

"Oh, don't get your panties in a twist. We're not really going to be talking politics. I saw it in his eyes today. He's falling for me. I'm going to be the mayor's girlfriend, and just think of the status. I'll probably get free parking. Wanda will have a fit."

Kiki looked happier than Hannah had seen her in weeks, and she hated to rain on the parade, but she had to. "I don't want you going out with him."

"Why?"

Hannah battled with herself over whether to tell her sister about that afternoon's fiasco. Kiki couldn't keep a secret, but Hannah didn't want her sister getting in the clutches of a jerk like Alex. She opted for the vague approach. "He's a difficult man."

"My favorite kind."

"Anything with sideburns is your favorite kind."

"Don't try to talk me out of this. It's my chance at happiness."

Hannah made a soft growling sound at the back of her throat. When it came to men, Kiki's brain was a hardboiled egg. "Well, at least, don't discuss my campaign." She leaned close to Kiki and whispered so Perez wouldn't hear. "And don't tell him that we went into his office or how I found out about his Signatech options."

"You think I'm nuts? Trust me, our conversation tonight will be strictly of a personal nature."

"I still don't like this," Hannah said. "You could get your feelings hurt."

"Stop worrying about me. I see Wanda and Lauren over there. I'm going to sit down with them. I'll save a seat for you, John." Kiki waved goodbye, then headed off down the aisle with a new bounce in her step.

"Don't take all this so seriously, Hannah," Perez said as soon as Kiki was out of earshot. "Your sister can take care of herself." He kissed her on the forehead, and Hannah looked up at him with affection. His encouragement didn't make her feel any better, but it was nice of him to try.

Perez left to find a seat, and Hannah started for the stage, but out of the corner of her eye she saw Naomi in the lobby just inside the entrance door, pulling on the corner of her brown caftan, which had gotten caught in the doorway. As she tugged, the turkey feathers on her scalp flopped around, the clump of them sitting lopsided on her head, as if she had put them on in a rush. In one hand she held her Hopi war stick. The war stick, about three feet long with bells and feathers attached at the top, was a bad omen. Naomi finally freed herself, and then saw Hannah. Naomi frantically waved her over. Struggling for breath, Naomi grabbed Hannah's hand and pulled her into a corner.

"I ran from the parking lot and I can barely talk. Hannah, don't go on that stage tonight," she said, panting. "Walk away."

"What are you talking about?"

Naomi gulped some air. "I was lying on the couch for a snooze about an hour ago, and I must have slipped into an alpha state. I was in a trance, and I felt Red Moon surging inside me, rolling through me like a giant wave. It was so powerful, I could hardly breathe."

"Are you sure you weren't having that Richard Gere dream again?"

Naomi lifted her chin. "I know the difference. This scared the wits out of me. Red Moon definitely gave me a warning."

The music in the main room stopped, and Hannah's stomach wrenched. The debate was about to start. "I'd love to hear about this, but I've got to go."

Naomi's grip on Hannah's hand tightened. "It was a warning about tonight. Something about the black coyote coming down from the hill, and the coyote killing the fox." Her eyes drifted off. "Or maybe the fox killed the coyote. Or it bit the coyote's paw really hard. Oh, hell, I don't know. The point is, something bad is going to happen tonight."

Hannah glanced at the stage. Charlie was already seated, and Mary stood behind the lectern, looking Hannah's way. "Naomi, I know you're just trying to help, but I've got to get up there. The debate's going to start."

"Don't risk it!" Naomi gave the war stick a shake, the bells jingling. "Red Moon was so emphatic. And you know he's always really liked you."

"Have you told him I'm dating someone?" Hannah said coyly.

"This is serious. The negative frequency was just like that day you filed for the election, but much stronger. So much stronger. Red Moon feels an evil blackness, and it's associated with the mayor's race."

The tremor in Hannah's stomach grew into a more potent rumble. "He's always feeling something terrible," she said. "He's a worrying old woman sometimes."

"I'll tell him you said that. You know he doesn't mess around. He means what he says."

That much Hannah agreed with, but she couldn't back out of a public debate at the last second because a dead Hopi shaman suggested it. It could raise questions about her leadership skills. "Naomi, I appreciate the warning, but I have to go up there."

"I knew you'd be stubborn, so I've taken precautions." Naomi dug into the velvet backpack hanging from her shoulder and pulled out a small burlap bag hung on a thin leather strap. "Put this on."

Hannah sniffed it. "It stinks."

"It's a talisman."

"It's herbs and bacon fat. I smelled you wearing it last week."

Naomi slid it over Hannah's neck just as Mary called Hannah's name over the microphone. "I'll be performing the ceremony in a minute. I'm going to invoke the healing energies of White Buffalo Woman and ask for her guidance and protection. That, along with the talisman, might just keep the metaphysical shit from hitting the fan. But I make no promises."

"All right, do the ceremony," Hannah said hurriedly, putting the leather strap over her head, then tucking the talisman down the neck of her dress. She looked at the stage and saw Mary waving her up. "But do me a favor and do your dance in the lobby so you don't distract people from the debate." Naomi nodded.

Hannah scooted up the center aisle, bounded up the two stairs to the stage, and sat down in the chair next to her lectern. Charlie sat with his hands twisting in his lap, red blotches breaking out on his face. Alex's chair was empty.

A few stragglers came in the backdoor and found seats, and

Hannah saw about a hundred people in the audience, a decent turnout. It should have made Mary happy since the debate had been her idea, but she appeared grim and restless, her expression alternating between grimaces and faked smiles.

At last Alex made his entrance, striding up the center aisle and onto the stage, looking casual and confident in slacks and a mock turtleneck topped by a leather jacket, his signature outfit, the one he always wore when he led his seminars. His relaxed garb made Charlie look like a choirboy in his dark suit, white shirt, and striped tie knotted tightly at his throat.

There was a smattering of applause when Alex sat down. He smiled and waved at the audience, raising his "I've Been Busted" water bottle for all to see.

Alex doesn't look well, Hannah thought. His face was as white as his dental work, there was sweat on his forehead, and he kept opening and closing his fist. Hannah found it strange that everyone on stage seemed so agitated, when it was just a small town political debate. Mary looked on the verge of tears. Charlie shifted impatiently in his seat, the red blotches creeping up his bald scalp, and Alex looked just plain sick. To control her own nervousness, Hannah tried to ignore the fact that a hundred people were staring at her by looking past the sea of faces to the end of the room. Through the rear door she saw Naomi in the lobby, swaying with her arms raised, the Hopi war stick bobbing. Naomi's mouth was working and Hannah felt sure she was chanting.

Mary laid a few papers and a glass of water at a small table to the left of the lecterns. The audience was seated but there was still a rumble of conversation, and Mary walked to center-stage and asked for their attention, her voice amplified through a tiny microphone clipped to her blouse. The candidates were supposed to use the microphones attached to their lecterns.

The room now quiet, Mary first reminded everyone to turn off their cell phones, then introduced the three candidates. There was huge applause for Alex, followed by only a smattering for Charlie. Hannah had an even less enthusiastic reception, but Perez, Lauren, and Kiki whistled and hooted in the second row, which kept it from being embarrassingly quiet. She also noticed Detective Morgan clapping with enthusiasm. Hannah got a good look at his date and thought she had seen the young redhead before in uniform. Morgan was dating a cop. They probably had loads of fun telling each other to assume the position.

Mary explained the debate format to the audience. Each candidate had fifteen minutes of speaking time with an additional twenty minutes for questions from the audience and the other candidates. They had drawn lots to determine speaking order. Hannah was relieved to be going last. Poor Charlie was going first.

Charlie slowly stood up from his chair and stepped to his lectern as if it were a hangman's scaffold. He stumbled over his speech, talking mainly about his number of years in the community and how he supported the Signatech move. Rattled by someone's cell phone chirping Mozart, he dropped his notes, the papers gliding across the floor. Hannah retrieved them, whispering a reassuring "You're doing great" in his ear. It didn't look like he believed it.

Somewhere in the middle of his talk he worked in a bit about his business experience, and how he could use the skills as mayor. From where Hannah sat, he would have been better off trying to sell the crowd discounted transmission overhauls, since from their glum expressions it didn't look like they were buying his political sales pitch. Hannah thought it was a shame that people couldn't see past his exterior, because Charlie would have made a pretty good mayor.

She knew when Charlie finished his speech, because it was the only time he looked up from his notes, his giant sigh of relief shared by the audience. He looked grateful when there were only a couple of easily answered questions.

Alex was up next. Hannah felt the audience's anticipation as he moved to the lectern. She studied him, trying to figure out what it was about the man that had grabbed everyone's attention. Maybe it was his good looks, maybe his forceful personality. Maybe it was that folks were used to paying a couple of hundred bucks for one of his seminars, and now they were going to get fifteen minutes of psychobabble for free. But they would be disappointed, for tonight Alex lacked his usual shiny bright pizzazz. He didn't gesture, he faltered when he spoke. Hannah considered the possibility that she had misjudged him when it came to women. He could be upset about what happened between him and Mary. A lot of men displayed an outward coolness that hid their true feelings.

His voice thin, Alex spoke about Hill Creek's prosperity, the generosity of its citizens, its atmosphere of celebration and growth that served as a model for the rest of the county. Sitting stick straight in her chair, Hannah clasped her hands in her lap and tried hard not to roll her eyes. It was the usual Portman pep talk, high on hyperbole and shy on substance. He said nothing about any past accomplishments or future plans. He didn't even mention Signatech. He was rattling on about love again when a shout came from the back of the room.

"Killer! Murderer!"

Everyone gasped, turning their heads toward Althea as she chugged up the aisle with such a lumbering force they expected to see a trail of smoke behind her. Knowing all eyes would be upon her, Althea had accessorized her walking shorts and her "Portman Is A Prick" sweatshirt with a baseball hat topped with a foot-long plastic cricket that wiggled as she moved. She carried a placard that read "The Sin of Signatech." Hannah had to hand it to her. Althea knew how to get attention.

Like everyone else, Alex was startled, but quickly resumed his gracious smile. "Now, Althea, I appreciate your concerns, and you know I'm always one for an open discussion."

"Hah!" Althea shook her sign. "You've refused to even speak to me! My message to the people will not be suppressed!"

Detective Morgan stood up and squeezed past the people seated in his row.

"I'm sensing a troubling hostility from you," Alex said to Althea. "I think it's time for us to celebrate our sense of community. Why don't we all close our eyes, take a few deep breaths, and visualize—"

"Crickets!" Althea shouted. "That's what we should be visualizing, you ignoramus! Because there won't be any more of them if you get your way!" A couple of shouts from the audience for her to sit down only inspired her to higher volume. "We can't let innocent wildlife be trampled in the name of so-called progress!"

"I trampled a cricket just the other day," someone in the audience joked. Althea spun around to see who had made the remark, ready to clobber somebody in the name of insects everywhere.

Like Gary Cooper in an old Western, Detective Morgan made his way up the aisle and, without fanfare, grabbed the sign Althea now shook threateningly at the man she had decided was guilty of the cricket comment.

"We all appreciate getting to hear your view of things," Morgan said to her, "but you've made your point. It's not fair to disrupt the entire debate, now is it?"

At first Althea grabbed back the sign and glared at him, but his gentle firmness and Gerber baby face calmed her. Hannah caught sight of Lauren watching Morgan with lovesick longing. He continued soothing the savage beast in Althea, his head bent close to hers. Hannah couldn't hear everything he said, but his voice was gentle and his manner full of authority. It occurred to Hannah that if she had ever had a son, she would have wanted him to be just like Detective Morgan. Of course, Morgan as a nephew-in-law would be the next best thing. But how to get rid of that little piece of gutter fluff?

Althea, now meek as a puppy, followed Morgan back down the aisle, rested her sign against a wall, and politely took a seat in the back row.

Still behind the lectern, Alex tried to laugh, but he wasn't pulling it off. *He's sick*, Hannah decided. *He's got the flu or some virus.*

He made a flattering remark about Althea's commitment to her beliefs and then closed his remarks, even though he had a good eight minutes of speaking time left. Mary stood up and opened her mouth to say it was time for questions, but Alex beat her to it, opening it up for questions himself. You could have cracked a walnut with Mary's smile.

Hannah tensed. It was show time. If she was going to confront Alex on Signatech she had to do it now. A few people from the audience asked benign questions, which Alex answered quickly. One brave soul asked him about potential traffic congestion as a result of Signatech, but Alex ducked it, saying the town was doing a study. Alex had lied, Hannah was sure of it, and even if there was a study, what good would it do? The city didn't have easements to widen the roads. Did Alex think they would tear out the sidewalks? Hannah's heart thumped. She had to make her move with that bogus remark fresh on his lips. He thanked everyone then turned to sit down. Hannah scooted to the edge of her chair and cleared her throat.

"I have a question," she asked.

"What was that?" Mary asked, trying to resume her moderator role.

"I have a question for Mayor Portman," Hannah said more loudly.

She could tell that it threw him. A frown flashed across his face. He followed it up with a smile, then took a big drink from his bottle.

"Of course, Hannah," he said.

"Why don't you come to the lectern and use the microphone so everyone can hear?" Mary said, gesturing to the lectern with Hannah's nameplate.

A few pints of blood rushed to Hannah's face. She was in high school again, with toilet paper trailing out her skirt and everyone in the audience laughing at her. She swallowed hard. *Just get up there and do it*, she told herself. *You're sixty, not sixteen.* She rose from her chair and walked to the lectern. Taking a second to steady her nerves, she glanced at the back of the room, and through the doorway saw Naomi dancing and swirling in the lobby, her movements fast and frenetic, her knees raised high, one hand swinging the Hopi war stick over her head like a sword.

"Mr. Mayor," Hannah said, her voice cracking, the words sounding like a hiccup. Perez gave her an encouraging thumbs up, and Kiki mouthed the word "naked." Lauren was so busy staring at Detective Morgan she wouldn't have noticed a terrorist attack.

Hannah coughed. "Mr. Mayor, you have actively promoted the idea of Signatech moving to Hill Creek."

Alex started to speak, but Hannah, afraid to lose momentum, didn't give him a chance.

"But isn't it also true, Mr. Mayor," she said, her voice gaining volume. She gripped the lectern's edges with both hands, her knuckles whitening. "That Signatech recently gave you a substantial number of stock options?"

Portman's shocked expression told Hannah he hadn't intended the information to be public. There was dead silence. Portman took a big gulp from his bottle.

Signatech had bribed Alex, Hannah now felt completely certain. She had taken a risk by mentioning the stock, but it had paid off. He had no innocent explanation. All color had drained from his face and she saw his hands trembling. He looked awful, and the nice girl in her wanted to back off, but if she did, he would find some way to brush off the accusation, to tell some lies and save himself. She forced her mouth to open and form words. Dr. Love was going down.

"And wouldn't that give you a conflict of interest, if not worse, in making any decisions regarding that company?" she asked. "Can you explain why you accepted a large gift of stock options from them when the town council is making a critical decision concerning Signatech and the future of our town?"

She glanced at Mary. Mary didn't look happy at all, her eyes darting between Alex and Hannah.

Portman started to reply but the words froze in his throat. He seemed strangely bewildered. Movement in the back of the lobby caught Hannah's attention, and through the doorway she saw Naomi dancing wildly, hopping and waving her arms as if doing jumping jacks. Hannah looked back at Alex. He grabbed at the top of his sweater, pulling it away from his throat.

"Have you a response, Mr. Mayor?" Hannah pressed. "I demand a response."

Portman made a choking sound as if he couldn't breathe. He walked a few steps toward her, his legs stiff, then he stopped and stared down at his hands. He looked back up at Hannah, his eyes frightened, just before his legs buckled and he collapsed. There was a horrified silence, and then a woman screamed. Rushing to him, Hannah kneeled down beside him.

Kiki scrambled out of her seat, her legs sailing over the woman in front of her, planting a high heel in the woman's thigh just before she bounded up the steps to the platform.

"Alex, honey! Don't do this," she said, dropping to her knees beside him and patting his face. Then, with the irony of at last being in the position for which she had so longed, she gave him mouth to mouth.

Hannah shouted for someone to call an ambulance, and at least fifty people pulled out their cell phones. Hannah, Charlie, Mary, and a handful of people in the audience gathered around Portman and Kiki. Charlie started to pull Kiki away, but Hannah held him back. She had made Kiki take a CPR class with her, and although Kiki had jokingly done some regretful things with the male dummy, she had learned basic skills.

Kiki breathed into his mouth again and again. After a couple of minutes, she stopped, too out of breath to continue. Alex's eyes were closed, his face gray. Kiki looked up at Hannah with panic. Charlie knelt down and pressed his head against Alex's chest. He looked up, his eyes wide and frightened.

"His heart's not beating. I think he's dead."

Six

$\mathscr{H}$ER INITIAL RESENTMENT WAS DIRECTED at the alarm clock. Eyes closed, her hand fumbled with the books, the glasses, and various pens and papers on her nightstand, at last felt the clock, and gave its alarm button a punitive slap. The ringing continued. With a groan she rolled to the other side of the bed, grabbed the cordless phone and pressed the talk button, growling hello into the mouthpiece.

"Are you all right?" It was Perez.

"I don't think so." Hannah opened her eyes, the light pouring in through the window making her squint. Twisting around, she asked forgiveness from the clock for hitting it. She'd had that clock for over twenty years and had affection for it. When she saw the time, she muttered a "damn" and knocked the clock onto the bed. It was an up and down relationship. "It's already nine. Half the day's gone." Her head dropped back into the pillow.

"Trouble sleeping?" Perez's voice was strong and kind, resonating with the promise of some deeper knowledge, like FM radio in heaven.

"Didn't catch a wink until three," she said groggily. "I kept thinking about Alex."

"You should have come home with me."

Hannah pulled herself up on her elbows and pressed her hand to her forehead, the previous night's horrific details coming back with a nauseating clarity. The god-like Alex lying motionless on the platform, mouth open, saliva on his face. The arrival of the paramedics with their equipment, pushing everyone out of the way. A woman shrieking, throwing herself at Alex's feet and kissing his tasseled Cole Haan loafers. Hannah remembered someone trying to drag the woman away, but she kept holding on to Alex's foot, and they couldn't get her off him until finally she pulled off his shoe. Oh, yes, that was Kiki. The sharpening image made Hannah cringe. The paramedics had put something that looked like irons on Alex's chest that jolted his body, causing it to arch off the floor. Hannah and Kiki had stood in the crowd clutching each other as the paramedics tried to bring him back to life. At that moment Hannah forgave Alex for hurting Mary, for taking that bribe. She forgave him for any awful things he planned to do in the future.

"They weren't able to revive him at the hospital," Perez said.

Hannah felt a stab. But she knew Alex was dead when they put him in the ambulance. She just knew.

"Was it a heart attack?"

"They think so," Perez said. "Maybe it was."

"You're not telling me everything. What is it?"

There was some dead air.

"That's why I called you," he finally said. "There's something I want to tell you. Something about Alex."

Hannah sat up, now wide-awake. A gust of chilled air blew through the open window, and she pulled down the sleeves of her flannel pajamas, her favorites with the cowboys and bucking broncos, the ones she would never let Perez see. "What is it?"

"I spoke to Louis, my friend from the coroner's office, just now. He's an investigator. He told me that Portman died of heart failure. He also told me that it doesn't look right to him. They're going to do a postmortem. Louis has asked for tests."

"What kind?"

"Toxicology. They'll check for the usual overdose stuff— opiates, amphetamines."

"They think Alex was a drug user?"

"They don't know. You see, Louis knew Portman. He called Portman's doctor, woke him up last night, and found out that Portman was healthy as a horse."

"And he thinks Alex could have taken something that caused a heart attack?"

"Hannah, doesn't it seem odd to you that a perfectly healthy guy would drop dead like that?"

Hannah sipped her espresso and stared at the *New York Times* crossword puzzle, trying hard to focus on number four across, a five-letter word for "fatal surprise," and not the fact that everybody in the Book Stop Café had their eyes stuck to her. And it was the way they were looking at her, the way Greenpeacers would stare at someone who had just slapped a baby seal.

Kiki had awakened that morning right after Hannah, and it felt too late for making breakfast. They dressed, fed the pets, then drove to the Book Stop bookstore and café, one of Hill Creek's main nerve centers. The Book Stop provided pretty much the same informal news retrieval service as Lady Nails, but for the town as a whole rather than just the postmenopausal manicure crowd. With its old tile floor and salmon-colored walls, the Book Stop was the playpen for the town's pseudo-intellectuals, boasting an atmosphere of New Age chic and tattered erudition. Hannah went there because it was locally owned and the coffee was as thick as motor oil, just the way she liked it. Kiki tagged along because the café was a watering hole for male senior citizens, a place where retired professionals in jogging outfits sat at wobbly tables and discussed politics and kept up on the stock market with their WAP Palm Pilots.

The sisters had commandeered their favorite table, the large one by the arched windows where they could watch the bustling town plaza as well as what went on in the café.

"I loved my Alex and he loved me. Or he would have loved me," Kiki muttered, her eyes moist. She raised her fist. "We were going to bust some love barriers, blast through them like dynamite through whipped cream." She took a shuddering inhalation. "And now he's gone and my life is ruined. Not to mention that everybody hates us. I just don't want to live." She sipped her hot Lemon Lift, then tossed a peeved glance at the kitchen. "What's taking so long with that waffle? They flying it in from Belgium?"

"That's such a hunk of baloney," Hannah said from behind the newspaper. "You and Alex didn't even have one date."

"We shared a translucent fun-ness."

"The term you're thinking of is 'transcendent oneness.' "

"Don't tell me what I'm thinking. You never wanted us to be together." Kiki loudly blew her nose into a wadded paper napkin. "You discouraged me from the start."

"I was trying to protect you. And as far as everyone hating us, I can't imagine what you're talking about," Hannah replied. She kept her face hidden by the paper so Kiki wouldn't see her own torment. "Give me some black cohosh."

Kiki took a dark capsule out of her purse and slapped it on the table. "I'll tell you what I'm talking about. I always get blamed for the things you do. It's been like that since we were kids. You get caught with a pack of Marlboros, we both get grounded. You shove Mitzy Walstein into the boys shower, we both get detention. You kill Alex." She threw up her hands. "We both get blamed."

Hannah's insides wrenched. She put down the paper and glanced around to see if anyone was listening. Everyone was, or at least trying to.

"First of all, Mitzy went into that shower of her own free will. And second, I didn't kill Alex," Hannah said, her voice shaky. She longed to tell Kiki about the suspicions of the coroner's office, but Perez had sworn her to secrecy, for now anyway. The toxicology scan wouldn't be ready until late afternoon at the earliest.

"Oh really, missy? Then who was it last night that gave him that nasty shock? His heart shut down so fast it was like somebody pulled out the cord on a Cuisinart."

"There's no way my simple questions could have killed him. Alex's doctor said he was in top condition, and—" Hannah stopped, knowing she had said too much. But Kiki was too lost in the pink haze of Kiki World to pick up on it.

A peanut-sized tear rolled down Kiki's cheek. "The doctor didn't plan on anyone shocking the life out of him," she blubbered. "Why did you have to keep hammering at him the way you did?" Her voice became a high-pitched whine. "Charlie was there, too. You could have killed him instead. I don't want to go out with him. But no, you have to kill the cute one. Sometimes I could swear you just don't want me to have a love life at all."

Hannah picked up the newspaper and gave the pages a snap. The truth was, even though it was irrational, in the pit of her stomach she felt some responsibility. She would never say it out loud, but she thought she might have been just a bit too pushy about those stock options. It was a bizarre coincidence that Alex dropped dead at that exact moment. And she couldn't believe that Alex, who everyone knew was a health fanatic, would have taken drugs. The toxicology scan would surely come up negative, and then she would have to live with the guilt for the rest of her life. Her second husband had often accused her of being able to drive a man into heart failure, and now, here she had gone and done it. Unless. She took a sip of coffee, her shoulders hunched. Unless Alex had gotten a drug inside him without realizing it.

"I feel so alone and hopeless. I swear I want to die," Kiki said, then brightened. "Oh, goodie, here's my food."

Randy, the seventeen-year-old who worked the café counter, glided up to their table on Rollerblades. His attention span truncated by years of MTV, he stared down with confusion at the plate he held, trying to remember what it was and how on earth it had gotten there. After a few seconds, his head bobbed. "Whoa, okay. One Belgian waffle with extra bananas and double whipped cream." He put the plate in front of Kiki, then stood there, uncaring of the long line of people at the counter waiting for him to make their cappuccinos. He put his hands on the table and leaned close to Hannah. "Whoa, Mrs. Malloy, is it true you, like, wasted Dr. Love last night?"

Kiki mewed with agony and stuffed a big dollop of whipped cream in her mouth.

Appalled, Hannah eyed Randy over the top of her reading glasses. "Who told you that?"

"Like the whole town, practically. Man, everybody's talking about it. They said you didn't even lay a hand on the guy. You just said something to him, and he, like, you know, freaking died like in some kind of psycho movie." He slapped the side of his head. "I mean, whoa."

The newspaper in Hannah's hands began to tremble.

"You better go," Kiki said to him, her cheeks ballooned with waffle. She gestured him away with her fork. "She's in denial."

"Oh yeah, cool, gotcha." He gave Hannah a blank look just before his eyes widened. It was the first time Hannah had seen him when he didn't look like he was waking from a coma. "No offense intended, Mrs. Malloy. I don't want to make you mad or anything." He looked skittish, as if she could put a death hex on him right there. Head bobbing, he glided off faster than he had arrived.

Her lips pressed together, Hannah folded her paper. "Let's go. I want out of here."

"We can't, I'm not finished eating," Kiki said, holding protectively onto the plate. "Let's look at the bright side. I mean, it's not like you murdered poor Alex. You just shocked him to death." She took a bite of waffle and as she chewed she noticed the agony on her sister's face. "What did I say?"

Hannah glanced around the café, then leaned across the table. "You used the word 'murder,' " she whispered. "That exact word's been on my mind all morning. I know it looks like Alex died from a heart attack, but I can't help but think that maybe, just maybe, there's more to it."

"Forget it, Hannah," Kiki said, disturbed at this conversational turn. "He died from shock, but that's natural causes." The idea that Hannah could think such a dreadful thing only increased Kiki's agitation. Now in full-throttle-stress-eating mode, she shoveled more waffle into her mouth.

Hannah stared at the tabletop and ran her hand up and down her cheek. Everyone in the café thought she had killed Alex. It was obvious. She could feel their stares, their accusing eyes. She looked up at Kiki, who was dousing the piece of waffle on her fork with syrup. "Come on, let's get out of here. I really mean it."

"But my waffle. I'm almost done."

"I'll make you another one at home. I can't take these stares, like I'm a zoo animal. So ridiculous and unfair. Let's go."

Hannah grabbed her purse and jacket while Kiki gobbled the last few bites. Hannah was halfway out of her chair when she felt hands on her shoulders pressing her back down. Green flakes floating around her as she was assailed with the aroma of thyme and sage and the sound of Hopi singing.

"Naomi, what are you doing?" Hannah asked.

Naomi responded by singing more loudly and waving one hand over Hannah's head. She was wearing her funereal caftan, a brilliant green she claimed represented growth of the soul. On her head sat a gauzy blue turban dotted with yellow flowers. Wanda, dressed in black from head to toe except for her yellow "I've Been Busted" button, walked up to the other side of the table. When Naomi gave the nod, she struck a match and set fire to a clump of dried sage she held in her hand. She began waving the smoking herbs over the table while Naomi chanted.

"Stop it right now!" Hannah whispered through clenched teeth.

"Wanda's only being a good friend," Kiki said with forced politeness, struggling to clear out her Wanda-love channel, but it was as blocked as a toilet with a pillow stuffed down it, especially with Wanda dancing around and making certain that everyone in the café was ogling them. Normally Kiki liked being the center of attention, but the events of the night before had left her so perturbed that her makeup was a mess and her hair not fit to be seen. She took a deep cleansing breath and visualized her daisy. "Wanda's always so kindhearted," she said sharply.

Wanda shook the burning sage more vigorously until Hannah grabbed it and drowned it in her water glass. Naomi clucked with sympathy, and she and Wanda pulled up two chairs.

Naomi grasped Hannah's hand. "This negative vortex around you is understandable, so I'm not insulted by your behavior. But, dear, you need a spiritual detox pretty darn quickish. You've had a terrible disturbance in your karmic energy field."

Wanda expelled a mirthless chuckle. "Her karma could have a skull and crossbones on it. She killed a man last night."

"I didn't kill him," Hannah said, trying to keep her voice low, enunciating each word. "He had a heart attack."

"That's right," Kiki said, more protective of her sister now that she was under attack. "It's not her fault."

"I hate to contradict you, Hannah, when your self-healing dynamic is in such need of nourishment," Naomi said, her eyes soft with concern. "But you did say some things that were awfully non-affirmative to Alex right before he vacated his earthly vessel."

"He *vacated* his earthly vessel?" Wanda said. "More like she drop-kicked him out."

"The point is," Naomi said, "in terms of the great Universal Oneness, Hannah, you're in the shit locker."

"I am not!" Hannah pounded the table with her fist, then regretted it. She closed her eyes a moment and tried to get a grip on herself.

Shaking her head with sympathy, Naomi rummaged through her velvet backpack, brought out another handful of herbs, and tossed them over Hannah's head. Hannah swatted them away.

"You could see he didn't feel well," Wanda said, arms crossed. "It was obvious to everyone. And then you made up that ridiculous accusation about the Signatech stock."

In the process of gasping with indignation, Hannah inhaled herbs. "Not stock. Stock options, and I didn't make it up," she said, spitting out green bits.

"We're not saying that you planned it, dear," Naomi said in the tone one would use with a knife-wielding schizophrenic.

"But you can't deny that your words had a somewhat lethal effect."

"Stopped his ticker flat," Kiki added with a pained sniffle, the discussion renewing her suffering. She dabbed at her eyes with a wadded napkin.

"Kiki, you can't believe that," Hannah said.

"Well, honey, facts are facts," Kiki responded with a pitiful sigh. "We all know you didn't mean to do it."

"Oh, really?" Wanda said, drawing out the last word. She saw Kiki's frown. "Okay, I suppose it could have been subconscious." Her eyes moved downward. "What's that little pill on the table? Anything good?"

"Black cohosh," Kiki told her.

"What does it do?"

"Can't remember."

Wanda popped it in her mouth, then downed the rest of Kiki's water. As she swallowed, she gave her throat dainty little pats. "What's so sadly ironic is that even after killing our fabulous Alex, Hannah's still not going to win the election."

"I didn't kill him," Hannah repeated, for herself only, since no one was listening to her.

Kiki drew herself up. "I don't like what you're implying, Wanda. My sister will beat the pants off Charlie. A dead squirrel could beat Charlie."

Naomi held up a finger. "Don't use the word 'dead' around Hannah. It only increases the negative vortex."

Hannah bristled. "Let me get this straight, Kiki. You think it's okay for Wanda to accuse me of murdering Alex, but when she accuses me of being a loser, then you get ticked off?"

"I'll admit," Wanda said to Kiki, "that Hannah is well-known in town. Especially now. But let's face it, she's hardly known for her abilities as an aggressive leader."

"I'd say that killing the mayor is taking the bull by the horns," Kiki replied with vigor.

Wanda made a tsk sound. "Kiki, such hostility. It sounds like you need to visualize your daisies."

"I could visualize them right up your——"

Hannah held up her hands. "Ladies, could we end this?"

Looking fretful, Naomi dumped her entire bag of herbs over the table, filled her cheeks with air and blew on the green flakes until they swirled around the women's heads.

"Hannah will never be mayor," Wanda snapped, her eyes throwing off sparks.

"You're just jealous," Kiki spat back. She picked up her fork and pointed it at Wanda. "Jealous that she'll have all that power that you want for yourself."

"I'm not jealous, and she won't win anyway."

"Want to bet?"

"Whatever you like."

"You name it, toots."

"Phew. You don't have any money."

"Money's not what matters," Kiki said, stabbing the fork in the air. "Hannah always says so. Let's bet something that counts."

"Like what?" Wanda asked.

"Like, I bet that Hannah wins, you bet she doesn't. Whoever loses has to—" Kiki paused, her eyes intense. "Has to moon the mayor's inauguration ceremony."

Naomi's mouth opened. Hannah rolled her eyes to the ceiling. Kiki's bets usually involved nudity of some sort. A hopeless exhibitionist, Kiki had been stripping off her clothes for general public viewing from the age of three.

"Mooning?" Wanda wrinkled up her nose. "Like back in high school?"

"Pants dropped and cheeks exposed," Kiki replied, then let the fork dangle between her thumb and finger. "Of course, if you're afraid to take the challenge . . ."

Wanda's lips squeezed together, and Kiki knew she had her by the short hairs. With a butt lift, two rounds of liposuction, and Mr. Chico, her personal trainer, one would think Wanda would jump with delight at the chance to show off all that work. But the idea of exposing her sixtyish body was abhorrent to Wanda, and Kiki knew it.

For a moment Kiki enjoyed the shocked look on Wanda's face, but then the reality of her impulsive words sank in. Her derriere was hardly her most attractive asset, and in a mooning situation it would be hard to control the lighting. And what about makeup? Application would be quite tricky. She suddenly wished she hadn't made the bet so loudly. Everyone in the café had heard.

There was an ugly silence. Both Kiki and Wanda leaned over the table, eyeing each other like two sumo wrestlers, neither woman wanting the other to see the trepidation bubbling inside her. It appeared that their love barriers had not been quite as busted as previously thought. With an anxious countenance, Naomi picked up some herbs off the table and halfheartedly flicked them in their direction.

The café's patrons watched this scene with silent jubilation, thinking that things couldn't possibly get more interesting, when suddenly they did.

"I want to see the woman who killed my husband!"

All heads snapped to the front of the café. A pint-sized woman with frizzy chin-length hair dyed an implausible yellow stood at the cappuccino machine, slapping her hand on the countertop and glaring at a terrified Randy. He pointed to Hannah's table.

With manic energy, the woman stomped over, pushing her way through the maze of chairs and tables, not caring who she jostled, stopping a yard from the women's table. She gave them a razor-edged stare, her small frame trembling with emotion. Over fifty hard years showed in her lined, tanned face, but her body was still compact and curvy. She displayed it in a low-cut sweater, skintight pants made of shiny stretch material, and white boots with red thunderbolts streaking up the sides. Hannah thought she looked like a go-go dancer from the planet Pluto.

"Time to loosen the lips, gals," the blonde demanded. "Which one of you did the deed?"

The café became so quiet you could have heard a butterfly sneeze in Fresno. Wanda pointed to Hannah. The blonde walked slowly over, the clomping of her boots reverberating in the silence. A couple of patrons reached for their cell phones to dial 911. The woman reached Hannah, gave her a steely yet tearful eye, then suddenly shoved her hand at her. Everyone at the table jumped. Kiki yelped.

Grabbing Hannah's hand, the blonde vigorously shook it. "Thanks, babe! I really owe you one!"

$\mathcal{S}$EVEN

$\mathcal{M}$OUTHS OPEN AND EYES POPPING, every Hill Creeker in the Book Stop café sat frozen, no one bothering to even pretend they weren't staring at the odd blonde who pumped Hannah's arm with the vigor of someone trying to wrench a bone from the mouth of a dog.

They couldn't help themselves. For months nothing had happened in their village, life pleasantly rolling along with a dull sameness, everyone desperate for the faintest whiff of gossip to break the unrelenting grind of day-to-day contentment. And now, in only a matter of hours, to have such a bucketful. Behind their shocked expressions they were all quite giddy, and they would have thanked God for this largesse, except that in these days of political correctness, to single out a deity would surely be offensive to someone.

Hannah, however, did not share their joy. She sat mute with bewilderment as the blonde gyrated her arm with inexplicable enthusiasm. Naomi, Kiki, and Wanda looked on, astounded.

After a couple of attempts, Hannah managed to wrench her hand back. "I didn't kill him."

The blonde shrugged. "Hey, I'm not saying you shot him in the head or anything. I mean, that would be violence, and I'm opposed to that. But from what I heard, you shocked the shit out of the bastard, then gave him a tongue-lashing until he up and keeled over." She slapped Hannah on the back so hard, Hannah could have filed an assault charge. "Go get 'em, girl!"

"Excuse me." Kiki held up her hand and wiggled her fingers. As a conversational topic, life and death was interesting, but there was an issue at hand she considered more critical. "You're Alex's wife?"

The blonde's grin retreated. "Ex-wife."

Wanda sat up primly. "Alex Portman was married to you?"

she asked, speaking slowly and enunciating each word to make
sure the blonde understood the question.

"If I'm lying, I'm dying. We were married in the courthouse
back in Big Spring, Texas. Only he was Al Pinsky back then,
and you would have hardly recognized him 'cause he was fatter
than a tick. He was Al Pinsky, extra-chunky style. Of course,
he still attracted the ladies. He had loads of charisma." On the
last word she pronounced the "ch".

Due to extensive plastic surgery, Wanda always wore the startled look of someone who had just had an ice cube dropped
down her panties, but at hearing this, her eyes bulged and she
began to choke. Alex Portman fat? Impossible. As far as Wanda
was concerned, you might just as well have said that the man
kept his mother chained in his basement or drank jug wine.

"Of course, I still loved him, blubber gut and all. He was my
man." The blonde stood stiffly a few seconds, then slapped the
side of her head, her hair making a crackling sound. "Where are
my manners? I'm just so worked up. My name's Lorna Donatello. Here's my card." She stuck her hand into a red eelskin
purse and pulled out some business cards, which she passed
around with gusto.

Hannah looked at the pink card and read, "Lorna Donatello,
Bail Bonds, Let Me Set You Free, Why Don't You Babe?"
Below that was an address and phone number in Big Spring,
Texas.

Hannah and Kiki exchanged a look, both incredulous that oh-
so-suave and spiritual Alex could have been married to the
bouncing bundle of low-class machisma in front of them.

After reading the pink card, Wanda raised wide eyes back to
Lorna Donatello, then leaned close to Naomi. "Call NASA. I
think we've made contact with another life form."

Kiki sat back in her chair and studied the visitor with skep-
ticism. "How long have you and Alex been divorced?"

"Let me see now, Al and me, we've been divorced twenty-
two years, three months, two days, and—" Lorna checked her
red plastic wristwatch. "Five hours. Wish it were longer, that
slime-sucking shit bucket. Mind if I take a load off?" She pulled
up a chair and plopped down into it. "Sorry to speak ill of a
guy who's on his way to a dirt nap, but I'd be lying if I said I
was sorry. Hell, I'm glad he's gone. The scum owed me money.
Not that money's enough for me to want somebody dead."

Oozing fascination, Naomi leaned forward and rested her chin on her fist. "If I could be so nosy, what *did* it take for you to want Alex dead?"

Lorna turned up both palms. "Love. Pure, sweet love. Ain't that always it? I was just a victim of amor-yay, and I got the perpetrator of the crime right outside." She stuck both pinkies in her mouth and let out an ear-piercing whistle. Once Hannah's ears stopped ringing, she, along with everyone else in the café, followed Lorna's gaze to the front door.

The door opened and Hannah saw a man clump through it. Six-four and in his late forties, he had a bull neck, wide shoulders, and a torso that looked thick and hard. He gave off the impression of being disheveled although his clothes were pressed and his cotton shirt was tucked neatly inside his pants. He looked around the room until his eyes fell on Lorna, then he lumbered her way, carefully working his huge body through the tables, mumbling "excuse me's," his head bowed and a shy smile on his face, like some big, dumb eight-year-old.

Her eyes swallowing him lustily, Lorna crooked her finger. "Come here, you big hunka love stuff!" She remained seated, but as soon as he reached her she grabbed his waist, pulled up his shirt, shoved her face into his bare stomach, and gave him a growling raspberry. His face turned red but he didn't try to stop her.

When Lorna finished, she took his hand, the size of a catcher's mitt, and returned her attention to the women. "This is Ox, and ain't he a looker? But hands off, girlfriends, because he's my fiancé." On the last word she gave him a slap on the behind, to which he responded with an embarrassed shuffling of feet, his smile never dimming. "We're gonna get married," she added, in case someone didn't understand French. She jabbed her fist into Hannah's shoulder. "Thanks to you!" she said with enough volume for the whole café to share in her joy.

Hannah gulped. "Excuse me?" she said, half expecting Alfred Hitchcock to walk in and shout "Cut!"

"I guess I ought to explain," Lorna said.

"Oh, yes, please do," Naomi urged.

Lorna rearranged herself in her chair, with Ox standing sentry behind her, tucking his shirt back into his pants. Kiki, Wanda, and Naomi all scooted their chairs closer, their faces bearing the rapt glow of slow-witted children at a Disney movie.

"Like I told you, I'm in the bail bonds line of work, but you see, I don't want to join my sweet Oxie here in the sanctity of the marital union unless we can start fresh. The bail bonds biz used to have some class, but I'll be honest with you." She leaned forward on one elbow. "It's gotten seedy. But Ox and me, we've got plans for something special. Something with real sophistication."

"What kind of plans?" Kiki asked. If she, Wanda, and Naomi had bent any farther over the table they would have been flat on their stomachs. Hannah remained leaning back in her chair.

Lorna arched a penciled eyebrow. "Novelty chocolates. You know, candy in snappy shapes—hearts, flowers, certain body parts. Real eye grabbers. But for that kind of quality getup you need capital. I never thought we could come up with enough, did I, Ox honey?" His basketball-sized head bounced up and down. "But then I found out that Al's been cheating me."

Up until now, Hannah had distanced herself at least physically from the conversation, but when she heard this last part she bent forward, her interest heightened. "How so?"

"Well, you see, when we got divorced, I got half the seminar business. It was all my idea anyway. I mean, bustin' your love barriers. Al could never have thought up something that good."

"How did you come up with the idea?" Wanda asked with suspicion.

"It was easy. One day I was thinking about that old TV show, *The Dating Game*. Remember that one? And on the back of the set they had these little flower things stuck to the wall, and I thought to myself, dating leads to love, love leads to flowers. If you get depressed or get your heart broke, just think about a flower, and it'll take your mind off it. But when we tried out the seminars in Big Spring, they didn't go over. Those losers around there just aren't romantic. Then we tried making it a diet clinic and we changed the name to 'Busting Your Belt Barriers,' but nothing happened with that either, if you can believe it. When Al and me split up, I said it was okay if he wanted to try the idea someplace else, as long as I got half the profits. We signed a paper and everything. All these years he told me the seminars were dead in the water, that he was making his living selling Tupperware knockoffs door-to-door, just like the old days."

Sniffing a dirty diaper wouldn't have caused Wanda's cheeks to suck farther inward.

"He sold Tupperware knockoffs door-to-door?" Hannah asked, beginning to enjoy herself a little.

Lorna gave the table a slap. "Oh, hell, yeah, he was the best. Old Al, he had a dozen scams, and he was an ace at working women, especially the older gals, no offense intended. I'm in my fifties myself, though I like to think my airtight packaging has sealed in the freshness, if you know what I'm saying." She tittered. "Ain't that right, Ox honey?" His head started bouncing around again, his mouth spread into a dumb grin. She went on. "But where we grew up in Texas, you didn't have much chance as far as a career goes, unless it was pig farming like our daddies did, and both Al and me, we'd had enough of that, believe you me. Although, I'll admit, I can't look at a slab of bacon without getting a pang."

Kiki shook her head in confusion. "But Alex said he grew up in Connecticut."

Lorna scowled. "Yeah, and I'm a lingerie model."

"Did he go to Harvard?" Wanda asked.

"Al was always a first-class liar," Lorna said, cackling. "He took one year of trade school learning how to rebuild car engines, but he flunked out, failed a test on spark plugs or something. He was never the bookish type."

"How did you find out he was here in Hill Creek?" Hannah asked.

"It was like fate or something, you know what I mean? I was getting my hair done a couple of weeks ago back in Big Spring, and someone had brought in this newspaper from California, just as a joke to show us how wacko the people are here, no offense intended, and I saw this article about Al. You could have tipped me over like a teapot. It talked about how successful Al was with his seminars and how he was mayor of a whole town and everything. When I read that the seminars were called 'Busting Your Love Barriers,' I thought, 'Man oh man, old Al Pinksy owes Lorna some moolah.' So I dug out the divorce papers, and Ox and I hopped in the Buick and drove straight here, lickety split. We barely stopped for pee breaks."

"Did you get a chance to talk to Alex?" Naomi asked, and, liking to think the best of people, added, "maybe he was planning to pay you."

"Yeah, and maybe the Easter Bunny's going to hop in here and French kiss me. Al was planning to pay me a big fat nothing. I talked to him day before yesterday. First he tried to sweet talk me, and when that didn't work, he started saying how his lawyers would eat me for breakfast. What a slop bag. But now, thanks to you," Lorna said, directing the comment to Hannah, "my problem's over."

"No, not thanks to me," Hannah said firmly.

"Aw, don't be so modest. I checked the county property records yesterday and it looks like I've hit the jackpot. Al's seminar company, which I own half of, owns his fancy house and everything in it, so I get half of that, too. And don't think I don't appreciate it. When we get our business going I'm going to send you a big box of novelty chocolates." She gave Hannah a wink. "And we're talking the racy stuff." After seeing Hannah's expression, Lorna frowned. "Of course, if you're the prudish type, that's no problem. I'll send you plain old nuts and chews, but it won't be the same thrill."

"Oh, no, she'll take the other kind," Kiki chimed in fast.

"It's funny, though, him dying so quick like that." Lorna leaned her chair back on two legs, her expression turning thoughtful. "I saw him just the day before he died, and he was strutting around, bragging about how healthy and skinny he was, how he ran five miles a day. He said he had the body of a thirty-year-old and wasn't I sorry I'd been missing out on the goodies all these years. I'll be honest, when I first heard he was dead, I assumed it wasn't natural causes."

Hannah's ears pricked up. "Why?"

"Well, old Al had a way of ticking people off, if you know what I mean. He'd had a few run-ins with the law. Hell, he'd scammed almost every guy in West Texas, and then slept with their wives. While we were married, I might add. I assumed he was up to his old tricks here. I mean, if there was one thing Al was good at, it was making enemies."

Sitting on the porch of her brown-shingled Craftsman cottage, Hannah wiggled her big toe, it peeking out the tip of her canvas shoe. She had first noticed the hole while inspecting the climbing rose that ran along the front of the house. She had found hundreds of new buds. In a few weeks the bush would burst into a fire of red blossoms, and the knowledge that those months of fertilizing and spraying had paid off brought her deep satisfaction. But thoughts of Alex had intruded on this pleasantness, and she finally gave in to them. She sat on the porch steps amidst the pink geranium-filled terra-cotta pots and looked out at her garden, allowing her mind to wander into the dark spaces where it wanted to go.

It was eleven-thirty in the morning, and the serenity of her small, lush front yard was at odds with her discordant thoughts. She heard birds chirping and the whisper of leaves while thoughts of death swirled in her head. Still, she was grateful for the time alone. Kiki was getting her nails done, her real objective that of telling everyone at Lady Nails about the date with Alex that never happened. With embellishments, of course, including him muttering her name just as he died.

The back garden was twice as large as the front, and Hannah planned on putting in new plantings that afternoon. She did her best thinking on her hands and knees, wrist-deep in dirt, surrounded by bugs.

Hannah lifted her foot and inspected the hole. It didn't look reparable. The old espadrilles were her favorite for clomping around the house, and she hated to give them up. She wasn't sure if she could find them in the stores anymore. That was one of the problems with getting older. Things wore out—shoes, body parts, life philosophies, sometimes even friends.

The gate hinges creaked. Hannah glanced up and saw Perez coming up the walkway with Winston, his brown and white spaniel, leading the way, tugging at its leash. Hannah brushed the dirt off her pants and smoothed back the lock of hair hanging in her face. She relished his unexpected visits, but he always caught her when she was in her old gardening clothes. But then, when she was at home she was in her gardening clothes most of the time.

"You look nice sitting there, surrounded by all those flowers. I should take a picture and put it on my desk." He sat on the step beside her, tugging up the knees of his blue jeans. Winston lay restlessly at his feet, whimpering with anticipation.

"Right next to the picture of Winston?" she asked wryly, scratching the spaniel behind his ear where she knew he liked it.

"Next to the photo of my daughter and grandbaby. Although next to the dog is a special place." Ruffling the dog's fur with his hand, Perez laughed then unhooked the leash, the dog bounding around the side garden to look for Teresa and Sylvia. The pets would wreak havoc on the lavender Hannah had planted last week, but she didn't mind so much. The dogs had such a great time chasing each other and rolling around. Even Sylvia got in the act, following the best she could, snorting all the way.

"Any test results on Alex's body?" Hannah asked.

Perez picked a leaf off the potted geranium and pressed it to his nose, giving it a deep sniff. "The postmortem was done late this morning. The report's not ready, but I spoke to Louis. He said they didn't find anything, like clogged arteries, which would have caused a heart attack. The way Louis described it, Alex's heart went into some sort of seizure. It started beating so erratically that he died. That sort of thing can happen because of an outside substance, like a drug."

"Then that means—"

"Hold on. They ran a set of toxicology scans and got nothing. No drugs, prescription or otherwise. Alex had gone for a long, hard jog just before he got ready for the debate. A couple of people in town saw him running. Who knows? Maybe that tough exercise along with the stress of the debate did something." He saw Hannah's pained look and tucked her hand in his. "But it wasn't your fault."

Hannah saw Donna Brown, a neighbor, walking past the house, probably on her way to pick up her little girl from pre-school. Hannah waved and Donna waved back, but Hannah noticed she quickened her pace so she wouldn't have to stop and chat.

"That's not what the rest of the town thinks," Hannah said.

"Yeah, I picked up a coffee at the Book Stop. What happened at the debate last night is the scoop du jour. This town can be awfully petty sometimes." He slipped his arm around her waist. When they were in public he didn't show much outward affection, but when they were alone he couldn't keep his hands off her. "It'll blow over in a day or two and they'll be gossiping about something else. I knew you'd feel like this. That's why I've been bugging Louis, so I could find out what really happened to Alex and get you off the hook. Louis and I used to work together, and he owes me."

"I guess I owe you, too." She kissed his cheek.

He pulled her closer. "That's the kind of debt I like."

"So what else have you found out?"

"That's pretty much it. Maggie, the housekeeper, says Alex took a lot of different herbs. She's going to round up the bottles for Louis this afternoon. Sometimes health nuts poison themselves with herbal remedies." Joyful barks came from the rear yard, and Perez looked concerned. "Should I go get them? They might tear something."

"It's okay. Don't worry about it. I have a question. Alex was drinking from a water bottle during the debate. Could that have had something in it?"

"It was a wheatgrass drink. According to Maggie, he mixed it up himself everyday from a powder. They're looking for that bottle now. It's disappeared. Don't look so worried. It probably just got thrown away. They'll find it. Listen, there's something else I need to talk to you about. When I saw Louis this morning he had me describe what Alex looked like right before he died. I went over it with him the best I could, but do you remember any details?"

"I remember everything. How can I forget? He looked like he was having trouble breathing and he was perspiring."

"I remembered that he moved funny, like his legs were stiff."

"And he looked at his hands a few times. He was opening and closing his fists, but I thought that was nervousness."

"Alex wasn't the nervous type, and he spoke in front of large groups all the time. He should have been cool as a cucumber."

"Was there anything else you remembered?" Hannah asked. "Any other details you told Louis?"

"I've told you everything I told him. To be honest, my eyes were more on you than Alex, but I think I covered things pretty well. Louis took a lot of notes. The problem is, he handles the whole county and he's got a pile of cases on his plate."

"This one's high profile. We're talking about a mayor."

"But if Louis can't get something substantial quick he'll be under pressure to write it off to natural causes. The thing is, maybe it was natural causes."

She shook her head. "Alex was fit and healthy."

"I expect Louis to be thinking murder, but not you. You're always telling me to assume the best in people."

"I've learned from you that sometimes it's smarter to assume the worst."

Perez pulled away from Hannah, rested his arms on his knees, and let out a gush of air. They heard more barks followed by the sound of Hannah's metal watering can clattering on the ground. Perez started to get up, and Hannah pressed him back down.

"Leave it," she said. "You were about to say something."

He pulled off another geranium leaf and started tearing it into bits. "Louis said that if Portman was somehow drugged, it would help to have an idea about what substance was used. They couldn't find anything in his stomach contents, but that doesn't mean much. Louis said there are hundreds of toxins, and that he can't test for everything. He needs something to go on."

She mulled this over, at the same time watching a furniture truck move slowly down the street. It stopped a few doors down, probably delivering some quaint little end table that cost more than her monthly pension check. Anxiety gnawed at her, the raw furtive kind that always struck her just before a bad event turned worse. In the middle of a nasty situation there's always that denial period, when in the back of your mind you tell yourself it's all going to be okay. Then suddenly you realize it isn't, that if anything, it's going to be worse. And Hannah loathed sitting around waiting for news. She was the type who needed to take action.

"Is there something I can do?" she asked, a new energy in her voice. "I could help look for the bottle."

"That's being taken care of. Listen, Hannah, don't let this upset you. Try to maintain some emotional distance."

Whenever a man told her not to get upset, it always gave her the urge to kick him in the shin. "I'm right in the middle of this whether you like it or not."

"You don't have to be."

"What do you mean?"

"I've got an idea," he said. He looked at her expectantly, and Hannah knew she was about to find out the real reason behind his visit. "I want to do some hiking in Colorado, and I was planning it for summer, but why don't you and I go now, together? We could leave next week."

She laughed at the thought of it. "I could never keep up with you on a hike."

"Don't kid yourself. You're strong as a horse." He paused, smiling. "And I mean that in the nicest way."

"It's impossible. The election's only two weeks away."

His face grew somber. "That's the point, Hannah. Forget the election. You don't want to be mayor, and you know it. You just signed up for it because you felt so strongly about Signatech."

"I still do."

"You would detest being mayor. You hate the limelight, and you've never liked politics."

"So I just walk away and let Signatech ruin the town?"

"Hannah, the truth is, it's going to happen whether you like it or not. The town wants it. Even if you managed to win the election, the town council isn't going to go against the voters' wishes."

"Okay, it's more than the election."

"Then what is it?"

"Something bad is happening in this town. I know it. I can feel it."

"You sound like Naomi."

"Sometimes, in a weird way, she makes sense."

"So if you think there's something bad happening here, why stay?"

"Curiosity."

"About what?"

"About whether I'm right."

She could see Perez heating up. Pressing his hands against his thighs, he stood, walked a few paces, then turned to her. "Let's not dance around. You think Alex was murdered, but there's no proof. It could have been an accident."

"I don't think so."

He came back and sat down on the step below her, laying his hand on her knee. "This is all conjecture, and you have a way of getting your mind set on something, and then turning into a Sherman tank. Let it sink into your brain that sometimes people just die. There doesn't have to be anything dark and sinister going on. They've done a background check on Alex. He had no life insurance, and in spite of those seminars, he didn't have any money because he spent every cent he made. He only had some equity in that house, and not that much, so it's not like anyone would want to kill the guy."

"Not according to his ex-wife," Hannah said, then told him about that morning's scene with Lorna Donatello.

EIGHT

THE SUN HOT ON HER back, Hannah plunged her spade into the hard earth, cursing when a rock sent a shock wave up her arm. A gentle soul but a ferocious gardener, Hannah roughly dug it out, tossed it by the fence, and resumed her frontal assault on the neglected far corner of the back garden. The soil had hardened over the winter. She was going to recondition it and plant it with foxglove whether it liked it or not, by chopping it until it was crumbly and adding a homemade compost mixture from the plastic tub beside her.

She worked vigorously, letting out her frustration as she broke up the soil. Perez had left an hour earlier, annoyed with her, making an excuse about not staying for lunch. She knew he was only concerned about her, but the friction between them had left her even more on edge.

Kiki had brought Lauren home for lunch, and Hannah had spoken little as the three women ate in the back garden, sandwiches filled with a mixture of tuna, apples, walnuts, and a hint of curry. Hannah had been equally silent as she ate Lauren's homemade devil's food cake, but that was from her mouth being full.

Hannah scooped some compost from the tub, spread it on the ground and began mixing it into the dirt, first with her spade, then her hands. Alex's death, the Signatech stock options, Lorna Donatello sweeping in, along with her steel-teddy-bear boyfriend. It all gave off a distinctly foul odor. Yet there was no evidence of anything out of kilter except for the stock options, and Alex's death had put an end to those. The smart thing to do was to take Perez's advice and forget about it, go hiking in the mountains. Yet she couldn't. She had made a commitment to herself to see the election through, and she couldn't back out, especially now. As the years piled on, laziness crept up on a person, and it became so easy to let things slide, to watch from the sidelines and criticize rather than take action. Hannah hit a particularly hard clump of dirt and decapitated it with her spade. Well, not Hannah Malloy.

She felt a nuzzling under her arm and found Teresa begging for a snuggle, soon realizing it was a diversionary tactic so Sylvia could nose through the dirt for treasure. She felt certain that the dog and pig schemed together, speaking their own secret language of barks and snorts. After shooing them away, she yanked up the knees of her Japanese gardening pants, took off her gloves, and continued mixing in the compost with her bare hands, savoring the feel of the dirt between her fingers.

Stopping to catch her breath, she ran her eyes over the rosa cressida that clambered up the cedar fence. One bud exposed a tease of apricot, and in a month the whole fence would be covered with blossoms. Even though there were a hundred different plants in Hannah's garden, the roses took the starring roles. Showy and confident, they drew your eye, turned every other plant into a backdrop for their glory. Like Alex, Hannah thought. So very much like Alex. Only someone decided they didn't want to be his backdrop any longer. She felt sure of it.

"The good news is that I don't think Larry's relationship with that woman is serious," Lauren said from her lounge chair on the patio, remnants of a second helping of cake on the plate in her lap. Lauren could eat whatever she wanted and never gain an ounce.

"You talked to him?" Hannah asked. Sitting back on her rump, she critically assessed the current plant layout, wondering if she should dig up the daylilies. She suspected that the plants trembled with fear when she gave them that particular look, because it meant she was going to rip them out and move them.

"Oh, no, not really," Lauren said, with an audible unease. "Are you sure you don't want some help, Aunt Hannah?"

"No, thanks. I don't want you to get dirty. Shouldn't you be at work, anyway?"

"I'm taking half a day off. I thought you might need the company after what happened last night. If you'll loan me some old sweats I'd be glad to help."

"I'm fine, really. And your Aunt Kiki is helping." Hannah glanced at her sister, on her knees at the other end of the flowerbed, pounding at the dirt with the spade handle. Kiki looked out of place in a pair of Hannah's old gardening clogs, a sweatshirt, and the old toreador pants that had shown off her assets fifteen years and three sizes ago. Their current snugness impeded all stooping and bending, but they were the only pants Kiki would wear near dirt. "So if you didn't talk to Larry," Hannah said. "How do you know he and that girl—"

"The slut puppy," Kiki said.

"Don't say that," Hannah told her. "Detective Morgan wouldn't go out with her unless she was nice. As I was saying, how do you know that he and that slut, I mean girl, aren't serious?"

Lauren didn't say anything. Averting her eyes, she sipped her iced tea, the ice cubes tinkling.

"Because she tailed him," Kiki finally said, delighted at any distraction from the awful digging. She couldn't understand her sister's fascination with flowers when you could buy such nice silk ones that didn't get dirt and manure under your fingernails.

Bent over an unsuspecting dianthus that was about to be transplanted, Hannah's head popped up. "She what?"

Lauren took a big gulp of tea. "It was Aunt Kiki's idea. She explained it to me last night when I was in the ladies room."

Kiki looked at Hannah with upturned palms. "I had to convince her to come out, didn't I?"

Lauren went on. "After the paramedics took away the mayor last night, I wanted to come home with you, Aunt Hannah, you looked so frantic. But Kiki said that John was taking care of you and that a better use of my time would be to follow Larry and—" There the story dangled.

"There's nothing to be ashamed of," Kiki said. "Your Aunt Hannah is always saying that a person can't have too much information."

"I was talking about investing your IRA," Hannah told her, digging the dirt away from the dianthus.

"Like Lauren's love life isn't a little bit more important than that," Kiki said. "Lauren needed to take action, to know where she stood. So she got in her car and followed them."

Hannah stopped digging. "So that's all?" she asked Lauren. "You just followed them in your car?"

"Until they got to the café," Kiki answered, before Lauren had the chance. "Then you got out of the car and kept after them, didn't you, Lauren honey?" Kiki looked at Hannah with pride. "So assertive. Our little niece takes after me."

Hannah frowned. "But with counseling and medication, maybe she can be saved." She pulled out the dianthus and placed it in the compost tub, putting extra soil around its exposed roots.

"Well, I had to get out of the car," Lauren explained. "Aunt Kiki said that if they went to a restaurant I should make sure I saw what they were eating."

"To see if it was friend food or lover food," Kiki said.

"There's a difference?" Hannah asked.

Kiki shook her head at Hannah's stupidity. "Friends pound down hamburgers with onions. Lovers pick at salads. Fortunately for Lauren, Detective Morgan had a pastrami sandwich with pickles and French fries. That means there's still hope."

Hannah put down her spade. "You got close enough to see pickles?" she asked Lauren.

"Well, I was crouched down beneath the café window, but I managed to get a few peeks, before, well, you know."

"Before the manager threatened to arrest her," Kiki said, wanting the story to move a little faster.

"But after I told him I was your niece, Aunt Hannah, he decided to let me go."

"Why would knowing me make a difference?"

"He heard about the mayor's debate, and he didn't want any trouble from you," Lauren said. "He even offered to give me free pie."

"Did Detective Morgan see you?" Hannah asked.

"Yes. I told him I'd dropped something outside the café, but I don't know if he believed me."

"Grannie sucking eggs," Kiki said.

Hannah dug her spade into the earth. "My feelings exactly."

"No, I mean I see worms." Kiki stared at the ground with her face screwed up.

"Worms are good for the soil, so don't hurt them," Hannah told her. "Kiki, why don't you go inside and make us some more tea? I can finish this myself."

Kiki had been digging for half an hour and had yet to accomplish anything except getting herself filthy, heightening Hannah's suspicion over her insistence on helping. Kiki had always lumped gardening in the same category as adult education and flat-heeled shoes—boring and of no possible benefit. Something was brewing in Kiki's fluffy pink brain.

"No, Hannah, I want to help. See?" Both hands gripping the

spade's handle she struck at the ground, the blow's force causing her to fall back on her behind.

Hannah went over to her sister. "There's a hidden agenda here," she said, grabbing Kiki's arm and trying to pull her up, but she was dead weight. "Tell me what it is."

Kiki plopped back onto the ground, her plump legs splayed. "I just want to help, that's all," she said halfheartedly, scrunching her nose as she looked down at the streaks of soil on her sweatshirt. Brushing it off with her dirty gardening gloves just made the problem worse. "Why are you always so distrustful? Of course, I shouldn't be critical of you when you're under stress. It's natural, having just killed a man."

Hannah repeated the words that were becoming her mantra. "I didn't kill him."

Lauren swung her legs over the side of the lounge chair. "Of course you didn't."

"I didn't mean it like you murdered him," Kiki said. "You just nagged him until he croaked. Those are two different things."

"And one's better than the other?" Hannah asked.

"One's a felony. The other's just being bitchy."

Eager to discuss what was really on her mind, Hannah sat on the grass next to Kiki, pulling her knees to her chest. Not wanting to be left out, Lauren pulled over a lawn chair and joined them, while Teresa and Sylvia stretched out nearby, soaking up the sun.

"That's what's bothering me," Hannah said. "I can't get my mind off it."

"You've always been a little bitchy," Kiki said. "Mother said it was because you didn't eat enough roughage as a toddler."

"I'm talking about Alex's death." Hannah picked a ladybug off Kiki's sweatshirt, leaned over, and put it back on the rosebush where it could feast on aphids. "I'm telling you, he was too physically fit to drop dead."

"People drop dead all the time," Lauren said.

Kiki shook a finger. "Remember Aunt Betsy? She was fit as a fiddle and then one day, bam, she was a goner."

"She was hit by a truck," Hannah said.

"So nickpick. Let's drop it, Hannah. I can see how much it's worrying you. The thing to do is to just get it out of your mind."

"That's what John keeps telling me, but I can't, not after what

Alex's ex-wife said." Even though Perez had reacted badly to her suspicions, Hannah decided to voice them to, hopefully, more receptive ears.

"What do you mean?" Lauren asked.

"Lorna Donatello said Alex had a way of making enemies," Hannah said. "Maybe someone didn't like Alex's true authentic self as much as everyone else did."

"Do the police think he was murdered?" Kiki asked.

"I'm sure they haven't ruled it out."

The three women fell into a momentary silence as this information settled in. A cloud passed over Kiki's features.

"Okay, let's say that the police did think that Alex might have been murdered. Let's say if. Would they go through his things, like his office?" Kiki took a long breath and held it. "Or his computer?"

Hannah's eyes slid to her sister, her Kiki-radar on full alert. "Is there something you want to tell me?"

"No."

Hannah knew Kiki was fibbing, but before she could probe further she heard a thud followed by a clatter, and recognized the sound of Naomi kicking over her tin bucket.

"Naomi, you're eavesdropping," Hannah announced. She heard a muttered "damn" followed by the sound of the bucket being uprighted. Naomi used the bucket as a step stool to see over the fence during neighborly chats, ever since Hannah had raised the fence so Teresa wouldn't jump over it. Naomi's purple-turbaned head soon emerged over the cedar lattice.

"I wasn't eavesdropping," she said with indignation. "I was sitting on the bucket meditating. I was deep into my spiritual center when the two of you broke my focus, and I couldn't help hearing the last part." She gave Kiki a meaningful look.

Hannah glanced at Kiki and saw her mouthing "no" to Naomi with a pleading expression.

"Kiki, why did you ask about Alex's office? Tell me what's going on?" Hannah said.

Kiki frowned. "Nothing."

"Tell me now."

"Just spill it, dear," Naomi said. "You shouldn't keep it a secret."

Giving Naomi a menacing stare, Kiki kicked the ground with her heel. "Oh, all right. It's such a piddly little thing. You'll laugh when I tell you, Hannah. Really, you will. You see, I sent Alex some emails."

Hannah didn't laugh.

"But you don't have an email account," Lauren said.

"I just used Hannah's."

Hannah now understood how a recent email from her address had shown up on Alex's computer, but she still didn't get how Kiki had managed it. "You don't know how to use email," she said.

"Ellie showed me on her computer at the salon. I didn't realize it was so easy, and so much fun." Kiki worked hard to keep her tone light and breezy. "You know, Hannah, that email thing's going to catch on."

"I'm not understanding the problem here," Hannah said. "You sent him some emails. So what?"

Kiki chewed her lip, while Hannah, Naomi, and Lauren watched her intently.

"She sent him poetry," Naomi said.

Both Hannah and Lauren looked confused. "Aunt Kiki wrote poetry?" Lauren asked.

Kiki lifted her chin with pique. "Why does that surprise you?"

"Because you think a metaphor is a bullfighter," Hannah replied.

There was a pregnant lull before Naomi, unable to handle all this dillydallying when she knew a bomb was about to explode, finally spoke. "She didn't exactly write them."

"Anybody thirsty? I'm parched," Kiki said. "I'll just go in the kitchen and get us something."

She tried to stand, but she couldn't get up from a sitting position on the ground without assistance, and neither Hannah nor Lauren offered help. Kiki struggled up a few inches, then plopped back down.

"You're not going anywhere," Hannah said. "So you had better spit it out."

Kiki's lip chewing accelerated. "Okay, okay, if you're going to be so pushy. It was your poetry, Hannah. I found some of your old poems on your computer, and Ellie showed me how to add things to emails. Really, it's so easy, and so I sent some poems to Alex. You always say poetry is the best way to express your feelings."

"Kiki, how could you?" Hannah stood. "You realize that

when Alex saw the emails he also saw the address they came from, which includes my name."

"It's okay," Kiki replied. "I didn't sign them with your name."

"Tell her how you signed them," Naomi said.

Kiki's eyes shot daggers at Naomi. She squirmed, preparing herself for further unpleasantness. "Lushlips."

Hannah closed her eyes. "My God. That's why Alex was treating me so strangely. He thought I'd sent him poetry signed as Lushlips."

"It gets worse," Naomi said gravely.

Lauren muttered an "uh oh."

"Don't you have some astral plane to go to?" Kiki spat at Naomi.

"I'm sorry, Kiki, but you need to tell," Naomi said. "The secrecy is making your aura an unattractive brownish color that perplexes me."

Hannah didn't really want to ask, but had to. "How does it get worse?"

"Well, you know that I think your poems are great, Hannah, but they can get a little dry," Kiki said, fidgeting with a blade of grass, "so I changed them just a bit." Seeing the horrified expression on Hannah's face, she hastily added, "Only a few lines. A word here and there. It really perked them up. You know that poem where at the end you say something about someone's need being an empty room or something?"

"Your need is a windowless room, pitch black and fearsome, swallowing and silent," Hannah said.

"Yeah, that one. So depressing. Jeezus, what did you have for breakfast that day? I changed it to this." Kiki gazed upward, stretching out her arms. "I need you in a windowless room. We won't need any light. I'll bring the chips and gin, cause we'll probably go all night."

Hannah inhaled sharply and buried her face in her hands. Lauren stroked her back, and Naomi muttered a series of "oh my's." Sensing trouble, Teresa and Sylvia got up and trotted to the other side of the yard.

"You don't like it?" Kiki asked.

Hannah's cheeks reddened with anger. "There are limits, Kiki, boundaries that should not be crossed. And turning a person's heartfelt poems into tawdry gutter smut and sending them off over email exceeds that boundary. It pole vaults over it."

"I'll accept the tawdry bit, but you better take back that gutter smut remark," Kiki said, but without any force behind the words. Hannah had that frightening look in her eye that always made Kiki want to squeal and run.

"Alex thought I wrote those poems to him," Hannah said, her blood heating up. "He thought I wanted to take him to a motel room."

"Now, Aunt Hannah, it's not that bad," Lauren said.

"Yes, Hannah, dear, calm down," Naomi added, now regretting that she had initiated this painful revelation. "The man's transcended his physical manifestation. What could it matter now?"

"Because the poems are still on his computer," Hannah said. "I saw one of them when I looked through his laptop."

"Why did you look through his computer?" Naomi asked.

"That's how I found out about his stock options. Someone could go through his computer, find those poems, and think they're from me."

"It's a tempest in a teapot," Naomi said, her voice soothing. "Who would go through his computer now that he's left his earthly vessel?"

Hannah held up one hand, fingers fanned. "His family, his accountant, his lawyer, his ex-wife," Hannah said, ticking them off on her fingers. "Kiki, how many poems did you send?"

"I just started a couple of weeks ago, so there weren't that many. Eight or nine. Maybe more. Okay, more."

There had been various times in Hannah's life when she had an urge to stuff her sister's lower body in quick-setting concrete, but never so much as at that moment. She was saved from this terrible impulse by a loud voice that sounded like a chain-smoking poodle bellowing from the side of the house.

"Howdy, girls! What's cookin'?"

The women saw Lorna on the other side of the gate, with Ox behind her. Surprised, Hannah brushed the dirt from her pants and said hello. What was Lorna doing at her house?

"I knocked out front but no one answered." Lorna opened the gate, and she and Ox walked through. She had changed her outfit into shiny black leggings topped with a hip-length red shirt unbuttoned past the point of decency. "But I'm not the type to give up too easy." She took a gulp of canned diet soda. "You can't be the skittish type and last in my biz. Don't get up." She directed the last part to Kiki, who was still sitting on the ground, and had neither the intention nor the ability to lift herself. Kiki eyed Lorna's outfit with envy.

"I just love your shoes," Kiki said, admiring Lorna's white boots with the red thunderbolts streaking up the sides.

"Thanks." Lorna stuck out one foot, resting it on the heel. "I call these my signature boots, kind of my own personal fashion statement. Anybody in Big Spring asks, 'Who's Lorna Donatello?' and people say, 'She's the gal with the white boots with the red thunderbolts.' Makes it easy to find me."

"Speaking of finding things," Hannah asked. "How did you find out where we lived?"

"That kid at the café, the one with the skates, told me."

Hannah made a note to cut back on Randy's tips. She introduced Lorna and Ox to Lauren, and then shooed away Sylvia and Teresa, who were sniffing at the visitors.

"Nice pig," Lorna said. "He's about fat enough for slaughter." She aimed her eyes at Hannah. "It's you I came to see. Could we talk?"

"Certainly," Hannah answered after some hesitation. Ox went over to the flowerbed. Hannah glanced at Naomi, knowing she was dying to hear the conversation, and not wanting her to. "We'll go in the house."

"Oh, no, you stay out here," Naomi said. "It's such a beautiful day, such positive energy. I have a client coming in a little while and I need to fluff the pillows and get the incense started."

"Are you a hooker?" Lorna asked, with no detectable censure in her voice.

Naomi flinched as if someone had just given her a hard pinch on the backside. "I'm a psychic. My clients are looking for spiritual awareness and healing. I channel the spirit of an ancient Hopi snake shaman."

"Hey, I've heard of that on cable TV." Lorna moved closer to the fence. "Like a dead guy talks through you?"

"I am the physical vessel of Red Moon, his connection to this earthly plane," Naomi said with her special I'm-a-psychic voice, her hand sweeping the air. "I move between dimensions, and bring messages from the ancient one to this corporeal world."

"Wow. You know, I could use some spiritual healing," Lorna said. "In my biz your spirit gets in piss poor shape. I may not even have one anymore. Could I make an appointment?"

"Well, I'm terribly booked up," Naomi said. She tried to appear blasé when she was overjoyed at the prospect of a new client. Her battered Volvo needed new brake pads. "I have no appointments available today."

"What about tonight?" Lorna asked.

"I'm sorry, but tonight we're having a séance at Hannah and Kiki's house."

Bent over, his nose buried in a rose, Ox looked up. "A séance?"

"Wow, could Ox and I come?" Lorna asked.

"It's about a family matter," Hannah said, trying to discourage her.

"Lauren is having man trouble and we're going to ask Red Moon for help," Kiki said in a grand whisper. Pink-faced, Lauren pretended to be examining her ankle. "Personally all I think she needs is to dress a little sexier. A man likes a woman who lets him know her engine's running."

Lorna let out a low hoot. "There's not a man–woman problem around that can't be handled with a pair of thong panties and a squirt bottle of Crisco. Too bad I don't have any of my novelty chocolate samples yet." She winked. "I have a couple of chocolate designs that could fix love problems pretty damn quick. So can we come to the séance? We'll sit real quiet and just watch."

"I don't know, Lornie," Ox said nervously.

"Aw, it'll be fun," she told him.

"As long as you're there just to watch," Naomi said. She gave Hannah an imploring look.

Hannah knew Naomi was hoping that if Lorna attended the séance she would then set up a channeling appointment or two.

"I guess it's okay," Hannah said, ignoring the chastising looks coming from Kiki and Lauren. She empathized with Naomi's constant money problems, and wanted to help her round up a new client, even if Lorna's business was temporary. A buck was a buck. Naomi had refused all Hannah's offers of a small loan.

"That's settled, then," Naomi said. "Well, got to run. Other dimensions await." She disappeared behind the fence.

Lorna's gaze wandered off as she busily tapped the top of her drink can with her fingernail. Hannah wondered when she was going to find out the real reason for Lorna's visit. She watched Ox bend down to smell another blossom on her "Peace" rosebush. He had the strength to crush a person with his bare hands, yet she thought his big brown eyes would water up if he heard a sad story. Hannah wasn't sure if she should fear him or give him a motherly hug.

He drank in the rose's fragrance, then straightened. "This rose you got here smells great."

"I have others even better," she told him, always happy to discuss her plants. "It's the antique roses that smell the best."

"I've got a rugosa in my front yard," he said, his pride obvious.

"Which variety?" Hannah asked.

"Listen, Oxie babe, we can talk flowers later," Lorna interrupted. "I've got some pressing issues here, and I'm ready to get started."

"Sorry, Lornie."

Lorna took a long fortifying gulp of soda, then turned to Hannah. "Okay, here it is. I need to go into Alex's house."

"Why?" Hannah asked, puzzled.

"Because I need to get proof that his seminar business was making money, so I can stake my claim. His relatives are low-life vultures, and I don't want them waltzing in with one of those hotshot lawyers who advertise on TV and freeze everything up. I can't wait years before Ox and I get our new life started. I need money now." Lorna's words had come out in an aggressive gush, but she swiftly turned bashful. "And I want some company. Not that I'm scared or anything. I'd just like a pal along, and you're my only friend in town."

It stunned Hannah that Lorna put her in that category. "Why not take Ox?"

"He won't go in the house of a dead guy." She poked him in the ribs with her finger. "He's such a softie."

"I spook easy," he said. "I'm not even too sure about this séance tonight." He gave Lorna an entreating glance, but she was too focused on Hannah to notice.

"I've got to have someone with me," Lorna said. "To prove I didn't steal anything."

"Sounds to me like you'll be stealing documents," Hannah told her.

"Those papers are as good as mine. I'm only getting back my property."

Hannah concurred with that philosophy, since she wanted to

retrieve documents of her own. She noticed that one of the knot-holes in the fence had filled with purple and knew that Naomi was eavesdropping.

Grunting and groaning, Kiki struggled to stand. Ox stepped over, grabbed her from behind, and lifted her as if she didn't weigh a thing. She thanked him and gave him a flirtatious smile that fortunately Lorna didn't see.

"How do you plan on getting in Alex's house?" Hannah asked.

"That's the easy part. When I was there the other morning, you know, when Alex and I had a chat, I stole a set of keys from the table in the entryway. When he told me to kiss off I knew I'd have to take things into my own hands." She looked at Hannah. "So will you come?"

"Of course," Hannah said. Both Lauren and Kiki looked amazed. There was a thump from the other side of the fence. "And Kiki should come too." Kiki mouthed a "what?" "In case any questions are raised later, it will look better if you can say that two people were with you."

"Good idea," Lorna said. "I knew I liked you. You're a thinker. Somebody told me you're the town poet."

The mention of it caused Hannah and Kiki to exchange a churlish glance. "Only in a small way," Hannah replied with modesty. "My poems are published in a small weekly newspaper."

"Yeah, well, I got a few poems inside me, too. I got a soft, vulnerable side." Lorna took a gulp of soda, then hit her chest with her fist and belched. "Which is why I think I can be so good in the novelty chocolates line. Deep down I'm the creative type." She cocked a thumb in the direction of the street. "Let's get humpin', girlfriends. We got papers to steal."

NINE

"*I* DON'T CARE IF ALEX was a fat door-to-door sales-man who couldn't pass a spark plug exam. I still can't believe he'd marry someone trashy like that Lorna," Kiki said. "She's so pushy and obnoxious, and her clothes are just plain vulgar." Kiki gave her striped miniskirt with the beaded fringe a thigh-relieving tug.

This opinion delivered, Kiki returned her attention to her re-flection in the Cadillac's lighted makeup mirror, and ran her tube of Tahiti Pink over her lips one more time to achieve the desired grammar-school paste consistency. "And now we have to have her and that lug nut boyfriend at our séance tonight." She snapped on the lipstick's top with a punctuating click. "Al-though, I'll admit, that Ox is awfully cute in a caveman sort of way. How did she manage to snag a younger guy? You think it was those signature boots?"

Hannah didn't answer. Hannah didn't even hear. Having tuned out her sister shortly after backing out the driveway, her brain received these remarks only as vague background bleating. She pressed the Cadillac's accelerator, trying to keep up with Lorna's dented, smoke-belching Buick with its missing tail light and loose rear bumper covered with a minimum of thirty stickers that all bragged, "I Bopped at Billy Bob's."

Once the decision had been made to go with Lorna, Hannah and Kiki had hurriedly changed clothes, Hannah into slacks and a cotton sweater, and Kiki into a skirt and low-cut blouse that showed even more cleavage than Lorna's did. Hannah knew that far from disliking Lorna's wardrobe, Kiki was envious of it, and not about to be out-tarted by some upstart who had just blown in from Big Spring.

They had followed Lorna to her motel, the Marin Inn, where she had dropped off Ox, and then followed her back through town toward Alex's. Hannah shifted the car into a lower gear as the Cadillac struggled up the hill to Alex's neighborhood.

"How does she get that old car to move so fast? I wish she'd slow down," Hannah said.

"She's not the slow type. That woman is out to get what she wants, and she doesn't care who gets hurt."

"You don't like her because she was married to Alex."

"How do we know she was married to him at all? She just waltzes into town telling some big story and everybody swallows it whole," Kiki said. "You want my opinion?"

"No."

"My opinion is that this Lorna person is trouble, trouble coming at us like a Mack truck with its brakes out. And going to Alex's house with her is a big mistake."

"Thanks to you, we have no choice," Hannah replied. "I've got to get those poems off his computer, and I need you to distract her while I do it."

"Oh, piddle," Kiki said, sweeping the air with her hand. "No one's going through his emails. You've got to think more positive."

Hannah clamped her mouth shut. She was dying to tell Kiki about the coroner's suspicions regarding Alex's death. The juicy news was about to burst out of her, and she regretted that when she made her promise of secrecy to Perez she hadn't included a sister-only exception. The important thing right now was to find those humiliating poems and erase them off the face of the earth. If it turned out that Alex was murdered, the police could very well sift through his personal communications. They would also make the house off-limits, and Hannah would never get inside.

For years Hannah had endured the embarrassment of Kiki's behavior, but in spite of her sister's antics, Hannah had always held a certain respect in town. If it ever got out that Alex had received those poems from her email address, she would be the butt of jokes for years. She couldn't bear the idea of people in town thinking that she had been one of Alex's adoring groupies. And what would Perez say? He would believe her story, at least outwardly, but what if he had even the tiniest doubt?

With fresh resolve, Hannah downshifted, talking encouragingly to the Cadillac as it complained its way up the steepest part of the hill. It was Monday afternoon and Alex's street was livelier than the day before, with gardeners busily trimming lawns and a gaggle of kids on Rollerblades whooshing down the street. A high layer of clouds had drifted in from the Pacific, the trees and houses looking washed out under the milky sky.

Hannah pulled to the curb behind the Buick, and as soon as she turned off the ignition, she looked at Alex's house, a flutter of doubt stirring inside her. It looked the same as the day before—pristine, elegant. Only today it was the house of a dead man. Like Ox, she was spooked at the idea of going inside, but if she missed this opportunity to erase those poems there would be no others.

With no apparent qualms, Lorna hopped out of her car and marched jauntily up the sidewalk, her boots clomping against the pavement. She waved over the sisters. They got out of the car and joined her at the front door. Hannah noticed a newspaper wrapped in plastic lying on the porch, its headline announcing Alex's death, the gruesome irony making her shiver.

"Just act natural, like you're doing nothing wrong. Trust me, I know what I'm doing," Lorna instructed. She pulled a shiny key from her handbag. A squirrel loudly prattled as it scrambled up a tree, its fussing sounding like a reproach. Hannah took a few deep yoga breaths to calm herself.

"You've done this sort of thing before?" Kiki asked her, sliding her eyes to Hannah.

"In the bail bonds biz, sometimes you have to do the occasional illegal enter." Lorna took a quick peep up and down the street to make sure they were unobserved, unlocked the door, and pushed it open. "That's why I've got to latch on to a new career opportunity, pronto. Ox is too much of a pussycat for questionable behavior. Although technically this house is half mine. And if I get a good nasty lawyer, the whole thing might be mine." She started to go inside but Hannah stopped her.

"Lorna, that key looks brand new."

"The whole damn lock is new," Lorna said with pride. "I had it changed first thing this morning, as soon as I heard that Al had bought the farm."

Hannah couldn't believe what she was hearing. "How could you do such a thing?"

"Listen, babe, don't go all high and mighty. I've got my property to protect. I've been screwed out of my rightful share for twenty-five years. I won't be screwed out of it anymore."

Kiki gave Hannah another glaring, open-mouthed look that

said, "I told you so." "But how did you get the locks changed when, at least officially, you're not the owner?" Kiki asked.

Lorna shook her head and made a tsk sound. "You girls lead such sheltered lives. I just used the key I stole to get inside, then called the locksmith. When he got here I told him that I'd lost my purse and was *sooooo* afraid a big bad man had gotten my keys. Then I shook my boobs at him. He didn't ask any questions."

"But how did you even know that Alex was dead?" Hannah asked. An ugly thought crossed her mind.

"Heard it on the radio late last night and got the rest of the scoop at the mini-mart this morning when I was buying my breakfast Snickers. The guy at the register was telling the story to everybody who walked in."

Hannah and Kiki hung back while Lorna walked inside the house with a breezy gait, as if she already owned it. Hannah was beginning to think Kiki was right in her assessment of this woman. There was something heartless about her changing the locks before Alex's body had cooled. On the other hand, not many women had warm fuzzy feelings about ex-husbands.

No time for second thoughts. Hannah filed away her apprehensions for later review, and followed Lorna, pulling Kiki with her. She closed the door behind them.

The three women halted in the entryway. Hannah felt Kiki's fingers wrap around hers. Smelling the masculine aroma of cinnamon and musk, Hannah felt chilled by the eeriness of being in a house of the freshly deceased. The rooms looked so lived in, as if Alex were only away for a few hours. A newspaper on the entryway table, coats on the coatrack. A few dirty wineglasses and used cocktail napkins were scattered on the coffee table and bookcase, obviously left from the party. There probably hadn't been time for a complete clean up before the debate, and after the debate, no reason to do it.

"You keep saying how Ox is a pussycat," Kiki said. "But I thought you said he worked with you as a bail bondsman?"

"Bondsperson," Lorna corrected, thumbing through some mail lying on a cherry drop leaf table pushed against a wall near the door. "And officially Ox is just my assistant. I hired him to do a little rough stuff, but that part of things didn't work out. Ox looks tough enough, but he doesn't have the gonads for dealing with criminal types. He did catch one guy for me.

Climbed up a fire escape, grabbed the guy, and held him by the ankles until he gave up his gun. But he let the guy go when the son of a bitch told some sob story that was a complete load of hooch. A twelve-year-old could have seen through it." She put down the mail and shot the sisters a smile. "Ox ain't got much upstairs, but he's loaded on the ground floor, if you know what I mean. But enough sentimental stuff. I got work to do."

Lorna moved into the living room. She inspected each piece of furniture, stopped at the baby grand, running her hands over its gleaming black surface, already calculating the value of her fifty-percent ownership. Hannah remembered Perez saying that Alex didn't have a great deal of equity in the house, and she wondered if Lorna knew it. But even small equity in a high-priced property would probably be a fortune to a Big Spring bail bondsperson.

Hannah warily stepped to the edge of the living room, running her eyes over its expensive contents. The house itself was part of the enigma, she thought. Understand the house and you understand the owner. The furniture, the books, the small artsy objects that looked like they had come from exotic places. They were the accoutrements of a sophisticated, educated man. But it wasn't really a house as much as a stage set, with everything in it a prop to complete the image that Alex fought so hard to project. The man had battled to rid himself of the old Al Pinsky. Hannah wondered what it had cost him along the way.

"Look at all this fancy stuff," Lorna said, the words coming out with a bite, the sight of Alex's lavish belongings vexing her. "It must have cost a bundle." She pointed to an abstract oil painting, brilliant colors splashed wildly on canvas. "Why that over there probably cost a couple a hundred bucks."

Hannah felt sure the original oil had cost several thousand, but didn't say so, not wanting to increase Lorna's mounting indignation.

Lorna approached a mahogany chest to the right of the piano and reverently stroked the antique clock sitting on top. The clock looked French, made of black marble and trimmed with ornate curls of brass.

"He thought he could leave everything behind in Big Spring, dump his old self like some junk car on the side of the road. But Big Spring caught up with him." Her fingers rested against the clock, and she seemed transfixed, the object representing some quality of life she had only seen in magazines. The clock chimed and she jumped. She looked frightened for a second, then chuckled at herself. "I guess I better get started. You girls make yourself comfortable, and I'll start looking."

"There's a big buffet in the dining room with a lot of drawers," Hannah told her. "He could have kept papers in there."

"Good thinking." Lorna took off.

Once Lorna was gone, Hannah pulled Kiki close. "You keep Lorna busy while I handle Alex's email."

Kiki sniffled into a wadded tissue. "I can't. I'm too upset, being here." She pivoted around. "Just think, this is where I would have lived if he and I had been married."

You and the Pope would have been married first, Hannah thought. "Talking to Lorna will help keep your mind off the pain. Besides, we're here because of you. Now keep her out of Alex's office."

"But won't she go in there next?"

"She doesn't know he has an office or she would have looked there first. When she's done with the dining room, tell her you think he hid documents in his garage or his bedroom. Tell her anything. Just give me fifteen minutes."

Kiki blew her nose and trundled off. Hannah hurried into Alex's office, praying he had left his computer powered up. A thrill of relief ran through her when she tapped the keyboard and the screen flashed with color. She sat down and clicked on his email, quickly scrolling through his inbox. There was only one message there from her email address, and she couldn't resist opening it. It started out all right, Kiki sticking fairly close to the original poem until she got to the end. Hannah remembered the last two lines of her original verse reading, "When I finished my white journey, I lay breathing in the bluest night." But to her aggravation, Kiki had changed it to "When I put on my white teddy, you'll lay there breathing hard, all right."

Hannah's blood pressure shot upwards. She sifted through Alex's entire file of deleted emails and found two dozen messages from Kiki sent over the past two months. Muttering curses, Hannah wildly thumped the keys, deleting the messages one by one, not having the time or the stomach to read them. When finished, she scrolled through one last time to make sure she had gotten them all. Near the bottom of the screen, a subject line caught her eye. It read "Signatech." She hesitated, started to close the computer, then clicked on the email and opened it.

"We need more than verbal assurances. It will take your re-election followed by a successful council vote. On our end, we're still working through zoning restrictions on the Camden Road site, but we don't anticipate problems. Let's talk at the end of the week." The message was signed "Paul," but at the bottom of the email it listed a business called Temple, Inc. and an address in Fremont, a suburban town not far from San Francisco.

"What the hell are you doing?"

Hannah jumped. Lorna stood in the doorway, arms crossed, hip jutted against the doorjamb. She looked upset.

"I'm, well, just—" Hannah let the sentence hang, unable to conjure up a quick and believable lie. In her younger years she could have easily reeled off some credible story, and she always suspected that her wild youth had killed off some brain cells. Of course, it could have been menopause. She gave it a shot. "I'm, um, checking my email. You know, you can dial into your own email from anywhere."

Lorna walked over and looked at the computer screen. "That's Alex's email. Time to sing it, girlfriend. I know when people are lying. And to be honest, babe, you're not that great at it."

For lack of any other option, Hannah told her the truth. She had a feeling Lorna would understand. She was right. After hearing the story, Lorna shrugged. "So Kiki sent him some dirty poems, so what? For Ox's birthday last year I had chicken salad molded into the shape of me naked from the knees up, and I used parsley—"

Hannah held up a hand. "The point is, I need to get these poems off his computer so no one gets the wrong impression and thinks I sent them."

"A gal like me understands a little life complication. You should have just told me instead of sending me to sift through Alex's fancy napkin rings and frou frou placemats. Was old Al turning into a girl, or what?" Lorna went to the door, then turned to Hannah. Lorna appeared frayed around the edges, and Hannah wondered what was bothering her. "Let me know when you're done so I can go through his desk," Lorna said, and left.

It took Hannah another five minutes to double-check her previous work. Before she left the office she scribbled down the name of the Fremont company on the back of a gas bill in her purse. The email message troubled her. It sounded like there was another proposed site for Signatech, and there was no Camden Road in Hill Creek. But if Signatech was considering another site, why hadn't anyone mentioned it?

She closed the laptop and went back down the hall. Halfway down she heard crying coming from the living room. She hurried in that direction, assuming it was Kiki lamenting her lost love affair with Alex, but when she got there she saw Lorna sitting on the sofa with her face in her hands. Kiki sat next to her, Lorna tucked into her arm.

Cooing soothing words, Kiki looked up at her sister. "Lorna's have a mini breakdown."

Lorna lowered her hands and sucked in some air, a big tear rolling down her cheek, leaving a shiny trail through her rouge. It touched Hannah that apparently Lorna wasn't as tough as she let on. With her frizzy yellow hair and teary blue eyes, Lorna looked like a haggard doll that had been dragged around by an eight-year-old.

"I'm sorry to get emotional, but being here just got to me all of a sudden, you know, remembering my days with Al." She sniffled, grabbed a tissue from inside her bra, and blew her nose. "There were good times." She blew again. "Though mostly they sucked. He dumped me, you know," she said, her voice hardening. "Dumped me flat on my face."

"Aw, honey, that's happened to every woman," Kiki said with particular empathy. "I've been dumped so many times I can't remember them all. Of course, not by husbands. Both my husbands died."

"That's such a nice way to end a relationship," Lorna said in a voice tinged with envy. "Al, he gave me the heave-ho for some hippie bimbo back in the early seventies." Lorna scowled. "Moonbeam was her name. I'll never forget the little druggie twit."

Kiki gave Lorna's shoulder a squeeze. "A guy dumped me for a hippie girl named Sunflower."

"No kidding?" Lorna said.

Kiki nodded. "He was an insurance salesman, conservative as they come. And then one day he came over to get some things he left at my apartment. He told me we were through, that he was in love with Sunflower. They joined a commune."

"Old Al was never conservative. He was always a flake. The

day he left he took every cent out of the house. I was crying when he walked out, but he didn't give me a look. I followed him outside and I hung on to him, but he slapped me off, knocked me clean to the ground. Then he and his new girl took off in a beat up VW van with a license plate that said 'Be Kind.' Can you believe that? And he left me flat with all the bills and no money."

And he never really changed, Hannah thought.

"That's why I've got to fight for my share now. He screwed me once. I can't let him do it again." Lorna punched her fist into the couch. "Men are dirt. You just can't trust the bastards." She paused, her eyes fixed in front of her, and then her features softened. "All men except my Ox. He's a pussycat deluxe. He'd do anything for me."

Lorna fell silent, a condition Hannah felt certain was temporary. Kiki patted Lorna's hand, oozed more empathy, then started another of her own numerous tales of love gone rotten. Hannah had heard all of Kiki's stories a hundred times before, or worse, had lived through them. To escape, she walked toward the conservatory where the tables were still set up from the party. It was like telling war stories, Hannah thought. Women their age chewed over past loves the way old soldiers hashed over battles, reliving the old wounds, keeping the bitterness alive. Did men remember their past loves with such fresh pain? She didn't think so.

Seeing the party tables, Hannah felt a wave of sadness. They had been cleared of dishes, but the flowers and the soiled tablecloths remained. She thought of Alex, the way he must have been twenty-five years before, living what he considered a dead-end life in Big Spring, and dying to get out. She pictured him taking off in that van, and she wondered if he found what he was looking for. So few people did, especially in California. For a second she thought she felt him in the room, felt his ego along with his frustration. And anger. She felt that too. His anger at having his life cut off before he had finally gotten what he wanted. Whatever that was.

Her throat constricting, Hannah made her way through the tables to open the backdoor and get some fresh air. She noticed the flowers starting to wilt and could tell from the cloudy water in the vases that the water hadn't been replaced. The flower-lover in her made her want to change it so they would last another day, but there was no point, the idea depressing her. She moved toward the glass door leading to the garden, but as she passed the last table her eye rested on the vase that sat on top of it. The flowers stood tall, the water clean and clear. Why would someone have changed the water in that vase only? She stared at the flowers, her thoughts spinning. Then her hand moved to her cheek. She muttered, "Oh, God."

"Hannah, what is it?"

Hannah spun around and saw Kiki in the doorway.

"One of the vases has had the water changed," Hannah told her, her voice breaking. She pointed to the vase. "Look at it."

Kiki looked at the vase and then her sister. "Listen, hon, I've still got Wanda's doggie Valium right here in my purse. I was saving it for my physical next week. You know how upset I get just before they weigh me. But I think right now you need it more."

"I don't need a Valium. I need to call John."

"Why?"

"Because I want to talk to him before I call the police."

"The police? Are you nuts? That's the last thing we need."

"Kiki, listen to me. I think someone used that vase water to murder Alex."

TEN

TRIBAL FLUTE MUSIC FLOATING IN the air around them, Hannah, Kiki, Lauren, Wanda, and Naomi sat cross-legged and barefoot in a circle on the floor of Hannah's small living room, preparing for the séance. With its rose-colored walls and overstuffed chairs, the room felt soft and womanly, saved from frilliness by a lack of knickknacks and an imposing brick fireplace. On the walls hung a few family photos and two large watercolors of irises done by their great aunt Hildie. In one corner sat a television and a small stereo, and next to the sofa two cedar chip-filled cushions for the dog and pig.

The women possessing derrieres of varying breadth and thickness, each cushioned her bottom with a corresponding pillow—small throw pillows for Lauren and Hannah, a folded towel for skinny Wanda, a down bed pillow for Kiki, and for Naomi, a plump red silk meditation pillow reportedly blessed by a Tibetan lama. The rosy walls shimmered from a cluster of tall candles glowing in the center of their circle, and smoke curled from a bowl of burning herbs that Naomi insisted would cleanse the room's energy, its grassy smell mingling with the sweet, dense odor of incense.

Only in the past year had Hannah allowed Naomi to hold Red Moon sessions in her house, and until now the séances had been in the dining room around the old oak table. But tonight Hannah had put her foot down about burning herbs near the curtains, since the smoke made the room smell for days like a Girl Scout cookout. So after they had their dinner—Lauren's special scampi with lemon wine sauce followed by her strawberry rhubarb pie—they moved into the living room where there were more windows that could be cracked opened.

Since the coffee table wasn't big enough for all of them to get around, they shoved it to one side. After much mutual assistance, grumbling, and the releasing of Kiki's snaps and zippers, they arranged themselves on the floor, and Naomi streaked everyone's face with ashes.

Eyes closed, one hand held chest level, palm outward, and the other gripping the Hopi war stick, Naomi chanted softly as part of her pre-channeling meditation. Her voice was calmly rhythmic in the half-lit room, as soothing as the sound of rippling water, but the mood among the women was far from serene.

Hannah and Kiki traded feverish looks, that afternoon's scene at Alex's house still vivid, especially for Hannah. In her bones she had known Alex's death was murder, but the sight of that vase of fresh water gave a chilling solidity to what earlier had been only a suspicion. It was like supposing you might have a ghost in the house, thinking you felt its presence, and then turning down a hallway and suddenly seeing its pained, hollowed face.

Apprehensive about her tête-à-tête with Red Moon, Lauren sat rigidly next to Naomi, her fingers fidgeting with the feather and bead necklace around her neck. To enhance Lauren's receptivity to the spirit world, Naomi had dressed her in a brown tunic accessorized by the necklace and an additional clump of feathers pinned in her hair, so that she looked like a human sacrifice from some long gone primitive culture. Consulting Red Moon about her love life had sounded like a good idea to Lauren when Kiki and Naomi first proposed it, but Naomi's séances scared the wits out of Lauren, and now, faced with being the center of psychic attention, she wanted to bolt.

Lauren leaned toward Kiki, who sat on her other side. "Maybe we should call this off. I don't feel well."

"That's just nerves," Kiki said. "Buck up. If Red Moon can't give you advice on how to trap that cute Detective Morgan, who can?"

"Yes, dead Hopis are known for their matchmaking skills," Hannah said dryly.

"When is this Lorna person showing up?" Wanda asked as she readjusted the folds of the wool shawl she had bought at a chic vintage clothing shop especially for psychic sessions. She felt certain it had an electromagnetic field that was stimulating her sixth chakra, then found out after she got it home that it had bugs. The dry cleaners did a nonchemical cleansing and restored its positive vibrations.

"If she and Ox don't get here in five minutes I think we should start without them," Hannah replied.

Naomi stopped chanting, wrinkling her nose. "What do you think I'm doing here, chopping wood? Meditation is a delicate state and I require total quiet. Lorna and Ox will be here very soon. Now could you all put a lid on it while I concentrate?"

Everyone quieted, and in the silence Hannah tried to relax, but the image of the vase kept flashing in her head. A moment after discovering it she had called Perez, and he had called the police before coming over to Alex's.

When the police arrived, Lorna had laid out an elaborate fabrication about what they were doing in Alex's house, something about old photographs, a dead grandmother, and not being able to go in the house alone without having a nervous breakdown. Lorna expertly reeled off the lies, never mentioning that she had changed the locks. Lorna also didn't mention that Hannah had gone through Alex's computer, an omission for which Hannah was grateful, though Hannah knew if the police dusted Alex's computer for fingerprints, they would know she had used it. But she could explain that by saying she had tried it out at Alex's party, that she was thinking about getting a laptop and wanted a test run. Once the lies were told, the police hustled them out.

Burning to know if any connection had been made between the vase water and Alex's death, Hannah had called Perez three times later that afternoon. She knew she could get the information from him long before she would get it out of the police, if she ever got it from them at all. The first time she called Perez he had told her there was no news. The second two times he hadn't answered, and she assumed he was at the police station. But he should have been finished hours ago. Why hadn't he called?

"You haven't forgotten our little bet, have you, Kiki?" Wanda asked, eyes glinting.

Kiki shot Wanda a stiff exposure of teeth she hoped would pass for smiling indifference. It had been only sisterly zeal and a stomach full of waffle that had fueled that ridiculous bet. Now with half the town thinking Hannah had badgered Alex into a heart attack, Kiki figured the Unabomber had a better chance of winning the election than her sister. Kiki found the idea of mooning absurd for a woman her age, not to mention humiliating. Surely Wanda wouldn't hold her to it. Even if Kiki didn't have to moon the inauguration, the idea of losing the bet was revolting on its own. Wanda would harp on it for months.

Wanda took off her shawl, and to everyone's incredulity, displayed on her sweater a bright red button that read "Walter Backus for Mayor."

"Walter's running against Aunt Hannah?" Lauren asked, appalled.

"I hope none of you will be angry," Wanda said. "Especially you, Hannah, but someone had to fill the gap left by poor Alex. And Walter has such executive ability."

Hannah forced herself not to say something curt. She was certain that Wanda had pushed Walter into the election. If left to himself, Walter wouldn't run for anything except the closest cocktail.

"Hannah will whip him," Kiki said haughtily. The sight of the button had her seething.

"Perhaps," Wanda replied, polishing the button with the edge of her shawl. "Of course, I'm financing Walter's campaign, and I'm really thinking big. We're talking radio and print advertising."

A distressed squeak came from the back of Kiki's throat. Due to several lucrative divorces, Wanda had virtually unlimited funds, and all Hannah could afford were the flyers she had put up around town.

"Is he supporting Signatech?" Hannah asked the only question she considered truly important.

"He's not sure yet what he's supporting," Wanda replied with less smugness. "We're still working out his platform."

Hoping to change the subject, Kiki poked Naomi in the leg. "Isn't it time to start the session?"

"You can't avoid it, Kiki," Wanda said. "A bet's a bet. I'd like for you to wait until after Walter's inaugural speech before you actually drop *trou*, if you don't mind. I'm sure he'll be saying something poignant and we wouldn't want him interrupted."

"You can't possibly hold my sister to that ridiculous bet," Hannah said.

"I can and I will," Wanda replied. "And if she reneges, she'll never be able to show her face at Lady Nails again. I'll make sure of it. Of course, Hannah, if you win, then I'll be the one who embarrasses myself. But it's hardly likely to happen, is it?"

Kiki's lower lip trembled as she conjured the image of her largish bottom exposed to the Hill Creek population.

"And of course, the press will be there," Wanda tossed in like a firecracker.

"Darn you, Wanda Backus," Kiki spat. "Hannah's still going to win the election, just you wait."

Naomi spewed out some air. "That's it. The negative energy in here is thick as mud. You've destroyed my meditation. Now I'll have to start completely over."

"Well, try to speed it up," Hannah said, ready to get the séance over with so she could call Perez.

"Yes, please," Lauren told Naomi. "I've got to be home by ten. It's *Cops* night."

The women all bestowed pitying looks on Lauren. Ever since she had fallen in love with Detective Morgan she had become addicted to the *Cops* television show, turning it into a self-destructive ritual, gorging on Cheetos and hot cocoa while she watched it, weeping whenever the program showed a young uniformed policeman.

The doorbell rang. Hannah answered it, finding Ox and Lorna on the doorstep. Hannah welcomed them inside, noticing that Ox had worn a tie for the occasion.

Naomi jumped up to greet them. "It's so nice to add some new members to our little group," she said as she settled Ox and Lorna on either side of her, making the rest of the women shift over. "Red Moon appreciates new faces. Things get dull for him."

"One of the downsides of being dead," Hannah said. Naomi's lips pursed. She gave Hannah a warning look and then smudged Ox and Lorna's cheeks with ashes. Ox sheepishly looked left and then right, straining his neck to see in the dining room. "So where is he?"

"Who?" Hannah asked.

"The dead Indian."

Naomi smiled benevolently. "Red Moon prefers the term 'Astral American.' And he's not here physically. He fuses into my energy field and speaks through me. I'm his vessel. His temporary physical form."

Ox tugged worriedly at his chin.

"Oxie's a little scared," Lorna explained. "That's why we're late. I had trouble getting him out of the car, and let me tell you, the man can hang on to a door handle. But I've told him there's nothing to be afraid of."

"Of course there isn't," Naomi said, with maternal concern. "To speak with the spirit world is the most natural thing in the world. We all have the ability to communicate with the unseen. I'm more receptive than most, of course, it being a gift I was born with. But I can assure you that Red Moon is a gentle spirit of the light, and he only wants to do good in the earthly world."

"You see, babe, nothing to worry about," Lorna told him. "It's kind of like listening to the radio."

"Except you're tuned to KDEAD," Hannah said. Naomi's nostrils flared.

"Oxie's going to be A-okay," Lorna said, then pointed a finger at Lauren. "You're the one with the man trouble, right?"

Lauren meekly acknowledged her predicament, and Kiki gave her a pat on the knee. "Don't worry, sweetie. Red Moon will tell us what's going on with Detective Morgan. Won't he Naomi?" Kiki and Naomi swapped a glance laden with unspoken communications, and Hannah wondered what was cooking between them.

Hannah doubted that Red Moon could help with Lauren's love situation, unless he was a combination of Dr. Ruth and Uri Geller. And even if he did hand out any useful insights, Lauren wouldn't be able to recognize them since they would be veiled in obtuse coyote metaphors. But Kiki and Naomi had been adamant that Lauren needed a session, and Hannah agreed, with the caveat that no one would bring up Alex's death. Wanda was such a gossip, a human megaphone bleating whatever newsy tidbits she knew or suspected. Hannah didn't want her running around town telling everyone that Red Moon had named the killer, or some other nonsense.

Naomi drew in a long breath, slowly releasing it with the extra theatrical flair she always liked to throw in for neophytes. "All right, I'm ready to begin." She scooched her rear end more comfortably into the pillow. "Hannah, if you could switch off that lamp."

Hannah got up and turned off the table lamp, throwing the room into a deeper darkness, the candles glowing yellow in the center of the circle.

"Thank you, Hannah," Naomi said, waiting for her to settle herself back on the floor. "All right now, sacred sisters and brother, let us join hands and allow our eyes to rest on one of the candles. Focus on the circle of light surrounding the flame. See only the glow, and feel your inner spirit. Feel the sacred god or goddess that dwells within." Naomi saw Hannah roll her eyes. "Your inner goddess seems a bit bitchy tonight, Hannah, if you don't mind my mentioning it. Try to stay centered."

"I've got things on my mind," Hannah told her.

"Don't we all," Wanda said, her smile wicked.

"Let's all close our eyes," Naomi said. "I'm going to start off by calling on the energies of the magic white buffalo. It will help prepare Red Moon. He feels a bit strange tonight." She took in another deep breath and let it out slowly through her mouth before closing her eyes. "Smile on us, oh, white one. Our feet are on the golden plain, our hearts in the clouds. Let us be a human bridge between the spirit beneath and the spirit above. Let us walk into the sacred world where the animals speak and the trees whisper prayers."

Naomi fell silent for a moment, then began chanting, the rhythmic sound starting out soft and hypnotic, gradually building, becoming louder, deeper. This part always gave Hannah the creeps. Even though she had doubts about Red Moon, she believed that Naomi's trances were usually real, and it was a simple fact that Red Moon's predictions were often on target. Naomi's voice grew more masculine, no longer sounding at all like herself. Lauren's hand tightened around Hannah's. Hannah heard Ox swallow hard.

"Spring comes to yellow mountain," Naomi said in a voice strong and masculine. "River of laughing rock talks to the eagle, sings to the wind."

Hannah opened one eye and saw Ox's face, his brow creased with awe and worry.

"Young warrior runs naked in the wind," Naomi à la Red Moon said. "Male eagle perches on golden mounds."

"Is he talking dirty?" Ox whispered to Lorna. "You know I don't like dirty talk."

"It's dead Indian talk, baby," she replied. "Now shut up. You'll learn something."

"Dance with the wind," Naomi said, her voice gaining an unusual lilt. "Fly with the hawk. Laugh with the water rippling over smiling rock."

Hannah raised an eyebrow. She hadn't been to as many Red

Moon sessions as Kiki and Wanda, but she knew that Red Moon's metaphors were usually dark and ominous, which was understandable coming from someone deceased. Now suddenly all this upbeat talk about spring and laughing rocks. Was Red Moon on Prozac? Hannah again opened one eye and inspected the other women to see if anyone else was noticing the odd giddiness of the dead snake shaman. But Lauren only looked frightened, and Wanda wore an intense expression, both the usual reactions. Kiki, on the other hand, smiled mischievously.

"Earth mother runs happy through the field," Naomi said. "Her breasts raised high to greet the sun."

"It's dirty, Lornie," Ox whispered. "I don't like it."

Hannah didn't like it either, but for different reasons. Naomi wasn't in a trance at all. She was faking to convince Lauren to get a push-up bra and spike heels. Kiki had to be the one behind it. Hannah straightened her leg and gave Naomi a little kick, but it had no effect.

"Earth mother feels free, released from inhibition," Naomi continued, caught up in the moment. Enjoying herself, her voice got a singsong quality that sounded as if Red Moon had gotten a nightclub gig in Reno. The next step was for Red Moon to break out into a Hopi shaman rendition of "Feelings." "Earth mother runs naked, naked toward brown coyote. Earth Mother wears loin cloth."

From Frederick's of Hollywood, Hannah thought. Reaching over, she pinched Naomi's thigh. Naomi let out a loud "Ouch!"

Lauren's eyes popped open. "What happened?" she asked, terrified. Everyone opened their eyes. Ox was breathing hard. Lorna chewed a fingernail.

Giving Hannah a haughty but guilty look, Naomi cleared her throat. "I'm so sorry. Red Moon had a sudden insight that startled him."

"Something to do with me and Larry?" Lauren asked.

"Oh, no, nothing like that," Naomi assured her. "It was a random scene from a buffalo hunt. It had nothing to do with you. It was—" She paused, trying to think of some good way to finish the sentence.

"A drug flashback," Hannah said. "Something bad in the old peace pipe."

"Exactly," Naomi said quickly. "We'll have to start over."

"Red Moon seems so enthusiastic tonight," Wanda said eagerly, apparently unaware of Naomi and Kiki's scheme. "I think we should try to speak to Alex."

Hannah saw the sudden alarm on Lorna's face.

"We agreed we weren't going in that direction tonight," Hannah said.

"But we should," Wanda told her. "It would be busting through the ultimate love barrier."

Ox squirmed. "I don't like it."

"And I'm with Oxie," Lorna said. "Speaking to somebody who's been dead a few hundred years is weird enough. But Al's awfully fresh. He might not be settled in good yet."

"But that's exactly why we should pursue it," Naomi said. "Alex is still close to the earthly plane. He may want to speak, to reach out to those who knew him. And I'm feeling so receptive tonight." Naomi saw the cynical look on Hannah's face. "It's true, Hannah. Red Moon is very strong this evening. Unusually strong. His energy inside me, it's like a river, and sometimes it's shallow and hardly moving. But tonight it's deep and clear, the water flowing with such force."

"Let's go for it," Kiki said, then faced Lorna. "Unless you're afraid."

Hannah didn't know about Lorna, but Ox looked close to wetting himself. Was he afraid of the séance in general or of what Alex might have to say? Ox tried desperately to make eye contact with Lorna, but she was looking at Kiki.

"Deal me in," Lorna said roughly. "I'm not afraid of that jerk breathing or not breathing. But I'll warn you. I'm not taking any crap off him. I mean, it's not like he's sick. He's just dead."

"Is it okay with you, Lauren?" Naomi asked. Lauren nodded, seeming relieved to no longer be the topic of discussion. Naomi moved her eyes to Hannah. "And you?"

"Fine by me," Hannah answered. She knew if Naomi said she was feeling receptive, that she meant it, but Hannah was more interested in seeing the reactions of their new guests to this new direction of the séance, than in hearing what Red Moon had to say.

After everyone once again held hands and closed their eyes, Naomi began chanting. Like the first time, her voice started out low and natural, and then the chanting gradually became deeper and throatier. After a few minutes Naomi's voice grew with a masculine resonance that had been lacking previously, and Hannah knew that this time Naomi was going into the trance for real. Naomi's body rocked back and forth, the Hopi war stick keeping tempo, rapping against the floor, its bells ringing. Naomi's voice expanded, intensified, until Hannah could feel the sound of it penetrating into her bones. There was no longer any detectable trace of Naomi's own voice. Hannah opened her eyes and saw that even Naomi's face seemed to have altered, her mouth held differently, her eyes squeezed shut, every facial muscle tensed, distorting her features. A prickle ran up the back of Hannah's neck. She knew it was her imagination, but the flickering shadows on the wall seemed larger, forming into the shapes of animals.

Suddenly the chanting stopped. Naomi took in a long breath. Her body shuddered, and she began again. "Hay-ya, ha-ya, mel-lo. Hay-ya, ha-ya, mel-lo." The war stick rapped hard against the floor, the sound reverberating against the walls. "Snake man moves, no sound, no sound. He lead the people away from wisdom. All go down dark path. Snake clan, bear clan, fire clan. Animals run. Spider woman *criiieeesss*." The last word came out with a long, sad wail that scared even Hannah. Ox sat wide-eyed and pale.

A knock at the door made everyone jump. Naomi was so enveloped by the trance that she didn't react to it. Quietly, Hannah got up, tiptoed to the door, and found Perez.

"I just got back from the police station. I have to talk to you."

Her finger to her lips, Hannah pulled him inside, past the séance group and the dining room and through the closed door leading to the kitchen, where Sylvia and Teresa happily greeted him. Closing the door behind them, she gave him a few seconds to give each pet a head rub, then let the animals out into the backyard.

She noticed dark circles beneath his eyes. "Want some tea?" she asked, then decided he needed something stronger. "Or there's wine in the refrigerator."

Perez shook his head. Kiki was well known for drinking cheap rosé and apricot-flavored spritzers.

"You were right," he said. "Alex Portman was murdered, and it was done with the water from the vase."

Hannah's legs turned rubbery. She sat down at the kitchen table. There was a basket of bread left from dinner in the center of it, and the kitchen still smelled like garlic and wine sauce. "Do they know who did it?"

"No. Tomorrow they'll start questioning everyone who was at his party. Morgan wants you and Kiki at the station at eight-thirty in the morning. I told him I'd deliver the message to you. You'll have to be there."

"We want to be there. Where did they find the poison?"

"In a water pitcher, the kind you use to filter tap water."

"I have one. They use charcoal filters. Wouldn't that filter out the poison?"

Perez leaned back against the kitchen counter, his arms folded. "I asked Louis the same thing. He said if the charcoal was extremely fine, yes. But this filter used little pellets. It was enough to take out the plant debris from the water but not the toxin. The water wouldn't have looked different, but it should have tasted funny. According to Alex's housekeeper, he used the filtered water to mix up a wheatgrass drink from a powder. He always put it in that water bottle with his seminar logo."

"I tried wheatgrass juice once at the health food store," Hannah said. "It's bitter. It probably masked any taste."

"And Alex drank a lot of the stuff. Louis thinks he probably chugged a bottle after his jog. The toxin took effect quicker because his metabolism was speeded up."

"And he drank from that bottle all through the debate. We all saw him."

"That's why he was walking strangely and looking at his hands. Louis said he must have been feeling numb in his hands and feet, and his heartbeat was speeding up. He might have thought he was nervous or catching a bug."

Hannah heard Teresa scratching at the backdoor, but ignored it. It wasn't cold out, and the pets could wait. Perez lowered himself into a chair on the other side of the table. Under the glare of the ceiling light, he looked completely wrung out.

Hannah reached across the table and touched his hand. "Can I fix you something to eat?"

He smiled. "Thanks. I didn't have time to get anything. Can you just slap some cheese on bread for me?"

"I can do better." She got up and went to the fridge, getting out the curried tuna left from lunch. She was glad to be doing something to distract herself from the sick feeling growing inside her. She took the breadbasket from the table and sliced two whole grain rolls.

"Do the police have the water bottle?" she asked as she spooned tuna onto the bread.

"Get this. The janitor took it. Luckily he didn't drink from it or wash it. The police found it this afternoon, but they're pretty sure it'll turn up the same toxin that was in the pitcher." Resting his elbow against the tabletop, Perez ran a hand down his cheek in a gesture of fatigue. "It seems like the whole world is going down the stink hole. I can understand when people get killed over drugs or in a fight. But this? I don't get it."

She set the sandwiches in front of him. "Will you be working on the case?"

"They haven't asked, not yet."

Hannah went back to the fridge and got out a pitcher of Red Zinger tea. The sound of Naomi's chanting filtered through the door. Hannah tried to keep her face immobile, realized she couldn't, and took the tea to the counter, turning away from him so he couldn't see her.

"You want tea?" she asked, feeling his eyes on her back. They hadn't known each other very long, less than a year, but he was learning to read her, to know her moods. It made her uncomfortable, but still she welcomed it, knowing that the intimacy was something she needed, something everybody needed. Neither of her husbands had ever known her that well. She realized now that she had never let them. She found that with Perez she wanted to open herself up, the way she would air out a house closed up too long. Of course, there were drawbacks. Even turned away from him she felt he was looking right inside her head, knowing she was hiding something.

"What is it, Hannah?"

Men could be so irritating. She poured reddish tea in a glass. Naomi's voice grew louder. Hannah had already told Perez about her suspicions regarding Alex and Signatech. She told him over the phone before the debate, but she hadn't gone into details about how she got the information. She didn't want Perez to know how much snooping she had really done, but now she didn't see a way out. She got an ice cube tray from the freezer, giving herself that small amount of time to think of how she was going to phrase things. She was able to buy herself another twenty seconds while she emptied the tray and refilled it, but she knew Perez was waiting for her to speak. She put some cubes in the glass and sat down at the table, sliding the tea over to him. He looked excessively alert. She told him about snooping in Alex's office the day of the party, Kiki's emails to Alex, and her trip to Alex's house that morning. She also told him about the strange email she found from the Fremont company. For the purposes of dignity preservation, she left out two items. First, the juicy part about hearing Alex and Mary bust love barriers in his office, and second, about Kiki sending the emails from her email address.

"Did you get a copy of the Signatech email giving him the stock options?" Perez asked.

"No, but the police can get it easily enough."

"What's your take on that second message you found, the one from that company in Fremont?"

"Alex was obviously working on a backup site for Signatech in case the first one fell through."

"You think he was that worried about Althea and that stuff about the endangered cricket?" Perez started in on the sandwiches.

"That's the strange thing. I don't think it was that big a threat. His problem was getting general approval from the council, and as far as I know, they were all pro Signatech. And this second site, if that's what it is, isn't in Hill Creek. Why would Alex be involved?"

Perez swallowed, pausing to let the information and the sandwich sink in. "You realize that I have to pass all this on to Morgan, and that I'm going to have a hard time explaining why you were going through Alex's email."

"I'm not exactly proud of what I did, but I think I was justified. I was trying to protect the town as well as my sister."

"Sounds to me like you were trying to protect yourself."

"Why?" she said, more sharply than she intended.

"A candidate for mayor breaks into the computer of the incumbent and turns up some dirt."

"It wasn't like that. That first time I was in Alex's office, I was helping Kiki fix her bra."

"By going through Alex's trash?"

"I was looking for paper clips, and that led me in a roundabout way to his computer." Said out loud, it didn't sound too good even to her. She threw a concerned look at the kitchen door. Naomi's chanting had become thunderous.

"Listen, Hannah, I believe you, but you have to admit that on the surface your story's a little thin. Plus you lied to the police today about why you were in Alex's house."

"I didn't lie. Lorna did."

"It's the same thing, and you know it," he said, his voice heating up. "You withheld information. And now this is a murder investigation."

"Don't raise your voice at me. I've done nothing wrong."

"I don't agree."

Their eyes locked. She needed to tell him about the nasty scene she had heard between Mary and Alex. It struck her that now that it was certain Alex was murdered, Mary had a decent motive. But in his current state, Perez would give birth to triplets when he heard how she hid under the desk while Alex and Mary had sex. Perez had a conservative side to his nature that didn't understand such things. She steeled herself, prepared to dump it all out and take the consequences. But before she got started they heard shouts from the living room.

Hannah ran toward the sound, with Perez on her heels. When she reached the living room she saw Wanda and Lauren still sitting on the floor across from Naomi, both looking alarmed. Kiki stood a few feet away, watching Naomi, her hands over her mouth. Naomi, in her Red Moon voice, was shouting something unintelligible. The trance was intense; Naomi's eyes rolled back in her head. It scared Hannah, and she considered shaking Naomi out of it, but she didn't know if that would help or make things worse. She considered dialing 911. In Marin County, they probably got channeling emergency calls all the time.

Ox stood by the front door, Lorna at his side, stroking his chest, talking soothingly to him. When she saw Hannah, she glowered.

"You crazy people scared my Oxie half to death. We never should have come here. Talking to dead people. What a bunch of California whackos." Lorna hustled Ox out the front door.

Once Lorna was gone, Kiki hurried to her sister. "Oh, Hannah, I know you told us not to talk to Red Moon about poor Alex," she said. "You were so right. Red Moon's out of control. He keeps spouting off about Alex and saying the most terrible things."

"He mentioned Alex by name?" Hannah asked.

Kiki nodded. Hannah knelt down by Naomi and touched her arm. Within a few seconds, Naomi's shouting quieted to a threatening rumble.

"Evil flies silent on wings, the deer scatter," Naomi said in Red Moon's bass voice. "Evil lies in the field."

Hannah looked at Kiki. "It's Red Moon's usual—" she started to say, but stopped when she heard the next words.

"More will die," Red Moon said, the words throbbing, the sound coming from someplace so deep inside Naomi, it couldn't have existed. "More will die."

ELEVEN

THE SISTERS SHOWED UP AT the police station promptly at eight-thirty, Kiki clothed in a tight dress, bulky jewelry, and a fantasy about a tawdry romance with a hard-boiled cop. Hannah reminded her that most of the local police officers were young enough to be her sons. Kiki's fantasy shifted to a tawdry romance with a hard-boiled cop with bad eyesight and a penchant for much older women.

In separate interviews, the sisters told Detective Morgan what had happened at Alex's party, including being in Alex's office and finding the Signatech email. A lot of the basics Morgan had already heard from Perez. Hannah gave Morgan the nuts and bolts about going through Alex's emails the day before and why she had done it, leaving out the fact that Kiki's poems were bawdy rewrites of Hannah's poetry and that they had come from Hannah's email address. Kiki's poems had nothing to do with Alex's murder, and with them erased, there was no point in getting into the humiliating details.

Hannah also omitted what she knew about Alex's affair with Mary. She knew she had to tell Morgan, and she planned to do it later that day after she had a chance to discuss it first with Mary. Hannah considered Mary a friend and knew it would look better if Mary told the police herself. And if Mary told them, then Hannah wouldn't have to, and with some luck she could keep secret the regrettable episode under Alex's desk. Hannah called Mary several times that morning, but had no luck. She knew Mary would be at the rummage sale after lunch. She would talk to her there.

These events and decisions had occurred with a minimum of discussion between the sisters. They moved from bed to breakfast to the police station in a grim silence, their distress bottled up inside them.

It was a box of Choco Crunch that brought it all to a head.

After the police station, Hannah and Kiki had gone to the Hill Creek Grocery. They were in the cereal aisle discussing the health advantages of organic granola versus Choco Crunch, the latter being Kiki's choice as breakfast of champions. Nerves being raw, the discussion degraded into an argument. When Kiki ripped open a box of Choco Crunch and stuffed handfuls of chemically processed, nonnutritious wheat by-products into her mouth, tears running down her face, they both realized that it wasn't fiber intake that was upsetting them. Unable to wait another moment to discuss the explosive topic, they hastily pushed their cart to the meat counter, which was, if one was having a breakdown, even better for privacy than the shelf with the Cheez Whiz and the canned vegetables.

Although most Hill Creek residents would gladly sneak a T-bone into their grocery basket if no one were looking, few would risk the social censure of standing at the meat counter and openly buying the stuff. Like picking your teeth or being Republican, it was one of those things Hill Creekers didn't do in public. This was in spite of the signs on the meat counter ensuring potential buyers that the cows were farm raised, ate organic grass, and led lives of frolicking bovine freedom before they volunteered to be food so they might achieve their next karmic level. The savvy store management recognized that to its fashionably enlightened clientele, grocery purchases were eco/socio/political statements. Hill Creekers wanted to be seen buying vegetables that were organic, eggs that were free-range, and toilet paper made from recycled newspapers made from wood pulp that didn't come from the rain forest. Anything else could be ordered from the store's web site and, like porno magazines, discreetly delivered in plain wrappers, which was how the meat section maintained such a flourishing business.

"I still don't get it," Kiki said, her voice hushed but high-pitched with tension, gray streaks of tear-diluted mascara staining her cheeks. "Exactly how did somebody kill Alex with the flower water?"

"Monkshood is an extremely poisonous plant." Her eyes still closed, Hannah formed the words slowly and carefully. "According to what I read on the Internet last night, the plants are especially poisonous in the spring. It's the plant juices that are so lethal. I remember Mary saying that Maggie had cut the flowers the day before the party so she could get the house set up ahead of time. That means the flowers sat in the vases overnight, long enough for the juices from the leaves and stems to seep into the water."

"But who knows that?" Kiki asked, digging into the cereal box for a handful of stress-relieving Choco Crunch. "Only you know that kind of weird plant thing, and you didn't murder him."

A woman walked up to the adjacent fish counter and rang the bell. Nick, dressed in a clean white apron, came out from the back, wiping his hands on a towel. Hannah knew if she and Kiki rushed away Nick would know something was up, and he was as bad a gossip as Wanda, broadcasting everything he overheard to the men's transformational bodywork session participants at the fire station where he volunteered.

Nick gave them a look. Hannah lowered her voice to a whisper. "Pretend to be examining the sausages."

"How do you pretend that?"

"Keep your eyes on them, and every once in a while point and say 'mmmm good.' " Both women turned to the counter. "I know about poisonous plants," Hannah continued, her voice so low, Kiki had to strain to hear, "because I don't want anything poisonous in the garden that Sylvia and Teresa could nibble. But lots of people know these things. That information is in books, in the library, on web sites."

"Hannah, you have this awful look on your face. What are you thinking?"

"I hate to even consider this, but we both know there's another way someone could have known that the water was poisonous. We've both been thinking it since last night, which is why we've been afraid to discuss it. At the party, Walter was joking around about drinking the vase water, and I warned him it was dangerous. I said it pretty loudly because I thought he might actually drink it. You know how he is. There were dozens of people in the conservatory and all of them could have easily heard me say the water was lethal."

"Did you tell Detective Morgan that?"

"Of course."

Nick finished up with the customer and came over to the sisters. "Have you converted to the other side, Hannah? You seem awfully interested in those sausages."

Hannah looked up, embarrassed. "Yes, well, we have some relatives coming to visit, and they're from—"

"Poland," Kiki chimed in, proud of such creative thinking. "You have Polish sausages?"

"Let's buy the sausages tomorrow," Hannah said. "What fish is on special today?"

"I've got some nice tuna in the back that just came in," Nick said. "Dolphin free."

"I'll take a pound," Hannah told him. Nick nodded and went into the back.

"But Hannah, that means that it was probably someone at the party who killed Alex," Kiki said as soon as they were alone. "But Alex was the most loved man in town."

Hannah's expression was grave. "Obviously not. And there were a couple of people who might have wanted him out of the way."

"Like who?"

"Like Althea, for one."

"Aw, come on. Althea wouldn't hurt anybody."

"You don't know that. Environmentalists can get very aggressive these days. Look at the protesters in Seattle."

"But Althea was chained to a tree when you warned Walter about the vase water."

"Being an environmentalist, she might know her plants. And she said that she had gone inside his house once during the party to use the bathroom. She could have seen the monkshood."

"I don't know. Althea seems so goofy and harmless."

"You never can tell what's going on inside someone. Althea seems in general pretty bitter. I say that when you're looking for a murderer, find the person with the deep emotional wound." Hannah's thoughts turned to the pathetic scene between Alex and Mary. After being so rudely dumped, Mary could have a wound so big you could herd cattle through it.

This disturbing thought was broken when Margo, a fortyish belly-dancing instructor, pushed her cart up to the fish counter. Margo wore leggings and a crop top that provided full belly button exposure. After a quick hello to Hannah and Kiki, she turned to examine the fish.

Nick handed Hannah a package wrapped in white paper. "Here's your tuna," he said loud enough for Margo to hear, probably so she wouldn't think Hannah was buying meat. He told Margo he would be right with her and then disappeared again into the back.

The sisters started for the checkout so they could continue their discussion in privacy, but before they got out of the fish section they saw Lorna coming their way, arms pumping and boots stomping with the fury of lighted dynamite.

"Hannah! Kiki! I found you!" Lorna looked frazzled, her yellow hair standing out from her head at right angles, and her lipstick smeared at one corner, as if she had swiped it on without a mirror. "You gotta help me."

"What's wrong?" Hannah asked. She noticed Margo staring.

"They think Ox killed Alex. But he didn't. He couldn't. He looks big and tough, but inside he's tapioca." Lorna clutched the front of Hannah's shirt. "You've got to help him. I've asked around. I know you've worked with the cops before. And you're local. You write poetry. The cops will listen to a poet." Lorna pulled Hannah closer. "My Oxie won't last in jail. He's too pretty." Hannah removed Lorna's hand. "Sorry about that," Lorna said, stroking Hannah's shirt to smooth out the creases. "But I'm going crazy."

"Have they arrested him?" Hannah asked.

"No, but they're going to, I can tell. I know how these cops work." With shaking hands, Lorna pulled a cigarette and a plastic lighter from her purse, frantically clicking the lighter until it produced a flame. She touched it to her cigarette and took a drag.

Margo's previous expression of keen interest turned to keener horror. "You put that out right now," Margo demanded.

"Cool your jets," Lorna said with a snort. "I'll be out of here in a minute." She sucked on the cigarette like she was sucking venom from a snakebite.

"You'll leave right now," Margo snapped. "Secondhand smoke is a killer. And it's going to make my crop top just reek."

Lorna crossed her eyes. "Listen, Barbie, why don't you go home and exfoliate something?"

Kiki stifled a chuckle. Margo sucked in her cheeks with self-righteous indignation. "How would you like it if I called the manager?" Margo threatened.

"Gee, grocery store managers, they just scare me shitless," Lorna said with sarcasm, then held up her cigarette and gave

Margo a warning glare. "Now scoot, Barbie, before I put this out on your plastic tits."

Margo came close to frothing at the mouth. Lorna turned back to Hannah and started to speak, but then heard Margo maniacally ringing the bell on the counter and calling to Nick for help.

Lorna pivoted back to Margo. "Listen, what is this? You want a piece of me? You want a piece of Lorna Donatello? Because we can make that happen, Barb."

Just as Nick came back out, Lorna, her expression rabid, took a couple of steps in Margo's direction. Margo shrieked, reached into her shopping basket, and began shaking the business end of an organic carrot at Lorna's face.

Nick looked on in wonderment. There had never been a catfight in the grocery before. He thought maybe he should try to stop it, but then considered if that would be interfering with some sort of Amazonian goddess development, creating a spiritual obstruction he could be sued for later. While he pondered it, Lorna's right hand curled into a fist. As her arm cocked back, Hannah seized it.

"Let's get out of here," Hannah told Lorna. "We have more important things to worry about."

With Lorna muttering descriptions of the pain she could inflict on Margo with a carrot, Hannah paid for her fish and the half-eaten box of Choco Crunch, and then the three women hurried to the parking lot and over to the far side of the large green recycle bins.

"Now tell me why the police suspect Ox," Hannah asked.

"Who knows?" Lorna said. It came out angry, the incident with Margo sparking her hot temper. "Maybe because he's from out of town. Friggin' cops." Her face softened. "You don't think they'll rough him up, do you? Oxie could take it physically, but it would really hurt his feelings."

"Aw, honey, they won't touch him," Kiki said. "This is Hill Creek. The cops' idea of rough treatment is no Parmesan on the pasta."

"Well, Oxie won't like it, and he can't sleep good if he doesn't have a cushy pillow. But I won't let it come to that. I just can't."

Hannah studied Lorna puffing furiously on her cigarette. A teenager approached the first recycle bin and dumped in a bag, the cans clattering. Hannah waited for him to leave before she spoke. "I know our local police well enough to believe they wouldn't suspect Ox of murder without good reason. There's something you're not telling us."

Lorna shrugged. "Yeah, well, one of Al's neighbors saw Ox wandering around the backyard."

"When?"

"The day Al died. That afternoon, you know, after everyone left his hoity-toity party." Lorna took a final long drag off her cigarette, reducing it to a glowing stump. "Bad timing, huh?" The last sentence came out choked because she was holding the smoke in her lungs. Finally she exhaled.

Kiki waved away the smoke. "What was he doing there?"

"Nothing to be ashamed of," Lorna said, tossing the cigarette to the ground, stamping it out with her heel. "I asked him to go over and sweat Al a little."

"Sweat him?" Hannah asked.

"You know, put a little pressure on him. No rough stuff. Just some heavy-duty suggesting that he give me my share of the business."

Kiki turned up a palm. "So why was Ox wandering around the yard?"

"Because he rang the doorbell and no one answered," Lorna explained like it was a stupid question. "Ox thought maybe Al was just being cagey, so he went around the back and looked in the window."

"That hardly seems enough to suspect him of murder," Hannah said.

"Yeah, well, as luck would have it, the window was open," Lorna said. "And Oxie thought that if Al was in there hiding, he ought to go inside and force him to have a man-to-man talk."

"But you had taken a key to Alex's house," Kiki said. "Why did Ox have to break in?"

"I didn't think he'd need a key, so I didn't give it to him. He was just supposed to ring the doorbell, nice and polite. And he didn't break into anything. The window was open. That's like an engraved invitation. It was just Oxie's piss poor luck that he left fingerprints on the windowsill. But that proves that it was innocent. If he was up to no good he would have worn gloves. He's dumb, but he ain't brain-dead."

"Was Alex there?" Hannah asked.

"Yeah. Ox said it scared him pretty good when he showed up in his bedroom. Al had just gotten back from a jog and he was doing exercises or something. Ox said he was prissing around like a goddamn ballerina. Al always was half wimp."

"Then what happened?"

"They talked, no big deal."

"So what's the connection between Ox being in Alex's house and Alex's death?" Hannah asked. It was a trick question. She already knew the answer, but she wanted to find out how much Lorna knew. That morning's newspaper article hadn't mentioned the water pitcher.

Lorna's face crumbled. "They think Ox poisoned something while he was there. Can you believe it? Like he put rat poison in Al's Wheaties or something. Ox said he wasn't sure what they were talking about. And my being in the house yesterday didn't look so good either."

"Now that this is a murder investigation, you'll have to tell the police the truth about why you were there," Hannah said.

"I already told them. As soon as I knew they were grilling Ox, I told the cops everything. Well, not everything. I left out the part about you getting the poems off Al's computer. I figure that's none of their beeswax."

Hannah felt a shot of guilt. "We shouldn't hide anything," she said, remembering that she had hidden a few things herself.

"I've got nothing to hide. All I've done is go after what's rightfully mine, and that's nothing to be ashamed of. But you've got to help Ox," Lorna said, her eyes pleading. "My pookie's innocent." She paused. "But there are some additional factors that might not look so great for him."

"Like what?" Hannah asked.

"Like the fact that he's on parole for assault and battery. Remember I told you how he held that guy by the ankles?"

"That's considered assault?" Hannah asked.

"Yeah, well, I forgot to mention that at the time he was holding the guy over the edge of a five-story building. The cops got nitpicky and Ox did a little jail time. That assault charge could be, you know, misinterpreted by unenlightened law enforcement officials. That's why you've got to help him."

Hannah shook her head. "Help how?"

"I'm going to do some investigating myself, but I'm an outsider. Whoever killed Al was one of these high-class local yokels, like that Barbie bitch in the grocery store. The cops never mess with people like that. But you know these folks. You can nose around and nobody's the wiser."

"I think you should be talking to the police," Hannah said.

"I don't trust the cops."

"You can trust our cops."

"Yeah, and I'm Christie Brinkley. You and your sis here are my only friends in town. You've got to help me."

"It's a lawyer you need," Hannah told her. "Not us."

"There are things you can do a lawyer can't."

"Listen, Lorna, I know what you're going through," Hannah said with sincerity, remembering how she had felt when Kiki had been accused of murder. "But I can't help you. If Ox is innocent, I'm sure the police will figure it out without my help. There's nothing I can do."

A knot formed in Hannah's throat. She wanted to help Ox. There was a childlike sweetness about him, but even though he didn't seem like a killer, he had a decent motive for wanting Alex dead. Lorna's motive was even better, since murdering Alex would get her revenge as well as money. And the woman certainly seemed capable of the deed, since she had almost crammed a carrot up Margo's privates over a cigarette. Hannah didn't want to get involved with a possible murderer, and at that moment Lorna had a sting about her that Hannah didn't like.

Hannah again told Lorna that she was sorry, and then she and Kiki turned to leave.

"You got no choice but to help me."

Hannah turned back. "What do you mean?"

Lorna reached into her handbag and pulled out some folded papers. "When you erased all those poems to Al you forgot something. He printed them. I looked in his desk and found a whole mess of poems from Lushlips, some of them pretty naughty. Especially that one about Al being naked and your lovin' leaving him wreck-ed." A distressed squeak escaped Kiki's lips, and Hannah threw her a disgusted look. The sisters' reaction emboldened Lorna. "You told me yourself, Hannah, that everyone would think they came from you. For all I know, maybe they did. You're the type that's cool on the outside but burns hot deep down. Could be you were just burning, yearning for old Al. You know what I mean?"

Hannah drew herself up. "I didn't send those poems. It

doesn't matter anyway. What can you possibly do with them?" she said with much more calmness than she felt. "It's not like you can plaster them all over town."

"I can do better than that." Lorna's tone contained no pleasure. "I'll just hand them over to that Wanda Backus, the twenty-four-hour human news station."

Kiki inhaled sharply, her hand going over her mouth. Hannah felt a similar jolt.

"I'm good at sizing people up," Lorna said. "And I can tell that what old Wanda knows, the whole town knows. She'll probably even exaggerate some. Though she won't need to when she sees the one that says, 'you have me in your power, when we're done we'll take a shower.' "

Head hung low, Kiki tried sidling away, but Hannah, her eyes remaining locked on Lorna, grabbed the strap of her sister's handbag.

Lorna held up the emails and shook them. "I hand these over to your friend and the whole town will be whispering 'Lushlips' behind your back. Lushlips, lushlips, lushlips." With a flair for theatrics, she whispered the last part to give Hannah the full, appalling imagery. "And don't think about tackling me for these, because I have copies," Lorna added, seeing the fury on Hannah's face. She quickly stuffed the papers back in her purse and zipped it shut. In a worried gesture, she tried to run her hand through her bobbed hair, but like poking a thumb into a Brillo pad, her fingers couldn't get through the stiffly lacquered perm, and she pulled them out, leaving a tuft of hair sticking straight up. "I don't like playing hardball. I like you, Hannah. I can tell you're a straight shooter, but I'm desperate. Oxie's my man." Large tears welled up in her eyes. "I know he ain't exactly Albert Eisenstein, but I love him, and I won't let him go to jail." She raised her entreating baby blues to Hannah. "Haven't you ever loved a man that much, like you would rip somebody's eyes out and stomp them like grapes if you had to do it to save him?"

Seeing Lorna's misery, Hannah realized that she had never felt that way about a man. The truth was that she hadn't truly loved either of her husbands. She knew she loved Perez, but would she rip somebody's eyes out for him and stomp them like grapes? The very thought made her cringe. She wanted to feel intense, eye-stomping love like that, and if she couldn't feel it, she at least wanted to embrace those who did. Lorna's imploring words and the devastation on her face were turning Hannah's heart to Jell-O. Every corpuscle in her body wanted to help this woman, but how could she allow herself to be blackmailed?

"No," Hannah said, her voice faltering. "I won't do it."

Lorna's shoulders reared back. She wiped away her tears. "You'll be sorry," she said, but her words came out with more agony than threat. Hannah's heart ached as she watched the despair seeping through Lorna's crusty facade. It was like watching a fox weep. Lorna turned and walked away.

"You did the right thing," Kiki said. The sisters walked to the middle of the L-shaped parking lot and watched Lorna disappear around its corner. "We should stay away from that woman. She's nothing but trouble."

Hannah didn't answer. She headed for the Cadillac with Kiki beside her, the forlorn image of Lorna stuck in her mind. When they rounded the corner Hannah stopped. At the far edge of the parking lot, she saw Lorna and Ox.

"Darn it, there they are," Kiki said. "He must have been waiting for her. Come on, let's go back in the store until they leave." She tugged on Hannah's arm, but Hannah didn't budge.

Ox and Lorna stood close together, Ox holding Lorna's hands as she cried. He pulled her to him, her small body like a child's pressed against his large, thick form. The sight melted Hannah. She thought about Perez and the lengths she would go to in a similar situation. Okay, maybe she wouldn't stomp on somebody's eyes, but she would do everything just short of that.

She started for Lorna, but Kiki lurched in front of her. "Hold it. Where do you think you're going? You know we have to be at the rummage sale in an hour, and we'll barely have time to load up the car. Come on, Hannah, let's go."

"I have something to do first." Hannah moved forward, but Kiki again blocked her, holding her hands out from her sides.

"I know what you want to do, and you can't do it."

"Why not?"

"Because that woman's no better than dirt, that's why. There's a term for people like her."

"White trash? Is that what you're trying to say? That's beneath you, Kiki."

"White trash? If Lorna took community college courses she could work her way up to white trash. She's a blackmailer."

Hannah gestured to Lorna and Ox embracing. "She's a black-mailer in love. She's only doing it for him. How can I not help two people that much in love?"

"Bonnie and Clyde were in love, too, but it didn't make them a cute couple. What if it turns out that Ox killed Alex? You're feeling softhearted for that big thug because he likes to sniff roses, but he also likes to dangle people off the edges of build-ings. That's a bad sign."

"If we find out something incriminating, we'll turn it over to the police."

"I don't like this 'we' stuff. I heard you tell Lorna that the police could handle it, that there was nothing you could do."

"I was trying to discourage her. The truth is, there's a lot I can do, that you and I can do together. We can question every-one who was at that party, at least the ones who had motives to kill Alex."

"The police will do that."

"But we can wheedle information out of people the police can't. We've done it before. It's our civic duty to do it again."

Hannah detoured around her sister and took off across the parking lot. For a moment, Kiki stared after her in frustration, then hustled to catch up. Kiki knew that once Hannah got some-thing in her nut, she wasn't going to give up on it until she was good and ready, so there was no point in fighting. And though Kiki didn't approve of mixing with Ox and Lorna, if mixing was to be done, she planned to be right in the middle of it.

Both Ox and Lorna looked surprised when they saw the sis-ters coming their way.

"I'll do it. I'll help investigate," Hannah said. Kiki looked on, tut-tutting in disapproval.

"Good," Lorna said. "I'm glad you're seeing it my way." She tried to say it sharply but her face shined with gratitude. "You should start by talking to the people at the party. Any one of them could have gone into his kitchen. It makes sense that the poison was put into something he ate. Right now Ox and I gotta go. The police want to talk to him again this afternoon and we need to strategize."

"If you want me to help, I'll need Ox to answer some ques-tions," Hannah said.

"We don't have time for that now," Lorna replied. "We've got the cops, we've got to find a lawyer, then I'm taking Oxie to see the Golden Gate Bridge." She gazed up at Ox and ran her finger down his shirtsleeve. "Then tonight we're having a romantic dinner at a place called Frank's by the highway. The lady who runs the motel said it's really good. She says they have candles on the tables."

"I can answer questions," Ox said, showing a strain of independence. "We need to help all we can. What do you want to know, Mrs. Malloy?"

"First, what time did you see Alex the day he died?"

"About five-thirty, six."

"Why did you go see him?"

"I already told you why," Lorna said.

Hannah tilted her head toward Ox. "I'm asking him."

"Just to talk," Ox said. "To ask him for Lornie's money."

"Was anyone else in the house?"

"I don't think so. I didn't see or hear anybody, and I looked downstairs pretty good before I heard Al upstairs."

"When you asked him for Lorna's money, what did he say?"

"At first he laughed at me, said there was no chance. Then I took him by the collar and lifted him off the ground." He saw Hannah's disapproval. "I didn't hurt him none, but it scared him. As soon as I got him up in the air, he said in a couple of weeks he'd have lots of money, and he'd pay her then."

"What did he mean?" Hannah's blood pumped faster. "Where was he going to get the money?"

"I asked him that, too, because I wanted to make sure he wasn't playing with me, but he wouldn't say where. So I lifted him a little higher and shook him some, and he kind of squealed like a pig. Then he said it didn't matter where it was coming from, but that he'd have the money right after the election."

TWELVE

"CAN'T YOU SLOW DOWN? EVERY time you brake I get a table leg smack in the neck." Kiki reached around and shoved back the wooden leg, but it moved only an inch, the table wedged forward by two large boxes of paperbacks, bric a brac, and kitchen odds and ends that Hannah had salvaged for the rummage sale.

The used goodies, which included a floor lamp as well as the little table and the boxes, were piled so high on the backseat that the sisters had to put down the convertible top, a risky business since they could never be sure if it would go back up again. Fortunately the morning clouds had burned off, leaving the sky sparkling and the air warm, this perfect weather contrasting starkly with the gloom hanging over the town. The murder of a loved mayor wasn't the sort of gossip Hill Creek had wanted.

"We look like Yugoslavian refugees," Kiki said with testiness, still miffed at Hannah for agreeing to help Lorna. Her hair whipping in the wind, she tied a bright flowered scarf around her head, then studied its effect in the visor mirror. After adjusting her Sophia Loren–style sunglasses, she pushed out her lips into a sultry pout. With the convertible top down she always liked to strike a glamorous profile, since the Cadillac land yacht always turned heads. But this afternoon she was only going through the motions, Alex's murder weighing heavily on her mind and heart.

"Stop griping," Hannah said. "I'm having enough problems driving with this ceramic walrus in my lap. Where did we get this thing? It's atrocious."

"You bought it at a garage sale years ago."

Hannah gave the walrus a closer look and then remembered. It had been bought during her drinking days. That particular Saturday she must have had a whopping hangover that blurred her eyesight. Giving the walrus a pat on the head, she decided to keep it as a reminder of why she stopped boozing. All those mornings when her brain felt like it was covered with sludge. "I don't know why you're being such a fussbudget. You were thrilled to the gills about this rummage sale only a week ago."

"That was when I thought Alex would be there." At the mention of her former love, Kiki inhaled with a long, woeful sniff, followed by a sigh. "They shouldn't even have the rummage sale, not with him dead."

"Remember, the sale is benefiting a cause that Alex supported. And the truth is, because of Alex's death it's now going to attract a huge crowd. All that publicity. The crickets will ride to their new location in a stretch limo."

When Kiki didn't crack a smile, Hannah reached over and gave her shoulder a squeeze. She knew that behind the dramatics, Kiki truly mourned Alex's death.

"Oh, don't you act all sweet and nice, Hannah Malloy." Kiki pulled her compact out of her purse and opened it with a flick of her wrist. "You didn't like Alex one bit. You thought he was taking bribes."

"That doesn't mean he deserved to die. Whoever committed the murder will be caught and punished, if I've got anything to do with it."

"Oh, here we go." Kiki scowled as she patted her nose with her powder puff. "Now that you've made that promise to Miss Blackmailer Lorna, you'll be poking your nose in things you shouldn't, when what you ought to be doing is concentrating on the election. You've got to do whatever it takes to win so I don't have to humiliate myself in front of the whole town."

"You're the one who made the bet."

"You're the one who's always jumping into things and wreaking havoc on our lives. First you've got to save the town from Signatech, now you've got to catch Alex's murderer. Maybe tomorrow after coffee you can plug up that hole in the E-zone."

"It's the ozone. And we wouldn't be up to our necks in this mess if you hadn't sent Alex your raunchy poems."

"*Our* raunchy poems. You wrote part of them, too. And they weren't raunchy. They came straight from my heart."

"You've got your body parts confused."

Hannah braked at a stop sign, and the table leg hit Kiki in the back of the head. "Ouch! You did that one on purpose."

"Honestly, I didn't. Sorry." Hannah pulled away from the intersection as gently as possible, but then quickly resumed her speed. Perhaps Kiki had lost her enthusiasm for the rummage sale, but Hannah's interest had heightened to a fever. As much as Kiki wanted to avoid trouble, Hannah longed to swan dive right into it. She hadn't admitted even to herself that she was dying to get involved in the murder investigation, and now that she had promised Lorna to help, she felt exhilarated. Taking action, fighting for something, righting wrongs, that was the way to live. Being over sixty didn't mean she had to sit around crocheting doilies, especially when, in so many ways, she had never felt more vigorous in her life.

Kiki loudly blew her nose into a tissue, then smiled broadly as she waved it at Derek, the postman, who was bicycling down the sidewalk, with two saddlebags bulging with mail. It was amazing how good postmen could look when they wore those shorts.

"Let's use this time productively and talk about the investigation," Hannah said. "If I'm going to help find Alex's murderer, I've got to get the current facts straight."

"I'll give you the current facts," Kiki said, still peevish, digging through her handbag for her lipstick. "Lorna's boyfriend, that homicidal Jolly Green Giant, killed my poor Alex so he and his trashy girlfriend could get their hands on Alex's money. Ox admits he went in Alex's house after everyone left. Obviously Ox dumped the vase water in the water pitcher, then went upstairs and, just for fun, carried Alex around by the neck. The no-good bum. I've never trusted men that bulky. They have way too much testosterone."

Hannah stopped at a red light, pressing on the brake as lightly as possible, but the table leg still hit Kiki. "But would Ox know that monkshood was poisonous?"

"You've got a point. Ox couldn't find his butt with both hands and a tour guide, but that Lorna is one sharp cookie. Maybe the two of them went to Alex's together. If they crawled through an open window, Ox, coming from a southern state, would have helped in Lorna first, and that's why the neighbor only saw him and not her. One of them distracted Alex while the other poisoned the water jug." Kiki jabbed her lipstick in the air at Hannah. "That's what happened. And you say I'm the gullible one. You see Ox and Lorna making kissies in the parking lot and think you have to help them because they're in *looooovvve*. But the truth is, both of them are lying through their teeth."

Hannah thought Kiki might be right, but refused to say it out loud. "You're forgetting that there are other suspects. Both Althea and Mary had decent motives for wanting Alex dead, and Mary definitely heard me say that the vase water was poisonous."

"As long as we're accusing friends, what about Charlie? He probably heard you, too. And remember when he yelled at Alex at the party? He sounded mad enough to kill. With Alex out of the way he has a much better chance of being mayor."

"I can't believe that Charlie would kill Alex over the mayor's race. If this were New York or Chicago, maybe, but it's Hill Creek."

"It could still be a moneymaking position," Kiki said, looking into the visor mirror and applying a thick layer of Tahiti Pink lipstick. "You're the one saying that Alex was going to make all kinds of money off Signatech. Not that I believe it for one minute, but you have to admit that a crooked mayor could get some payoffs in any town."

"But did Charlie have access to Alex's water pitcher? Whoever poisoned it had to have done it after the party. During the party there were too many people around."

"It could have happened before the party," Kiki said. "Maggie was probably alone in the kitchen all morning."

"Why would she kill her employer?"

"Maybe he wouldn't give her a raise. Maybe she was secretly in love with him and he rejected her."

Considering this, Hannah turned left onto Center Avenue, then turned the corner toward town hall.

In the past twenty-four hours, the rummage sale had been touted as a memorial to Alex, and Hannah suspected that many of the people who attended his party would be there, perhaps even his killer. Being council members, Mary and Charlie would definitely attend, giving Hannah an opportunity to talk to them both. With any luck, a few other suspects would be there as well hoping to pick up a few treasures on the cheap. Murderers probably loved a bargain as much as anyone did.

Hannah parked in the no parking zone in front of town hall and switched on the hazard lights so they could unload the car. The sale started in ten minutes, and a crowd, mostly women, was already gathering on the sidewalk behind the ropes. A huge plastic banner strung across the stucco building read, "Help the Cricket AND Move In Signatech." Above it, "Alex Portman Memorial Rummage Sale," had been hand lettered.

About thirty tables along with several clothes racks stood in the small parking lot to the right of the building, along with stands serving sushi, pasta, wine, and soft drinks. Tony Bennett crooned "I Left My Heart in San Francisco" from a boom box. The tables, laden with items, were separated into books, clothes, kitchenware, toys, and sports equipment.

Even with everything she had on her mind, the sight of so much used merchandise made Hannah's mouth water. The old adage that one man's trash is another man's treasure was never truer than in Hill Creek. Since many residents were prosperous, their castoffs tended to be high quality. Half of Hannah's furniture, Sinatra records, and gardening tools had come from savvy garage sale shopping, and Kiki was always turning up with French scarves and only slightly worn Gucci shoes she had bought for a pittance.

Hannah pushed shopping from her mind and refocused her attention on finding a murderer. Searching the group of volunteers setting up the sale items, she spied Charlie about twenty yards away behind a table piled with books, thumbing through a paperback. Hannah was about to walk over but a policeman stopped her, telling her politely that she needed to move her car. She turned back to the Cadillac and started unloading. A stack of gardening books in her arms, Kiki walked around the front of the car.

"I heard that the Ross Women's League made some donations," Kiki said, her face flushed, the excitement of shopping overwhelming her depression. "That means designer labels. You think they'll let us buy things before the sale starts? Since you're running for public office, you should get some rummage sale perks."

"I'm sure that's always been Hillary Clinton's motivation," Hannah said, pulling the floor lamp from the backseat.

"I might find some cheap things to spice up Lauren's wardrobe." Kiki wiggled her eyebrow in a manner indicating that "cheap" was the operative word and she wasn't talking price.

"Before you start shopping, we've got to get the car unloaded. Let's carry the table first. I'll get those books later." Hannah opened a back door, two frying pans clattering to the sidewalk. Once she had retrieved them, she and Kiki pulled out the table and carried it to an area near the back reserved for furniture. Then, like a hound after a squirrel, Kiki zoomed to the clothes racks for a pre-sale peek. It was useless to keep Kiki away from clothes, so Hannah headed for the Cadillac to haul the remaining donations herself.

Hannah opened the car door, pushed the front seat forward, and slid the first box closer to her. It held a collection of the sisters' attempts at self-improvement. There were the electric hair rollers that were supposed to make Hannah look like Susan Sarandon but instead made her look like Janis Joplin. Underneath those sat the "Boogie Your Way to a Better Bottom" video that had made Kiki's bladder hurt so much she had to go to the doctor, and then there was the electric foot massager Hannah had received as a gift. Kiki had used it in such an unwholesome manner that now Hannah could barely stand to look at it.

As Hannah took Kiki's tawdry romance novels off the top to put them with the gardening books, she noticed an old Brita pitcher and remembered putting it in the box last week. She picked it up and examined it. It was clear plastic with a white plastic lid and filter, and although scratched, still usable. Hannah's stomach tensed up when she realized that something like it had been the means of Alex's murder.

"Traitor!"

Startled, Hannah dropped the pitcher onto the car seat, spun around, and saw a beet-faced Althea, her fists on her hips, her mouth wrenched into an accusatory pucker. "What are you doing here?"

"I'm here because if it turns out that we can't stop Signatech, we have to do what we can to save the poor crickets," Hannah said. She noticed that Althea had the good taste not to wear her "Portman Is A Prick" sweatshirt.

"The newspaper said he was poisoned," Althea said, her previous gruff tone turning apprehensive. "The police called me and want to talk to me this afternoon. I know lots of other people from the party who've gotten calls. Have the police telephoned you?"

"Kiki and I were at the station first thing this morning. They have to talk to everyone at the party." Hannah's eyes slid over to the Brita pitcher lying on the car seat, and an idea popped

into her head. Turning away from Althea, she picked it up and
clutched it to her chest. It could be as good as a confession. The
water pitcher hadn't been mentioned in the newspaper, so only
the killer knew about it, and only the killer would react when
he or she saw it. Filled with investigative zeal, Hannah turned
and faced Althea, the pitcher in plain view.

"I think he might have poisoned himself," Althea said, not
missing a beat. "Committed suicide. It would be like him to do
it in front of everyone. Such an exhibitionist."

"Isn't that the cabbage calling the lettuce green? You interrupted a town hall debate by marching down the center aisle,
shouting out 'murderer,' and wearing a big plastic cricket on
your head," Hannah said. She held the Brita pitcher a little
higher. Althea glanced at it, but gave no visible reaction.

"I was promoting a social cause," Althea replied. "It's a completely different thing."

"What's important now is that we show some respect for a
community member who's passed away," Hannah said. "And
this rummage sale is a memorial to Alex."

"This rummage sale's a sham. Nobody knows if the Yellow-
bellied can be moved at all. No one's tested it."

"Then it's only reasonable to give it a try."

"It's not reasonable to a cricket," Althea said angrily, then
she stomped off, not giving the jug another glance.

The experiment's failure disappointed Hannah, but just because Althea didn't react to the jug didn't necessarily prove her
innocence. And Mary or Charlie might not be so blasé when
they caught sight of it.

"You need to get your car unloaded and moved, Mrs. Malloy," a young male police officer told her. "You could get a
ticket."

With no budget for parking fines, Hannah assured him she
would speed up the unloading. She put the Brita jug on top of
one box and had just picked up the whole thing when she saw
Maggie walking up the sidewalk, her long flowered dress flapping around her legs. In her arms she held a brown grocery
bag filled with clothes. Hannah called out to her, and Maggie
veered over to the Cadillac. She looked awful, her eyes red
and swollen.

"I'm so sorry," Hannah said gently. She put the box on the
Cadillac's hood. "You worked for Alex a good while."

"Five years," she answered. "He wasn't always the easiest man to be around, but he had a good heart, deep down. The police say he was murdered, poisoned. It had to have been something he ate at home, because he didn't go anywhere between the party and the debate except to jog. I went to the emergency room late last night and tried to get my stomach pumped, but they said I was okay and didn't need it. But I sampled everything at the party."

"The police talked to you last night?"

She nodded. "They called and asked me a lot of questions about what Alex ate, who went where at the party, but I didn't know much, and they didn't tell me Alex was murdered, not directly. I tried to get into Alex's house this morning. I had some personal things I wanted to get out, but somebody had changed the locks. I was at the front door when a police car pulled up. That's how I found out he was actually murdered. They swarmed all over me like I was a criminal. That Detective Morgan took me aside, along with a woman officer. They were nice, considering, but they drove me to the police station and asked me all these questions."

Hannah reached over to the box and picked up the water jug, eager to test it on another suspect. "What kinds of questions?"

"About the kitchen mostly, who was in it and when. But that was a ruse. I've seen them do things like that on television, you know, to catch the suspect off guard. I'm not stupid. I know they think I poisoned him. You should have seen the police, Hannah, going all over Alex's house and yard. And I'm the logical suspect because I fixed most of his meals and all the party food." She clutched the bag more tightly. "But I didn't do it, Hannah. Why would I? I'm out of a job now. I can't go for more than a couple of weeks without money coming in, and who's going to hire me thinking I might poison their food?"

"Maggie, please, try and relax. First of all, this will blow over and people around here will be fighting for your services. You're the best cook in town. The Rose Club has a luncheon coming up. I'll recommend you as the caterer. That job will be some good public relations for you."

"Thanks, Hannah," Maggie said, sounding more composed.

"You've always been a friend to me. A lot of people around here don't want to get chummy with someone who's just a housekeeper."

"You're a housekeeper *extraordinaire*, and I'm proud to be your friend. The police will find out who killed Alex in no time, and this will all be over."

"But how will they do it? Anybody at the party could have slipped something into Alex's food."

Obviously the police hadn't mentioned the pitcher to Maggie, Hannah thought, unless she was being very cagey. And Maggie was showing no reaction to the pitcher in front of her. "Has anyone else at the party gotten sick?" Hannah asked.

"Not that I know of, but it could have been Alex's toothpaste or the brandy by his bed that was poisoned. The police took a lot of things out of Alex's bathroom and bedroom, and if that's how the killer did it, it will make it worse for me because I had access to the whole house. Since Alex was such a big shot the police will want to arrest someone right away. Hannah, I'm scared."

Hannah put her arm around Maggie's shoulders. "We just need to find out who did it, and you know more about what went on in his house that day than anyone. You probably knew Alex better than anyone."

Hannah stopped talking and gave Maggie a chance to calm down. This was her opportunity to get information that the police might not have thought of. Maggie was known for keeping an eagle eye on things, the woman never missing a detail when it came to Rose Club functions. Maggie always remembered who wore what, who flirted with whom, and who sneaked into the garden with somebody's wife.

"Maggie, did anyone arrive early for Alex's party?"

Maggie shook her head, her long beaded earrings bouncing. "Not that I know of, and I got there early that morning to start cooking."

"Was there anybody at the party acting strangely?"

"Only about half the people there," Maggie said, and she and Hannah exchanged a smile. They often chuckled together at Rose Club meetings over the foibles of the locals.

"What about after the party?" Hannah asked. "Did anyone stick around once the party was over?"

Maggie gave her a quizzical look. "Only Mary, and she was upstairs. She didn't feel well."

"Was she ever alone in the kitchen?"

Maggie's head tilted slightly. "If you're thinking that Mary poisoned Alex, you're dead wrong. And why are you asking these things? Are you helping the police?"

"I'm just trying to figure it out, like everyone else. A friend was murdered, and we all need to help the police, especially those of us who were at the party. We're the ones who may have seen something important."

Maggie looked down at her bag of clothes, fiddled with a T-shirt lying on top, then lifted her gaze back to Hannah. "Look at Signatech," Maggie said, her voice lowered. "If Alex was murdered, it was over that. This is just between you and me, but if I were you, Hannah, I'd find out who owned the land Signatech wants to build on."

"I already know who owns it. The town does."

"Not all of it."

"How do you know?"

"When I clean house, I see things." Maggie started when she heard her name called.

The two women saw Mary only a few feet away. Hannah wondered how long Mary had been there and how much she had heard. Hannah was anxious to talk to her, to tell her what she would later have to tell the police, but she couldn't do it in front of Maggie. It wouldn't be right.

"How are you holding up?" Mary asked Maggie, her expression full of concern. Maggie shrugged. Mary looked over at Hannah, not appearing to notice the Brita pitcher. "We need to get everything on the tables as soon as possible, Hannah. The sale starts in a few minutes and people are practically pulling down the ropes to get in. Can I find someone to help you unload the car?" Mary glanced at the backseat of the Cadillac and gave Hannah a warm smile. "It looks like you've been especially generous."

"That's okay, I can get it myself," Hannah said. "It's not as much as it looks."

"Let me know if you change your mind," Mary told her. "I've got some high school kids helping and they have strong arms."

"Can we talk later?" Hannah asked Mary. "It's important."

"Sure," Mary replied. "I'm managing the sports equipment.

I'll be there all afternoon." She took Maggie's bag and, linking her arm in Maggie's, steered her off. Maggie looked over her shoulder at Hannah as they walked toward the tables, leaving Hannah wondering why Mary seemed so anxious to get Maggie all to herself.

THIRTEEN

"*I* FOUND IT!" KIKI SHOUTED, her purse flapping from her shoulder as she scuttled past the rummage sale tables toward Hannah, scuttling being the only rapid movement her high-heeled ankle-strapped sandals allowed. In one hand she carried a large plastic bag and over her head she waved something orange and sparkling. When she reached her sister by the Cadillac, she dropped the plastic bag to the ground and held up the top with both hands.

"Isn't this completely, utterly fabulous?" Kiki said, panting from the jog. From her hands hung a garish sequined tube top that had been fashionable during the disco days of the eighties.

"Don't you love it? It says, I'm a looker and I'm available, caress me." Kiki punctuated the last part with a shoulder shimmy.

Hannah's face puckered. "Are you sure it's not saying 'I'm a hooker and I'm available, oh, no, don't arrest me'?"

"You've always been repressed, fashion-wise, Hannah."

"And you're delusional. You can't fit into that thing."

"It's not for me, silly. Although if it were just a size or two larger—"

"You could get it around your thigh."

Kiki lifted her chin. "May I remind you that I buy my clothes in the petite department."

"That's because you're short, but you wear a size fourteen."

"A fourteen *petite*. And this is for Lauren, anyway. It's just the thing she needs to lure Detective Morgan into a web of love." She put a husky inflection on the last few words. "And for only two dollars. Betty let me snap it up before anyone else had the chance."

"I'm sure the editor of *Vogue* is weeping at her loss."

"And look at these." Reaching down, Kiki pulled a pair of black patent leather boots from the plastic grocery bag. The

boots were the dream footwear of any well-dressed sadomaso-
chist, with silvery metal studs running up the sides, and steel
tips covering the toes. "These are going to be my signature
boots, just like Lorna's. They're really going to make me stand
out in a crowd. And they have flat heels so I won't fall down."

Hannah nodded with approval, even though she thought the
boots more appropriate for a motorcycle gang moll. She was
always badgering Kiki to wear flat-heeled shoes, afraid that one
day Kiki was going to hurt herself on her ridiculous high heels.
"The boots are fantastic. They scream you. Now help me get
the boxes unloaded so I can park the car. The rummage sale's
going to start. You get the paperbacks and the box with the
wicker baskets. If the box is too big for you just take the things
out and carry them to the right tables."

Hannah lifted the remaining box from the Cadillac's backseat
and carried it to the housewares area, where she said hello to
Nancy, a nurse at the hospital, who was busily rearranging pots
and pans on the table. Hannah put her box on the ground and
was unloading it, keeping the Brita pitcher safely aside, when
she spied Mary and Maggie huddled near the town hall entrance.
Hannah watched them as she applied white stickers to a wok, a
blender, and a vegetable steamer so Nancy could price them.
Mary was holding Maggie's hand, both women wearing the
same beleaguered expressions. Their relationships to Alex had
been similar, Hannah decided. In a way, they had both been in
his employ, although Hannah had a feeling that Mary had enjoyed an extra special benefits package. It still bothered her that
Mary had pulled away Maggie so quickly, as if she didn't want
Hannah talking to her.

Kiki whizzed past, her arms loaded with three wicker baskets
and a framed photograph of Andy Williams. She plonked it all
down on the table next to Hannah's box.

"I got Randy to carry the lamp over to the furniture section,
so that's the last of it," she said, breathless. "Now I've got to
get back to the clothes racks. Betty just told me there's an orange plastic miniskirt and a pair of spike heels that will be
perfect with the tube top. Can you believe the luck? They just
came in, so I've got to snap them up for Lauren before somebody else with real fashion sense beats me to it."

Kiki took off just as the gong sounded and the rummage sale
officially opened. The waiting throng of people quickly clumped

around the tables, dreaming they would find some castoff that would turn out to be a priceless gem. Holding the Brita pitcher, Hannah scanned the crowd, seeing many Rose Club members and a few of the Lady Nails regulars. Ellie was already combing through the toys, thinking of her grandchildren. Bertha was scrutinizing a denim jacket, as if she actually needed one.

Standing a few feet away, the police officer got Hannah's attention and tilted his head meaningfully toward the Cadillac. Hannah hurriedly got inside the car, started the engine, and drove it across the street to the public parking lot. As she was walking back she glimpsed Walter Backus crossing the street, in the opposite direction of the rummage sale. After looking behind him guiltily, he dashed into O'Reilly's, an upscale Irish-style pub on the corner.

Just as Hannah walked past the sushi stand, Wanda glided up, holding a half-eaten tuna roll between two fingers. Her presence astounded Hannah, since normally Wanda wouldn't have touched anything at a rummage sale with a solid gold fondue fork. She had dressed for the occasion in a long frothy white skirt, five pounds of pearls, and a T-shirt that read "Chanel" on the front and "Vote for Backus" on the back.

"Here to pick up some used lingerie on the cheap?" Hannah asked with a laugh.

"You're so droll sometimes, Hannah. Isn't this a wonderful event, the whole town working together to save the poor sweet little crickets? By the way, you better keep an eye on your sister. I just saw her elbow old Mrs. Watson at the skirt section, and she almost knocked the poor woman off her walker. Someone could get hurt. This is a public place, and Kiki's a safety hazard."

"Maybe we could hang orange rubber cones on her."

"There you go, being droll again. It's so cute the way you do that. But some of us have to deal with serious issues. We have to consider the town's insurance premiums." Wanda popped the rest of the tuna roll in her mouth.

Hannah's lips curled up. "I thought Walter was the one running for office, but you're sounding very political yourself. This is a new side to you."

Wanda swallowed and pressed her perfectly manicured hand against her chest. "Because of the incredible strength of our marriage, Walter would want me to act as co-mayor, naturally.

We are two people fused into one. He insists on my advice on everything." She peered over the top of her dark glasses. "By the way, have you seen Walter anywhere? I can't find him, and I think he should talk to the council members about widening the left turn lanes on Walker Road. He must be campaigning somewhere."

"I'm sure he is," Hannah said, not wanted to squeal on Wanda's co-candidate. With steely eyes Wanda grazed the entrance to O'Reilly's, then suddenly looked as if a cold draft had just blown up her skirt.

"Well, must be off. I've got campaigning to do," Wanda said before marching in the direction of O'Reilly's as fast as her Bruno Magli sandals would take her.

Once Wanda was gone, Hannah looked around for Mary, but couldn't spot her, so, Brita pitcher in hand, she took off for the books table where she had last seen Charlie. He wasn't there, but Frannie stood behind one of the book tables hurriedly scribbling inside the front covers. There was already a small crowd looking at the volumes.

"Have you seen Charlie?" Hannah asked her.

Frannie shook her head. "He was here a few minutes ago, but I don't know where he went, and he's supposed to be helping me. Hannah, could you help me price these? I just put a dollar fifty on a Danielle Steele, then I remembered that I priced a Hemingway for only a dollar. It doesn't seem right from a literary perspective."

"How about two dollars for the hardbacks and fifty cents for the paperbacks? That way you don't have to write a price in each one. You can just put up a sign."

Frannie slapped her forehead. "Of course. I'm so stupid today. But with everything that's happened, it's hard to keep from bursting into tears. To think that someone could kill such a wonderful man as Alex. What's next? Is someone going to murder the Pope?"

"I know how you feel. Is there something more I can do to help?"

"Could you stay here a minute and let people know the prices while I go make a sign? You can put your things right here under the table. I'll only be a minute. When people are ready to pay, send them to the cashier's desk by the sushi booth."

Hannah preferred to search for Charlie, but Frannie looked

on the verge of hysterics. Frannie left, and Hannah sat on a stool behind the table, putting the Brita pitcher and her purse at her feet, regretting the time she was wasting. The table had at least ten people looking at the books, and Hannah explained the prices, at the same time looking through the crowd for Charlie or Mary. She didn't see either of them. As people selected their books, Hannah directed them to the cashier's desk.

The books were mostly paperbacks of the self-help variety, including, *Biomorphic Body Transformation, Feng Shui Your Way to Better Sex*, and *The Craniosacral You*. There must have been thirty copies of *Women Are from Venus, Men Are from Mars*.

At last Hannah spotted Mary at one of the tables set aside for sports equipment, staring down in confusion at a collection of metal and plastic contraptions that Hannah recognized as Thigh Busters. Kiki had two different models, and neither had ever made contact with Kiki's thighs. Barely used health equipment was always abundant at Marin County rummage sales.

Standing up, Hannah was anxiously searching for Frannie, when a little girl about eight years old walked up to the table. She stared at Hannah a moment then looked halfheartedly at the books.

"I haven't seen any children's books here," Hannah told her, trying to steer the child's attention away from *The Tantric Art of Self-Pleasuring*. Strangely, the little girl seemed much more interested in Hannah's chest, her brown eyes fixed upon it. Hannah looked down to see if there was food on her shirt, but saw nothing.

"What are you staring at?" Hannah asked.

The little girl tugged on the straps of her denim overalls. "My mommy says you don't have any breasts."

At first shocked, Hannah looked closer at the child and realized she belonged to Alice Crandall, a friend from the Rose Club. Alice had obviously told her daughter about Hannah's surgery, which Hannah didn't mind, but she still didn't know what to say.

After floundering a few seconds, Hannah finally said, "It's true." Having never had children of her own, she had no idea how to talk to them, and usually spoke to them with the same directness she would use with an adult. "The doctor removed them because I had cancer."

The girl's face turned troubled. "I don't have any breasts either. But I'm going to grow some."

"I'm sure you will. Breasts are good things. They have numerous uses."

"Will you grow some?"

Hannah laughed. "Not likely, but I'm fine without them. I have flowers now where my breasts used to be. Want to see?"

As the little girl looked on in amazement, Hannah unbuttoned a few buttons of her blouse and revealed the upper part of the tattoo of roses, lilies, and ivy on her chest. Hannah was in the middle of explaining the tattooing process when Frannie returned. After quickly saying goodbye to the child and wishing her luck with her future breasts, Hannah collected her purse and Brita pitcher, then hustled off in Mary's direction. The crowd was thickening and she had to bob and weave, dodging a woman holding five handbags and ducking past a man swinging a putter.

Now at full steam, the rummage sale had gained a festive air, with at least a hundred people milling around the tables, and Latin-beat music pouring from the loudspeakers. When Hannah neared Mary, she stopped by a table of hand tools to gather up nerve. What she was about to say was going to be unpleasant, but it had to be done. She took a deep, fortifying yoga breath and went over.

On her knees, surrounded by Thigh Busters, Mary put a sticker on each one, which could have been the first actual contact with human flesh any of them had ever had.

"I'd keep them cheap," Hannah said. "Now everyone just has liposuction."

Mary looked up and gave Hannah a quick smile. "I used to have one of these myself. I donated it to Goodwill two years ago." She returned her attention back to a Thigh Buster still fresh in the box.

"Mary, I need to talk to you."

"Not now, Hannah. I'm too busy. Maybe later."

"It's about Alex's murder."

Her hand out to place a sticker, Mary froze. She straightened and aimed her eyes at Hannah. She didn't look at the Brita pitcher tucked inside the crook of Hannah's elbow. "It's sickening, isn't it? That sort of thing happening here."

"That sort of thing happens everywhere."

"You're right, I guess. I'd like to talk to you about it some-time, but not now."

"It has to be now."

Mary blinked. "Why?"

"Because there's something I'm going to tell the police. I should have told them this morning, but I put it off." Hannah paused. "It has to do with you and Alex." She saw the muscles in Mary's face tighten, and her own discomfort grew. "I know what happened between you two at the party."

Mary looked like Hannah had slapped her. She stood up, and Hannah got a whiff of her perfume. Roses with a hint of vanilla. "Nothing happened at the party."

"Mary, I heard it all." Steeling herself, Hannah told Mary about being under the desk while she and Alex made love and then war. Mary turned the color of cooked salmon, which made her face only a shade pinker than Hannah's. Hannah felt com-pletely humiliated, but she figured that neither of them was over-flowing with dignity just then.

It took Mary a second to regain the power of speech. "What were you doing in Alex's office in the first place?"

Hannah explained about her Signatech suspicions.

"You're still accusing Alex of taking a bribe?" Mary asked.

"I'm saying it's possible. I've told the police as much."

"I don't have a high opinion of Alex on a personal level, but I can't believe he'd take a bribe. I didn't believe it when you brought up those stock options at the debate. There could be a simple explanation. But regardless, the man is dead. Leave him in peace."

"I have to tell the police the whole story."

Mary stared at Hannah while this registered. "Not about my relationship with him?"

"What choice do I have? This is a murder investigation, and you have a motive. It's better for you to get it out in the open. You should go tell them yourself."

"My affair with Alex is nobody's business, especially yours. Okay, I was angry at Alex," she said, then realized how loudly she was talking. "Who wouldn't have been?" she said with a lowered voice. "When Signatech first approached the town council about relocating here, I was against it. Alex knew I had influence with the rest of the council, so he decided to make sure I saw things his way. Me being single at my age, I guess

he thought I'd be an easy target, and he was right. It took awhile
for me to get it, but the truth is that Alex only cared about Alex.
He started cooling off on me as soon as he was sure he had the
council votes for Signatech. When he was done with me, he
tossed me aside. That day in his office, I'll admit, I hated him.
But I didn't kill him."

"Doesn't it seem strange to you that Alex cared so much
about Signatech?"

"Not at all. He wanted the glory of bringing a big company
to town. It meant a lot of publicity, which would have helped
his seminar attendance."

"What did you do after you left his office that day of the
party? You didn't sit down to lunch."

"I did what he told me to do, like always. I went upstairs and
got two Valiums from his medicine cabinet. I guess I should
have only taken one, because they knocked me out. I laid down
on his bed and didn't wake up until after everyone had left the
party."

"What time did you go home?"

"I'm not sure. Around five, I think. Alex came up to the
bedroom to change clothes for his jog. We exchanged a few
words and I left. Although I don't know why I should tell you."

"Was Maggie still there?"

"Yes, she was, but she was getting ready to leave."

Mary was sounding increasingly angry, like she wanted to
thrash Hannah, and Hannah wondered how much it would hurt
to have a Thigh Buster banged against your head. She pressed
on anyway. "What were you talking to Maggie about a few
minutes ago? You pulled her away from me pretty fast."

"You have no right to ask me those questions. You're not the
police, Hannah. But I don't mind telling you. I have nothing to
feel guilty about," Mary said, but the fear in her eyes said differently. "When I went up to Alex's bedroom I was pretty upset
and I was crying. Maggie came up and saw me. She knew Alex
and I were seeing each other, and I told her what had happened."

Maggie had just told Hannah a different version, that Mary
had gone upstairs because she felt ill, but Hannah knew it was
natural for Maggie to not want to tell such a humiliating story
about a friend. Hannah would have done the same thing.

"And Maggie consoled you?"

Mary nodded. "She told me that he wasn't good enough for

me, that I'd find someone else. The usual things you say to someone who has just been dumped. So just now I thanked her for her kindness." Mary's eyes turned watery and for a moment Hannah thought she was going to cry, but she didn't. Instead she stood tall, the look in her eyes toughening. "I've got to get back to work. Tell the police whatever you want, but I'm not the one who killed him."

A woman the size of a Volkswagen Jetta walked over and picked up a Thigh Buster. Mary answered a few questions for her, then the woman stared at it a moment, put it back down, and walked off in the direction of the food booths.

As Hannah watched Mary talk to another potential customer, she felt badly about upsetting her, but she had found out at least some of what she wanted to know. Mary was definitely bitter toward Alex, and she had an opportunity to put the poisoned water in the pitcher.

The customer left. Mary stepped close to Hannah. "While you're going around accusing people, remember something," she said, the words coming out full of grit. "With you running against him for mayor, you have a good motive yourself to want Alex dead."

FOURTEEN

HANNAH AND KIKI STOOD AT the bottom of the steps that led to Alex Portman's small, elegantly columned porch. The sun had started to drop behind the mountain, and Hannah knew that if she was going to snoop, she needed to snoop fast. She hadn't been able to drag Kiki away from the rummage sale clothes racks until six-thirty. Now it was close to seven, and dusk would be quickly falling.

Slipping her car keys into her purse, Hannah wondered if this was the right thing to do. A lone bird perched in a nearby tree warbled a melancholy song, its lilting voice singing of human folly, of past troubles and future ones to come. Hannah wished it would shut up.

"See that sign?" Kiki said, wagging a sausage-shaped finger at the front door that had belonged to Alex Portman during his last earthly manifestation. Kiki pointed to a large and ominous white sticker pasted over the door. "Read it, Hannah. It says 'Crime scene. Do not enter.' Did you hear that last part? Do-not-enter."

"Which is precisely why we're not entering," Hannah replied. Tucking her purse under her arm, she stepped over to the low trimmed hedge running along the left side of the porch, just beneath the windows. The two-foot-wide shrub hugged the front of the house and would have made the windows difficult to break into. No one would have prowled around the front anyway, not in broad daylight. If someone broke into Alex's house they did it from the back.

"We should be at the Rose Club meeting," Kiki said. "It started ten minutes ago."

"This is more important."

"More important than winning the election? You're on the Rose Club board, and people will notice you're not there. You can be sure Wanda's there, sucking up to everybody, getting them to vote for Walter. And what are we doing?"

"Trying to catch a killer."

"My point exactly. You should leave it to the police. Besides, I'm starving and I know for a fact that Irene is bringing her spinach dip to the meeting, the one with the homemade croutons."

"This won't take long. I just want to look around the backyard." Hannah continued walking along the shrubbery.

"Why?" Kiki asked, right behind.

"Because the killer might have been there."

"You mean Ox. He admitted that he was prowling around outside the house. Are you looking for evidence against him?"

"I'm looking for evidence, period."

"And you think you can find something the police can't?" Kiki let out a long whistle. "Talk about an ego. Mother always said you were a little full of yourself."

"It was daddy who used to say that. It's simply that I know gardens. I know what belongs there and what doesn't. I know where a gardener wouldn't step, which plants have been disturbed," Hannah said, her eyes on the ground, her pace quickening. Not only was it getting dark, but she had left Detective Morgan a voicemail message asking him to call that evening, and she didn't want to miss him. "It's possible that I can find a clue the police missed."

Hannah turned the corner, going down the side of the house. With the sigh of the long suffering, Kiki tramped along, but it was hard to keep up. While in the car, she had put on her new rummage sale signature boots, and they didn't fit as well as she had originally thought. "If your knowledge is so essential, then why aren't the police calling and begging for your services?"

"Because they lack vision. Trust me, I need to do this."

"Oh, yes, I forgot," Kiki said with sarcasm. "You've got to help Lorna, the blackmailer."

"As far as I know, no one at Alex's party went outside the house, except for Althea, who was in the front yard, and Charlie, who stepped only briefly outside the conservatory with Alex. If I can find some evidence in the backyard, it might mean there was an intruder who got in the house and poisoned Alex's water before or after the party."

"Like Lorna and Ox."

"Or someone else."

Hannah stooped down by a large rosemary bush growing just below a window, examining the ground underneath.

"What if one of the neighbors sees us?" Kiki said. "They'll call the police and we'll end up in the slammer."

"The fence is too high for anyone to see us. Besides, like you told Lorna, you were in jail once and you liked it." Hannah raised an eyebrow. "I had a hard time getting you to leave."

"That's because I lost five pounds, and I happened to hit it on a good week when there were so many fun girls around. And the gossip. You don't have that kind of luck twice."

"We won't go to jail," Hannah said, straightening up. "There's nothing wrong with what we're doing."

"So why did you park the car down the street and not in front?"

"Because some small-minded people might misconstrue our intentions."

They came up to a high wooden gate. Hannah was just tall enough to reach over and unlatch it, and the sisters moved down a sand-colored flagstone walkway past a large gardening shed, then around to the back.

A soft "ooh" came out of Hannah when she saw the garden. She had only glimpsed it through the window the day of the party and hadn't realized how large it was and how beautifully designed. There were at least two dozen varieties of roses, including a few hybrids that Hannah couldn't identify, and an abundance of other flowering plants, almost everything with white blooms that glowed in the softening light. The landscaping was gorgeous, yet there was a controlled showiness to it, a lack of abandon and romance that told Hannah the garden wasn't an act of love on Alex's part, but just another thing in his life meant to impress. Any gardener who worked from the heart could never resist having the odd plant here and there, something he or she had fallen in love with, even though it didn't fit in with the rest. You could tell a lot about a person by looking at their garden, and it was love that was missing from this one. Probably the same thing that had been missing from Alex's life.

"It's getting dark. We need to get moving. Keep your eyes to the grass and look for anything that could show a stranger was here. Cigarette butts, gum, anything like that," Hannah instructed, mostly to keep Kiki busy. She was sure the police had already done a thorough search of the lawn. It was the flowerbeds near the doors and windows she was after, where the police might not have known what to look for.

Kiki frowned, but aimed her eyes at the ground. The quicker they got it over with, the quicker she'd get her dinner. "I don't know why you're wasting time doing the police department's job when you should be campaigning. With Walter in the race, you could get clobbered. Wanda will do anything to win, and I'm going to end up buck naked in front of the whole town, and it's going to be your fault." She threw up her hands. "But do you care?"

The truth was, Hannah didn't. Her enthusiasm for politics had paled compared to her desire to know who killed Alex. It wasn't that she no longer cared about Signatech coming to town. She did. But for the moment, the idea of such a concentrated evil as murder seized her more. No sense in spending her time worrying about traffic congestion when on those same streets a killer was running loose.

Hannah and Kiki searched for twenty minutes. Kiki kept to the lawn, while Hannah inspected the flowerbeds. Neither woman found anything.

Kiki plopped down into a teak chair next to a small garden table. "See? All that trouble and we get zip, zero, nada. You could have been handing out campaign flyers, kissing some hands, shaking some babies, but no, not you."

Hannah crouched in front of the flowerbed near the conservatory and examined the dirt, careful not to disturb anything. She looked closer at a rock that could have been a button, but turned out to be only a rock. When she straightened she noticed the rosebush underneath the kitchen window, the same rose she had admired the day of the party.

"Can we go now?" Kiki asked. "My signature boots are killing me. I think there's a nail sticking in my toe."

"I want a quick look at that rose. I've got to know what it is." Hannah walked over to the rosebush and contemplated the large white blossom tinged with deep red, the petals luminous in the dwindling light. Gorgeous. Delicate beauty coupled with strength. A bush like it would be perfect next to the blood red blossoms of her Mr. Lincoln. Able to see the rose up close, she recognized it as a Boule de Neige, an antique Bourbon rose that, until now, she had only seen in pictures. Touching the velvety petals, she felt a catch in her throat, the same she always felt when confronted with a perfect rose. Seeing such beauty made her certain that God was a woman.

As she leaned down to drink in the fragrance she noticed that a low branch of the rosebush had been broken off, petals scattered to the ground. She bent down and carefully picked up a petal by its edge. She supposed the police could have broken off the branch while doing their search, but she could tell by the petal's brown edges and the discoloration of the branch that the damage was at least a couple of days old. The police had only come to the house that morning. It seemed unlikely that a policeman would step that close to the window if he were looking for evidence in the narrow flowerbed. He would keep his feet on the grass, just as she had. She heard fingers snapping.

"Hey, earth to Hannah," Kiki said. "Why are you staring at that rosebush like it owes you money? Let's go home. I'm starving and I just remembered there's some of Lauren's lasagna left in the freezer."

"You ate that last week in the middle of the night."

"How do you know?"

"I found old noodles when I changed your sheets," Hannah replied distractedly. She peeked in the window at the kitchen, and saw dishes from the party stacked on the countertop. Moving closer, her hands braced against the window ledge, she saw silvery fingerprint powder on a white toaster, a blender, and around the edges of the cabinet doors. Then Hannah felt a thorn in her leg. She looked downward and realized that in order to look into the window she had been forced to step into the flowerbed, close to the Boule de Neige. "Someone looked in this window."

Hannah said it only to herself, but Kiki heard. She limped over to Hannah, her foot hurting from her boot.

"No big mystery. It was Ox. He looked inside, saw that no one was in the kitchen, climbed in, and poisoned the water pitcher."

"Or he looked in the window and saw who did poison the pitcher."

"Then why didn't he tell the police? Can we go now? This darn boot's killing me."

Hannah stepped back from the flowerbed, her attention remaining fixed on the window. She would talk to Ox and find which window he had crawled into. She hadn't noticed any footprints in the soil, but the police had probably already checked for that. It was the broken rose branch that was intriguing, and she would tell Detective Morgan when she spoke to him later. He wouldn't like the fact that she had been in Alex's garden.

"We'll go in a second, Kiki. I'd love a rose like this one next to my Mr. Lincoln, and I need to get a cutting."

"That's stealing."

"Digging up a rosebush is stealing. Taking a cutting is a gardener's right. I'm sure Alex would approve. There's a gardening shed by the side of the house. We passed it on the way. I'll find some clippers in there. It'll just take a second."

Limping behind her sister, Kiki prattled on about wanting to go home, but she knew that Hannah wouldn't be deterred from a good rose cutting. Hannah was never shy about such things, and equally generous in giving them out from her own garden.

The shed door was closed, held in place with a metal gate latch. Hannah lifted up the latch and entered with Kiki in tow. It was dim inside, the only light coming from a small window high on the back wall. The shed was large, about eight by twelve feet, with a wood counter along one side and a single row of drawers underneath. Beneath those were two shelves filled with pots, plastic tubs, and seedling trays. About ten big bags of soil sat neatly stacked against the opposite wall.

"This is too well organized for my taste," Hannah said, squelching envy. She would have preferred a large potting shed like this one to a marble bathroom with a Jacuzzi and a towel boy, but didn't have the room or money for any of it. "All the tools are put away."

"Not like your gardening stuff, which is scattered everywhere," Kiki said.

"It's controlled chaos, and I like it," Hannah said defensively, opening a drawer, then closing it. "The clippers have to be somewhere.

Kiki leaned over, braced herself against the wall with one hand, and with the other, grabbed her foot. "I think what's hurting in these boots is the little metal part on the toe. It's got a nail or something that's digging into my skin."

"Maybe your signature boots are actually carving their signature," Hannah said, rummaging through another drawer.

"You're so hilarious."

"Pry off the metal piece. It will stop hurting for now, and you can take the boots to the shoe repair tomorrow."

"I'm not good at prying things off. Would you do it?"

"We're in a hurry, remember? Just take off the boot."

"I'm not walking around with one bare foot. I could step on a bug," Kiki replied, then noticed a metal spike with a small red flag at the top, the only object lying on the counter. It was about three inches long, the type of tool used to mark watering systems during installation. Bracing her foot against a low shelf, she inserted the spike underneath the tip of the boot and tried to pry off the offending piece of metal.

Hannah opened a few more drawers, finding spades, trowels, wire, everything but clippers. "All his tools are the best quality." She held up a hand spade. "Take a look at that handle."

"Yeah, fabulous," Kiki said in an irritated monotone. Still laboring with her boot, she gave the spike a shove and it broke in two. "Darn!" She threw the pieces on the ground in disgust.

Hannah opened another drawer, then froze. "Do you hear something?"

"That was my stomach rumbling."

"It sounded like footsteps."

"I didn't have much lunch."

The shed door slammed shut. Hannah heard the sound of the metal latch falling into place.

Kiki pushed on the inside door handle, but it didn't move. "Somebody's locked us inside! Probably some neighborhood kid." She pounded on the door. "Delinquent! This is what happens from listening to that rap music!" She looked at Hannah. "Now what are we going to do? I need food."

Kiki seemed only upset that dinner would be delayed, but Hannah's instincts warned her of something more malevolent. She stood perfectly still, ears tuned to the sound of more footsteps outside.

Kiki kicked the door. "This isn't funny. Let us out this minute! My sister is practically mayor!"

Hannah heard a splashing sound, and then, with a sickening dread, inhaled the fumes.

"My God, that's gasoline," Hannah said. Kiki looked at her in total noncomprehension. "Scream, Kiki! Scream your head off!"

FIFTEEN

FOR A LONG SECOND, KIKI looked dumbly at Hannah, but as the gasoline's odor filled her nostrils, her eyes widened and her mouth formed a silent "Oh, God." Then she started shrieking.

Her sister's screams resounding in her ears, Hannah fought her own panic. Jerking open a drawer and grabbing the heaviest of the spades, she shoved it into a small gap between two door boards to lift up the outside latch, but because of the spade's curvature, it wouldn't fit. Her heart hammering inside her chest, she checked out the door and found fresh hope. The screw in the top hinge was loose. She jammed the spade's tip underneath the flat metal that attached the hinge to the door, and pressed as hard as she could against the handle. If she could pry off the top hinge, she thought she could knock the whole door loose from its frame with her body weight.

Between Kiki's screams, Hannah heard the sound of metal hitting the flagstone, followed by footsteps heading away from the shed. She thought with relief that whoever had locked them in had been frightened by Kiki's shouts and run away, but a low crackling sound and burning smell brought new horror. Through the gaps in the wallboards, Hannah saw flames.

Seeing the horrified look on Hannah's face, Kiki followed her sister's gaze. Fear combined with Kiki's howls roared in Hannah's head as she kept shoving against the hinge with the spade. Feeling the fire's heat on the back of her legs, Hannah threw every bit of her strength into it. The wood behind the hinge splintered, but the spade broke. Hannah grabbed a pair of long shears that hung on the wall, stuck the metal end behind the hinge, and shoved against the wooden handles with her shoulders. The length of the shears provided more leverage, and she saw the hinge starting to move outward.

"Kiki, help me!"

Kiki grabbed the handles and pushed with her sister as smoke seeped in through the wallboards. The bags of soil kept out the flames, but Hannah knew they wouldn't for much longer. With a groan, Hannah gave the shear handles another heavy push, and the board split.

"Get back!" Hannah shouted. Kiki moved back to the end of the shed. Hannah rammed her shoulder against the door, but it didn't give. Gray smoke swirled around their heads. Kiki started coughing, covering her face with her hands. Hannah picked up a terra-cotta pot from a shelf and hurled it through the small rear window. The glass shattered and the smoke began to thin.

"We're going to die," Kiki sobbed. Hannah wedged the shears behind the lower hinge and began the same process, the smoke creeping into her lungs. She pressed all her body weight against the wooden handles, and the metal bolt on the hinge loosened. She stepped back a few feet and rammed her shoulder at the door. This time it flew open, and she fell through, landing hard on the ground, the grass cushioning her fall.

Kiki tumbled out, collapsing on the ground next to Hannah, both of them coughing, their eyes burning.

A woman in a terrycloth bathrobe, her hair dripping wet, burst through the gate. "What happened? I heard yelling when I got out of the shower," she said, the words coming out in a rush. She halted, clutching the collar of her robe. When she saw the saw smoke pouring out of the shed, she yelped.

Hanna stood up, pulling up Kiki with her, and they stumbled a safe distance from the smoke and flame.

"Are you all right, sweetie?" Hannah asked Kiki. "Are you okay?" Kiki nodded. Her arms around her sister, Hannah turned to the woman.

"Call an ambulance and the fire department. Better call the police, too. Someone just tried to burn us alive."

Detective Morgan pulled up an Adirondack lawn chair close to Hannah's. "You need more water?"

Hannah lowered the glass she had just emptied and placed it on the grass at her feet. Leaning her head against the chair's back, she breathed in the cleansing air. A whisper of a breeze felt sweet against her skin, but it didn't soothe the grinding in the bottom of her gut. The idea that someone wanted you dead. It was the sort of thing that set a person's mind to heavy thinking. But what cut into Hannah more was the way that someone had intended her and her sister to die. Who could hate them that much?

She leaned forward, her hands clasped in her lap. "I'm fine," she said, lying outright.

Gently, he lifted her left arm and examined the long bloody streak. "What about that scratch? Does it hurt?"

In escaping the shed, she had managed to take a few inches of skin off her arm. "No, it's alright. I'm more concerned about my sister."

"The paramedics say she's fine. They've given her some oxygen and a saline drip, to be on the safe side. But I think she's just shaken up. I'd be pretty shaken up myself. I still don't understand how you got out."

"I can't remember everything. I guess whoever did it got skittish when he heard Kiki screaming, and just dumped the gasoline on that one side of the shed. The bags of soil slowed the fire. It gave us some extra time."

A fireman in a black and yellow suit walked past. The air had a strange smell of stale smoke and fresh water. Her elbow propped on the chair's arm, Hannah pressed her fingers against the spot on her scalp where a throbbing pain was just starting.

Morgan put his hands on the knees of his khaki slacks and let out a gush of air. Hannah knew she was about to receive a disciplining chat. "I don't need to tell you how lucky you are, Mrs. Malloy."

She lowered her hands. "You call what happened to us lucky? Maybe tomorrow we'll walk away from a head-on car crash."

"You were damn lucky to survive. You shouldn't have been inside that shed in the first place. I may have to charge you."

Hannah watched his eyes, steady and kind, and his threat didn't disturb her. She knew he would no more charge her than he would charge his own auntie, at least not for this infraction. He saw her as a mother figure, and he was possibly infatuated with Lauren. He would give her a break, at least as long as this was the end of her investigating.

Morgan stared at the ground a few seconds, working something out in his head. He picked up a twig off the ground and rubbed it between his thumb and finger. "Are you sure that this time you told me everything?"

Hannah nodded. She had started from the beginning, telling

him about the fight she heard between Mary and Alex, about her agreeing to help Lorna, although she didn't say exactly why, only that she thought Ox was innocent. The only secrets she clung to were her email address being on Kiki's poems and the poems' unabashed raunchiness.

"The broken rose beneath the kitchen window could mean something," Hannah said. "You should re-question everyone."

"I know how to do my job, Mrs. Malloy."

"Of course you do. I didn't mean—"

He held up a hand to stop her. "Anything else about the shed you can tell me? Something you forgot?"

"I've told you everything. I heard the door slam shut, then heard footsteps. I don't remember much else after that except trying like hell to get out. Did Kiki give you anything useful?"

"She remembers it the way you do." He snapped the twig and dropped the pieces on the ground. "We've been down this road before. Don't make my job any tougher. I don't want you helping Lorna Donatello and her boyfriend. I wouldn't trust them if I were you. They're both suspects for the mayor's murder. You were at the mayor's party, and that makes you a suspect as well. You realize that?"

"And I tried to burn up my sister and myself to distract the police?" she told him, her anger showing. "How did I lock myself in the shed?"

"You know what I'm saying. You're on the suspect list. Keep your hands clean. We'll find out who did this. I have more questions for you, but they can wait until tomorrow. Go home and get some rest. I'll have a patrol car watch your house for the next few days."

"Are you going to tell John?"

"He'll like it better if he hears it from you."

Hannah cringed at the thought of the tantrum Perez was bound to throw. They had had arguments before over her involvement in police issues.

Morgan left. Hannah sat quietly, holding her hands together to try and stop the shaking. She needed to calm herself before she saw Kiki. Kiki would be hysterical, and with good reason, since she had warned Hannah not to meddle in the first place. Hannah's taste for investigating Alex's murder was definitely on the wane. Funny how a brush with death could give even the most curious of women a strong inclination for staying safely at home, curled up with a cup of hot tea and the doors bolted. Maybe she could learn how to knit tissue box covers or macramé plant hangers.

Hannah looked up at the black outline of Mount Tamalpais, a red light blinking from the peak. She had always felt that Mount Tam had some magical power that watched over their little town, like some kindly mother, keeping them safe and separate from the world's evil. But where was the mountain mother tonight, when there was a monster loose in Hill Creek?

Hannah heard the familiar click of Kiki's step. She emerged from the side of the house clutching a blanket around her shoulders, her makeup cried off. When she sat down in the chair next to Hannah, the sisters embraced.

"Kiki, I'm so sorry."

"I just can't believe that someone tried to kill us," Kiki said. "And we would have gone the hard way."

Hannah pulled away to arm's length. "I should never have gotten you involved in this. I shouldn't have been involved myself. I'll drop it and—"

"Drop it? Are you nuts?" Kiki said, giving Hannah a punitive slap on the shoulder. Hannah mouthed an ouch, her shoulder bruised from the shed door. "Where's your spunk? Your sense of justice?"

"It passed out from smoke inhalation."

"Hannah, we have to go after this animal who tried to kill us."

"Didn't what happened in that shed scare you just a little?"

Kiki turned up a palm. "Well, sure, but you were there. I knew you'd get us out."

"So all that screaming you did was a display of confidence?"

"Let's focus on what's important, which is that somebody tried to barbecue us like we were all-beef wieners. We can't just sit on our hands. You're the one who this morning said we can find out things the police can't. We've got to catch the son of a bitch and put him behind bars. And I'm not talking about some country club prison. I want this guy to have some boyfriends and be nicknamed Sweet Cheeks."

"Why did you keep saying 'him'?"

"Because it was a man," Kiki said in a grand whisper. She moved closer. "I saw somebody, at least I think I did. I haven't told the police yet because I thought I should talk it over with you first. You see, I'm not completely sure. There was this gap in the boards down near the ground, and I saw a leg or an ankle. Probably an ankle, because I think I saw some sock. And there was a bright red mark, like he had scratched himself." Hannah thought about the broken rosebush near the kitchen window as Kiki continued. "But I'm telling you, it was definitely male."

"How could you tell?"

"The same way you can tell a hybrid tea rose from a floribunda. Experience and expert knowledge. And when it comes to male body parts, it's hard to slip one past me. Whoever tried to shake and bake us was a card-carrying member of the male gender. And he's also the same person who killed Alex."

"How can you know?"

"Wake up, Hannah. It's too much of a coincidence that we start investigating Alex's death and then somebody tries to kill us." Hannah had already come to the same conclusion. Kiki went on. "Still, I don't understand how they knew we were investigating. Of course, you do have a reputation for prying."

Hannah was fairly sure it was more than that. She told Kiki about the game she played with the Brita pitcher at the rummage sale. She now wondered if it had almost cost them their lives.

"But the killer wasn't at the rummage sale," Kiki said. "I already told you, it was a man's ankle I saw, and all the suspects at the sale were women. Althea, Maggie, and Mary."

"But Charlie was at the rummage sale and he probably saw me."

"I don't think it was Charlie's ankle. Charlie's too pale and wimpy. The ankle I saw was strong and tan and macho. So take a look at the list of suspects and ask yourself these questions. Who has a motive for wanting Alex dead, who's been seen sneaking around Alex's house, and who has enough testosterone to float the HMS *Pinafore*?"

$\mathscr{S}$IXTEEN

$\mathscr{D}$ARKNESS HAD FULLY SETTLED, A few stars glittering like diamonds against deep blue velvet. It was that time of night when Marin's older single women settled in for evenings alone with their cats and reruns of *Frasier*. Some discovered a quiet fulfillment. Others grew bitter. And then there were those genetically predisposed to getting themselves into buckets of trouble, regardless of age or marital status.

Fresh from a narrow escape with death, Hannah and Kiki slid into the Cadillac, not needing much more fulfillment than the relief of being alive. Hannah started the engine and steered the car away from the curb past two squad cars still parked in front of Alex's.

Hannah rested her arm against the open window, her other hand on the steering wheel, maneuvering the car slowly down the hill. She felt like driving through town, past the town limits, then stomping the accelerator until she reached someplace safe. But where would that be? Fantasyland, maybe. She used to think of Hill Creek that way, a magical place isolated from the world's cruelty. But even Disneyland has to get real sometime.

Detective Morgan had offered to drive the sisters home, but Hannah didn't think Kiki, in her current state of mind, should be that close to a billy club. It was a different woman who sat next to Hannah. She studied Kiki a few seconds while stopped at a stop sign at the end of the street. Kiki stared straight ahead, body bent forward, hands braced against the dashboard, her plump, small-featured face steely with aggression, like some rabid Pekinese dog. This wasn't the usual I-only-care-about-clothes-men-and-Ding Dongs Kiki. This was combat-ready, commando Kiki, pissed off and ready to rumble.

Seeing her sister in this militant condition made Hannah believe that something had gone horribly awry in the universe, like the Pacific Ocean had dried up, or Saturn had dropped onto

Pluto and squashed it flat. It was supposed to be Hannah charging ahead with all pistons firing, and Kiki doing the finger shaking. Maybe it was only because Kiki had cried off her false eyelashes, but Hannah thought she saw a peculiar wildness in her sister's eyes. Jack Nicholson had worn the same look in *The Shining*.

"We're gonna get him, Hannah." Kiki pounded the dashboard with her fist. "I'm going to look at Ox's ankle, just for confirmation, and then I'll bring the bastard to his knees, make him beg for mercy, make him wish he'd never heard our names."

Hannah wondered if smoke inhalation could cause the immediate mutation of brain cells. After reaching the bottom of the hill, she navigated through a neighborhood of glossy new wood-framed condos, then turned left, reaching the edge of the town center. She stopped at a stoplight next to a car of teenage boys and blaring rap music, then stuck a finger in her left ear and rolled up the window. Not that she had anything against rap music. She actually liked some of it, only at volumes that didn't make her fillings hurt.

"Um, I see some problems with your plan, Kiki."

"Don't say problems." Kiki shook her fist. "There are no problems, Hannah, only temporary obstacles. Isn't that what you've been telling me for the past fifty years? We must seize the moment. Lorna said this morning that she and Ox were going to Frank's tonight for dinner. It's not even nine o'clock, so they're probably there right now. Here's the plan. We go in and look at his ankle. If he's the one who locked us in that shed, we call the police. And while the cops have him handcuffed we kick him, and kick him good." Kiki whacked the dashboard and made a growling sound.

Hannah considered the possibility that the paramedics inadvertently slipped something into Kiki's oxygen. Those medical canisters must all look so similar.

"First of all—and please stop punching the air like that, you'll exhaust yourself—to bring Ox to his knees and make him beg for mercy will require a confrontation with him," Hannah said carefully. "I don't think that's advisable if the man really is a cold-blooded murderer. A murderer might react badly to that kind of thing. It would be better to let the police handle it."

"Since I didn't tell the police right away about seeing the ankle, they might not take it that seriously. They might not immediately arrest him. I know now that not telling them about it was a mistake, but that's spilled milk. And we're not going to confront Ox, not directly. We're just going to look at his ankle, and then we'll force him into confessing."

"What if he doesn't like displaying body parts?" Hannah asked with increased fervor. "What if he attacks us?"

"He won't. It's a public place." Kiki patted her handbag. "And don't forget, we're packing heat. I've got my pepper spray, and I'll keep one hand on it the whole time. One false move and the big guy gets it."

"There's another issue. Detective Morgan told me not to be involved in this anymore, Kiki. He was quite firm about it. He said that if he caught me doing it again he was going to charge me."

Kiki made a "ppffft" sound, then gave Hannah a withering stare. "Is itty bitty Hannah scared? Afraid the big bad policeman will slap her hand?"

"Sweetie, are you taking any new hormones you haven't told me about?"

"Where's your sense of justice, where's your rage? Remember that old bumper sticker you used to have, the one you left on your car for years, even after it was in tatters? It said 'Question Authority.' That's always been one of the qualities I admired about you. You've never just accepted things. You've spoken your mind, kicked a little butt, and taken some names. So when did you start cowering in front of bureaucrats?"

"When they started threatening to put me in jail." Hannah held up a finger. "Okay, Che Guevara, let's go over the plan and check it for flaws. We think Ox is a crazed killer. He's the size of an ice cream truck and has Lorna with him, who's a bail bondsman and is probably licensed to carry a gun. But we have your pepper spray. If he tries anything we're going to serve him up *au poivre*."

Kiki shrugged. "Works for me." With loud grunts, she managed to work off her signature boots and put on her high-heeled sandals. She couldn't catch a criminal with shoes that hurt.

Hannah thought things over as she drove and quickly realized that Kiki's plan did make some sense, although not in the way Kiki intended. If Ox was after them, he would probably try again, and soon. Morgan having the police patrol their house was a nice gesture, but not all that comforting. If Ox wanted to

kill them he would find a way. It would be better for them to
get evidence against him that night when they could catch him
in a public place. He couldn't do much about it in a crowded
restaurant. Plus they would have the element of surprise. He
would never expect two sixtyish women to take bold action. She
was starting to like the plan better.

"Okay, I'm in," Hannah said. "Let's go to Frank's."

Kiki let out a cheer and gave Hannah a military salute. Turning off Center Avenue, Hannah headed for the freeway, occasionally casting a concerned glance at Kiki, who kept punching
her fist into her hand. It was just plain strange.

Although Hannah hadn't said it out loud, there was another
reason she wanted to confront Ox without the police. In spite
of Kiki's certainty about seeing Ox's ankle, Hannah, deep down,
couldn't believe it. If Ox had killed Alex, it was possible he did
it without Lorna knowing, which would explain why Lorna had
asked for Hannah's help in finding the murderer. But would Ox
be so worried about what Hannah would uncover that he would
want her dead? And she couldn't believe that Ox would deliberately hurt anyone. She knew it wasn't coldly logical, but when
she saw him smelling that rose in her garden, she felt she had
glimpsed into his soul, and she hadn't seen a killer there. She
had seen warm puppies and lollipops. Kiki seemed certain it
was him. Hannah was certain it wasn't. They couldn't both be
right. Best to find out the truth before causing Ox trouble with
the police.

"You still hungry?" Hannah asked. "We can stop for something."

"Don't need food," Kiki replied, hands on the dashboard, eyes
glinting. "Livin' off my rage."

"You realize you've cried off all your makeup?"

This time Kiki looked at Hannah with real fear. She flipped
down the visor and stared into the lighted makeup mirror. "Darn
it! Why didn't you say something?"

Frank's restaurant sat on the frontage road just north of Hill
Creek, its red neon sign a beacon to hungry highway drivers,
and like every Friday night, its parking lot was jammed with
cars. Hannah pulled the Cadillac up to the valet parking sign,
something she normally never did, but she was starting to feel

the day's traumas, especially in the shoulder, and didn't want
to walk more than she had to.

Frank's wasn't a valet parking kind of restaurant. A local
institution, it was deliberately unfashionable, with red vinyl
booths and a menu of steaks, chops, and fish, one of the few
old restaurants in Marin that had escaped transformation into an
Italian trattoria or high-tech sushi bar. This meant that the trendy
young stayed away, so you could enjoy your food without
twenty-somethings flitting about and looking at you like you
needed carbon dating. It attracted customers from all over the
county, and the valet parking was more to convenience its aging
clientele than any pretence to elegance.

The shed incident had left the sisters disheveled and smelling
of smoke, so before reaching the restaurant they had pulled into
a 7-Eleven to make themselves presentable. Under the parking
lot lights they combed their hair and performed general rehab,
which for Kiki meant a complete reapplication of the makeup
she carried in her purse. Hannah put on some lipstick and a little
powder. Afterward, Kiki liberally sprayed them both with perfume to hide the smoke odor.

The sisters walked inside the restaurant, the room noisy with
cocktail-fueled conversation and the clinking of dishes, every
table full and a boisterous crowd in the bar waiting for tables.
Hannah told the black-suited hostess they were looking for
friends. The hostess sniffed them, then made a face, and Hannah
didn't know if the woman was reacting to the smell of the
smoke, the heavy perfume, or the combination of the two. Scan-
ning the tables, she saw Lorna and Ox sitting on the same side
of a booth next to the window that looked out onto the parking
lot.

"Let's go get him," Kiki said, then started to take off, but
Hannah held onto her.

"We're not here to start a fistfight," Hannah warned. "We
don't know if either one of them has done anything wrong, and
if they have, that's even more reason to proceed with caution."

"Okay Miss Calm-and-Cautious, have it your way, but if I
recognize his ankle, he gets the pepper spray right in the kisser."

Dodging waiters shouldering loaded trays, they made their
way toward Lorna and Ox's table. The two were still working
on dinner, Lorna digging into a huge steak and Ox halfway
through a burger with fries. Seeing the food made Hannah ac-

knowledge her own ravenous hunger. Even red meat looked good.

"We need to talk," Hannah said.

Her hand wrapping around a glass of amber liquid, Lorna smiled when she saw them. She wore a lipstick-red sweater with two rows of rhinestones marching down a plunging V neck. Seeing Lorna's cleavage, Hannah guessed that Lorna's breasts had been purchased, same as Kiki's, only Lorna had gone for the economy size. Kiki beheld them with envy.

Ox gave them a grin, then sipped something that looked like cola.

"Didn't expect to see you gals here. Take a load off." Lorna pointed to the booth seat opposite. The sisters slid in. Kiki sat stiffly, everything about her, inside and out, curled into a fist.

"You guys want to order something?" Ox asked.

"We're only staying a minute," Hannah told him, her voice measured.

Ox saw Kiki surveying his food. "Want a French fry?" Kiki started to nod, then remembering her rage, shook her head.

"So have you found out who killed Al?" Lorna asked. Her expression grew puzzled and she gave the air a sniff. "You two smell funny, like you've been grilling gardenias."

"It's called Eau de Human Barbecue. Ever hear of it?" Kiki said with belligerence, slapping the tabletop. Hannah gave her sister a warning look.

"I haven't found out anything new, but something's happened," Hannah said before Kiki could get physical. "A couple of hours ago someone tried to kill us."

Ox's forehead corrugated. "No kidding?" Hannah saw Kiki ease one of Ox's French fries off his plate and pop it into her mouth.

"No kidding," Hannah replied. Tired, hungry, and still thoroughly shaken, she wasn't in the mood for small talk, so she jumped right into it. "I need to ask you something, Ox. Where were you this evening around seven?"

"Back off, girlfriend," Lorna said, stabbing the air with her finger. "No one accuses my pookie. Why would I ask you to help us and then have Ox try to kill you? That would be stupid, not to mention inefficient. And he would never try to kill anyone without asking me first. For your information, he was at Gold's Gym working on his pecs." She looked at him, her eyes getting all soft and gooey. "And they're real nice ones, sweet stuff, I can vouch for that." She turned back to Hannah. "It's too bad that someone tried to kill you. If I get my hands on the loser I'll crack his nuts for you at no charge. But it wasn't Oxie."

"I want to see his leg," Kiki said. Before anyone could comment, she slid under the table.

"What the hell?" Lorna said, her face screwed up.

Ox jumped up in his seat. "Lornie, she's touching me."

Lorna dove under the table. A youngish waiter glided up and asked if anybody needed anything just as angry voices came from beneath the table. There were a few knocks that shook the glasses, followed by a thud and a loud "ouch" from Kiki. Both women reappeared and slithered back into their seats. Kiki's hair was sticking up where Lorna had pulled it.

His eyebrow arched, the waiter flared his nostrils and feigned a look of disdain, but there was high amusement behind it. "Cocktails, anyone?"

"If only I could," Hannah replied. The waiter gave her a commiserating wink.

Kiki smoothed her hair. "She wouldn't let me see it," she said to Hannah.

Lorna tossed back her drink. "Listen, girlfriend, that's private property," she said, crunching ice with her teeth for punctuation. "What's his leg got to do with it?"

"Someone locked us in Alex's gardening shed and then tried to burn it down," Hannah told her. That shut Lorna up, and she sat back in her seat. Ox's eyebrows knitted. "Kiki saw a leg through a gap in the wallboards and she noticed a mark, a red mark. Just let her take a look at Ox's leg and this will all be cleared up."

Lorna gave her head a hard shake, her hair not moving. "Oxie didn't do it."

"It's us or the police," Hannah said.

"It's okay, Lornie," Ox said fast. "Let her look. They have a right to check everybody out, and I've got nothing to hide." His words did the trick. Lorna agreed, although it was obvious she didn't like it. He moved sad eyes to Kiki. "Right or left?"

"Both," Kiki told him. Lorna watched with aggravation as Kiki dropped again under the table.

Lorna bent down to check up on her. "Lookie, but no touchie."

Ox tried to eat a French fry but he kept squirming, and Lorna looked about ready to break somebody's arm. Even Hannah thought Kiki was being a little too thorough. How long does it take to look at a man's ankles?

"Oh, my God!" Kiki shouted from under the table. "Hannah, I found something!"

It was one of those moments. Hannah didn't know exactly what happened inside her head, but when she heard those words, she snapped. Maybe she was so tired she was irrational. Maybe some emotional string inside her had been pulled so tightly it finally broke. But all of a sudden it didn't matter how big Ox was or what weapon Lorna might have in her handbag. Hannah lunged over the table and grabbed Ox by the collar, sending a glass tumbling, water spilling. Looking back on it, Hannah couldn't remember every detail, only her anger that he had tried to hurt her sister.

Ox pulled back, while Lorna, a definite stand-by-your-man type, grabbed Hannah's wrist. Lorna swung back her arm, ready to plant her fist on Hannah's jaw, but Ox took hold of her elbow.

Kiki came up from under the table, her mouth forming an astonished "oh" when she saw her sister's hand on Ox.

"Gee, sorry, Hannah. I meant I found this." Kiki held up a twenty-dollar bill. "There weren't any marks on his ankle. Guess I was wrong."

Although reluctant, Lorna released Hannah, and Hannah sat back onto her seat. Feeling guilty and wanting to be Girl Scout helpful, Kiki started mopping up the spilled water with a napkin. The waiter came up to the table.

"Now ladies, you need to calm down or you'll have to leave," he said.

"Oh, yeah?" Lorna snarled. "Well how would you—"

Ox hushed her with a look that made Hannah wonder who really was the dominant partner in the relationship. "It's okay," Ox told the waiter. "There won't be any more trouble."

"It was just a misunderstanding," Hannah said, the words directed at Ox. "A terrible misunderstanding for which I'm very sorry."

The waiter left.

"You ought to be sorry," Lorna said sharply, looking ready to throw another punch. "That sort of thing hurts Oxie's feelings."

"It's okay, Lornie," he said, stroking Lorna's head like she was a hyperactive rottweiler. "She thought I tried to kill them. You can understand her getting worked up."

"Did I hurt you?" Hannah asked Ox. Both he and Lorna got a good chuckle at that one, their amusement breaking the tension. "I've never done anything like that in my life."

"It shows," Lorna said. "You fight like a sissy."

Hannah thought the word "sissy" inaccurate. Since she had tried to throttle a man three times her size, she thought she deserved points for effort, but decided not to press the issue. "The reason Kiki and I were almost killed is because we were investigating Alex's murder," Hannah said. "So you owe us a little understanding."

Lorna didn't appear convinced. "Did you find out anything?"

"Maybe, but I have some questions for Ox."

"Ox isn't answering any questions," Lorna replied.

Ox rested his hand on Lorna's arm. "It's okay. Let her ask me what she wants."

Kiki finished mopping up and put the wet napkin on the empty table next to them. Picking up a sugar packet from a little ceramic bowl, Lorna tapped it against the table.

"When you went to Alex's house that day of his party, you got in through a window. Which window was it?" Hannah asked Ox.

"The living room. I know because of the sofa and the big piano." Ox shifted in his seat and worried his shirt collar with his fingers. Lorna's sugar packet danced on the tabletop.

"You didn't look in any other windows where you stepped into a rosebush?" Hannah asked.

Lorna stopped the tapping. "What are you getting at?"

"No, no rosebushes," Ox answered. "I know for sure because I noticed the flowering maple by the living room window, and the leaves were a little yellow, and I thought Alex ought to give it an iron treatment. Otherwise, you know, he won't get good flowering this summer."

"So, enough lip flapping," Lorna said. "You found out what you needed. Oxie didn't try to kill anybody and wasn't hanging out by any rosebushes. You better go find the real killer before I decide to go into the poetry publishing business." She gave Hannah a meaningful glare. "Now we'd like to be alone. We're discussing wedding plans."

Hannah and Kiki got up.

"One more thing," Lorna said. "If I ever catch either of you laying a finger on Oxie again, I don't like to think what'll happen." Hannah didn't like thinking about it either.

The sisters walked out of the restaurant into air thick with mist and the thundering of cars on the freeway. Hannah gave the college-aged valet her car ticket. She looked in the restaurant window and saw Ox and Lorna talking, and from their faces, the exchange was angry.

"I can't believe I made such a mistake about Ox. Do you think old age is creeping up on us?" Kiki asked.

Hannah rotated her shoulder and winced. "I think old age is sitting in our laps and giving us a hickey."

"Maybe it was an arm I saw," Kiki said. "Whoever it was could have been bending over and that's why I thought it was an ankle."

"I thought you were an expert on male body parts."

"Well, ankles and arms aren't my main specialty. But I saw Ox's wrists and there was nothing on them. Should I go back and have him roll up his sleeves?"

Hannah saw Ox get up from the table and walk off. "I think we should leave him alone for now."

Ox came out the front door and looked around. When he saw the sisters standing by the valet parking sign, he hesitated a second, then came their way. He looked even bigger at night, a lumbering walrus of a man, half teddy bear and half warrior. When he reached them he didn't speak right away, but stood quietly a few seconds. Kiki stepped behind Hannah for protection.

"I want to apologize for Lornie," he said at last.

"I'm the one to be apologizing," Hannah replied. She glanced back at the restaurant window where Lorna vigilantly observed them.

"Lorna shouldn't have talked to you the way she did. You've been trying to help us. But she's not the apologizing type. It's just not in her." He studied his loafers a second. When he raised his eyes again they had turned hard, the teddy bear gone and the warrior full frontal. "You just have to understand that when one person loves another person, they'll do anything to keep them from getting hurt. They'll do anything, even if it's stupid, because they've got to protect them. Right or wrong doesn't come into it. That's just the way it is."

The glow from Frank's neon sign fired Ox's face into an angry red. The toughness of his voice made Hannah tighten, and she wasn't sure if what he said was a veiled explanation for the past or a threat for the future. She wasn't particularly fond of either option.

Hannah started to say something, but Ox cut her off by turning around and heading back into the restaurant. Just then the valet drove up in a polished Mercedes and handed it over to a well-dressed redhead swathed in about three cows' worth of beige leather. The valet then snatched another set of keys from a rack and trotted off.

"This outing was a bust," Kiki said, her arms wrapped around her. "We found out nothing."

"We found out a lot," Hannah said.

"Like what?"

"That Ox knows his plants. He knew that a flowering maple was a regular plant. Most people would have thought it was a tree. The two have different botanical names, but are both called maples, and Ox knew the difference. And if he knew that, he might have also known that monkshood is poisonous."

"But if he's the one, how come I didn't recognize his ankle?"

"Don't know."

They fell into silence. It was close to ten and it hadn't been the easiest of days. The valet drove up in the Cadillac, the exhaust letting out a blast just to embarrass them. Hannah tipped him two dollars because she thought he was sexy, then he helped her into the car like she was ninety with a broken hip. She hated that, the assumption that because you're a certain age you're frail and sexless, when underneath your aging exterior your blood still runs hot. She hoped the valet had been looking in the window when she grabbed Ox by the collar.

Hannah drove while Kiki stared out the window, both of them mulling over all that had happened. The lighted streets were filled with cars—teenagers on the prowl for fresh excitement, exhausted professionals just getting home from work, having put in the extra hours to keep up the payments on the house, the car, and platinum American Express card. Everybody wanting more of the things they already had plenty of. It was Kiki who finally spoke.

"Now that I think about it more, I'm realizing that I was wrong about the ankle. I must have seen something else completely. This is why you're better at investigating than I am."

"I don't know about that. You have your own way of accomplishing things."

"Let's face it, I was dead wrong, and I almost got you pummeled by Lorna. And the woman looked like she could throw a punch."

"So all that talk earlier about finding the person who tried to kill us is down the drain?"

"Listen, there's a point when pluckiness turns to stupidity. We both know it's better if you did the investigating. I need to focus all my energies on your campaign."

"Focus how?" Hannah asked warily.

"It's time for me to fulfill my duties as your campaign manager. I know up until now I haven't really jumped into it headfirst, but there's one thing I've been working on, and I've got some ideas I think you'll like. But let's talk about it tomorrow. I'm too tired right now to think about anything. I just want a bubble bath, some cocoa, and then bed."

Hannah agreed, but for her it would have to wait. As she pulled into their driveway she saw Perez's Subaru station wagon parked out front, with him leaning against the front fender, his hands in his pocket. Even in the darkness Hannah saw his turbulence. Kiki wanted to stay outside and hear the argument she felt sure was coming, but Hannah made her go in the house.

Running her hands over the top of her hair, Hannah smiled as she approached him. He stood under the street lamp, bathed in the amber glow of an energy-saving light bulb. He didn't have his usual smile.

"A late night visit, kind of like high school. Did you throw pebbles at my window?" she said, trying to sound lighthearted. He didn't say anything, which had her worried until he pulled her to him, enfolding her in his arms.

"Jeezus Christ, what the hell happened?" he whispered, his breath warm and tingly on her ear. She told him she was fine, but the truth was, she was fighting the beginnings of tears, the strength of his arms causing the day's emotions to well up. She had spent her whole life taking care of everyone else, and had never known what it felt like to have someone take care of her.

Perez held on tightly for a while, her face buried in his shoulder, neither of them speaking.

"Detective Morgan told you?" Hannah asked when she finally pulled away.

"I went to the station after dinner, and I could tell he was shook up about something. I made him tell me," Perez said. Hannah could hear the old cop's impassiveness in his voice, but his face told a different story. "Why did you go to Alex's? It was a stupid thing to do."

"I know, and I'm not going to do anything like it again."

"We both know that's a lie."

"But I'm going to be very careful. Extremely careful. I was scared to death in that shed. I thought I was going to die."

He pulled her to him again and pressed his lips against her hair.

"I did find out something," she told him. He stepped back to arm's length. "A rosebush just outside the kitchen had been disturbed. Someone was looking in that window."

A patrol car turned the corner and cruised slowly past the house. Perez nodded to the officer behind the wheel.

"The point is," Hannah said, "whoever looked in that window could be the one who poisoned the water."

"Or saw who did it," Perez said, coming to the same alternative conclusion she had. "It probably happened in the kitchen. They're still interviewing people from the party, and they interviewed Maggie again this afternoon. She says she refilled the water pitcher that morning after she had used it to make coffee. So, if she's telling the truth, we have proof that the water was poisoned that day."

Hannah's gaze strayed to the yellow light streaming from her house windows. Was that the reason Ox looked uncomfortable when she talked about that rosebush? Had he looked in the window and seen Lorna poison the jug?

"I want you to spend the night at my house tonight," Perez said, his words snapping Hannah out of her thoughts.

"I can't leave Kiki."

"Bring her along. I've got the spare bedroom."

"I can't do that either."

"Why not?" he asked.

"Because I want this relationship to last. One night with Kiki in your house would be the end of it."

"Don't joke about this, Hannah."

She laid a hand against his chest. "I'll keep the doors and windows locked, and you just saw the patrol car keeping an eye on us." He shook his head with irritation. "I'll be fine. Is there any new information on the case that you can tell me?"

"Not much. They've done background checks on everyone at the party and no one had any connection to Signatech that they can find. And they didn't pull any fingerprints off the pitcher except for Maggie's and Alex's, but that's not a surprise. The killer wouldn't grab it barehanded. But they found some smudges, probably from gloves or a cloth."

"The smudges could be innocent. Maggie could have picked it up wearing rubber gloves or wiped it with a dishtowel."

"Or the smudges could have come from the killer. Right now the main suspects are Alex's ex-wife and boyfriend. Those two had the most to gain, and she stole a key to the house and had the locks changed. Of course, Morgan is still questioning everyone at the party, focusing on the people who were in the room when you announced that the monkshood was poisonous."

"I wish I could go back and change that."

"You couldn't have known you'd inspire a murderer. So far they've questioned Mary Katowski, Charlie Wright, Wanda and Walter, and Maggie. Oh, and Althea Lamont. Charlie had a motive to get Alex out of the mayor's race, and Maggie had more opportunity than anyone to poison that jug."

"She also had more opportunity to notice anything that was amiss in his house. Or with Alex, for that matter."

"You think she knows something she's not telling?"

"What I know is that Maggie's the type who always has her eyes and ears open. She might have seen something important the day of the party and not realized it." Hannah remembered what Maggie had told her earlier that day at the rummage sale about the Signatech land. With everything that had happened, she had forgotten about it.

"What are you thinking, Hannah?"

"How great a long, hot bath is going to feel." Hannah didn't think she should casually repeat what Maggie had told her since it had been said in confidence. She would check out the ownership of the Signatech site the next morning. If it turned out to be important, she would pass it on to the police. "You know, John, you're being awfully nice about this, considering. How come you're not yelling at me for interfering with a police investigation?"

"Because I've tried yelling before and it didn't work." Hannah was standing in the shadows, and he took her hand, pulling her into the light. "This time I'm trying something else. I'm asking you again to come to Colorado with me. We could leave tomorrow."

"I can't." She saw everything in him tighten. "I can't leave Kiki, not with what's gone on."

"I've got the same solution as before. She can come with us."

"I've got the same response as before. Twenty-four hours with Kiki and you'd be homicidal."

"If I have to, I'll carry you to Colorado."

Hannah ran the back of her fingers down his cheek. "Your knees are too bad for that."

"Not since my surgery. I've got the knees of a thirty-year-old. Will you come?"

"The safest path for me is to stay in town and help find out who's doing these things."

"You'll be safer far away."

"Am I supposed to move permanently? Whoever wanted to kill my sister and me is still going to want us dead when we get back. We're better off doing all we can to help the police. I'll only be safe when this person is caught."

He started to say something but stopped himself. She knew he was measuring his words, trying not to get angry, and she loved him for it.

"How can you help the police without exposing yourself to more danger?" he asked.

"By being careful, by staying in public places. I won't let myself be caught alone like I did today at Alex's."

"You're a lot of trouble, Hannah."

"More than I'm worth?"

He drew her to him and kissed her with an intensity that was new for them. It was a letting go, him telling her how much he needed her, and by her own ardency, she told him the same. A boundary had been crossed, their love for each other at last admitted, if only silently.

Gently, she pulled away, feeling shy. "I should go in."

"We'll talk again tomorrow," he said, not meeting her eyes. She smiled inwardly. They could have been sixteen-year-olds too embarrassed to discuss that they were now going steady. "You've had a tough day. I don't need to tell you not to let anybody in the house, male or female."

He kissed her one last time, then waited by the car until she made it up the walkway and was safely inside. As soon as she shut the door, fear washed over her, and she reconsidered Perez's offer of letting Kiki and her stay over. By the time she made up her mind to do it, she heard the Subaru's engine start, followed by the sound of the car taking off down the street. It would be all right, she told herself, not truly believing it.

She checked on Kiki and found her sister already asleep. Kiki's brain was like a phone wire, with everything, good or terrible, passing through at max speed. Hannah figured her sister would wake up the next morning bright and optimistic, while the foreboding in her own heart would linger.

SEVENTEEN

❧

"SORRY, BUT I DON'T WANT to go with you to the town clerk's office and look up property," Kiki said. "It sounds too much like going to the library. A woman like me requires more stimulation."

Looking for her hairspray, she pivoted left, then right, stumbling when her silver boot tip snagged on the pink bathroom rug. Hannah had fixed the boot right after breakfast by using a screwdriver to bend the offending nail into submission. That, along with a Band-Aid on Kiki's big toe, put her back in high-speed signature-boot action.

Hannah took Kiki's arm, amazed that her sister had such trouble staying upright even in flat-heeled shoes. Once steadied, Kiki admiringly surveyed her reflection in the mirror that took up almost the entire wall over the sink, the opposite pink wall lined with shelves to capture the arsenal of hairsprays, gels, mousses, foundations, eye pencils, and mascaras she considered life essentials. A basket hanging by the doorjamb held more than fifty lipsticks, some of amazing vintage, and all variations of the same shade of peachy pink more suitable on a sixteen-year-old than a sixty-year-old woman. Hannah's bathroom was the same size, yet felt roomy as a bus station in comparison. Her makeup included foundation, one shade of blusher, and a selection of two red lipsticks.

Studying herself in the mirror, Kiki ran her hands along the sides of her tight, long sweater, and gave herself a "foxy lady" wink, not cognizant of the way her plump body bulged inside the red sweater with the lumpiness of an overstuffed Christmas stocking. Hannah noticed that the sweater was similar to the one Lorna had worn at Frank's restaurant.

"Like I said last night, I've decided to let you work on the investigation on your own," Kiki said. Finally locating her maxi-hold hairspray, she gave her coiffure another spritz, officially giving it the consistency of wire mesh. Hannah watched from the doorway, arms crossed and thoughts dubious. Kiki's hair was pulled on top of her head and fluffed into a miniature tornado, its funnel shaped by a single long tendril hanging down one cheek. It was all very Ivana and had taken two hours to construct. Hannah mused upon why her sister had gone to such extra trouble. There had to be a reason. There was always a reason.

"But I need your help," Hannah told her, waving away the hairspray fumes she felt sure could kill brain cells. It would explain a lot about her sister.

"Hannah, I'm not a twelve-year-old." Kiki held up some dangly Mickey Mouse earrings to her ears for consideration. "I know you just want me to be safe, and that's sweet, but I have plans."

"Like what?"

"Somebody has to work on your campaign, and you haven't lifted a finger on it since Alex died."

"I don't want you hanging around the house by yourself."

"I won't be. I'll be at Naomi's for about an hour." She discarded the Mickey Mouse earrings, opting for some dangling black ones instead. "You're as much a worrywart as your cute John. How many times has he called this morning?"

"Only three."

Dabbing a third coat of blusher on her cheeks, Kiki sighed. "It must be so fulfilling to have a man's love. Alex and I would have shared that kind of devotion if he hadn't taken a dirt nap."

"Dirt nap? That's a term Lorna used. I thought you didn't like her."

"I don't, but she has a certain *savoir flair*. And you've got to give her credit. She nabbed Ox, and he's got to be ten years younger than her." Kiki blew a kiss to herself in the mirror, then shooed away her sister. "So go. I'm heading straight to Naomi's, then I'll probably drop in at Lady Nails for a while. The girls will want to hear about what happened yesterday." Kiki's brush with death was the kind of delicious story that came along once in a lifetime, and she planned to tell and retell it with suitable embellishments. "And after that I have another appointment in town."

"What kind of appointment?"

"An appointment. Don't be so nosy."

Something was stewing. "You're not going to be afraid, after someone tried to kill us yesterday?"

"I'll be surrounded by people. Nothing can happen."

"I don't understand your casual attitude. What's going on?"

"All right, if you're going to nag, I'll tell you. While you were in the shower, I went outside to get the paper and saw this cute policeman driving by the house." She picked up her bottle of "Eau de Madness" and squirted it behind her ears, elbows, and knees, then gave herself a shot down her sweater on the off chance that some man might stick his head down there. You just never knew what a day held. Hannah backed up a few feet. "You know, keeping an eye on us," Kiki explained. "So I waved him down, and mentioned that I was going to town late this morning after my visit with Naomi. I told him how scared I was, so he's coming with me to town to make sure I'm safe. Isn't it exciting? Police protection. Wanda will be pea green. And he's *sooo* cute. Butt like a Greek statue. So go investigate, Hannah, and don't worry about me. I'm fine and dandy."

Satisfied that Kiki would be safe, although she wasn't so sure about the policeman, Hannah took off for the town hall. She managed to snag a parking place in the adjacent lot, and when she walked inside she saw with sadness all the smiling photos of Alex on the walls. When she opened the door to the town clerk's office, she heard Alex's voice welcoming her to Hill Creek, the sound of it giving her the creeps.

"No one has the heart to turn it off," Frannie said from behind the counter. Still wearing mourning black and her yellow "I've Been Busted" button, Frannie looked careworn.

Hannah told her that she wanted to check on the ownership of some land, and without her usual gossipy banter, Frannie led her to the huge bound books that contained maps of every parcel within the town limits. The books were laid out on a table, and behind that stood a counter with three computers where you could look up details on any particular parcel. It took Hannah over an hour to flip through the books and match the parcels to what she knew was the proposed Signatech land. Once she had the reference numbers she looked up the tracts on the computer. The proposed site was made up of five separate parcels, and as she already knew, the town of Hill Creek owned all of them. At least the large ones. According to the map there was an irregularly shaped half-acre sitting between the town's land and

the road, and this parcel, vital to the site, belonged to someone
else. She jotted down the reference number and returned to the
computer. When she saw who owned it, she muttered an invol-
untary "good grief."

She felt Frannie's keen eyes on her, and knew she was dying
to know what could be so interesting in the town records. Hannah pushed her glasses farther up her nose and looked again to
make sure she was seeing right. But there it was, the fact printed
in white letters pulsing against a neon blue background. The
parcel was owned by none other than Charlie Wright.

Hannah stepped hard on the gas pedal, noticed the school zone
sign, then braked, praying that the policeman two cars behind
hadn't noticed her speeding. She was impatient to find Charlie,
but the last thing she needed was a speeding ticket, and the local
police were rightfully strict about school zones.

Charlie's garage was on the edge of town center. Hannah
stopped at a red light by the Book Stop, her mind wrapped up
in what she had just learned. Being on the town council, Charlie
had a direct conflict of interest with the proposed Signatech
move. But surely the rest of the council knew he owned the
property. You couldn't keep that a secret.

A block up, a stooped old man walked his yellow Labrador
across the road, and Hannah slowed the car to a crawl, still
wracking her brain, feeling that mental buzz that had always
been more addictive to her than liquor. Charlie's ownership of
that land fit into the whole Signatech drama, that much was
obvious. But how? The old man and dog safely across the street,
she speeded up again. Tapping on the steering wheel to the beat
of Jimi Hendrix on the radio, she glanced at the sidewalk and
saw a giant photo of herself emblazoned on a three-by-four
board. That in itself was peculiar. What was even more peculiar
was that the board appeared to be walking toward Lady Nails.

Pulling the Cadillac to the curb, Hannah turned off Jimi and
blinked a few times to make sure the music wasn't causing a
drug flashback, but when she looked again, her face was still
moving down the sidewalk. Then she recognized the black patent leather boots beneath it and the pouf of bottle-blonde hair
bobbing from the sign's top. She got out of the car.

"Kiki, what are you doing?" Hannah stopped and looked

around, hearing music and wondering where it was coming from.

"Campaigning," Kiki replied, then, spying Mrs. Polanski from the catering shop moseying down the sidewalk, she raised a small Forty-Niners megaphone to her mouth and bellowed, "Vote for Hannah!" Mrs. Polanski screamed and jumped a good foot off the sidewalk, dropping her packages. Once she realized the source of the yelling, she smiled and waved good-naturedly. Hannah hurried over and helped her gather up her things. As soon as they approached, Kiki reached into the black and orange plastic pumpkin she carried and handed Mrs. Polanski something. Mrs. Polanski accepted it with smiling gratitude, but Hannah noticed that in Mrs. Polanski's other hand she carried a clump of white cloth which she hastily stuffed into her shopping bag as if she didn't want them to see it. She then waved stiffly at the two sisters and hurried off down the street.

"Where did you get the sign?" Hannah asked.

"Naomi and I've been working on it for a couple of days, and we just finished this morning. We wanted it to be a surprise. I surprised you, right?"

"Almost as much as you surprised Mrs. Polanksi."

Kiki tugged on the vinyl shoulder straps that held together the two signs, one sign in front and a matching one in back. "Do you think this makes me look fat?"

Hannah chuckled. "Poster board is always so slimming. What's in the pumpkin? It's a little early for Halloween."

"Candy. This pumpkin's the only thing I could find in the house that was big enough and had a handle. You see, you need to have a freebie to get people's attention." She handed Hannah a small cellophane-wrapped candy. "Things were going swell until Wanda spread a rumor that the candies were wrapped by sweatshop labor. Then she set up that hideous booth on the plaza."

Kiki pointed across the street past the Book Stop to a slick white Plexiglas "Vote for Backus" booth, Wanda standing inside. Classical music blared from two tall speakers, and several people had lined up in front. Wanda was handing them something.

"What's she giving away?"

"T-shirts," Kiki said, spitting it out the way she would have coughed up a hairball. She tried to cross her arms in pique but the sign was so wide, her hands wouldn't meet, which only aggravated her further. "One hundred percent unbleached cotton, made in America. On the back the shirts have a big picture of Alex with 'In memory of our loving mayor' written underneath, and on the front they have a photo of Walter and 'Vote for Backus.' Doesn't it just make you sick?"

On the contrary, Hannah admired Wanda's marketing savvy. Wanda busily shook hands and passed out T-shirts as well as bottles of designer water for those potential voters who might be thirsty. Hannah also noticed stacks of campaign literature. It all must have cost a fortune. Wanda had come up with everything. Everything except the candidate.

"Doesn't Walter do any campaigning himself?" Hannah asked.

"He started out at the booth, but he only lasted ten minutes. Wanda says he's in high-level meetings with town officials, but I saw him sneak into O'Reilly's."

"Campaigning probably makes him thirsty."

Kiki smiled. "What doesn't? Did you find out anything good at town hall?"

"Plenty. You want to hear about it?"

Kiki spied a couple of Hill Creek residents rounding the corner. "Later. Potential voters straight ahead. Got to scoot." Kiki forged down the sidewalk, the rear sign bouncing against her tush.

Hannah got back in the Cadillac and took off, waving to Wanda as she drove by.

Charlie's garage was only five blocks away, and within a couple of minutes Hannah pulled into its parking lot, the Cadillac looking like a parade float next to the row of sleek European cars awaiting repairs. She went straight to the office.

The sign out front read "Charlie's Garage," but the cozy name belied the establishment's sophistication. Charlie's office was clean and stylish, with thick taupe carpet, art prints on the walls, and Italian leather furniture, all of it designed to give his upper-crust customers the sense of quality and comfort they demanded. Charlie was savvy enough to know that his clients didn't want mere repairs on their ego-nourishing luxury cars. They wanted surgery.

Charlie was nowhere in sight, so Hannah headed for the shop, a huge white room cleaner than her kitchen. She saw several mechanics fiddling with cars, then recognized two long legs attached to a pair of red Adidas sneakers sticking out from under a new blue Jaguar. They belonged to Tulley Lundmark. The garage didn't handle American cars. Much too gauche. But a few years back young Tulley had fixed the Cadillac's transmission when Hannah had been in a bind. Tulley figured he owed her. Ten years before, she had done volunteer tutoring at the high school and had struggled with Tulley to get him through algebra. He managed a B, and he never forgot her.

Even though she was in a rush she took a few seconds to lust for the Jaguar, a spanking new peacock blue convertible with an elegant sloping nose and rolled leather seats the color of butterscotch. Hannah wasn't a car fanatic, but there was something deliciously sexy about this one. Sexy and expensive. She couldn't afford the gearshift knob.

She called Tulley's name, and he rolled out from under the car, lying face up on a flat dolly. When he saw her he smiled broadly.

"Hi, Hannah. Got a problem with the gold boat?" He smoothed back his straw-colored hair and in the process streaked it with grease. Hannah had always liked him.

"No, it's running about as well as it ever does. I'm looking for Charlie."

"He's not coming in until later."

"Where is he?"

"Home, I think. I heard him say he needed to clean out his fishpond. He's crazy about those fish. He left his home phone number in case something came up."

Something was about to come up for Charlie, and he wasn't going to like it. Hannah said goodbye and Tulley disappeared back under the Jaguar.

Hannah had been to Charlie's house when he had a garage sale a few years before. The sale had been mostly tools, so she hadn't stayed long, but she remembered the location. A small wood-framed bungalow nestled on the slope of Mount Tam just behind town, Charlie's house was meant for comfort and not for show, and lacked the polish of his business. When she pulled in front, she saw weeds infusing the landscaping and an old lawnmower standing sentry near the front door.

Hannah gave the door's peeling surface a quick knock, relieved when no one answered. She would never have gone into the house alone with Charlie anyway, and she wasn't sure how she would have explained it to him. She felt silly being afraid of Charlie, but since he was a suspect for Alex's murder, he was a suspect for the shed incident as well. She had to be cautious.

She went to the east side of the house where she heard the neighboring children playing behind a tall hedge, the friendly sound making her feel safe. There was no fencing, so she walked through to the back. The yard was mostly gravel. She found Charlie on his knees by a round cement-edged pond, about five feet across, filled with green water, algae, and lily pads that floated on the surface. Charlie plunged his arm up to the elbow into the water then quickly raised it, the small net in his hand holding a flopping fat goldfish. He wore old shorts and a stained T-shirt that revealed puny pale arms. Cautiously, Charlie placed the fish in a bucket of water by his feet.

As soon as she walked toward him, he looked up, hearing her feet crunching the gravel, concern drifting across his face. His mouth began silently working and she knew he was trying to figure it out. *Hannah. Here. Why?*

"Uh, nice to see you." He stood up, water dripping from his right hand onto his leg. Hannah looked down at his ankles and saw no marks. Kiki's assumption about his legs had been on target. They were so thin and pale, they wouldn't have looked half bad coming out of a pair of saucy high heels. He followed Hannah's eyes downward and misconstrued her thoughts. "Sorry about the sloppy clothes. I'm in the middle of something here, but if you'll just let me clean up."

She followed him into a backdoor leading to a small kitchen. He gestured to a stool next to a Formica breakfast bar, and she perched there, reminding herself that she was close to an open door with people in the next yard. If he made a move she could scream and people would hear.

While he washed his hands at the sink she took stock of the place. The inside of the house was better kept than the outside, everything looking worn but cared for, with the patina of settled bachelorhood. The kitchen was homey and well stocked, with glistening pine paneling and an array of well-used pots hanging from a rack over the sink.

Charlie dried his hands then offered her coffee, which she accepted since it was already brewed. After pouring the steaming liquid into two mugs that read "Charlie's Garage," he handed her one. He stood by the sink and sipped his, holding the mug with both hands. He still reeked of pond water.

"So what can I do for you?" he asked, trying to sound friendly, although his body language was distrustful. It struck her with amusement that he probably saw her as competition, since they were both still in the mayor's race. She found it less amusing that perhaps he thought she could be Alex's killer. It was understandable. She was thinking the same thing about him. She tried the coffee. It tasted like he had made it with the pond water.

There was no roundabout way of putting it, so she just hit him with it straight on. "I found out that you own land that's part of the Signatech site."

Charlie's jaw quivered just slightly. He set his mug on the countertop. "It wasn't a secret. Everyone on the council knew. I exempted myself from that vote."

"Will you make a lot of money if the Signatech deal goes through?"

"Yeah, so what? Lots of people here make lots of money. I'll be getting mine later than most." He dumped the rest of his coffee down the sink, a good place for it by Hannah's reckoning, then dropped the mug in after it. His bitterness on the subject of money didn't surprise her. Hill Creek was divided into two groups, the Haves and the Have-Much-Mores, with members of the first group often harshly envious of the second. It was something Hannah had a hard time understanding when there were people ten miles away living in shacks and dodging crack dealers. Seemed like people would count their blessings.

"Your garage looks like a profit maker." She was trying to sell some look-on-the-bright-side optimism, but Charlie wasn't buying.

"Well, it's not. With overhead and insurance my margins are slim. These days people want to go to the dealerships for service. I don't see where it's any of your business anyway."

It's my business because you may have tried to kill me yesterday, she wanted to tell him, but didn't. "I only brought up your garage because I was just there. It was Tulley who told me you were home."

"Tulley should keep his mouth shut." Charlie stared so hard down into the sink that Hannah thought the garbage disposal was speaking to him. Finally his shoulders relaxed, and when he looked back up he seemed regretful. "I shouldn't have said that. Tulley's a great kid. I'm just on edge. Listen, I've got to be back at the garage in an hour, and I need to finish cleaning the pond. Can we talk outside?" Not waiting for an answer he headed out the backdoor, and Hannah followed, mug in hand. It was bad coffee, but it still contained caffeine.

Kneeling by the pond, he peered inside the bucket. Using a baby voice, he asked the fish if they were okay, which Hannah thought was sweet, then he picked up the net and dipped it in the water. After swishing it around a while, he stopped and looked at Hannah. "I promise you, I've had nothing to do with the decision on Signatech. Like I said, I exempted myself from that vote. So if you're planning to bring this up as a campaign issue, well, I guess I appreciate your letting me know about it, but it's not going to win you anything. It's all been aboveboard."

Hannah sipped coffee, watching Charlie over the mug's rim. He pulled a couple of fish out of the water, the shiny orange creatures twisting in the net. Perspiration clung to his forehead, one rivulet creeping down toward fretful eyes. He hurriedly put the fish into the bucket. She could almost see the thoughts writhing in his head, like those fish in their torturous moments out of the water.

"It's all been aboveboard," she said, pausing. "Except for the Fremont connection." She threw it out blindly, not knowing what nerve it would strike, if it struck at all. It turned out to be a bull's-eye. Charlie tensed, his body perfectly still, yet at the same time jittery, everything inside him in motion.

In Hannah's years as an executive secretary to a string of CEOs at a large corporation she had learned to read men, at least when it came to certain things, like when they were in trouble. Charlie was a man with a secret, the burden of it becoming too much to bear.

Hannah kneeled down next to him, feeling the grass's dampness creeping through her pants legs. "Tell me the truth, Charlie," she pleaded softly. "I know part of it anyway. I know that Alex got stock options from Signatech. Was it a bribe to make sure they got building approval?"

He waited a few teeth-grinding seconds before replying. "Yes, of course it was."

"How long have you known?"

"I suspected it for a couple of months. Alex jumped on the Signatech bandwagon a little too quickly to be believed, and he never did anything that didn't have a personal payoff. I didn't know it was stock options until you said it at the debate. But, you see, it didn't matter to me. I didn't care if he was taking bribes as long as the Signatech deal went through. I need that money, Hannah. I'm tired of fixing cars."

"It's an honest business."

"I'm sick of working on cars that cost more than my mortgage, tired of sucking up to arrogant thirty-year-olds who think they can treat me like an errand boy because they lucked into high-tech stock or inherited money from their daddies. If I sold my land I was going to turn the garage management over to Tulley and do something else."

"You said if. I thought the Signatech deal was solid."

"It was until that Temple outfit came into the picture. I was in Alex's office a couple of months ago and noticed the return address on an envelope on his desk. It was from Temple Land Development, and addressed to Alex's house, not the office. That got me curious, so I called information, telephoned the company, and asked for the man whose name was on the envelope, and pretended I was Alex. I learned enough to figure out that Alex was playing both sides. The Temple people owned a tract in Fremont that Signatech was interested in as a backup site in case the Hill Creek parcel fell through. If Temple was willing to pay a bigger bribe, then Alex would put an end to the Hill Creek location."

"Did he have that much power?"

"He had Mary in his pocket, she was so infatuated with him, and he told her which way to vote. And everyone else on the board he'd charmed, except me. It surprised me that Mary didn't see through him. She's smarter than that." His voice grew tender as he spoke of her. His eyes wandered off into the land of the lovesick, then he gave his shoulders a shake and returned to earth. "Not that she would have ever had any luck with him. He'd never give her the time of day."

It surprised Hannah that Charlie didn't know Mary and Alex had been sleeping together. She became aware that the sounds from the neighbor's yard had stopped. She and Charlie were alone.

"I knew what Alex was going to do," Charlie went on, "and

you entering the race made it easy for him. Once he had the Temple bribe confirmed, then he would have this sudden insight about saving the village atmosphere of our charming little town. And the Signatech deal for Hill Creek would be down the tubes."

"Is that why you decided to run for mayor, so if you won you could swing the deal the other way?"

He nodded. "At first I actually thought I might win. Then it became obvious that I didn't have a chance against that slick, two-faced braggart."

"Unless Alex dropped out of the race."

It struck Hannah that Charlie had a strong motive for wanting both her and Alex dead, and here she was, alone with him. Not smart. Perez had wanted to spend the day with her. She should have let him.

"I didn't kill him," he said, as if reading her mind. His tone was yielding, his eyes wounded. "But I think I know who did."

"Tell me."

He looked down at his hands, shaking his head. "I can't. I can't say anything. You see, I'm not sure."

Hannah studied him, looking for any facial tic, any gesture that would tell her he was lying. "What makes you think you know who did it?"

He stayed silent a moment while dread settled on him. "At Alex's party I confronted him with my phone call to Temple," he then said. "He was a stone wall, wouldn't admit to anything. After the party I came home and got to thinking. By that time I had a few drinks in me. I drove back to his house about an hour later."

"To do what?"

"To get in the house and go through his office, to find some proof of what the bastard was doing." Hannah wanted to tell him that she had already done that job, but couldn't risk it. "That way I'd have some leverage with him to make sure the Signatech Hill Creek deal went through," Charlie continued. "I heard him at the party say something about going for a long jog before the debate, so I waited in my car down the street. When I saw him leave I went up to the house. I knew Maggie was still there cleaning because her old Toyota was in the driveway, and I figured she'd leave the doors unlocked. My plan was to slip into his office without her seeing. She wouldn't have been cleaning in there."

"And did you?"

"I couldn't. Maggie was all over the house picking up dishes, wiping off furniture, vacuuming. She was moving from room to room, and I lost my nerve."

"You looked in the windows?"

"Yes." He stopped, drawing in a long breath. "That's when it happened."

"What?"

"I saw something. But you see, I could be wrong about it, and I won't hurt someone without being certain. I could so easily be wrong."

"If you tell me what you saw, maybe I can help you."

"You'd like that, wouldn't you? You'd love to tell everyone you solved Alex's murder. Then you'd have the election in the bag. And where would I be?"

"Okay, don't tell me. Solve Alex's murder yourself and take the credit, but you need to talk to the police, Charlie. Tell them what you know."

"If I go to the police I may cause trouble for an innocent person."

"If you don't you may let a murderer go free and somebody else might get hurt." She watched him, knowing he was struggling with the decision. His hands trembled, his lips sucked in with tension. It made her think there was more involved here than what he had told her, but it wasn't the time to press him. She had to get him to the police. "You need to go now, Charlie. It's the right thing to do. You'd never forgive yourself if somebody else got hurt. You could be in danger yourself."

The last part did the trick. His eyes darted to her. "You're right," he said shakily. "I'll go now. The fish will be okay for a couple of hours, and I really don't need to go to the garage. Tulley can handle—" He looked down in panic. Hannah looked down as well and saw a fish lying in the grass, motionless. "I dropped her. She's dead," he said, his voice quaking. He picked up the fish and reverently placed it in the bucket, but the fish floated on its side. He began weeping, burying his face in his hands.

The sight of this man crying over a goldfish made Hannah's heart ache, but she had to get him to the police station before he changed his mind. She placed a hand on his back. "I'm so sorry, Charlie. You're in no condition to drive, so I'll take you. We'll go right now. You can talk to Detective Morgan. He's a good man. Come on, let's get your hands washed."

Charlie sat stiffly in the passenger seat. He had put on a fresh shirt and topped it with the green tweed coat he had worn to Alex's party, and his hair was wetted and slicked back like a school kid's. He kept his eyes out the window and was mostly silent. When he did speak, the conversation centered on the dead fish. Her name was Suzy Q. Hannah wondered how you assigned gender to a fish, but Charlie seemed certain that Suzy was all-woman, and she wondered if there was anything kinky a lonely man could do with a fish. He was more eccentric than she had ever suspected. It made her ponder what other oddities Hill Creek residents secreted behind closed doors. She had a hundred questions to ask him, all concerning what he knew about Alex's murder and not about fish, but in his current emotional state, she thought he might go completely off his rocker. The important thing was to get him to the station. Then maybe her involvement could be over. Murder solved, everybody happy.

She pulled the Cadillac into the parking lot. A van blocked the drive in front so she let him out near the lot entrance. "You want me to wait for you?"

"No. I'll call a cab when I'm done." He stared at the police station like it was a concentration camp.

"You've got to do it," Hannah said, her voice softly urging.

He twisted in the seat toward her. "I know you've had a hard life in some ways. You were sick for a while."

"I had cancer."

"You must have been so afraid. How did you handle it? Not knowing if you would live or die, dealing with the uncertainty? The chemotherapy and all that?"

"By taking things hour by hour, by fighting off self-pity. Some shit just happens, Charlie. Cells mutate, friends disappoint you, life doesn't turn out the way you want. You can't take it personally. You just do what's right and stop analyzing."

His hands lay in his lap palms up. He gazed at the police station a second, and then back at Hannah. "Thanks for making me come here. I wouldn't have done it, otherwise. I said earlier that I didn't want to talk to the police because I didn't want to cause trouble for someone who could be innocent, but that's not the whole truth. It was myself I was protecting."

"How, Charlie?"

"By talking to the police I'll end up telling everything I know, and it will get out that I knew Alex was taking bribes and didn't say anything. Well, I'll never be mayor, and the Signatech deal will go south and I'll be stuck in that garage forever."

"Talking to the police is the right thing, Charlie. You have to do the right thing."

He got out of the car and crossed the parking lot toward the station's front door. About ten yards in front of it, he halted, but then resumed walking. Feeling sad for him, Hannah figured his thoughts were full of death—dead fish, dead mayors, and one really dead dream.

EIGHTEEN

THAT EVENING HANNAH FORCED HER mind from murder and took off for the county hospital's breast cancer support group, which she now led every other week. The group was small, its participants always changing, usually about five women who had recently learned of their cancer. Hannah didn't try to hand out medical information. The group's purpose was to let these women know they weren't alone and to provide emotional support in the early stages of treatment. Hannah did her best to educate and encourage, helping them to accept the fear and start working through it, to understand that they could survive the ordeal and emerge stronger. She was walking proof.

It was after nine when the group broke up, and Hannah stayed late to talk one-on-one with a woman in her early forties who had just been diagnosed. By the time Hannah left she felt mentally and emotionally drained, not just from the group, but from everything that had happened over the past week. She needed time alone, right then needed it as much as food and air, so she just drove for awhile, the convertible top up and the windows down, with the wind whipping through the car. There was a swarm of cars on the road, making her wonder where everybody was going that late at night. Maybe, like her, they were going nowhere, just driving around all alone in their metal cells on wheels, trying to figure out why sometimes they felt so isolated. Welcome to California.

She tuned the radio to her favorite talk station and heard a caller prattling about aliens, how the government should spend more money trying to contact alien beings this guy felt sure were out there. Hannah chuckled, not understanding why anyone would waste time on finding life on other planets when humans themselves remained such a mystery to each other. And if you were so desperate to communicate with another species, try convincing a dog and pig not to make the occasional Tootsie Roll in your house.

She was tired to the bone, but thoughts about Charlie still played pinball in her head. He hadn't phoned. During the group break she had called Kiki to check, and there had been no messages. It wasn't as if he had promised to call. Still, she thought he would have, just to say how things had gone. She rationalized that maybe he was too upset to talk about it. Maybe he didn't want her to know what had happened. Maybe he blamed her for what happened to his goldfish.

It was now ten-thirty and she didn't want Kiki worrying, so she headed home, pulled the Cadillac into the garage, closed the heavy metal door, and went into the house through the back. As Sylvia and Teresa greeted her with joyful nuzzles, she heard soft music and voices drifting from the living room. The sound of Johnny Mathis put Hannah's Kiki-radar on full alert. Kiki played that music when there was a man in the house. Hannah put down her coat and purse on the kitchen table and went to investigate.

When Hannah walked in, Detective Morgan, sitting on the couch with Lauren, chirped hello, looking very relieved to see her. She knew why. The room had been transformed into a Kiki-Special, take-no-prisoners love zone. Scented candles flickered in every corner, pink handkerchiefs had been thrown over the lamps, giving the room a rosy glow, and Kiki's set of Erotic Scrabble was laid out on the coffee table with a few tawdry words arranged on the board, a couple of them misspelled.

Kiki leaned against the ancient oak chest, two fingers grasping a champagne glass filled with something frothy and dangerous, her pinkie outstretched and her body moving to the music with the drowsy sway of a sedated reptile. Her other hand swished the folds of the purple caftan that Naomi had given her for her last birthday. Kiki let out a gurgling hello when she saw her sister. Hannah observed the half-empty pitcher on the coffee table, recognizing the reddish brew as Kiki's strawberry margaritas, a recipe she called Love-ade. Eau de Madness floated in the air thick as fog. It was going to take a SWAT team to get Morgan out of this one.

"I asked him to stop by on his way home because I was feeling so incredibly anxious," Kiki said, sounding as cool and smooth as the cocktail in her hand. "Wasn't it sweet of him to come? We're having such fun!" Kiki gulped some red liquid and snapped her fingers to the music, even though the song was a slow one.

Things didn't look that fun to Hannah. There was an eerie subterranean buzz in the room, as if some basic universal law had been violated, a cosmic karma shoved out of whack. Hannah half-expected to see a two-headed cow dressed in a tutu playing checkers in the corner. Then she got a good look at Lauren, who was sitting in the shadows at the far end of the couch, and she realized the situation was weirder than that.

Lauren was swathed in the fashion catastrophe that Kiki had snapped up at the rummage sale—orange sequined tube top, tight orange plastic skirt the size of a Kleenex, and red spike heels with ankle straps. The whole thing had cost less than ten bucks, and it was apparent that Kiki had overpaid. To complete the effect, Lauren's makeup had been slathered on with a plaster trowel, her eyes topped with false eyelashes that looked like miniature roadkill. She wore a typical coiffure à la Kiki, her brown hair piled onto the top of her head then teased and sprayed so that it shot upward. Ordinarily Lauren wouldn't have been caught dead in a ditch looking like that. It showed the depth of her desperation that she had fallen to the gutter level of a Kiki Beauty Blitz.

Lauren sat on the couch as far from Morgan as possible, hands between her knees, feet together, her dress and comportment that of a contrite hooker hoping to pass the convent entrance interview. Now Hannah knew why Morgan had been so relieved to see her. Instead of attracting Morgan, Lauren's outfit was having the opposite effect. On another woman the tawdry outfit might have been alluring in a one-night-stand-boy-am-I-a-slut sort of way, but on Lauren's thin, childlike form the clothes didn't inspire lust. More of an urge to call social services. Poor Detective Morgan wore a hunted look, and he clung to the edge of the couch, his eyes occasionally darting to the door, or in his mind, escape hatch. Hannah didn't blame him. The only hope for him now was to fall to his knees and pledge himself to the priesthood.

Hannah walked farther into the room and Morgan stood up. "It's so great to see you, Mrs. Malloy," he said in a voice lacking his usual professional tone.

"It took some convincing but we managed to talk him into a little drinkie," Kiki said, her lips curling up.

"I'm off duty," Morgan added, probably more to explain why he wasn't arresting Kiki and Lauren for solicitation. "We still have a patrol car coming by your house every half hour, but I thought I should check up personally, and make sure you're all right."

Kiki edged over to Hannah. "Could you help me in the kitchen for a minute?"

Realizing he was to be left alone with Lauren, Morgan inhaled sharply, obviously yearning for the relative safety of handling armed criminals. Hannah gave him a sympathetic nod, then followed her sister. Just before they left the living room, Kiki pivoted, wiggled her fingers at Morgan, then quickly pulled Hannah through the dining room and into the kitchen, the only room besides the bedrooms and bathrooms that had a door. When they were safely inside, she shut it behind them.

"What's going on out there?" Hannah asked.

"You told me not to stay here alone, so I invited Lauren over, and then Detective Morgan called to check on us, so I asked him to drop by. As long as he and Lauren were both going to be in our living room, I thought we should take advantage of it, and, you know, grease the love skids a little."

"A little? Why didn't you drench them in Wesson oil and ask them to wrestle?"

"I just don't understand it," Kiki said, ignoring the remark, going over to the cabinet next to the stove and rummaging through its contents. "I've got Morgan liquored up, and Lauren's looking so good, and yet nothing's happening. I'm thinking we need some finger food. I know I've got some Ding Dongs in here somewhere."

"Morgan's scared to death of Lauren in that outfit."

"Oh, piddle," Kiki said, tossing out a few bags of pasta as she continued her search. "Everyone knows that policemen like their women raunchy."

"She looks like she needs penicillin. And you shouldn't be pouring drinks down Morgan."

"He's only had one drink, but I think he's drunk. He can't hold his liquor."

"One of your margaritas would knock a cow to its knees."

Finding no Ding Dongs, Kiki tossed the pasta back in the

cabinet and closed it. She leaned against the counter, her arms crossed. "He looked so tired and stressed when he came in, I think he needed a toddy for the body. But what can we do to get the love fires burning?"

"It might help if you left them alone."

"I tried that, but when I eavesdropped, all they were doing was making silly small talk, and Morgan kept saying how he needed to go home. I'm completely stumped. I thought Lauren's outfit would bring out the animal in him."

"It did, only the animal is a catatonic gerbil." Hannah grabbed a glass from the dish drainer and filled it with water from the tap. "Did Charlie call?"

Kiki paused before answering, sizing up Hannah. "No. Why are you so interested in Charlie all of a sudden?"

The kitchen door opened. Lauren hurried in, closing the door behind her. She threw her arms around Hannah. "He wants to leave!" she said in a furious whisper. "What am I doing wrong?" Putting down her glass, Hannah gave her niece a few consoling pats.

Kiki shook her head and tut-tutted at her protégé's ineptitude. "Honey, did you shimmy your shoulders like I taught you?" she asked. Lauren nodded. "And you put your hand on his leg and called him baby?"

Hannah closed her eyes and mouthed an "ugh."

Lauren started sniffling and Hannah increased her patting tempo. "Stop trying to be something you're not, Lauren. Your Aunt Kiki meant well, sort of, but this fashion statement just isn't you." She pushed Lauren to arm's length. "It isn't anyone outside of certain parts of Tijuana."

"So what do I do?" Lauren asked.

"Go out there and tell him that the accountant's society is putting on *Irma La Douce* and that you're trying out for a part. Tell him you were testing the outfit."

Lauren's eyes brimmed with hope. "You think it will help?"

"You have no place to go but up."

Lauren headed unsteadily out the kitchen door. Hannah got the phone book off the counter and looked up Charlie's number and dialed. No one answered.

"You're calling Charlie, aren't you?" Kiki asked with mounting suspicion. "Why are you so darn interested in him?"

"I can't tell you, not yet. Come on, I've got to talk to Morgan."

"I thought you said Lauren and Morgan needed to be alone."

"Love will have to blossom later. As long as you've got him tipsy, I might as well take advantage of it."

They returned to the living room. Morgan appeared more relaxed and had moved to the center of the couch closer to Lauren.

"I didn't know Lauren was interested in acting," he said to Hannah, his words a little slurred.

Hannah sat in a chair directly across from him. "Yes, Lauren has a wide range of interests." Actually, Lauren's interests included only accounting, cooking, and Detective Morgan. Getting a closer look at him, Hannah saw the fatigue in his face, and felt affectionate sympathy. With a murder investigation, he had to be working long hours.

"How did things go with Charlie Wright today?" she asked him.

"What do you mean?"

"He came to see you this afternoon."

"No, he didn't. Was he supposed to?"

"That's what he told me. He'll probably call you tomorrow."

Hannah shifted in her chair, unable to understand why Morgan didn't know about Charlie's visit. Maybe Charlie had spoken with someone else, but surely Morgan would have heard about it. She decided to drop the subject until she spoke to Charlie and found out what had happened, but she wasn't about to let Charlie squirm out of talking to the police. If he had gotten cold feet, then she would go to the police and do the talking for him.

Morgan sipped his margarita and gave Lauren a lingering look that told Hannah the man might really care for her niece. Lauren blushed. Hannah hated to interrupt the moment, but there was a murderer running loose.

"Is there anything new in the investigation?" Hannah asked.

Morgan unglued his eyes from Irma La Douce. "I can't talk about that, Mrs. Malloy. I know you and Mrs. Goldstein are concerned about your safety. Understandably so."

"Whoever did it may try again," Lauren said, with new animation. She stood up and walked over to Hannah, putting a tender hand on her aunt's shoulder. "You've got to protect them."

He gave Lauren another puppy dog gaze. "I won't let any-thing happen." His smile came out lopsided. It surprised Hannah that he was such an easy drunk. She thought all young men learned to handle their liquor in college. But then, young women were supposed to learn to handle men in college, and Lauren sure hadn't. "The problem is, we just don't have that much to go on yet. Mrs. Goldstein told me tonight about seeing some-body's leg through the wallboards."

"You haven't turned up any evidence at the shed?" Hannah asked.

Morgan shook his head. "No fingerprints on the gas can and none of the neighbors saw anything. But don't worry. We'll catch whoever did it."

Lauren smiled with pride, but Hannah didn't share her con-fidence.

"What about evidence in Alex's murder?" Hannah asked. "We have a right to know. The two crimes are connected. They have to be."

Morgan was quiet, and Hannah knew he was deliberating on how much to say. He took another sip of Love-ade and the booze worked in her favor.

"I'll tell you this much. We have a suspect and we're keeping a close eye on them, so you don't have to worry."

"You mean Ox," Hannah said. "Lorna Donatello's boy-friend."

"Oh, yeah, well he's a suspect, too, and so is she." Morgan took another sip. Love-ade grew tastier the more you drank. That was the beauty part. "But we've got a new one."

"Who is it?" Hannah asked, trying hard not to sound over-eager when she was about to fall out of her chair. In sync, Kiki hurried over with the pitcher and refilled Morgan's glass.

"Yes, tell us who it is," Kiki said, hovering over him. "We'll feel so much safer if we know." She winked at Hannah.

"I'm sorry, but I've said all I can. Well, I guess it's time for me to be getting home. I've been putting in sixteen-hour days." Pressing his hands against his knees, Morgan stood, but Kiki quickly slammed down the pitcher on the coffee table and pushed him back into the couch.

"Not yet, honey. You just got here," Kiki said with the staunchness of a drill sergeant. "What you need is a little relax-ation. How about a shoulder massage?"

"No, thank you," he said. "I really need to get home."

When it came to getting her mitts on a man, Kiki Goldstein seldom took no for an answer. He tried again to rise, but she shoved him down and grabbed hold of him. After twisting his shoulders so he faced away from her, she pressed the heels of her hands into his shoulder blades and began massaging. "How does that feel?"

He opened his mouth to protest, but feeling the soothing pressure, only a small groan of pleasure came out. "Feels good," he said, his eyes closing.

Kiki continued kneading, leaning into it to increase the intensity. "Just relax. There you go, big fella." Morgan's head fell forward, and Kiki grinned at Hannah and Lauren. "Now surely you can tell us who that new suspect is. We won't breathe a word." Kiki kept up the massage. Hannah and Lauren watched expectantly, but Morgan didn't speak. At first Hannah assumed he was thinking it over, then she realized what had happened.

"He's asleep," Hannah said.

Kiki stooped in front of him. "Detective Morgan. Oh, Larry." She snapped her fingers by his ear. His head jerked back with a start. After mumbling something unintelligible, his head fell forward again.

Lauren kneeled down near his face. "The poor thing. He's dead to the world."

"I'll put some ice down his undies," Kiki offered. "That'll wake him up."

"Leave him alone," Hannah said. "He's exhausted."

"Poor baby," Lauren cooed.

"Poor baby, nothing. This is no time for him to be snoozing," Kiki hissed. "We've got to get the name of that new suspect."

"We won't find out tonight," Hannah told her. "Look at him." He fell back onto the couch, his head rolling to one side.

"I don't think he can drive home," Lauren said.

"He'll have to stay right where he is," Hannah said. "Let's stretch him out."

Hannah pressed his shoulders down onto the cushion and placed another pillow under his head while Lauren lifted his legs onto the couch. Lauren then lovingly took off his shoes.

"He has a little bit of spittle in the corner of his mouth," Lauren said wistfully. "Isn't that adorable?"

It must be true love, Hannah thought, *if Lauren was captivated by the man's drool*. But just then Hannah was much more interested in what was inside the man's head than on the outside. She wanted to know the name of the new suspect, since whoever it was could be the sisters' would-be murderer. But a question looming bigger for her was this: what on earth had happened to Charlie?

NINETEEN

❧

WRAPPED IN HER PINK CHENILLE bathrobe, with bunny slippers on her feet and lavender hair curlers piled on her head, Kiki poked a lump of bran muffin in her mouth, chewed a second, then made a face. She pulled off another piece, slathering this one with jam, and gobbled it with satisfaction.

Hannah insisted on making muffins out of bran and sunflower seeds, ingredients Kiki felt were more suitable as kitty litter than breakfast food, but one of Kiki's life philosophies was that anything could be made palatable if you just put enough jam on it. To test the theory she had once covered parts of herself with marmalade after a cozy homemade dinner for two with Alfred Jenkins, who owned the pharmacy on Barclay Road. When she walked in the dining room, Alfred took one look at her, claimed he was diabetic, and exited so fast he tripped on the porch steps, fell flat in the flower bed, and spent a half hour searching for his dentures. There was no figuring men.

Kiki sat opposite Hannah at the old wooden table where they ate breakfast most mornings. The small kitchen was the most pleasant room in the house, with cornflower blue walls and windows facing the garden. The last of the spring rain splashed against the windows, and Sylvia and Teresa lay contentedly under the table, certain they would eventually get bites of something tasty.

Kiki swallowed another lump of jam-covered muffin. "Too bad Detective Morgan ran off so early. I went out there to massage his feet, but he was already gone."

"He left before we were up," Hannah replied, hidden by the *New York Times*. "A foot massage wouldn't have gotten the new suspect's name from him anyway. If he didn't tell us when he was drunk, he wouldn't tell us sober."

"A lot of good things might have happened last night if he hadn't fallen asleep so early. Lauren's outfit would have completely won him over if we had given him more time." Kiki dropped two pieces of bran muffin by her foot for the dog and pig.

"Or given him a shot of morphine and some Spanish fly." Hannah gave the newspaper an irritated snap. Two glasses of orange juice, the newspaper, and a plate of muffins weren't the only thing standing between the sisters that morning. Hannah woke up testy. As soon as she had rolled out of bed she decided for certain that Charlie had changed his mind about talking to the police, scampering away like a frightened squirrel, and Hannah blamed herself. How could she have been foolish enough to trust him? He was so skittish in the car, she should have known he would back out. She should have personally walked him into the station, dragging him by the hand like a naughty schoolboy.

Hannah rose from the table and carried her plate to the sink, greeting the two spiders lolling around the faucet base. The spiders had made the sink their home for a week now, and Hannah had grown to like them, naming them Fred and Ethel. She rinsed the dish then dribbled a little water near them for when they got thirsty. "You shouldn't meddle in people's lives," she told her sister.

Kiki faked a laugh. "Like you don't stick your nose everywhere it doesn't belong. It was you running around asking questions about Alex's murder that almost got us roasted."

Hannah sat back down at the table. "I've already apologized for that."

Kiki saw her sister's hurt expression. "I know, honey. It's not like you can help yourself. It's like me with men. Men just make my motor run. You're that way when it comes to other people's troubles, so I'm not blaming you for the fact that some crazed person wants to kill us. I'm not so worried about it since we have the police driving by the house. But I think we need some additional protection. I was thinking about a big gun."

"You know I won't allow that. You'd shoot somebody. By accident, of course."

"I knew you'd say that. That's why I had Lauren bring these over last night." Kiki went to the kitchen drawer and pulled out two meat tenderizers. They had wooden handles and metal heads similar to a hammer, except the heads were covered with sharp points designed to beat the most intractable chicken breast into submission. She carried them to the table and gave one to Hannah. "Keep it in your purse during the day and by your bed at night. They're better than billy clubs. You hit somebody in the head with this baby and—"

"Turn them into Swiss steak?"

"I'm serious here. Lauren says she accidentally hit the dishwasher repairman with one, and he talked gibberish for a good ten minutes. You're not listening to me, are you? You're lost in space, and here I am talking about something important like personal protection. What's in that head of yours?"

"Charlie. I called him again before I put the muffins in the oven, and he didn't answer."

"So, he's not at home."

"Oh, he's home all right. The spineless weasel's avoiding me."

"Why?"

"I don't feel right about discussing it, not yet. Charlie wouldn't want me to. But I'll fill you in as soon as I can."

"I want to know now. You know I don't tell secrets."

"You spew them like a fire hose."

Using the meat tenderizer, Kiki gave the table a small yet definitive rap, geared to defend her honor, but a banging at the backdoor preempted the debate. The sisters exchanged a surprised look, neither imagining who would call so early at their back door. Only Naomi took that liberty, and she always flew in without knocking.

There was more banging, and since Hannah was closest, she answered it. She found Althea on the porch step, standing in the rain with no umbrella, completely drenched, her wet shirt and shorts clinging to her skin, her hiking boots dripping.

"I've been accused," Althea said, barely able to speak, she was so upset. Water ran down her soaked gray hair and onto her cheeks.

"Of what?"

"Murder."

Hannah hustled her inside, got a clean dishtowel from the drawer by the sink and thrust it at her. "Dry yourself off, then tell me everything. Don't leave out a syllable."

"I'll make her some tea," Kiki said, thinking it couldn't hurt to warm up Althea's vocal chords. She started to get up but Althea waved her back down with the towel.

"Don't need tea," Althea said, choked. "Can't drink."

"Then at least sit," Hannah suggested.

Althea shook her head, sending out a spray. "Can't sit."

"Take a deep breath and get a hold of yourself, and then tell us what happened, please," Hannah said. Sylvia and Teresa trotted up to the guest to say hello, and Teresa licked the water off Althea's thick calves.

Pressing her hand against her diaphragm, Althea breathed in deeply, letting it out in staccato puffs. "The police questioned me yesterday afternoon," she said, twisting the towel in her hand while water puddled at her feet. "They think I killed Alex! I went to your backdoor because I think the police are following me."

Kiki's eyes narrowed into slits. She slowly rose from her chair, meat tenderizer in hand, then stealthily sidestepped to the counter. While a moaning Althea buried her face in the towel, Kiki held the weapon close to her side, ready for a surprise attack if Althea, although currently pitiful, suddenly turned bloodthirsty.

"Have something hot to drink. You'll catch cold," Hannah said. Now standing behind Althea, Kiki raised the meat tenderizer over the woman's head. In that ominous position, along with her hair rollers and bathrobe, Kiki looked like something out of a low-budget horror movie. After getting Kiki's attention, Hannah arched an eyebrow. Althea may have won Detective Morgan's vote as Most Likely to Kill, but Hannah considered the honor still up for grabs. She was determined to question Althea while she had the chance, and she could hardly do it if Althea was unconscious. Though, sharing her sister's concerns, Hannah hoped the police officer patrolling their house knew Althea's whereabouts.

"This is so awful," Althea groaned, holding the towel tightly between her hands, like she was about to strangle somebody with it. Hannah sidled a little closer to her own meat tenderizer, still on the table. "How could they think I could do such a thing?" Althea rolled her eyes upward and posed the question to the universe. "I'm an environmentalist."

And you reduced noxious gases by eliminating Alex Portman, Hannah thought but didn't say. "Why do they suspect you?" Hannah asked, retrieving the towel and rubbing it over Althea's wet arms. Although Althea may have been a homicidal maniac,

Hannah couldn't stand to see anyone catch cold.

"Personally, I think it's all politically motivated." Althea's voice vibrated as Hannah vigorously rubbed her wet head. "The town bigwigs want Signatech moving in, so they've set the police after me. I'll call the American Civil Liberties Union, that's what I'll do."

"Your shoes and socks are soaked," Kiki said, contemplating Althea's ankles. "Maybe you should take them off." She gave Hannah a look chock-full of unspoken communication.

"That's sweet of you to worry about me," Althea replied. "But I'll leave them on."

Frowning, Kiki plopped back down at the table. Hannah finished toweling Althea's hair, then studied the woman's baggy shorts covered with pockets of various sizes, and wondered if they held a knife or gun. In an inspired move, Hannah rubbed the towel against Althea's shorts pocket. She didn't feel anything. She rubbed the other side.

"Uh, thanks, Hannah, I'm dry enough now. I think I will sit for a minute," Althea said, puzzled, then collapsed into a chair at the table, letting loose a world-weary sigh.

Hannah put the wet towel on the counter. "Althea, are you sure there isn't anything you did that caused the police to be suspicious?"

Althea shifted left then right in her seat, concentrating on picking at some invisible lint on her shorts. "Well, you see, it's a little thing really."

Clutching the meat tenderizer, Kiki slid off her chair and very slowly dropped onto her hands and knees. Hannah gave her a "What are you doing?" glare that Kiki ignored.

Lost in her own misery, Althea didn't notice Kiki crawling on the floor as she told her story to Hannah. "It has to do with Alex's party. Someone said they saw me sneak into the kitchen while everyone was at lunch."

"But you were handcuffed to the tree," Hannah said.

Startled, Althea looked downward. "Kiki, what are you doing to my socks?"

"My, uh, contact lens. It shot off my eye," Kiki said. She pulled Althea's sock away from her ankle and peered down at Althea's skin. "Strangest thing. I thought it might have gone down here."

"And why are you holding a meat tenderizer?" Althea asked.

"Because, um, when I find the contact I'm going to smash it. It'll be so full of germs. Now let me check the other one. Hmm, not there." Disappointed, Kiki stood up, stepped behind Althea and mouthed "no marks" to Hannah.

"Where were we?" Althea asked with confusion.

"You were saying that you went into Alex's kitchen," Hannah said. "And I reminded you that you were handcuffed to the tree."

"Oh, yes, well, I unlocked the cuffs because they were starting to chafe. You know I've got skin like a baby, and I thought Maggie might have some hand cream."

"And did you ask her?"

"She was busy serving lunch and I decided not to bother her."

"You said earlier someone saw you sneak into the kitchen," Hannah said. "What's that about?"

"Could I have some water?" Althea asked sweetly.

Hannah knew she was stalling. "The glasses are in the cupboard to the right of the sink."

Althea went over to the cabinet, took out a glass, and filled it from the tap, wrinkling her nose when she saw the spiders.

"So why did you sneak into the kitchen?" Hannah asked, pressing her.

Althea gulped down some water. "It was all totally innocent. I was hungry, so I tiptoed into the kitchen. I didn't want anyone to see me."

"Why?" Hannah asked.

"Because I didn't want to be seen eating Alex's food."

"But people had already seen you eating his appetizers in the front yard," Hannah reminded her. "Maggie took food out to you, and I heard her say that Charlie had brought food to you as well."

For a second Althea looked highly miffed, then, bracing herself against the kitchen counter with one hand, she pressed the other against her forehead. "Okay, beat it out of me, if you must." Althea went on, unaware of Kiki standing behind her, tapping the meat tenderizer against one hand. "Maggie made those little meatball appetizers and I wanted some. There. Happy?"

Hannah tilted her head. "Sorry, I'm not getting you."

"My sister's slow sometimes," Kiki said to Althea, then turned her attention to Hannah. "Althea's a vegetarian, or supposed to be. She didn't want anyone to see her eating red meat."

"I'm so ashamed," Althea wailed. "I knew eating those meatballs was wrong, wrong, so horribly wrong. But they were seasoned with oregano and something wonderfully spicy, and simmered in a cream sauce." She lowered her hands and gazed plaintively toward the window, her tongue brushing over her lips as she relived the memory. "I think Maggie put in brandy and maybe just a pinch of nutmeg. I thought I could have one meatball and that would be the end of it. But I was weak. Still, should I be punished for simple human frailty? I don't know why the police are so against me. I have no motive to want Alex dead!"

"You were pretty emphatic about saving the Yellow-bellied cricket," Hannah said.

"I'm not going to jail for a goddamn cricket! It's an insect, for chrissakes, a stupid bug!" Althea looked wildly at the countertop until she spotted the spiders, then, leaping to the table, grabbed the second meat tenderizer and brutally squashed the spiders with two ear-splitting whacks. The execution completed, she turned to a shocked Hannah. "A dead bug is good bug, that's my policy. Now, tell me what I should do, I'm begging you. Tell me what I need to say to make the police understand that I didn't kill Alex."

Her hand to her mouth in disgust, Hannah walked to the sink and, with a small gasp, saw the two brownish splats that had once been Fred and Ethel. At least their end had been quick. She squinted at Althea, for the first time truly believing she could have killed Alex. The woman was a lunatic. Kiki crossed her arms, wearing a smug disdain that announced she had known it all along.

Althea went back to the breakfast table, dropping into a chair. "So what's your advice, Hannah? You know about these things."

"First, hand over the meat tenderizer nice and slow," Hannah demanded. Althea sheepishly obeyed, and Hannah put it in the sink safely out of Althea's reach, then wiped up Fred and Ethel with an extra-strength Bounty, muttering an inaudible but heartfelt "rest in peace" before tossing them in the trash.

"I have no idea what to do in this situation," Hannah told her. "Why would you suggest I did?"

"Oh, Hannah, everybody in town knows you start snooping

whenever there's any trouble, and you've helped the police in the past. Now will you help me or not? I'm thinking about making a run for it. I'd head for Mexico but the water wreaks havoc on my bowels."

"How about Canada?" Kiki suggested. "Nobody would find you there."

Althea touched her nose. "My sinuses shrivel up like prunes in cold weather."

"You have to stay right here, Althea, and face this problem head on," Hannah advised. "Tell the police everything you know. If you're innocent, you'll have no problem."

"If I'm innocent?" Althea said with indignation. "You think I'm guilty, don't you? You think I killed him."

"I didn't say that," Hannah replied.

"Well, I'm saying it," Kiki said tartly. "Look, Hannah, at the back of her left leg. I didn't notice it before, but I see it now. She's scratched!"

Althea looked down at the numerous red scratches on her calf, then back at Kiki, perplexed. "I was at the Signatech site the other day trying to catch some Yellow-bellies. I'm experimenting with re-homing them, to see if it can really be done. It was sheer hell trying to catch the little buggers, and I got scratched in the weeds."

Hannah stooped down and examined Althea's leg. There were several deep red scratches, and they looked fresh. She straightened. "Where were you Tuesday at dusk?"

Althea drew herself up. "I don't like your tone of voice, Hannah Malloy. What exactly are you suggesting?"

"I'll tell you what she's suggesting," Kiki said, pacing slowly in front of Althea. "Somebody tried to kill Hannah and me, and I know it was you." On the last part she pointed the meat tenderizer directly in Althea's face.

"How dare you!" Althea shouted with self-righteous fury. "I have never been so insulted in all my life. Slander is a crime."

"It's not slander if it's true," Kiki told her. Red faced, Althea jumped out of her chair, giving Kiki a threatening sneer. Kiki waved the meat tenderizer at her. "Not one step closer, missy, or you'll get the business end of this."

Althea lunged toward the sink and grabbed the other tenderizer. Assuming a fencer's sideways stance, she faced Kiki, holding the kitchen implement as if it were a saber. Kiki yelped and backed up against the wall while Hannah grabbed the weapon from Althea. Teresa yapped excitedly. Sylvia quickly waddled under the table.

"Be careful whom you threaten, ladies," Althea said, her breath coming in heaves. "If you go around making accusations you'll hear from my lawyer." Althea stormed out of the room, Hannah following. Althea marched out the front door and down the walkway, occasionally halting to stomp her foot against the pavement.

"You leave those bugs alone!" Hannah shouted from the doorway. "They're innocent bystanders!"

Althea scoffed then stomped on an unsuspecting centipede that, perhaps like Althea, had the rotten luck of being in the wrong place at the wrong time.

A few hours later Hannah strode down tree-lined Walnut Avenue toward home, a reusable, earth-friendly canvas bag of groceries in her arms, filled with fruit, cheese, wholemeal bread, and orange juice. Canvas shopping bags were the latest Hill Creek enforcement of socially sensitive eco-chic. Normally Hannah avoided outward displays of "PC." In her opinion, political correctness had become a type of social fascism, with a narrow-mindedness as rigid as that of any right-winger. Still, she disapproved of all plastic and paper bags and tried not to use them.

It was late morning and the fog had lifted, leaving a shimmering sky, the air scented with freshly mown grass and rosemary. Hannah shifted the groceries from her right arm to the left. The few blocks from town felt like twenty when carrying such a load, but with the past week's events, she had forgotten about groceries. Now there wasn't much to eat in the house except for the earthquake supplies and Kiki's supposedly secret stash of Ding Dongs. Hannah could have driven but decided that walking to the store would give her time to organize her thoughts regarding Alex's murder.

Althea's emergence as a prime suspect was tantalizing, and that silly meatball alibi, although original, was hardly believable. Charlie claimed to have seen something at Alex's house after the party, something that identified the murderer. Perhaps it had been Althea.

Jack Ulrich, a neighbor, jogged her way, and Hannah smiled

and greeted him, returning to her grim thoughts as soon as he had passed. She ran more of the Althea scenario through her head. Althea admitted that she had gone into the kitchen while everyone was having lunch, but she could have lied about the timing, hoping to make it sound more innocent. What if she had gone into the kitchen after the party, and Charlie had seen her? He could have been the one who tipped off the police about her the day before. The timing was right. But if Charlie had told the police, why didn't Detective Morgan know about it? Maybe Charlie had gotten cold feet about showing up in person and had called in the information anonymously. If so, Hannah planned to talk to Charlie and confirm it.

Earlier that morning, just after Althea left, Hannah had called the police station and left Morgan a voicemail about Althea's scratched legs. The next step was Charlie.

Hannah entered the house through the front door, sat the groceries on the kitchen table, and said hello to Kiki and Naomi, both women standing by the sink, sipping from dainty flowered teacups. As Hannah put the cheese and orange juice in the fridge, she noticed Kiki pulling worriedly at the strand of beads around her neck. Both she and Naomi stared at Hannah with the strangest expressions.

"Do I have raspberry in my teeth? I bought one of those little pastries at the bakery and ate it on the way home," Hannah said. She folded the shopping bag and put it in the cabinet over the stove. Kiki and Naomi responded to her question with only rapid sips from their teacups. Hannah tried a simpler question. "Did Charlie call?" Still no reply, not verbal, anyway. Naomi turned toward the window, while Kiki began chewing her knuckle and whimpering. Walking up to them, Hannah sniffed the air. "There's sherry in those cups. It's not even noon."

"We're drinking strictly for medicinal purposes," Naomi said.

"What's wrong?" Hannah asked.

"When I said you had to do whatever it took to win the mayor's race," Kiki said, her voice frail, "you know I didn't mean that literally." She burst into tears.

Naomi bit her lip, pressing her hand to her cheek. "We must consult Red Moon on this," she said. "Yes, he can help us. I'm sure of it."

"Oh, he can't do anything," Kiki said, the statement followed by a sob. She pulled the bottle of sherry from the breadbasket where she had stashed it as soon as she had heard Hannah coming, and filled her teacup to the brim.

"Then perhaps a cleansing. That's what we need," Naomi said, her voice getting shrill. "Maybe if I did the dance of the blessed falcon."

"You better do the dance of the kick-ass, high-priced lawyer," Kiki blubbered. She chugged the contents of her teacup. "It's all over now but the crying."

"Will the two of you tell me what's going on here?" Hannah demanded.

The sherry bottle in hand, a weeping Kiki led Hannah out the backdoor to the garage, with Naomi following. The garage door was open, the Cadillac parked inside where Hannah had left it the night before. An old wooden nightstand Hannah recognized from Naomi's bedroom stood a few feet away.

Hannah turned to Kiki. "Did you dent the fender again? Is that what this is all about?"

"Show her," Naomi said to Kiki.

Kiki heaved a shuddering breath. "You see, Hannah, the rummage sale took in so much money that Naomi and I decided to take her old nightstand to that antique shop on Bullard Avenue and see what she could get for it. We thought it could bring in enough to pay for new brake pads for the Volvo. But the trunk in the Volvo isn't that big, so we carried it over here because I thought for sure it would fit in the Cadillac's trunk."

"But it didn't," Naomi said, over-enunciating each word.

"Ridiculous," Hannah said. "There's plenty of room."

Naomi shook her head. "Don't think so."

"You just have to put it in sideways," Hannah explained, then pressed the trunk button. It popped open. "Let's carry—" The words froze in her throat when she saw the horrified grimaces on the women's faces. Hannah looked at the open trunk and cried out. Charlie Wright lay on his side, his knees pulled up, his hands beneath his chin in a praying gesture. There was an ugly brownish gash at the back of his head. Hannah felt like a cord had been twisted around her gut and pulled tight.

"Oh, Hannah," Kiki cried, clutching Hannah's arm. "He's dead."

"Are you sure?" Hannah asked, barely able to get out the question. "You shouldn't have closed the trunk on him. Why did you?" Her voice became high-pitched with rising panic. "We've got to call an ambulance."

"Forget it," Kiki said, choking back tears. "I slapped him a couple of times, then Naomi took his pulse. He's dead, dead, dead." She gulped from the sherry bottle.

"Not dead, dear," Naomi said. "But his physical vessel is most definitely kaput."

Hannah pressed her fingers against Charlie's neck. He felt stone cold.

"It wasn't worth it," Kiki said to Hannah, waving the bottle at her. "It's just a stupid mayor's job. It's not worth committing murder."

"I didn't murder him," Hannah said. Dread bolted through her, her legs were rubbery.

"Of course, she didn't," Naomi scolded Kiki. "Have some faith in your own sister. It was obviously manslaughter. He probably attacked you, Hannah, right? Of course, he did. It was self-defense, plain and simple."

"But she stuffed him in the trunk," Kiki whined. "That's going to look bad."

Naomi grabbed the bottle from Kiki and took a slug. "She was, um, going to drive him to the police station herself and save some tax dollars. She's always been civic-minded," Naomi said, fighting back her own hysteria. "But she had to do her grocery shopping first, right Hannah? You needed to eat a little something."

"That's right," Kiki said, getting the hang of it. "She didn't want to make her confession with low blood sugar. She gets so cranky."

Naomi snapped her fingers. "Which is exactly why she killed Charlie. Temporary insanity. Her blood sugar was dangerously low and she had no idea what she was doing."

"Poor old Charlie," Kiki said, sniffling. "To think that all that stood between him living and dying was a Snickers."

"Will you two stop it?" Hannah said in a ferocious whisper. "I didn't kill him."

"Of course you didn't," Naomi said with a cooing tone she would have used with a sick parakeet.

"I don't know how he got in the trunk." Hannah closed her eyes and tried to take a deep breath, but the air came no deeper than her throat. "I've got to keep calm. I've got to think. Kiki, why didn't you call the police as soon as you found him?"

"Don't get snippy. We were just trying to protect you, to come up with a decent story to tell the police. And we just found him a little while ago. We've hardly had time to think. Oh, Hannie, what will I do when you're in jail? Who will I talk to? What if the water heater goes out?" She tried to take the bottle from Naomi, but Naomi hung on to it. Staring down at Charlie, Naomi took another gulp.

"I'm not going to jail," Hannah said. She forced herself to look again at Charlie's gray face. He appeared in death the way he had in life—small, pathetic, and victimized. With sadness, she wondered if he had ever known any happiness, if he had family somewhere who would mourn him. It was these thoughts running through her mind when she noticed green slime clinging to the thin wisps of hair just above his ear. It had to be from his fishpond.

"Kiki, go call the police. Right now," Hannah commanded, her eyes still on Charlie. He was wearing the same green tweed sport coat he had been wearing when she dropped him at the police station the day before, the same one he had worn to Alex's party. Hannah leaned closer. She wanted to say goodbye to him, to tell him she was sorry for his unhappy end, but it was too late for that. She kissed her fingers, and as she pressed them against his head, she noticed several whitish rose petals scattered on the inside of his jacket.

TWENTY

ETECTIVE MORGAN HOOKED A THUMB in the waistband of his pants, his silver handcuffs jangling against his hip as he paced the interrogation room. The space was small with a tan floor, white walls, and all the quaint charm of a public urinal. Hannah watched him from her chair at a square metal table pushed against a wall. Across from her was a one-way mirror, and she wondered if anyone was back there observing her. She knew that her urge to make an obscene gesture at the window was infantile and she suppressed it.

Earlier, Morgan had someone type up Hannah's statement, and the single white page now sat in front of her. Her reading glasses still perched on her nose, she looked up from the document and told Morgan it was fine.

Stopping the aerobic exercise, he faced her, his eyes sharp. He had barraged her with questions for over two hours, occasionally with a gruffness she would have found insulting coming from anyone else. She was tired and hungry and wanted to go home. Yet it was Morgan she felt sorry for, his tough questions at odds with his baby face and the glimmer of regret she saw in it.

A video camera whirred gently in the background, music to be grilled by, and she closed her eyes and focused on the white noise, trying to clear her head. The image of Charlie remained in her mind. Charlie lovingly cleaning out that pond. Charlie alive and breathing. Charlie cold and dead. He lived alone and died alone, with only his goldfish to love. She wondered who would take care of them now that he was gone, and the idea of it made her want to cry, but she didn't let herself. She felt sure that Morgan thought of her as a mother figure, and seeing her cry might send him into some bizarre New Age therapy, like soul drumming or searching for his inner wolf.

When she opened her eyes again, Morgan stood by the mirror,

his hands on his waist. She knew he didn't like what he was doing. He cared deeply for Lauren. Hannah felt sure of it now, even if he was still unaware of it. Men were usually the last to know these things, but he might be suspecting that he cared for her, and if so, the last thing he would want would be to harass her aunt. But poor Charlie's body had turned up in the trunk of Hannah's car. Questions had to be asked. Morgan had driven her to the station almost immediately after arriving at her house and finding Charlie, and Hannah was anxious to cooperate. She wanted as much as anyone to find Charlie's killer. She wanted it more.

"You should smooth your hair," Hannah said in a hushed voice. For a second Morgan's capable cop demeanor melted into befuddlement. Hannah tapped her head with her finger. "You've been running your fingers through it and a few pieces are standing up. You'll be embarrassed when you play back the videotape in front of the other officers."

"We're getting off subject," Morgan said, checking his reflection in the mirror and then quickly smoothing his hair. "Now let's go over things again."

"All right." She said it with exasperation. Why was he keeping her when she had already told him everything she knew at least three times? His pig-headed need for repetition of simple facts might be annoying for Lauren after a few years of marriage. Yes, honey, we're having chicken tonight. Yes, chicken tonight, chicken tonight. "I want to cooperate in any way possible, but I have the Rose Club political forum this afternoon at three. Will I be able to make it?"

He checked his watch. It was the black plastic kind that probably showed the time in ten time zones and took his pulse. Hannah figured his pulse rate just then was in the high range. "Yeah, you should be fine." He picked up his little steno pad from the table and flipped back a few pages. "Okay, you say you dropped off Charlie at the station at what time yesterday?"

"About eleven-thirty. He was wearing the same clothes that he had on when I saw him in the trunk."

"I don't understand why he couldn't drive to the station himself."

"I told you. He was too upset."

"Because he killed his goldfish." The look on Morgan's face wasn't pretty.

"I know it sounds silly," Hannah said. "But I think he was upset mostly because he didn't want to identify Alex's killer."

The guilt came again, starting around her stomach and moving upward, filtering throughout her body. She should have made sure Charlie had gotten safely inside the station. She should have realized he was in danger, been more cautious. But from her car to the police station front door was a short walk. She twisted her hands together in her lap, the image of Charlie in the trunk of her car making yet another mental intrusion— his body curled up like a sleeping child's, his face ashen and streaked with algae. *I'm so sorry, Charlie.*

Morgan dropped his pad onto the table, the noise breaking Hannah's concentration. She found him staring at her with the kind of testosterone-infused ambiguity that men wore just before they started yelling and making no sense. Was he angry that she didn't have more to tell him? But she was the one who should be incensed. He was wasting time having her repeat details when they should be actively pursuing the killer, discussing next steps, comparing theories, going after evidence.

"I feel certain that Charlie was murdered in his backyard." She scooted forward in her chair, eager to lead Morgan into a more productive line of discussion. With two fingers, she pushed her reading glasses to the tip of her nose and viewed him over the rims. "When I saw Charlie in the trunk I noticed algae on his head. I recognized it from his fishpond. Here's how I think it happened. He was talking to somebody he knew, because from the gash on his head, I'm pretty sure they struck him from behind. That means he turned his back to them. And whoever did it didn't sneak up on him, at least I don't think so, because he was probably by the fishpond, and it's surrounded by gravel. He would have heard them coming. Somebody struck him, then held his head under the water. Of course, we won't know until we hear from the coroner. When do you think you'll be getting a report?"

"That's not your concern," Morgan said with an accusatory edge she found offensive. She wondered if she should confide in Lauren about this rather unpleasant side to him. But he was, after all, under stress.

She took off her glasses and set them on the table. "I've given this some thought," she continued, her patience wearing thin.

"Someone followed me yesterday, the same person who locked my sister and me in that shed."

"And this person followed you because they saw you with the Brita pitcher at the rummage sale?"

Hannah rubbed her chin. Was it her imagination or did she detect disbelief in his voice? *Relax*, she told herself. *You've done nothing wrong. He knows that. Everyone knows that.* "This man or woman believes I know more than I do about Alex's murder. Their first attempt to kill me failed, so they were going for a second try. They followed me to Charlie's house and then to the police station. Whoever it was realized that Charlie had evidence about Alex's murder, otherwise, why would he be going to the police, right?"

"So you dropped Charlie off at the station. Except nobody saw him there, and there's always someone at the front desk."

"He got cold feet and went home."

"How did he get home? He didn't have a car."

"Maybe he took a cab or a bus. You should check that out. Or maybe he wanted time to think, and he walked. I do that all the time, and it's not that far from town to his house.

"Problem is, there's no one to corroborate your story."

She stiffened. "Please don't refer to it as 'my story.' You make it sound like I made it all up. Why would I?"

Morgan didn't answer, and Hannah suddenly didn't like the vibes in the room. She recrossed her legs, trying to get comfortable, but the hard metal chair wouldn't cooperate. He gave no response to her question. He just looked at her, his silence an emptiness that felt like it would swallow her whole. The video camera playing its one note jazz in the background, the sickening truth sunk into her.

"You think I killed him?" Again, nothing from Morgan. No expression of horror at the mere suggestion, no shocked denial. She gave him a few seconds, just in case his reactions were slow, and then a ball of dread formed inside her. "What's my motive?"

"Mrs. Malloy, you could be in a lot of trouble."

"I'm asking you, what's my motive?"

"You were pretty emphatic about not letting Signatech destroy the town. You've lived here a long time. People get emotional about these things. And Charlie was all for Signatech."

"I'm not some crazy who goes around killing people for civic causes." She swallowed hard. "Are you arresting me?"

"Not at this time, but if I were you I'd get a lawyer."

"You're joking, right? My garage wasn't locked. The trunk wasn't locked. Anyone could have put Charlie in there."

"You don't have an alibi for the time he was killed."

"I had just left the cancer group and I needed some time alone."

"So you were just driving around. Okay. But you were seen with Charlie the day he died, Mrs. Malloy. One of your neighbors saw the police at your house this morning, and she told an officer she saw you driving down Center Avenue yesterday. She said Charlie was in your car."

"Just like I told you." She stopped there, realizing that he was no longer taking her words at face value.

"We found a battery-operated utility light by his pond, along with a bucket. So you're right that he must have been working on the pond at night," Morgan said. "And again, you're right, somebody met with him in the backyard and killed him. A neighbor saw him around nine-thirty taking out the trash, so we know it happened around the same time you were driving by yourself."

"How can you possibly believe I did such a thing?"

"You think I like this? I don't," Morgan said, his volume rising. He looked like he was in pain, but Hannah figured that, at this point, who wasn't? Only Charlie. "There's a lawyer in San Rafael. His name's Ramsey, and he's good. You're free to go now. We'll be in touch with you later in the day."

Hannah stared at him, her mouth gaping. "It's bad enough that you're suspecting me of murder, but I can live with that. What's worse is that by focusing on me you're wasting precious time and resources that should be used in finding the person who actually did this." She stood up and stepped toward him, getting right in his face. "Do you honestly believe I hit that little man with something and then held his head under the water until he was dead? Is that what you really think?"

It was a staring game between her and Morgan, and he flinched first.

"Call that lawyer, Mrs. Malloy."

Hannah grabbed her coat and purse, took a few steps, then faced the one-way mirror and made an obscene gesture, mild and of Italian origin, before walking out.

TWENTY-ONE

"YOU JUST MARCH RIGHT IN there, honey, and hold your head high," Kiki said, giving Hannah a little shove toward the door of the town hall assembly room. The Rose Club political forum started in five minutes. Hannah had been skulking behind a potted plant in the lobby for the last fifteen.

She knew she shouldn't, but she felt disgraced. Though Charlie's body had only been found that morning, the Hill Creek grapevine was fast and effective, and it seemed the whole town was gossiping about his murder along with Hannah being the prime suspect. As people filed past the sisters on their way to the main hall, some of them stared at Hannah outright, others struggled not to look at her, the way they would keep their eyes off a nasty wreck on the side of the highway.

Originally the forum was to be held at the Rose Club clubhouse, an old Tudor-style mansion donated to the club thirty years before. The club's ballroom easily held a hundred, but the murders insured a tremendous turnout, so the political forum was moved to town hall at the last minute. Hannah noticed the espresso concession that had been hastily set up in the lobby to turn a quick buck for repairs to the club's greenhouse. Hannah wondered if she should have volunteered for a photo booth. *Have your picture taken with Homicidal Hannah, only one dollar.*

At last Kiki successfully pushed Hannah into the doorway where she reluctantly faced the assembly room, with its wood paneling, vaulted ceiling, and peaked glass wall behind the stage. The sight made her feel queasy, reminding her of that awful night of the debate only a week earlier when the whole tragedy began.

"Now that I see you under strong lighting," Kiki said, "I think you should put on a little more lipstick."

Glad for any delay, Hannah headed back to the safety of the

potted palm, with Kiki right behind. Hannah fished through her handbag.

"Uh, no, honey, not your red one," Kiki advised, her tone politic. "Red lipstick screams guilty. Use my pink and then put a little gloss over it." She spelunked through the black nether regions of her own purse, retrieving a gold lipstick tube. "Pink has that air of innocence. I hear it's the color Mother Teresa always wore, though I doubt she went with gloss. On her it would have looked slutty."

Hannah snatched the tube of Tahiti Pink. Taking makeup tips from Kiki represented a new personal low, one dip below everyone thinking she was a killer. But if pink lipstick could stop the stares she was getting, like she was Lizzie Borden, Jeffrey Dahmer, and the Boston Strangler rolled into one, she would paint her face up like an Aborigine.

Using the gold cap as a mirror, Hannah applied the lipstick and handed it back to Kiki. Then, gathering up fresh nerve, she reminded herself of the motto she had lived by for the past thirty years. When tough women get knocked down, they pick themselves up and they keep on going. If she could face cancer she could face this, and she couldn't let these small-minded people frighten her when there was so much work to do. She had to find out who had committed the murders before she was arrested for them herself.

Kiki tugged excitedly on her sleeve. "Hannah, I've had an inspiration. Let's go into the ladies room and put lots of mascara on you. Then we'll splash water on your face and make it run so it looks like you've been crying your eyes out. That will get you loads of sympathy."

"Too Tammy Faye Baker," Hannah told her. "Besides, I think you need really big breasts and blonde hair to pull that off. I'm a little short on both."

"How am I going to get you out of this mess if you won't take my advice? You certainly didn't listen to me on your clothes." Kiki shook her head at Hannah's outfit. "With that dark pantsuit you might as well be wearing a sign that says, 'Killed him dead, no regrets.' Everyone knows that if you're a murder suspect, you wear pastels."

"I don't own pastels."

"Ever heard of shopping? In this situation the worst thing you can do is look strong and full of self-control. It screams 'I did it.' You want to look devastated, fragile, but still dressed to the hilt, so the women pity you and the men want to get you in the sack. My suit is a perfect example." Kiki swept her hands along her outfit, which was complete Planet Zsa Zsa, a brilliant yellow form-fitting suit with rhinestone buttons.

Hannah wasn't listening. Sweat had broken out on her forehead and her queasiness had worsened. *I should have stayed home.* But it would have made her look even guiltier, like she was afraid to show herself. She had to strut into that room, face those people, and find out which of them was the real killer. If only she could keep from throwing up on them first.

Kiki took hold of Hannah's arm, and together they walked into the assembly room doorway, chins held high and knees quaking. Most of the chairs were taken, with the rest of the crowd scrambling for the few vacant seats. Hannah spotted a reporter from the local newspaper as well as a San Francisco television reporter, the media obviously hoping another mayoral candidate would get bumped off *en flagrant* during the forum, to be caught on videotape for the six o'clock news.

Since it was a Rose Club event, vases of fresh-cut roses decorated small tables against the walls, with an extravagantly large bunch in a crystal vase on a table up front. A lectern stood at centerstage with a long table to its left for the candidates. A separate table and chair was set up to the right of the lectern for Bertha Malone, the moderator. The candidates' table had name cards, the candidates' names written in cursive and decorated with a colored drawing of a rose. When Hannah saw Charlie's name card, a knot formed in her throat. Why had they left it there? Surely Bertha and the other Rose Club members knew he was dead.

"Aunt Hannah!"

The sisters saw Lauren flying through the lobby with Naomi at her side. Lauren threw her arms around her aunt. The stares of people around them didn't bother Hannah, but a camera's flash rattled her and she quickly pulled away from her niece.

"That reporter's taking pictures. The nerve," Naomi said in a huff. Always loving a camera, Kiki unbuttoned the top button of her yellow jacket, then threw her arms over Hannah, swinging her around so they both faced the photographer. "Okay, Hannah," Kiki muttered through a big Prozac grin. "At the count of three, you faint."

Hannah grimaced at Kiki just as the camera flashed.

Lauren grasped Hannah's hands. "How could Larry accuse you of murder? I'm not going to date him. I don't care how much I love him." Tears welled up.

"You can't blame him," Hannah said. Her own ill will against Morgan had lessened once she decided that, even with just the current evidence, he could have arrested her, and didn't.

"Yes, Lauren, don't be too hasty," Kiki said. "Cute men don't grow on trees. I wouldn't hold a grudge unless Hannah actually ends up in the slammer." Kiki waggled a hand at her sister. "Not that you will. But even if you do, Lauren could marry Detective Morgan, and when you're paroled we just won't let you and Morgan sit next to each other at Thanksgiving."

Lauren brightened a little.

"I'm not going to jail," Hannah said, hoping deep down that saying the words out loud might help her believe them. "I'm going to help catch the murderer."

"Which of course you will, Hannah," Naomi said. "You know, even Red Moon supports you one hundred percent. He said just this afternoon that the trapped beaver would soon paddle free. He finds the white man's ways so fascinating. In fact, he wanted me to ask you your thoughts on the identity of the real killer. What he actually said was that he wanted to know the true direction of the black crow that flies so darkly, but I knew what he meant."

Normally Hannah would have qualms about answering Red Moon's question, but with her breathing relatives already discussing her parole, she was pleased to have anyone's support, even that of a dead person. "You can tell Red Moon that Lorna, Ox, Maggie, and Althea are all still possibilities, but that it's Mary I'm most interested in. She had a motive and opportunity," Hannah said, her voice low and serious. "She could have acted out her vengeance on Alex and then murdered Charlie because she thought he could identify her."

"And she's the one who tried to kill you in the shed?" Lauren asked.

Hannah nodded. "She saw the Brita pitcher at the rummage sale and thought it was my way of accusing her."

"You don't look completely convinced," Lauren said.

"I'm not sure I see her committing two murders and attempting a third just because a man broke up with her," Hannah explained, pausing, alert to Maggie entering the assembly room through a side door. "There had to be something else going on. Maybe it involved Signatech."

There was a lull in the conversation. It was Lauren who broke the silence. "Or maybe it had to do with when Mary and Alex knew each other in San Francisco."

All the women stared at Lauren.

"What are you talking about?" Hannah asked.

Pink crept up Lauren's cheeks. "Well, remember when I was following Larry after the debate, and I was crouched down beneath the café window? The window was open because it was a warm night, and I heard Larry tell his date that it turned out that Alex and Mary have known each other for years, long before they got involved in Hill Creek politics."

"Why didn't you mention this before?" Hannah asked.

"I didn't even think about it until today, and I was embarrassed that I was eavesdropping."

"But we encourage eavesdropping," Kiki said.

Hannah poked her in the side. "No we don't."

"Fantastic news!" Naomi said, waving her hands, her sleeves flapping. "This means Mary could have a deeper motive for wanting Alex dead. I'm getting a distinct spiritual message that the beaver will soon paddle free. But we must keep our positive energies focused. Let's all hold hands and do the sacred whoop of the healing white crow."

"You'll have to whoop without me," Hannah said, checking her watch. "I only have a few seconds before the forum starts and I want to ask Maggie some questions."

Hannah mumbled "excuse me's" as she edged her way through the crowd, her thoughts gyrating. Mary was looking like a better suspect all the time. But Morgan had known about her previous connection with Alex, and as far as Hannah knew, he didn't consider Mary a serious suspect. Unless he wasn't telling her all he knew, which was likely.

Hannah spotted Maggie in the second to last row, sitting one seat from the end, with the end seat vacant. Hannah went over and sat down next to her. When Maggie saw her she smiled. She had dressed up for the forum, wearing a beaded vest, her clipped gray hair shiny with gel.

"I want you to know that I'm still behind you all the way,"

Maggie told her first thing. "I know you wouldn't hurt anyone and the rest of these people do, too."

"I'm not so sure about that," Hannah said. "Everyone keeps staring at me."

"Oh, they're just drunk with gossip right now. They'll get over it and see the truth."

"That's what I'm hoping. Listen, I only have a minute and I want to ask you a question," Hannah said, making sure no one else could hear, "about the day of Alex's party, when Mary went up to Alex's room to lie down."

Maggie's face darkened. "I don't want to talk about this."

"Just one question, please. Mary says she took two of Alex's Valiums and that they put her to sleep for a couple of hours. Did you see her take them?"

"I know you're just trying to protect yourself, Hannah, but trust me, Mary couldn't kill anyone."

"Did you see her take the Valium?"

Maggie hesitated. "Alex didn't take Valium. He took Xanax, which is the same thing, but sometimes he called them Valiums. And Mary didn't take any of them."

"How do you know?"

Maggie glanced nervously at the man on the other side of her and fiddled with her earrings. She scooted closer to Hannah. "Because he only had a few pills left, and I finished them off. I was so stressed out trying to get things ready. I took a couple the day before the party and another two that morning. I couldn't have gotten through it without them."

"Could he have had some other pills in his medicine cabinet you didn't know about?"

"No, I kept his medicine cabinet organized, and I picked up his prescriptions. I know every pill in that house. There weren't any other tranquilizers."

"Have you told the police this?"

"Not exactly."

Maggie fingered her earrings again, her discomfort obvious.

"You took a lot of his pills?" Hannah asked.

Maggie looked at Hannah with beseeching eyes. "Sometimes, but I'm getting help with it. I know I should have told the police, but if the story got out I wouldn't be able to get another job." Maggie clutched her hands together in her lap. "The first time

I talked to the police I didn't even know that Mary claimed to have taken the tranquilizers. Nobody mentioned it then."

"But they did later?"

"The second time I was questioned. And I lied, told them I didn't know. I didn't think it was that important, and Mary has always been such a good person. But now with Charlie. If Mary's alibi is that she was knocked out on Alex's pills, well, it can't be true."

Kiki came over to Hannah. "You've got to go up on stage," she said. "Bertha says it's time to start and she's having a hissy fit because you're not up there."

Hannah wanted to finish things with Maggie, but Maggie didn't share the urge, because she stood up and hustled off down the row as soon as Hannah's head was turned. Hannah watched her make her way down another row, pushing past people's knees to a middle seat. As Maggie sat down, Hannah caught her eye. Maggie wore the same regret Hannah had seen on Kiki a thousand times when she had said too much to the wrong person.

TWENTY-TWO

"I'LL WALK YOU UP TO the front," Kiki said, linking her arm in Hannah's, the sisters facing the long aisle that led to the assembly room platform. "It'll look good to have family at your side. But please, try to make your lip tremble, and keep your head turned a little to the right. I see the television reporter over there."

They started down the aisle, Hannah keeping her head turned completely to the left to avoid the camera, Kiki facing directly at it with her mouth quivering and her bust shoved forward as far as it would go. By now most people were seated, but the sisters got stuck behind a woman struggling with a double baby stroller. Several people tried to help her, creating a bottleneck in the aisle.

Standing there, unable to move, Hannah sensed the unease in the room, and felt it was directed at her.

"I can't stand the way people are staring at me," she whispered to Kiki.

"Let 'em stare," Kiki whispered back. "You'll prove yourself innocent, and beat the pants off Walter. Then when you're mayor, it'll be payback time. You can have the cops give parking tickets to all the people who weren't nice to you."

"I'd never do that."

"Why not? Check out Frannie over there. She used to be our friend. Now she's looking at us like we're dirt. When you're mayor you can stop her garbage pickup. And that nasty Fred Timms, pretending not to see me when I waved at him just now. How are you going to like it, Freddie, when you don't have sewer service?"

"Keep your voice down."

"Imagine people thinking you could be a murderer just because Charlie ended up dead in the trunk of your car. That could happen to anyone."

"It's actually *your* car. Yet nobody's accusing you of murder."

"Because I spent the evening in question getting drunk with a police officer. That's what you call an ironclad alibi."

The young mother finally got her two babies out of the stroller, and the sisters made it the rest of the way down the aisle. For dramatic effect, Kiki threw her arms around Hannah once they reached the front. Then, just as Hannah mounted the stairs to the stage, she heard a hubbub at the back of the room and saw Wanda sweeping up the aisle wearing a business suit, the drab gray I'm-so-darn-professional variety that Wanda normally wouldn't have allowed herself to be buried in. Wanda marched forward, morphed into a small town Hillary Clinton, licking her lips with the taste of power, ready to steamroll over whatever stood in her way. Lacking any similar transformation, Walter followed his wife with the gait of a sick dog, flanked by two largish men in black suits and sunglasses. Halting, Wanda scrutinized the crowd, eager to shake hands and kiss babies. But the only woman with babies was seated in the middle of a row, and since babies couldn't vote anyway, Wanda manhandled a few conveniently located voters, shaking their hands and asking them to vote for her husband.

While Wanda worked the room, Walter slunk past her, saying hello to Hannah and Kiki when he reached the front, appearing thankful to have temporarily eluded his wife. The bodyguards followed him at a discreet distance.

"Who are the hunks?" Kiki asked him.

"Goons to protect my person," Walter replied gloomily. "Wanda insisted, you know, with the candidates all getting bumped off. She's so fixated on my being mayor. Just look at her." Wanda, still in high-schmooze mode, grinned madly for the cameras, seizing people's hands and joggling them whether they liked it or not. "It's like she's possessed by the devil," Walter said. "I mean, even more than usual. She hired the bodyguards because she thinks they'll attract attention. She says the murders have put Hill Creek on the map and that I've got to take advantage." He stuck his finger down his collar and tugged on it. "My bride seems alarmingly unconcerned that I could become a murder victim myself. I heard that old Charlie's skull got smashed in by your manure shovel, Hannah. That true?"

"Of course not," Kiki answered for her sister, since Hannah's mouth was currently hanging open in outrage. Kiki nudged him with her elbow. "Either of those bodyguards single and the type to appreciate an older woman?"

He nodded. "Marty, the big one on the right, he's a possibility. But be gentle with him. He looks tough but I know for a fact that he needlepoints."

Kiki gave her breasts a shove upward, then sauntered over to him. Walter inched close to Hannah.

"Sorry about the shovel remark, but I'm under stress," he said. "Are you sweating as much as I am?"

Hannah detected a slur in his voice and knew he had been drinking, maybe heavily. His preferred alcohol was vodka, so she couldn't smell it on his breath, but he had the moist-eyed, pickled-cerebellum appearance of the recently sloshed. He also seemed scared, his eyes darting about the room as if he expected someone to run in with a hatchet.

"If you're concerned about getting killed, why don't you just quit the race?" Hannah asked.

He cocked a thumb in Wanda's direction. "She says I've got the race sewn up now that it's just you and me. No offense. I'd love to see you win. I don't want to be mayor. But Wanda said she'll cut off my allowance if I drop out." He leaned his head close to Hannah's. "My love, I want you to know that I don't think for a minute that you're a murderer. The fact that people are saying it is absurd and cruel." He paused. "But just in case, I'd like to be whacked in my sleep, if possible. Preferably after I've been drinking heavily, which is every night, making scheduling easy. You could do that, for a friend?"

"I promise, I won't kill you," Hannah said with sarcasm. Wanda tossed them a nasty glance like it was a stink bomb. "I have a feeling your wife wants that honor."

Walter let out an unmanly sigh. "I almost wish you were the killer. If you bumped off a few people, well, at least I'd know you had a damn good reason, a solid rationale. It's scary to think some crazed maniac is taking an unusually personal interest in cleaning up local politics. And I could be next. Uh, oh. Eva Braun has spotted me cavorting with the Allies."

Wanda whisked up the aisle. First thing, she jerked Kiki's hand off Marty, then she huddled with the two bodyguards and pointed at Hannah. The bodyguards immediately flanked Walter.

After making sure everyone was watching, which naturally they were, she approached Hannah.

"Hello," Wanda said loudly, casting a disapproving eye on Kiki, who was once again fondling Marty. "How are you holding up, Hannah? You look so tired. I want you to know that I think it's just horrendous what they've done to your campaign flyers."

"What do you mean?" Kiki said, her head snapping around, but still keeping hold of Marty.

"You haven't seen them? So terrible. Someone has marked graffiti on them so they read 'Vote for Hannah or die.' People can be so vulgar. Walter will propose sensitivity training for all Hill Creek residents after he's mayor." Wanda turned to her husband. "Are you ready for your talk, dear? Maybe you should step into the back and do some jumping jacks to get your dynamism equalized." She looked again at Hannah. "Walter's such a mover and shaker these days. I know he worries that his duties as mayor could distract him from our relationship, but I've assured him that if Hill Creek needs him, we must be willing to make sacrifices," she said to Hannah, but loud enough for all to hear. "And a relationship as strong as ours could only be enhanced by civic duty. It's such a pleasure to watch him campaign, don't you think? His vitality, strength, and intellectual potency are a constant inspiration to me."

"I need to pee," Walter said meekly.

Hannah smiled at Wanda. "I'm sure it will be a powerful torrent."

"Make it fast," Wanda whispered gruffly to him. "Bertha says we're ready to start. And don't forget to zip."

His head bowed in submission, he hustled off, his bodyguards right behind.

Almost as anxious as Walter to get away from Wanda, Hannah handed Kiki her handbag, checked her pocket for her note cards, and then made her way up the short steps to the stage. Kiki took a seat next to Lauren and Naomi in the third row. After taking her place at the table, Hannah looked out at the hundreds of faces staring at her, her heart pounding, the sweat forming in her armpits. Just when she was considering running out of the room and making a break for Mexico, Perez hurried through the rear door. He smiled at her, gave her an apologetic shrug for being late, then found a seat at the end of an aisle near the back.

Walter returned, tripping on the stairs, and then again on the carpet runner as he took his seat next to Hannah.

Once Walter was settled, Bertha Malone walked to center-stage, swishing her long denim skirt, her silver and turquoise bracelets rattling. After a tap on the microphone and a call for everyone's attention, she welcomed everyone to the Rose Club political forum, then solemnly announced that Charlie Wright had passed away. A disturbed rumble was still traveling across the room when she introduced Hannah as the first speaker. When Bertha said that Hannah needed no introduction there was more rumbling and only a smattering of applause, except for Kiki, Lauren, Naomi, and Perez, who clapped loudly. Kiki and Naomi both let out energetic hoots.

Hannah walked up to the podium, squinting, the overhead lights directly in her eyes. Feeling hot all over as well as thirsty, she began her short speech, her voice cracking with nervous-ness, the note cards in her hand shaking. She kept to the issues, purposefully not mentioning the murders. Originally she had intended to publicly proclaim her innocence, but it had been Perez who insisted on the phone earlier that day that she not bring it up. He thought it would invite questions from the au-dience, and that in her situation she should say as little as pos-sible. If someone asked a question on the murders, she was to decline answering. Hannah didn't like the idea of backing away from a confrontation, but she trusted Perez's advice. She had yet to get a lawyer, since to her, getting a lawyer seemed an admission of guilt.

In the middle of Hannah's description of her plan for man-aged commercial growth, she noticed Mary in the audience, sit-ting near the back. The sight of Mary staring at her with such hardness on her face caused Hannah to stumble over her words. She paused a second before continuing on about not letting Sig-natech clog the streets with more traffic, about protecting the small town atmosphere that made Hill Creek special. She tried not to look at Mary, but she couldn't help herself, not after what Maggie had just told her. Why had Mary lied about taking Alex's tranquilizers?

When Hannah finished no one raised a hand for questions. At first she felt grateful, but then realized that people in the

audience were probably too embarrassed or afraid to ask anything. They thought Homicidal Hannah might kill them if they
crossed her.

She thanked everyone, and as soon as she turned to sit back
down, she heard the word "murderer" from the crowd. She spun
around to see who had said it. People twisted in their seats, but
no one seemed to know or wanted to admit who it was. Kiki,
Naomi, and Lauren all looked horrified and Perez turned red,
furious. He stood, issuing a silent dare to whoever it was to say
it again. No one took him up on it. He sat down, looking disappointed at having no one to punch.

Mortified, Hannah took her seat, her legs wobbly. She felt
like a defendant at a Salem witch trial, expecting the townspeople to all point at her and scream "witch!" Her heart beat wildly
and perspiration dripped down her back as Bertha introduced
Walter. He walked timidly to centerstage. He didn't look much
better than she did, and she decided that the shout of "murderer"
had rattled him as well. He stood behind the lectern, white-
knuckled hands gripping its edge.

"Firsts of all, I would like to say to the Rose Club member-
ship, that I don't think Hannah Malloy killed anybody," he said,
slurring his words. Hannah smiled her thanks, although his support would have meant a bit more if he hadn't been so obviously
drunk. "Our Hannah wouldn't hurt a fly." His forehead
scrunched. "Well, a rose-eating pest, yes. She'd kill 'em without
mercy. But humans?" He shook his fist at the audience. "Hell,
no, I say! I say, hell, no!"

The audience was quiet. Sitting in the front row, Wanda
glared at her husband. Avoiding eye contact with his wife, Walter forged ahead. "Secondly, I'd like to say, that I'm dropping
out of this election." His slurring was worse, the last word coming out "eluckzun." "I decided at the urinal only a few moments
ago that this mayor thing's just too dangerous, and to be honest,"
he leaned an elbow on the lectern and rested his chin on his
hand, "I'd make a lousy mayor. I'm not even completely sure
where town hall is."

Just as Wanda slapped her forehead, Walter's eyes rolled upward, his knees buckled, and he collapsed. There was a gasp
from the audience. As his body crumpled, a silver flask fell out
of his coat pocket and slid across the floor, its shiny metal casing
glinting under the overhead lighting. Hannah rushed to him, but

the bodyguards got to him first and pushed her away. Wanda flew up the stairs to the platform and knelt by her husband's side. For a moment there was an astonished hush, the same incredible idea in everyone's minds—Walter Backus was dead.

The blonde television reporter, praying for the worst, bounded to the stage, microphone in hand. The cameraman hurried behind her, the camera lens pointed at Walter. When Walter's eyes half-opened, Hannah let out an audible sigh of relief. The reporter, less appreciative of this sign of life, dropped to her knees and shoved the microphone between the bodyguard's legs to get it close to Walter's mouth.

"Have the bartender call me a cab," Walter said groggily, the reporter's microphone broadcasting it to the whole auditorium.

For a few seconds Wanda stared speechless at the spineless heap that was her husband, her rabid gaze still clapped on him as his bodyguards carried him off the platform. As they hauled him down the center aisle, Walter waved cheerfully to the voters, a lopsided grin on his face and spittle glistening on his chin.

Her aspirations for power flushed down the political toilet with a resounding whoosh, Wanda's shoulders slumped, and her mouth twisted with the agony of being thrust back into obscurity. Then suddenly her cheeks sucked inward, and she lifted her chin as if a voice had whispered to her. She strode to centerstage, took the microphone off the lectern, grabbed the cameraman by the neck, and swung him around so that the camera was aimed at the person it had been meant for all along, which was, of course, her.

"My husband has been under a great deal of stress, and I would like to announce that I will be taking his place as candidate for mayor," Wanda announced. "Naturally I represent the same platform as my husband." She pushed her shoulders back, looking regal, and stretched out both arms in front of her, a là Eva Peron. Then, curling her hands into fists, she said, "I am afraid of nothing, nothing except mediocrity. Together, my friends, we will take Hill Creek to new prosperity and ourselves to new zeniths of self-development!" She swept one arm through the air. "We will reconnect to the pregnant cores of our inner selfness!"

An initial smattering of applause quickly grew into a thunder. Nobody knew what connecting to the pregnant cores of their inner selfness was, nor did Wanda, for that matter. Still, it sounded hip and fabulous, qualities that in Marin County were prized far more than substance.

Kiki absorbed this new development with shock. Wanda had scooped up a disaster and turned it into a coup d'état. Hannah, on the other hand, felt only admiration for Wanda. Whatever Wanda's faults, you had to admit the old girl was fast on her feet. As if she had been a politician all her life, Wanda orated to the crowd, describing a political platform that was everything and nothing. Like a pro, she sidestepped questions, sashayed over issues, skipped her way over unpleasant queries that would force her to take a stand on anything controversial.

When Wanda at last relinquished centerstage, Bertha stepped forward and reminded everyone to vote and to be careful driving home. Relieved to have it over with, Hannah moved down the side aisle to find Perez, and within seconds the blonde television reporter caught up with her, the cameraman at her heels.

"Mrs. Malloy, have you been questioned by the police regarding the two murders?" the reporter asked, then shoved the microphone in Hannah's face. Seeing the camera pointed at her, Hannah's brain froze.

"Mrs. Malloy has no comment," Perez said, then looped his arm in Hannah's and steered her toward the door. The reporter tried to follow but Kiki grabbed the cameraman's arm, and, not to be outdone by Wanda, stepped in front of his lens.

"I'm Kiki Goldstein, Hannah Malloy's younger sister," Kiki said with an emphasis on the "younger" part. She patted her hair. "I'm also her campaign manager. I have time for that sort of thing because I'm single. I'm here to say that my sister is completely innocent of any crime. She will ride the shoulders of the people to victory, and I, her younger and single sister, will be right by her side."

While Kiki lobbied for votes and dates, not in that order, Perez pulled Hannah through the crowd. "We'll take my car. It's at the curb," he said as they reached the front door. His arm protectively around her, they moved swiftly down the steps. A few people had already spilled onto the sidewalk heading for their cars, but Perez and Hannah had beat most of the crowd. Never slowing, he led her down the walkway toward his station wagon, parked illegally at the curb. He pulled out his keys and

Hannah heard the doors click open. Perez had already opened the driver's door and Hannah had her hand on the passenger door handle when she heard her name shouted behind her. The voice was familiar, high-pitched and gravely, the way Minnie Mouse might sound after thirty years of chain-smoking. Hannah pivoted and there was Lorna only a few yards away wearing a tight purple sweater dress and gold high heels Kiki would have killed for. She looked incredibly trashy. She also looked small, vulnerable, and afraid.

"It was you all along," Lorna said loudly. "You killed Alex and tried to pin it on Ox."

The crowd on the walkway had thickened, some of them slowing their pace to eavesdrop. Others stopped and watched the scene with open-mouthed fascination, forgetting their Reiki appointments, the cat that needed feeding, and the kids waiting to be picked up from their African drumming classes.

Perez walked around the car and stood next to Hannah. Seeing the suffering on Lorna's face, Hannah couldn't hate her for the accusation. She knew Lorna was thrashing out at whomever she could. Hannah walked up to her and reached out her hand. "Lorna, I promise you—"

"You promised you'd help Ox," Lorna spat, "and that was a lie. They found that dead guy in your car. You're a murderer."

Perez moved in close. "That's enough," he said to Lorna, his voice cop-like. "You better go home."

"Sorry, pal, but I've got plenty more to say," Lorna said, not afraid of him. He inched closer to her, but Hannah put her hand on his arm. "I'll be watching you, lady, dogging your every step," Lorna said, now inches from Hannah's face. "You won't be able to lay the blame on my Oxie, you got it? I'll be following you."

"I think you've been following me already," Hannah replied softly.

"What are you talking about?"

The other times Hannah had seen Lorna, Lorna had worn boots or pants, but that day Lorna's strappy sandals revealed a small tattoo on her ankle. Hannah recognized it as an Egyptian symbol, an elongated loop with a cross at the bottom. It was done in red.

"What's that mark on your ankle?" Hannah asked.

Lorna looked down, then back at Hannah. "Don't try to change the subject."

Hannah asked again.

"Okay, if you want to get weird about it. Al had me get this tattoo when we were married. He went through this Egyptian phase. It's called an ankh or something. I was stupid to get it, because the next month he moved onto some Chinese stuff and wanted me to have a yin yang symbol tattooed on my butt. He was always into some schtick."

What Lorna called a schtick, Hannah called evidence. Kiki must have mistaken the tattoo for a scratch that day when she saw it through the gap in the shed's wallboards just before some-body set it on fire.

"If you think I'm guilty of murder, then let's go to the police," Hannah told her, looking for any excuse to get Lorna in front of Detective Morgan.

Lorna let out a mirthless laugh. "Like I'd go anywhere with you."

"If you're frightened of me, you can have Ox come with us to the police station."

Lorna sucked in her lower lip, her whole body starting to quiver. "He's already there, locked up in a jail cell."

"They arrested him?" Hannah asked. "For what?"

"For Alex's murder. The murder you committed."

"On what evidence?"

"The dumb lug confessed," Lorna told her, the words spilling out with a sob. "He walked in there a couple of hours ago and told them he killed Al."

TWENTY-THREE

HIS JAW SET WITH TENSION, Perez put on a pair of mirrored sunglasses, then pulled the station wagon away from the curb and made a fast and illegal U-turn. The policeman in the squad car parked down the street either didn't notice or pretended not to.

Hannah hadn't said a word since they got in the car. She looked behind and saw the town hall doors spewing people onto the sidewalk. At the fringe of the crowd stood Lorna, fixed as a statue as the people swarmed past, her eyes on Perez's car.

"I already knew about Ox's confession," Perez said. He had a death grip on the steering wheel and Hannah wondered if it could break in his hands. "That's why I was late. I was at O'Reilly's having a drink with Mack Guadarama. He used to work for me before he moved over to Hill Creek, and he gets chatty if you buy him a few beers. Ox's confession will take some heat off you." He stopped at a stop sign, taking off with a mild screech of tires. A vein throbbed at his temple. "The police are assuming that the murders were committed by the same person. So if this Ox guy confessed to Alex's murder, they'll start with the assumption that he killed Charlie, too. It's going to take some pressure off you, at least for a while."

"Except that Ox didn't kill Alex."

Perez looked at her. "Come again?"

"Watch where you're going!"

Perez slammed the brakes, the car screeching to a stop inches from the red Ferrari in front of them. The driver, about thirty and wearing jeans and a T-shirt, jumped out of the car and yelled something, but when he saw the look on Perez's face he shut up. Perez waved him back in the car, and the guy acquiesced, meek as a puppy.

Bracing his arms against the steering wheel, Perez let out a rush of air. "Jeezus, that would have been expensive." He pulled the car over to the curb and shut off the engine. "Okay, let's talk where I can't run into anything."

Hannah resettled herself into her seat, trying to calm down after the near miss. She hated to see Perez so worked up, and was sorry for bringing him into such a mess, but she knew he wouldn't have it any other way.

"For Ox to have put the monkshood in Alex's water, well, it doesn't make sense," she said. "He was inside Alex's house the day before the lunch party, sometime in the morning. Maggie cut the monkshood and put it in the vases late that afternoon, so Ox didn't even see the flower arrangements until the next day after the party. It's too big a leap to think that he knew monkshood was poisonous, saw the vases that day and figured the flowers had been there long enough to make the water lethal."

"Then why did he confess?"

"Because he probably thinks Lorna killed Alex and he's trying to save her."

Perez took off his glasses. His eyes, usually warm and kind, were now serious, unyielding. *Cop eyes*, Hannah thought. He must have scared the pee out of criminals he arrested. If she hadn't been so thoroughly disturbed, she would have found it all very arousing.

"Do you think she did it?" Perez asked her.

"I don't know. I have the same problem with her being the killer as I do with Ox. How did she know the vase water was poisonous?" Hannah looked out the window. "It's such a gallant thing for Ox to do, sacrificing himself for Lorna that way. What a sweet man."

Perez said, "Yeah, he's a doll. You just want to hug him. Let's keep going. Why would Ox think that Lorna murdered Alex?"

"Kiki thinks she saw a scratch on someone's leg through the boards of the shed. She and I confronted Ox about it."

"You what?" It didn't come out quite a yell, but close enough. The vein in his temple danced the cha cha.

"It was perfectly safe," Hannah said. "Ox was at a restaurant with Lorna and there were plenty of people around. Kiki checked his ankle and didn't find anything, but Ox obviously knows about Lorna's tattoo. He thinks she's the one who set the shed on fire, and she had no motive to do that unless she killed Alex."

"But you don't think she did it."

"Like I said, I don't know. There are a couple of big holes that have to be filled in. But Althea's still in the running as a good suspect and Mary's shaping up as well." Hannah told him about her earlier conversation with Maggie, and about the suspicious lack of tranquilizers at Alex's house for Mary to have zonked herself with. Therefore, Mary was lying about being zonked.

Perez pulled the car back into the traffic. "I'll tell Morgan that Mary lied about the drugs. He won't like the idea of you asking Maggie questions, so it's better that it comes from me. He'll check it out."

"I thought you were mad at Morgan for accusing me of Charlie's murder."

"I've cooled off. He's just doing his job, and, to be honest, I would have had the same suspicions about you."

"Oh, really?"

His eyes slid to her, then quickly back to the road. "I'm sleeping with you, and I know you better. I've got another question. Lorna asked you to investigate Alex's murder. If she's the guilty one, why would she do that?"

"I can explain it."

"I'm ready and waiting."

"She knows how gossipy this town is, and she knew the word would get out that she had asked me for help, and that it would get back to the police. It made her look innocent, and I was arrogant enough to think she really wanted my help. I feel so stupid. She's a bail bondsman, a law enforcement professional." Hannah struggled against her seat belt in order to turn toward Perez. "If she wanted an investigator she'd hire a real detective, not a sixty-one-year-old retired secretary."

Perez made a right turn onto Walnut. "You need to work on your self-esteem."

"Not really. That's the problem. I was egotistical enough to not question any of this until now. The more I think about it, Lorna has the best motive of anyone for wanting Alex dead— love and money. Alex dies and she gets Ox and her dream of a novelty chocolate business."

"Okay, take it easy. I'll go to the station right after I drop you off, and I'll talk to Morgan. But I want you to stay out of this. As soon as you get home I want you to call this number." He steered with one hand while he fumbled in his shirt pocket, then pulled out a slip of paper and handed it to her.

She looked at it. "Whose number is this?"

"Frank Jenners. He's a criminal attorney."

"Why do I need this now?"

They had reached her house. Perez pulled into the driveway and shut off the engine.

"If Ox's confession is false, Morgan will figure it out pretty fast," he said. "And that leaves the evidence pointing at you."

"What evidence?"

"Someone in town saw you driving with Charlie in the car the day he was killed."

"I know. Morgan already told me, but that just confirms what I told the police."

"It only confirms that Charlie was with you. Morgan knows you're smart enough to cover yourself in case the police found fibers from Charlie's clothes inside your car. And this person who saw the two of you said that Charlie didn't look happy. She said he looked scared."

"Scared because he was headed for the police station."

"Or scared of you. That's how the police could see it. And then there were those rose petals in his pocket. The police can't figure out how they got there, but you're well known around town for your roses."

"So now I'm a crazed killer who sprinkles rose petals on my victims?" The comment was supposed to illicit a chuckle from Perez, and didn't. Hannah didn't like where things were heading. "I can tell you have more. There's no sense in hiding anything. I'm already down about as far as I can fall." Perez's frown told her she still had more room to go.

"I learned something else from Mack. Something he told me as a personal favor. Right after her boyfriend confessed, Lorna gave the police hardcopies of the emails she says you sent Alex. They're all love poems."

Hannah squirmed in her seat. "I didn't send them, Kiki did, and Lorna knows it."

"When you told me about those poems, you forgot to mention they came from your email address. They make it look like you had a pretty serious thing for Alex. I think it's time you told me all about it."

Usually Hannah gave Perez the abridged version of events, but this time she put it all out, covering every detail. It was embarrassing, but humiliation didn't seem that big a deal compared to the prospect of arrest. She liked to think of herself as flexible, but she had a limit when it came to jail cuisine and showering with women.

"I believe you," Perez told her when she had finished. "Because I trust you and because I know you'd never screw up your poetry that way. Mack brought a copy of one for me to see. If you sent somebody love poems, they'd be beautiful. They wouldn't have phrases like 'if you love me really, I'll let you cop a feelie.'"

"I appreciate your confidence." Her smile rapidly faded. She looked at the rosebush climbing up the front porch of her house and tried to ignore the fresh fear gnawing at her. Maybe Perez believed her, but she doubted the police would.

"John, I need a favor."

"Name it."

"The rose petals in Charlie's pocket, can you get a look at them?"

"I'm not sure. Mack might help me out on it. Why?"

"If I can get a good enough description of them, I may be able to tell you how they got in Charlie's pocket."

"Are you arresting me now?" Hannah asked Morgan. She sat down in the same chair she had used that morning. Same chair, same walls, same look of regret mingled with accusation on Morgan's face. Everything the same and everything different, and not for the better. Hannah had received Morgan's call as soon as she walked in the house. That had been around five-thirty, and he insisted on seeing her right away. Hannah hadn't been hungry, but Perez made her eat half a cheese sandwich before he drove her to the station. He wanted to wait, but she made him go home.

"Do you recognize these?" With one swift movement Morgan slapped a stack of papers in front of Hannah and fanned them on the table.

"Did you practice that before I got here?" she asked.

He didn't appear to be in the mood for jokes, even tiny ones.

With his khakis, blue button-down shirt, and air of gloom, he looked like a frat boy who had just flunked the big final. "Look at them, Mrs. Malloy."

She took a quick look just to keep up his self-esteem level, since he seemed like the type who had been teased in grade school, but she already knew the papers' content. "My question is this, Detective Morgan. Why did Alex go to all the trouble of printing and keeping these?"

"Maybe he was flattered by the attention."

"Or maybe he thought he could blackmail me with them if I became a real contender in the election. Only I didn't send them. My sister did, and she'll swear to it."

"Your sister would say anything to protect you. But the letters are from your email address."

"My sister and I share it."

"Then you'll have no trouble coming up with friends who can show emails they received from your email address signed by your sister."

Hannah crossed then recrossed her legs. As far as she knew, the only emails Kiki had sent were the poems to Alex. Morgan took a set of keys out of his pocket and started nervously jangling them. She knew he had been hoping for a reasonable answer from her, one that might save her skin, and he had been disappointed.

"We've compared the poems in these emails to the poems you've published in the *Marin Sun* over the past few years," Morgan continued, his key jangling accelerating. "They're very similar."

"Kiki altered my poetry to suit her needs. She's been doing that kind of thing since she was twelve. Once in high school English when I wrote a paper on Albert Camus, she sneaked it from my book bag, changed some of it, rewrote it in her handwriting, then turned it in as a paper on Nehru. She got an F, of course. See, she got Camus confused with Nehru. Then there was the time—"

He kept rattling the keys. "We're getting off track, Mrs. Malloy."

She took the keys from him and put them on the table. They were making her crazy. "You're the one off track if you think I could write something as silly as this." She slid one of the poems from the table and scanned it. "Here's a good one. 'A

bird's glistening wings don't give me a zing. Oh, the freedom
of the sky, your pectorals make me high.' You think I wrote
that?" She grabbed another paper and slapped it with the back
of her hand. "Or this one. After having known me, do you
honestly think I would write a poem titled 'Ode to a Hunky
Buttock'?" She thumbed through the others. "Or would I write
something like this." Hannah glanced through another poem,
looking for the sections where Kiki had transformed her verse
into sailors' limericks, but nothing in this poem was familiar.
"Wait a minute. I didn't write this."

Morgan gave her a wry look. "So you keep saying."

"No, I mean this wasn't one of my original poems, and Kiki
couldn't have written it."

"How do you know?"

"Listen to it." There were two stanzas on the page, and it was
the first one she read out loud. "I have but to be by thee, and
thy hand would never let mine go, nor heart withstand the beating of my heart to reach its place. When should I look for thee
and feel thee gone? When cry for the old comfort and find none?
Never, I know. Thy soul is in thy face."

Morgan was quiet a moment, then he cleared his throat. "That
was beautiful. You say you didn't write it, but how can I be
sure?"

"Because you can find it in the library. I'm pretty sure this
poem's by Robert Browning."

"But isn't that your email address at the top?"

"No. See, the top is smeared. The paper must have jammed
when it was printed, and I don't think it was an email at all.
It's done in a different typeface."

Morgan took the page from Hannah and examined it. "It was
put in the same file as the others, so we just assumed."

"You assumed wrong. I didn't send those poems to Alex. My
sister did. I wasn't in love with him, and my sister wasn't in
love with him either. But whoever sent this poem to Alex probably was. And the only person I know of who felt that way
about him was Mary Katowski."

"Be wild and free, Hannah," Naomi said. She raised her arms
over her head and twirled, her tunic swirling around her legs.
"Lift up your arms, throw back your head and howl, howl, howl!

It'll connect you with your earth essence, balance your life force meridians. You'll feel so centered and whole."

Hannah, Kiki, Naomi, and Lauren stood in Hannah's backyard under the full moon's light. The sky was clear, a handful of stars breaking through the city lights, and cold air nipped at Hannah's skin. Wrapping her arms around herself, Hannah lifted her chin and breathed in the clean scent of eucalyptus. She wasn't about to do any howling, but at that moment her animal instincts were keener than Naomi realized. The night was still, and Hill Creek along with it, yet Hannah sensed something stirring in the town, something frightened and angry moving in the town's shadows.

"I don't want to howl," Hannah said to Naomi, pulling the top of her flannel robe close around her throat. "I appreciate you bringing me home from the police station, but my gratitude has limits. It's cold out here and my feet are getting wet."

"Since you refused to let us be nude, we have to at least be barefoot, to feel our skin directly against the breast of our Mother Earth," Naomi told her. "You need to get in touch with your spirit animal, Hannah, if you're going to free yourself from all that negative energy enveloping your chakras. If you howl long enough you'll go into a trance that will open a pathway to your inner animal power."

"My inner animal must be a toy poodle, because right now I feel like having a treat and curling up on the couch for a snooze," Hannah said.

"You just give howling one little try. Please, for me," Naomi pleaded.

Hannah smiled. "Maybe one small howl."

"Oh, goodie. But wait just a sec so I can get the sacred pipe ready and we can begin the power animal ceremony." Naomi pranced to the garden table and retrieved a long rough wooden pipe decorated with red paint and feathers. After packing the pipe bowl with dried leaves from a leather pouch, she sat on the grass cross-legged.

"Howling makes you feel better, Hannah, it really does," Kiki said. "Look how Lauren has thrown herself into it."

Lauren sat on the grass, feet tucked beneath her, head tipped back, howling like a cat with its paw in a trap. Hannah listened with heartache, knowing it was a howl for lost love. Hannah had told Lauren over and over not to let Morgan's professional behavior affect their romance, but Lauren couldn't forgive him for suspecting her aunt of murder. Hannah decided it was best to just give her time.

"I'm feeling some negative energy myself," Kiki said. "Wanda's going to win the election for sure, and I'm going to have to expose my tush to the whole town."

"Hasn't that always been your dream?" Hannah asked.

After tossing her sister a nasty look, Kiki sat in a chair near Lauren and Naomi and let out a wail, beating her chest with her fists. Naomi lit a match and touched it to the pipe, inhaling deeply.

"Hold it!"

Startled, the women jerked around and saw Perez by the gate. In blue jeans topped with a leather jacket, he stood with his legs apart, both hands gripping the handle of a gun held straight out in front to him, the moonlight catching the metal barrel. Lauren and Kiki screamed. Having shrieked in mid-inhale of the sacred pipe, Naomi began coughing.

"John, put that thing away," Hannah told him, giving Naomi a few restorative pats on the back. "They're just howling."

Perez pointed the gun at the ground. "Sorry," he said, embarrassed. "I was at the front door when I heard screaming. I thought somebody was in trouble."

"My, my, that was exciting," Naomi said, tapping her chest and sputtering a little. "We're just releasing primal energies, John. Hannah's a little depressed, and we're doing some howling therapy. I learned it from a certified wolf priestess. You should try it, John, and show Hannah how it's done. Men are so good at connecting with their primal sources. Just throw your head back, John, and howl like a wolf."

"But put the gun away first," Hannah suggested. Perez tucked the gun in the shoulder holster underneath his jacket. Hannah had never seen him wear it before, and it disturbed her.

"Thanks, but I'll pass," he said before going up to Hannah. Then he whispered, "What's in that pipe Naomi's smoking?"

"Dried basil," Hannah replied.

"Could have fooled me," he said as Naomi began wailing. "Hannah, I need to talk to you." Lauren and Kiki joined in the howling, and he looked at them like they were crazy. "Out here isn't a good spot. Can we go inside?"

They walked in the backdoor to the kitchen, with Teresa and

Sylvia following. He sat down at the table, settling into the chair and crossing one ankle over his knee. He studied Hannah as she leaned back against the counter.

"How are you doing?" he asked.

"I'm okay. What's new with the investigation?"

"That's what I want to talk to you about." He had to raise his voice as the howling got louder. "Lorna Donatello has an alibi for the time you and your sister got locked in the shed. She was bowling and several people at the bowling alley have vouched for her. Apparently when she bowls, she jumps around a lot and curses. A lot of people noticed her."

"What about Althea?"

"Similar story. She was in San Francisco protesting the building of some new freeway ramp. There are a dozen people who say she was there all afternoon chained to a fire hydrant. Morgan's still trying to confirm Mary's alibi. She claims she was shopping, and if she was, they'll find someone who remembers her. The person who doesn't have an alibi at all is Ox."

"Is he still in jail?"

"No. Lorna got him a lawyer and he retracted his confession. Morgan didn't have enough evidence without it, so he had to let him go. But that's why I came over. Morgan still thinks Ox could be our killer. He checked on some things back in Texas. A few years ago Ox won third place in a San Antonio flower show."

Hannah wanted to laugh. It was so hard to picture. "Third place for what?" The howling outside stopped, and she assumed they were catching their breath.

"Best hyacinth or something. The point is, our boy Ox knows his plants. Morgan has two officers following him, so it would be tough for him to get close to you, but Morgan doesn't have the manpower to put someone outside your house all night. Hannah, I want you to spend the night with me."

"Gee, when I was younger I used to get asked that all the time, but it was never for my safety."

"I'm serious about this, Hannah."

"I know, and I appreciate it, but like I told you last time, I can't leave Kiki, and bringing her to your house would be cruel and unusual punishment. For you."

"Then I'll sleep here."

"Sorry, but I have a rule with Kiki. No girl/boy slumber parties. If I break it, sometime in the future I'll come home and find a rugby team here for a sleepover."

"I'll sleep on the couch," Perez said. "I've brought my tooth-brush. Don't try to talk me out of it."

Another group howl erupted from the backyard, and this time Teresa joined in.

"You sure you want to stay here?" Hannah asked with a laugh.

His sober expression melted briefly. "I guess I should have brought ear plugs. There's something else I want to tell you. I got that other information you asked for, about the rose petals in Charlie's pocket. Mack took a look at them and jotted down some notes. He thought the information was for me. He said they were dried up and in an evidence bag, and he only saw them for a second."

"What else did he say?"

"That they were kind of whitish in the center and red on the edges. Does that mean anything to you?"

"Yes," Hannah replied, after a moment's hesitation. "That's the rosebush outside Alex's kitchen window."

A few hours later, Perez was asleep in Hannah's living room. Hannah had made up the couch with a sheet, pillow, and blanket, and Perez had settled in wearing his clothes. It amazed Hannah how fast he fell asleep. She supposed that's what came from a clear conscience.

"That's two men on the couch in one week," Kiki said dreamily as the two sisters stared at Perez's sleeping form from the hall. "That couch has never seen so much action." She watched him for another few seconds, then sighed. "When he was in the backyard tonight holding that gun on us, I thought I'd never seen anything so sexy in my life. Does he ever do things like that when the two of you are, you know, alone together?"

"All the time. I put on a nightie like a hooker's and then he threatens to cuff me. The fun part is when he tells me to spread 'em."

"Very funny." She put her hand on Hannah's shoulder. "I just want you to know that I'm closing my bedroom door tonight, so if you and John want to, you know, get cozy, I won't be listening."

"We won't be getting cozy, because first of all, that would

break the house rule, and secondly, you would be listening. You might even take pictures."

"I thought of that, but I knew you'd notice the flash. I'm going to bed and I'm going to sleep like a baby. I feel so safe with a man in the house."

Kiki and Hannah hugged each other and said goodnight, then Hannah watched Kiki pad down the hall, wishing she could share her sister's sense of security.

TWENTY-FOUR

❧

WHILE PEREZ SNORED ON THE living room sofa and Kiki dreamed of chocolates and pool boys down the hall, Hannah tossed in bed, unable to sleep. Around one-thirty she propped herself up among the pillows, her need for brain activity overwhelming her need for rest. It was after two when she bolted straight up in bed, her mind fixed upon the Robert Browning poem she had discovered among Kiki's lust-loaded emails. The poem was the key.

Hannah kicked off the covers and slipped out of bed. Missing the rug, she yelped as her bare feet hit the cold floor, and she made a mental note to get new house slippers to replace the ones Teresa had chewed. After a few minutes of rummaging through her bedroom bookshelf, she found the tattered copy of Browning bought at a garage sale years before. Crawling back in bed and pulling up the covers to her chest, she took a small battery-operated book light from her nightstand drawer and clipped it to the back cover. Kiki slept like the dead, but if Perez awoke, he would see any regular lamp light under her door and would want to be with her. Perez's company in the middle of the night was always a pleasure, but just then she needed time to figure out this puzzle before she risked sharing it with anyone else.

After putting on her reading glasses, she thumbed through the pages. At the police station she had only read the poem's first stanza, but the letter had included two.

The book light was no bigger than a thumb, and it cast a narrow yellow beam across the page, making Robert Browning's words glow golden in the darkness. She pushed her glasses farther up her nose and read the second stanza. "But the soul whence the love comes, all ravage leaves that whole; vainly the flesh fades; soul makes all things new."

She read the last part again, whispering the words and feeling the glow that beautiful poetry always gave her. But when she noticed the poem's title, a chill ran from the base of her spine right up to her scalp. Bold black letters at the top of the page read, "From Any Wife to Any Husband."

Already dressed in gray slacks and a white sweater, Hannah tiptoed into Kiki's dim bedroom, a ray of first light peeking through the pink ruffled curtains. A month before, Hannah, Kiki, Naomi, and Lauren had worked together in repainting Kiki's boudoir, as she liked to call it. Now it reminded Hannah of a strawberry sundae, all pink, red, and white, the walls dotted with framed photos of celebrities—Zsa Zsa Gabor, Warren Beatty, Sean Connery. An antique vanity stood against one wall with a plastic sign taped across the upper part of the mirror reading, "Go out there and make somebody love you."

Kiki lay sprawled on the bed, the frilly covers kicked off, her arms and legs outstretched like she had landed there after leaping from a tall building, a half dozen lacy pillows scattered around her. Her clothes from the night before lay rumpled at the bed's foot. Kiki hated throwing out old clothes, believing that everything came back in style if you just waited long enough. As a result, her bedroom functioned as one large haphazard closet, its furniture scattered with thirty-year-old miniskirts (that didn't fit even back then), boa scarves chic in the sixties, go-go boots that reigned fashion supreme in 1975.

Hannah moved next to the bed, chuckling at the dried brown gook covering Kiki's face that was supposed to shrink her pores. A U-shaped foam pillow lifted Kiki's neck a few inches off the bed to keep the mask from rubbing off in her sleep.

A faint, lurid smile wafted across Kiki's face. Hannah imagined her sister dreaming of dashing bachelors, chiffon dresses, and fluttering poms poms on a college football field. Kiki moaned, giggled softly, and pouted her lips. Hannah hated to interrupt such a rewarding dream, but she was in a hurry. She gently tugged at Kiki's pink simulated-satin nightgown. Kiki moaned, tipped her curler-topped head toward her sister, opened one eye, then closed it.

So much for delicacy. Hannah slapped Kiki's shoulder. "Wake up."

"What time is it?"

"Six."

Kiki groaned and swatted the air with one hand. "Go away."

"I have to talk to you."

"Later. I was just dreaming that I was taking a bubble bath in this huge heart-shaped tub in Las Vegas," Kiki said groggily. "And would you like to know who was in the bubbles with me?"

"Not really."

"Bill Clinton. He wanted me to scrub his back, and it was so strange. I told him, no, that Monica wouldn't like it."

"Kiki, I think I know who killed Alex and Charlie."

Kiki's eyes popped open, her dismay creating a seismic shift that sent a dozen cracks through her clay mask. She pulled herself up on her elbows.

"Who?"

Hannah sat on the edge of the bed. She told Kiki about the poem.

"So Lorna sent it to Alex? She was his wife," Kiki said.

Hannah shook her head. "I don't think Lorna would send a poem by Robert Browning. She's more the Dr. Seuss type. And she's too crazy about Ox to be making love noises at Alex."

"Then who sent it?"

Hannah hesitated, uncomfortable with what she was about to say. "Mary. It had to be Mary."

Kiki sat up. "I don't believe it. And even if Mary did send the poem, it doesn't mean she's a murderer. Mary's too nice. And the way she wears her hair, it's not killer hair. It's too soft and fluffy. Murderers wear their hair flatter, I'm sure of it."

Upset, Kiki was at the babbling stage, and Hannah held up a finger in front of her sister's face, a gesture that sometimes had a quieting effect, like dangling something shiny in front of a parakeet. "Listen to me and focus. The other day, Charlie told me that he left Alex's birthday party along with everyone else, but that he came back to Alex's house an hour later and looked in a window. When he did, he saw something he thought could identify Alex's killer."

Kiki pressed her hand against her throat. "What was it?"

"The rose petals in his coat pocket came from Alex's Boule de Neige rosebush."

"This is no time to start talking plants, Hannah. Get to the point."

"It is the point. That rosebush is outside Alex's kitchen window. Charlie must have looked in and seen someone putting the vase water in the pitcher. At the time he didn't realize what he was seeing. It was probably later when he found out Alex was poisoned that he put things together. And the party was over around three-thirty or four. That puts Charlie at Alex's around four-thirty or five when Mary was still there."

Kiki squinted, causing more cracks in her clay mask. "Maybe it's because I haven't had my coffee, but I still don't get why you think Mary's the killer."

"Because if Charlie saw what I think he saw, it means that for certain the killer poisoned the water after the party, and that narrows our suspects." Hannah stopped and took a breath. "We know Maggie was there."

"Now I'm confused. You think Maggie did it? Why would she kill her employer?"

"She wouldn't. But Mary was also there. She claimed she was upstairs sleeping off a couple of tranquilizers, but she lied about that. And I think she sent the Browning poem to Alex."

"But you said the poem was about wives and husbands. Does that mean she and Alex were secretly married?"

"She might have thought she and Alex were going to get married. Maybe he said he'd marry her just to get her help in getting the Signatech deal approved. And when Alex broke up with her that day, she was devastated."

"Who wouldn't be?"

"She had heard what I said about the monkshood and she decided to poison him."

"I'm not so sure about all this, Hannah. Killing a man just because he dumps you. Justifiable, yes, but also a little extreme. If I killed every man who had dumped me——"

"There be a trail of corpses from here to New Jersey."

Kiki scowled, causing bits of clay to fall onto her chest.

Hannah continued. "The point is, if Mary's the killer, it explains why Charlie lost his nerve at the police station. I think he was infatuated with her."

"You're so slow sometimes. Everybody knows Charlie was nuts about Mary. He turned to sap whenever she got near him."

"Which is why he didn't have the heart to turn her in to the police." Getting up from the bed, Hannah walked the floor while she described the scenario, her voice kept low so as not to wake Perez. "He probably went home and called her. She came to his house that evening. He was too crazy about her to realize she was a danger to him. Maybe he thought he could keep the secret and they could have a relationship. But when she found out what he knew, she killed him. They were out by the pond." Hannah raised her hand in the air, gripping an imaginary weapon. "She hit him over the head with something then held his head under the water."

Kiki's face screwed up. "And then Mary tried to kill us, too." Her gaze moved downward and she picked a few clay flakes off her nightgown before looking back at Hannah. "Except that I don't think that was Mary's leg I saw from the shed."

"You said yourself that you're not sure what you saw."

Kiki nodded, her face somber. "So what do we do now?"

"It's what *I'm* going to do, which is warn Maggie."

"Warn her about what?"

"Mary's trying to get rid of people she thinks can identify her, including us, then Charlie. Maggie could be next. She was in the house when Mary poisoned the water. She could have seen something, something she doesn't even realize yet is pertinent."

"But if Mary were going to hurt Maggie, wouldn't she have already done it?"

"While Ox was in jail, she couldn't, because then the police would have known they had the wrong person. But now that Ox is out, the timing to get rid of Maggie couldn't be better."

"You think Mary will kill Maggie and the police will think Ox did it. But Mary could also be after us."

"I don't think she considers us that big a threat anymore. She knows we're investigating and that if we had any real evidence against her we would have already told the police."

Kiki wrapped her arms around her knees. "You've got to call Detective Morgan and tell him what you suspect."

"If I tell him now about my poem theory he may not take me seriously. Ox may be his number one suspect, but I'm probably still number two." Hannah sat down once more on the edge of the bed. "By the time I explained it all and got him to listen, it could be too late for Maggie." Hannah paused, her expression worried. "It may be too late now. That's why I'm going to her house. Once I'm sure she's safe, then I'll start getting evidence against Mary."

After Hannah stood up, Kiki grasped her hand.

"Why not just call her?" Kiki asked.

"Because I'm driving Maggie straight to the police station and walking her inside. I'm not making the same mistake I made with Charlie. I'm not going to see another innocent person killed."

"I won't let you do it, Hannah. It's too risky."

"It's okay. I know the condo complex where Mary lives. I'm going to drive by and see if her car is there. Surely this early she'll still be home."

"If you believe killers are the type who sleep late." Kiki worriedly twisted the pink blanket in her hands, but her grip loosened and a sly smile crossed her face as an idea congealed. "If you solved the murder, then you would win the election hands down."

"I don't care about that anymore."

Kiki scrambled out of bed. "Maybe you don't, but I do. I'm going with you to Maggie's."

"Impossible."

"Why? You said there's no danger, and I wouldn't mind taking a little credit for murder-solving myself." Kiki winked. "That would put old Wanda in her place."

Hannah opened her mouth to argue, then changed her mind. Even though Maggie said she believed in Hannah's innocence, it would be normal for her to have a few doubts. She might feel more comfortable if both sisters were there.

"All right, but let me do the talking," Hannah said. "And just throw on some clothes. We don't have time for you to fix yourself up."

"I've got to rinse off my mask, and I can't go anywhere without my makeup."

"Put it on in the car."

"Hannah, we don't have a car."

She had a point. In her flurry of high-octane thinking, Hannah had forgotten that the police had impounded the Cadillac. "We'll borrow Naomi's car."

"She won't be up yet, but I've got a set of keys to her Volvo that she gave me in case she ever lost hers. We can take the car and leave her a note. She'll understand. But what about John? Should we tell him?"

"No," Hannah said. "He'll only try to stop us. He'll say it's too dangerous."

"What if he's right?"

"Kiki, we are strong, intelligent women with plenty of life experience, and we can take care of ourselves. And as long as we're careful and watch our backs, what can happen?"

Kiki considered this a moment, then said, "I'll bring the pepper spray."

"And don't forget your meat tenderizer."

Ten minutes later, the two sisters hustled into Naomi's dilapidated Volvo. Hannah backed out of the driveway, trying to ignore the constant ringing coming from the bells and feathers hanging from the door handles and the rearview mirror. As Hannah drove down Walnut Avenue she noticed Kiki digging through her handbag, which bulged even more than usual. Kiki pulled out a camera.

"Why did you bring that?" Hannah asked.

"I want to get a picture of you solving the case for the newspaper," Kiki explained, bouncing a little in her seat with excitement. "It's going to be great publicity, Hannah. Once everyone sees it, you'll knock the stuffing out of Wanda in the election and she'll have to expose her skinny little tush to everyone she knows. I wonder if all that liposuction left identifying marks."

"I doubt the doctor branded his initials on her. No photos, Kiki. This is serious business, not a campaign stunt."

"Have it your way, but if you ask me, your political instincts are plain awful. There could be plenty of good spin from this." Frowning, Kiki lifted her foot and adjusted the metal tip of her boot, which was coming loose again, but she wanted to wear the boots because they looked so good with her yellow jumpsuit. She had her pantslegs stuffed into them, creating a Kitten with a Whip effect she thought highly provocative. And if Hannah solved the crime and the police came to the scene, it would pay to look her best. "What if I write a story for the newspaper? Just a few paragraphs about you solving the crime. I brought your little tape recorder along so I could record my thoughts. That way I can make it a first person, I-was-there sort of thing."

"Oh, all right, if it will make you happy," Hannah said distractedly, eager to drop the subject, her mind on more critical issues.

She drove across town to Mary's condo complex. Although Hannah didn't know Mary's condo number, she did know

Mary's car, a cherry red Miata. Hannah found it parked in a carport.

Hannah headed back through town then turned the corner onto Maggie's street, a leafy road that winded through an old neighborhood just west of town center. The area was made up of remodeled smaller homes with the occasional cottage that had escaped renovation. Maggie's house fell into the latter category. The Volvo's transmission emitted a plaintive whine as Hannah pulled to the curb. "Everyone's got an opinion," she muttered to the car. The Volvo answered with a small explosion out its tail pipe.

"Naomi always says that Penelope runs better if you—"

"Penelope?"

"That's Naomi's name for the car. Penelope of the Whispering Leaves That Sing So Softly."

Hannah groaned. "More like Penelope of the Burning Oil That Brakes So Badly."

"Naomi says Penelope runs smoother if you put an offering of flowers and berries in the glove compartment."

"The only gift Penelope's getting is a tank full of gas, and it won't be premium."

Butterflies in her stomach, Hannah gathered up her purse and observed the freshly painted white cottage nestled among overgrown oleanders at the end of a gravel drive. She had been there two years before when Maggie had wanted advice on a shade garden for the backyard. Hannah had dropped by, studied the garden's layout and then recommended a variety of rhododendrons. The house was doll-sized with only a tiny kitchen, living room, a small bedroom, and adjoining bath the size of a phone booth, but the rear yard was huge. Maggie leased the house at a below average rent in exchange for keeping up the landscaping. At first Maggie hadn't known much about gardening and it took a lot of help from Hannah and other Rose Club members before she stopped killing things with overdoses of fertilizer.

Hannah and Kiki got out of the Volvo, and headed up the drive, their shoes crunching against the gravel, then turned down a short walkway. Before they reached the front door they heard faint clipping sounds coming from around the back. Walking toward the noise, they passed a couple of battered garbage cans and a wood stack, ending up in an unfenced rear yard. With relief, Hannah saw Maggie, safe and sound, hacking away at a boxwood hedge. Maggie reminded Hannah of an aged Alice in Wonderland, her gray hair wrapped in a blue bandana, a green canvas apron tied around a long cotton dress, and the clippers like huge scissors in her hands. A variety of tools, including a rake and a shovel, lay scattered on the grass, and in one of the flowerbeds Hannah spotted a pile of freshly turned earth. Hannah started in Maggie's direction, but Kiki stopped her.

"Now, Hannah, as soon as your conversation with Maggie reaches the critical point, I want you to give me a signal," she said in a hushed voice.

"What do you mean, critical point?"

"You know, when you're talking about stuff that should be in the newspaper article," Kiki explained. "I don't want to miss important info."

"Your job is to keep a sharp eye out."

"So I won't miss good quotes that I could use for the newspaper?"

"No, to watch for Mary. Even though we saw her car parked at her house, I'm still uncomfortable. Whoever committed these murders is capable of anything."

TWENTY-FIVE

HANNAH AND KIKI STOOD AT the rear corner of Maggie's house, as Maggie clipped away at the hedge, unaware of their presence.

Hannah pressed her hand gently against her stomach, doing her best to squelch her blossoming misgivings. She felt trouble close by, like a bomb ticking, heard but not seen. She realized that it had been dumb not to wake up Perez and bring him along, but it was too late now. They had to warn Maggie. Hannah reminded herself that Mary was safely at home, probably still in her bathrobe enjoying her first cup of coffee, mulling over who she would kill that day. Maggie stopped clipping and examined the hedge, rubbing her right shoulder.

After reminding herself again what a strong and capable woman she was, Hannah started for the garden, but Kiki held her back. They retreated a few paces along the side of the house. Her hands on Hannah's shoulders, Kiki pressed her sister back against the wall.

"What we're doing is safe, right?" Kiki asked. "Mary's at home, and this is not in any way a problem, right?"

"Do I look concerned?"

"Like you need an adult diaper and a tranquilizer the size of a kiwi. Listen, take my advice, and don't jump into the danger thing right away with Maggie," Kiki said, her voice hushed as more clipping sounds came from the yard. "Ease into it."

"Why?"

"I don't want to offend you, but with all the gossip floating around about you being a murderer, Maggie might feel a little cautious. It could scare her teeth loose if you right away spout off 'Mary's going to kill you.' You don't want to give the poor woman a heart attack. Make a little small talk first."

"Like, love your outfit, and oh, by the way, run for your life?"

"Exactly."

Sticking close together, the sisters walked into the garden. It looked just as Hannah remembered, a big square lawn of dwarf fescue with a hedge running along the back fence, flowerbeds bordering the sides. In the corner, up in a tall birch, a squirrel fussed at a bluejay over birdfeeder rights. Beneath the tree Hannah saw the patch of rhododendrons and ferns she had helped Maggie plant a couple of years earlier. The plants looked good, everything healthy and lush green.

Hannah called out Maggie's name, and when Maggie saw them she smiled and laid down the clippers. She checked her watch.

"You girls are out early. It's barely seven," Maggie said. She rubbed her shoulder again, then grasped Hannah's hand. "I was going to call you. I wanted to apologize for taking off the way I did yesterday at the Rose Club forum. I guess I was just nervous."

"This situation's making us all a little crazy," Hannah said.

Maggie looked down at her soiled clothes. "Sorry about the way I look, but I need to get my gardening out of the way early today. I've got an interview with a placement agency at nine-thirty. Wish me luck."

Maggie's open, friendly face made Hannah doubly glad she had come over. Maggie was a sitting duck for a nut case like Mary.

"You're trimming back that long hedge yourself?" Kiki asked.

Maggie pushed the bandana farther back on her head, exposing a tuft of gray hair. "I can't afford to pay someone. To tell you the truth, I could use some advice. I'm not sure how far to trim it back."

The small talk was making Hannah jittery, but remembering Kiki's advice, she fought the urge to tell Maggie a killer was after her, then drag her into the car and take off. Be cool, Hannah told herself. They were safe, at least for a while. Mary was probably at her breakfast table munching toast and planning which weapon to use.

Hannah walked over to the shrub spanning the yard's back fence. Always liking to get her hands on a plant, she took a sprig in her fingers and rubbed the cool smooth leaves. She pulled off one and held it to her nose. It smelled like citrus.

"I'd take it down a few more inches if I were you," Hannah

said to Maggie. "The shrub's so healthy, you're going to get a lot of growth in the next couple of months. If it gets too tall, the shade it casts will damage the lawn."

"That's not what I wanted to hear," Maggie said. "My arms are already killing me from holding these clippers."

"You need a power hedger," Kiki told her. "Hannah's got one, and she whacks down the shrubs in no time."

"I have one, too. The landlord gave it to me, but I don't feel comfortable using it. It's so loud and to me it seems dangerous." Maggie took off one of her gardening gloves and frowned at the hedge as if she could chide it into growing shorter.

Now unbearably antsy, Hannah chose to dispense with the chitchat. "Maggie, I have something to tell you and there's not much time." Out of the corner of her eye she saw Kiki take the camera out of her purse, and she gave her a frosty look.

"What about?" Maggie asked

Hannah took a breath. "Mary."

Maggie turned solemn. She jerked off the other glove, holding both in one hand. "Save your energy. The police asked me another hundred questions last night, and I'm worn out." She bent down to pick up the clippers.

"You need to listen to me," Hannah told her. "I think Mary is dangerous."

Maggie straightened. "There are people around town who think you're dangerous, Hannah, but that doesn't make it true. Why on earth would Mary want Alex dead?"

"Because he dumped her flat," Kiki chimed in. "That kind of thing irks a woman because of the marriage statistics."

"It was much more than that. Mary thought she and Alex were going to get married," Hannah said. Maggie tilted her head, looking at Hannah with puzzlement. "He had sex with her in his office during his lunch party, and then broke up with her before his pants were zipped."

Maggie threw the gloves to the ground. "How do you know all that?"

"Mary told me," Hannah fibbed. No reason to tell everyone that she had hidden under Alex's desk.

"God, I'm so tired of talking about this." Maggie pulled off her bandana and used it to wipe her forehead. "Listen, they had been seeing each other for months, but I knew Alex was just using her so she would vote his way on Signatech. The man was a bastard to every woman who got close to him. But Mary's a grownup. She knew what she was getting into." Maggie shook her head. "All those silly women chasing after him. They phoned him, wrote to him, even hung around outside the house sometimes. Such simpering idiots."

Offended, Kiki reared back her shoulders. "I wouldn't call them idiots. He was a very attractive man."

"He had charisma, I'll grant him that," Maggie said with bitterness. "But he was a two-faced liar who treated people like servants. I couldn't say it while I worked for him, and then, afterwards, it didn't seem right to badmouth the dead. But the truth is, Alex was a self-obsessed ass. I used to think Mary had a brain, but she was a stupid fool for not seeing through him."

The venom in Maggie's voice surprised Hannah. "I thought you and Mary were friends."

"We were friendly. There's a difference. If you're thinking she poisoned Alex, well, I guess that's a possibility. She stayed upstairs at least a half hour after everyone left the party. I was busy cleaning, taking out garbage, picking up as much as I could before I went home for the day. She could have come downstairs and poisoned the water pitcher, and I wouldn't have known it. She must have lied about taking the tranquilizers to cover herself."

Hannah started at a noise from around the side of the house. She spun around, saw nothing, but silently hoped Kiki had remembered to bring her pepper spray. When she turned back, Maggie was glaring at Kiki.

"What are you doing?" Maggie asked.

"Don't worry, honey, this is journalism," Kiki replied, holding up the camera. "Hannah, step close to Maggie, and the two of you get real serious looks on your faces," Kiki told them, but the instruction was unnecessary. Hannah already looked as serious as a double bypass, and Maggie appeared stricken.

"I don't want my picture taken," Maggie said angrily. "Put the camera down, now, or I'll take it from you."

Hannah and Kiki regarded Maggie with shock. Kiki lowered the camera. "I didn't mean anything."

"Better put it away," Hannah told her sister. Kiki slipped the camera back in her purse.

Maggie's hard expression collapsed. "I'm sorry I said that.

It's just that I can't stand to have my picture taken. I used to be pretty, you know, and look at me now."

Touched by the hurt in Maggie's voice, Hannah didn't know what to say. She always considered Maggie the type who didn't give a hoot about her appearance.

This being a subject close to Kiki's heart, she walked up to Maggie and put her arm around her. "Aw, come on now, honey, you're a good-looking woman. You just need a Kiki Beauty Blitz." Kiki winked. "We could dye your hair red and put some makeup on you. You'd look just like Raquel Welch."

Maggie smiled. "Somehow, I don't think so."

Kiki nudged Maggie with her elbow. "A little blue eye shadow and dangly earrings can work wonders."

Hannah was grateful that Kiki had pacified Maggie, but at that moment she was more concerned with the woman's safety than her looks. That noise she heard still had her spooked. It occurred to her that in Mary's large condo complex, it was possible that there could have been more than one red Miata.

"Maggie, if Mary did kill Alex, she may think you saw something that could be used against her," Hannah said. "It's possible that Mary is a very disturbed woman. A dangerous woman."

"A complete whacko," Kiki added, in case "disturbed" and "dangerous" didn't register.

"And if Mary thinks you could be a threat," Hannah said, pausing a beat, "you could be next on her hit list."

Hannah expected Maggie to respond with shock, fear, maybe a little hair tearing. Instead she looked at Hannah with contempt.

"So Mary's a whacko just because she got her revenge against a man who abused her?" Maggie asked.

Kiki turned up a palm. "Let's face it, honey, she killed the guy over a love spat. It's not like he beat her up or killed her cat."

"There are worse ways to hurt someone," Maggie replied.

"Like what?" Kiki asked, eager to advance a conversation that was starting to get juicy. Hannah watched silently, her high curiosity mixed with unease.

"A man can degrade a woman, can promise her love, and then give her nothing," Maggie said. "He can tear down her confidence bit by bit until she's just a shell of her old self. Who could blame a woman for lashing out?"

"You're being very protective of a woman whom you claim isn't a close friend," Hannah said.

"I may not be able to understand what she saw in Alex, but I understand her pain. I saw what he did to her. Something like that happened to me once. It's happened to a lot of us. We can all understand her motives."

"Can you understand her motives for killing Charlie?" Hannah asked.

"That was a terrible thing, if she really did it. But Hannah, you're just making guesses."

"What if I'm guessing right?" Hannah said. "We want to take you to the police station where you'll be safe."

"I appreciate you wanting to help me, but I'm not afraid of Mary." Maggie clipped a hunk of leaves from the hedge, leaving an unattractive hole. "Now, if you two could go, I've got to finish this up."

"Maggie, I can't leave you here," Hannah told her. "It's too dangerous."

Maggie again jabbed the clippers at the hedge and took out another ill-advised chunk. "I'm an adult."

Charlie was an adult, too, Hannah thought. *Now he was a dead adult.* There was no way she was leaving Maggie home alone. "At least let me show you how to use the power hedger. The work will go so much faster, you'll be finished in a few minutes," Hannah offered, stalling for time. Once Maggie had time to think things through, she might listen to reason.

Maggie hesitated before responding. Hannah felt certain that she wanted to throw them out, but then she saw Maggie soften. "I'm sorry I'm being rude, but the past week has been hell. You've always been kind to me, Hannah. The hedger's in the garage, hanging on the wall just left of the door."

"Will it need gasoline?"

"No, it's battery powered. Just pull it loose from the thingy it's connected to."

Hannah walked back to the garage, opened the door, and flipped the light switch. She found the power hedger on the wall just as Maggie had described. The "thingy" turned out to be a battery charger plugged into a wall outlet. After getting down the hedger, Hannah glanced around the garage. It was tidy, with neat shelves, and tools hanging on the bare-stud walls. Hannah wondered if it had been Maggie who had organized Alex's gardening shed. Hannah's own garage was chaotic.

Above a rack holding old paint cans, Hannah noticed an ancient and battered vanity license plate hanging cockeyed on the wall. A couple of old brooms partially obscured it, but Hannah could make out the words, "Be Kind," and it brought a smile to her face. It was so like Maggie. The hedger in hand, she started out of the garage, but stopped at the door. There was something familiar about those words. She walked closer and saw that the plate came from Texas. Lorna was from Texas, and she and Alex had lived there when they were married. But lots of people from Texas ended up in California. Lots of people from everywhere ended up in California.

Hannah walked back out into the yellow sunlight and found Maggie and Kiki huddled together. Kiki had just finished putting Tahiti Pink lipstick on Maggie. When Maggie saw Hannah, she backed away a few steps, lowering her head with embarrassment.

"I'm giving her a taste of the miracles that can be performed by the full Kiki Beauty Blitz," Kiki said. "Doesn't the pink make her look twenty years younger?"

"At least. You look great," Hannah told Maggie with sincerity. Maggie responded with a shy smile. She did look pretty with the lipstick. Hannah held out the power hedger to her. "To turn it on you just press this little switch," Hannah explained, turning the hedger on its side. "Remember to keep a solid grip on the handle and always hold it so the blade is away from you."

Hannah handed the hedger to Maggie. It was then, her hand brushing against Maggie's calloused fingers, that it hit her why the words on the license plate were familiar. Lorna had mentioned them the day she had sat on Alex's couch and cried about their relationship. Bawling like a baby, Lorna said that Alex had left her for some hippie girl back in Texas. She also said that the van they had driven had a license plate that read "Be Kind."

While Maggie warily examined the hedger, Hannah watched her, her eyes darkened, the first inkling of comprehension settling on her.

"When should I look for thee and find thee gone?" Hannah said, the words slow and soft. "When cry for the old comfort and find none?" It was the Browning poem. She wasn't getting every word right, but she was close enough. Maggie's eyes snapped up from the hedger. She looked like someone had just punched her.

"Are you okay, Hannah?" Kiki said, then sidled up to Maggie and cocked a thumb at Hannah. "Sometimes she overdoses on those Chinese herbs. Too much dong quai and she starts babbling Shakespeare."

Hannah wasn't listening, and neither was Maggie.

"Vainly the flesh fades. Soul makes all things new," Hannah continued, now louder. "But the soul whence the love comes, all ravage leaves that whole. You were talking about yourself, weren't you, Maggie? You used to be so beautiful, and you're not anymore. But your soul is the same as it was twenty years ago. That part of you never aged."

As the squirrel and bluejay resumed their squabbling at the birdfeeder, Hannah realized with melancholy that she had gotten the story of Alex's murder right. A woman in love had avenged herself against an emotionally brutal man, then killed Charlie because he could identify her as the murderer. Only Hannah had been mistaken about which woman. She just couldn't understand how the rest of it all fit.

Maggie stood transfixed, her lips parted.

"You knew Alex in Texas," Hannah said.

Maggie didn't respond. She just stood there holding the hedger, her eyes strangely empty. Years before, Hannah had traveled to New York City to attend a business conference with her boss, and on her afternoon off she had taken the subway to the Guggenheim. The people on the subway had worn that same look. Shut down. Nobody home.

"Hell, yes! The bitch knew him like a fly knows cow shit!"

Hannah looked over at the side of the house and saw Lorna, her fists on her hips, brimming with piss and vinegar.

"What are you doing here?" Hannah asked.

Lorna strode up, her eyes stuck to Maggie. "I've been following you for two days, Hannah, to nail you for trying to frame Oxie. You could have knocked me over with a feather when I clapped a gander on this bitch." She tipped her head at Maggie.

Maggie's blank look evaporated. Now she looked scared to death, which was reasonable, Hannah figured, since a stranger had stomped into her yard yelling obscenities.

"Hannah, I'm confused," Kiki said, her hand pressed against

her temple. "What you said a second ago. How could Maggie have known Alex in Texas?"

"Because she's Moonbeam McKenna," Lorna said.

Kiki squinted with concentration. "Where have I heard that name before?"

"From me," Lorna said. "Moonbeam McKenna is the dope-dealing, hippie bitch, low-life, scum-sucking bimbo who ran off with my lawful husband." Her hands on her waist, Lorna approached Maggie, glaring at her with hostility as she walked a slow semicircle around her. "I'll tell you, there's not much that surprises me these days, but it shocked the holy shit out of me seeing you after all these years, Moonbeam. I didn't recognize you until you put on that lipstick. It really took the years off. For a split second I saw the old you."

Kiki beamed. "I told you it was your color," she said to Maggie, who didn't seem pleased.

"I had no idea you were even still alive," Lorna said. "I mean, with your druggie lifestyle and all."

When Hannah saw Kiki's hand reach back into her handbag, she gave her a warning look. This was not the time for snapshots. Kiki hadn't even noticed Hannah, yet her hand pulled back empty. Hannah decided Kiki must have picked up some mental vibrations from her. She read once in a women's magazine that that kind of thing happened when you lived together long enough.

"Who are you?" Maggie asked, flustered, her voice cracking. She turned to Hannah for help. "Do you know this woman?"

Smiling, Lorna let out a low hoot. "You must have lost a few brain cells, Moonie girl. Let me refresh your memory. I'm Al Pinsky's former wife. Remember? The one back in Big Spring who stood in the street in her polka dot nightie bawling her eyes out when you took off with her husband."

"I think you've made a teensy mistake," Kiki said. "This is Maggie, Alex's housekeeper."

"His housekeeper?" Lorna said with disbelief. She followed it up with a belly laugh, like it was the best joke she had ever heard. "Well, haven't you come down off your pedestal? But you're Moonbeam, there's no doubt about it. You look like crap now, but I'd know you anywhere."

Hannah could tell that the last comment hit Maggie hard. Maggie's mouth tightened and she lifted her chin with indignation. "You're crazy," she said. "Get off my property or I'll call the police."

"You're Moonbeam and I can prove it," Lorna replied. Maggie's eyes grew large as Lorna darted over, reached down, and lifted up her dress. Lorna then gestured to a tattoo on Maggie's ankle like she was unveiling a new washer–dryer on a TV quiz show. Hannah gasped when she saw it. It was an ankh tattoo identical to Lorna's.

"Told ya." Lorna directed the smug comment to Hannah and Kiki. "Alex liked to brand his women like heifers. He was such a class-A shithook."

Maggie snatched back the hem of her skirt. "Get away from me or—"

"Or what?" Lorna shot back. She stood up, her body language cocky. "Come on and try it, Moonbeam. I've been waiting twenty-five years to sock you one."

Neither Maggie nor Lorna moved. They just gave each other the glowering stares of junkyard dogs.

Kiki tugged on Hannah's arm. "That's the mark I saw when we were in the shed! And see, Maggie has thick ankles and doesn't shave. That's the leg that tried to kill us!"

Hannah was way ahead of her. Maggie had the means and opportunity to kill Alex, but Hannah had never really suspected her because she never thought Maggie had a motive. But if she had once been Alex's lover? Maybe even more than that.

While Hannah mulled this over, Kiki's emotions got the best of her, and she let out a noise equivalent to squealing tires. "You! You tried to burn us alive!" she shouted at Maggie. "I swear to God, I'll slap you silly!" Her face purple, her arms stretched in front of her Frankenstein-style, Kiki bolted at Maggie. Seeing Kiki race-waddling her way, Maggie dropped the hedger in astonishment. Kiki, unskilled in physical contact outside that of a romantic nature, stopped just short of Maggie and began flailing her arms. The attack was supposed to be a terrifying flurry of punches but looked more like the result of neurological damage, Kiki's slaps never getting within a foot of Maggie.

"You get her, girl!" Lorna shouted with enthusiasm. "But, babe, you need to step into it!"

Maggie held up her hands to protect herself, the gesture hardly necessary since Kiki, even with Lorna's encouragement, was still only swatting air while emitting a high-pitched "yyyeee" noise. Hannah grabbed her from behind.

"Murderer! Killer! Fire bug!" Kiki shouted, shaking her fist as Hannah dragged her back. "Let me go, Hannah! I'm going to knock her flat!"

"Stop it!" Hannah shouted. "Stop it, stop it, stop it!" She took her arms from Kiki, but grabbed hold of Kiki's belt so she couldn't go anywhere. "You're not going to knock anyone flat."

"Why not?" Lorna said, sounding miffed. She stood a few feet away, watching Hannah with disdain. "I don't get you. Moonbeam tried to kill you. Doesn't that touch a nerve? What are you, made of ice? Always so cool and calm. You're not human."

"We don't have any real proof that Maggie did anything," Hannah replied. She let go of Kiki's belt, and Kiki stayed put.

"What does it take to convince you?" Lorna said. "You want Moonbeam to write out a confession?"

With a sickening clarity, Hannah realized that a written confession was probably what it would take. The facts were falling into place, yet nothing could be proven. She had to get more information from Maggie, and Maggie didn't look ready to spill out any murder confessions. Maggie had taken a few steps back toward the hedge, her eyes bright with fear. Slowly and cautiously, Hannah moved toward her, the way she would approach a frightened dog: She wanted information from Maggie, and she didn't know any way to get it except to just ask.

"Were you and Alex married?" Hannah asked her. "The poem you sent Alex was titled 'From Any Wife to Any Husband'."

"Al marry this slut puppy? No way," Lorna said, vaulting into the conversation.

Maggie's hands curled into fists. "We didn't need a piece of paper. Alex said we were married in the eyes of God."

"Yeah, and Al told me he'd be faithful forever and that the little sore on his lip was just a pimple," Lorna said. "But at least I knew he was lying. You never had a clue."

Maggie's body went rigid, everything about her quietly dangerous. Kiki had come up right beside Hannah, and Hannah pushed her sister back a few feet, not liking at all the way things were going.

"Don't talk like you know me," Maggie growled at Lorna. "You have no idea who I am."

"But I do know you. I kept up with you for years after you ran off with my husband. Think of it as tracking stolen property. I found out that you were a dopehead, that you went to prison in Arizona for selling drugs," Lorna said with a bitterness fueled by thirty years of hate. Lorna had waited a long time to get revenge upon Moonbeam, and this was her moment. "Then, as soon as you hit the slammer, it was goodbye Moonbeam as far as old Al was concerned. He dumped you like yesterday's garbage and took off for California."

There was an ugly silence broken by the ironically sweet chirping of a robin that had just landed at the birdfeeder, obviously unaware that it had entered a war zone. It made Hannah wonder if birds had chirped during the war in Bosnia. Probably so. You probably feel pretty sure of yourself when you can fly off any time you want.

Nobody was flying off from Maggie's backyard. Maggie and Lorna were rooted to the ground, staring at each other, each ready to tear out the other's vital organs. Feeling sorry for both women, Hannah watched skittishly from a few feet away, afraid to intervene, afraid not to. She wanted to call the police but was afraid of what would happen if she tried to leave. Lorna stood there coldly confident, the confrontation making her stronger, but Hannah could tell that Maggie was starting to emotionally fray, the trip down memory lane a place she hadn't wanted to go. Looking past Maggie's gray hair and lined face, Hannah could visualize how she must have been twenty-five years earlier—young, lovely, and full of hope.

Hannah decided to keep the women talking. With Maggie's frazzled state, maybe she could be manipulated into giving more information.

"How did you end up working for Alex?" Hannah asked. She kept her voice soft and earnest, mimicking the tone of a shrink she had once watched on the Lifetime channel.

"Yeah, Moonbeam, tell us how the woman who was once the temptress of men ended up scrubbing their toilets," Lorna spouted off, apparently unaware that Hannah was trying to create a safe space for Maggie to share thoughts and feelings.

This time Lorna truly hit the bull's-eye. Maggie's chin quivered, suppressed pain rising to the surface. She clutched at the front of her gardening apron.

"My life's been hard, too hard for one person," Maggie said

with audible torment. "Yes, I went to prison, and after I got out I had a drug problem, but I cleaned up. I was broke. I had no place to go. I heard that Alex was doing well in California, so I called him for help. He owed me."

"Al owed *you?*" Lorna said, then let out a low whistle. "That's a joke."

"He did owe me! When I got caught selling drugs, I'd been doing it for him," Maggie said, spewing out the words, her voice thick. "He made me sell the drugs. He said we needed the money."

"So Alex owed you so much he let you be his maid," Lorna said. "Are you that stupid?"

"She was much more than that," Hannah said quickly, wanting to settle Maggie down, to keep her talking. "You took care of him, didn't you, Maggie? He depended on you."

Maggie nodded. A tear spilled onto her cheek and she rubbed it away with the back of her hand. "I was like a wife. I loved him. I looked out after him. I fixed his meals, washed his clothes. I helped him with ideas for his work. He needed me. He said he did. He said we still had a spiritual bond that could never be broken." Maggie's hands reached out in front of her, palms upturned, and this gesture, along with her pleading tone, made Hannah suspect that Maggie was trying to convince herself as much as anyone. Hannah couldn't imagine what turned this supposed spiritual bond to murder.

Lorna tried to laugh but it came out more as a cackle. "Save it for *Oprah*. I hate to break this to you, but you were just a toilet scrubber to Al. That day I was at his house to demand my money, he tried to sweet talk me. Typical Al Pinsky. Like I would fall for that shit. But while he was bullcrapping around, I asked him what happened to old Moonbeam. I guess he didn't want me to know you were in the house. He thought it might tick me off, might make me come down harder for the money. You know what he told me? He said he came across you a while back. He said I would laugh my head off if I saw you, that you were an old, fat, worn-out dopehead. He told me that he'd never given a flying fart about you. You should have heard it, Moonbeam."

A dead stillness fell on the small group of women, as if the earth had stopped turning. The pain on Maggie's face wrenched

Hannah's heart, but Maggie didn't seem shocked by what Lorna had just told her.

"I did hear it," Maggie said. "I heard everything he said about me."

Hannah drew in a breath, starting to understand Maggie's motive for killing. She felt Kiki come up behind her and touch her arm. Hannah turned and they exchanged a brief look.

"When he realized it was you at the front door, he told me to stay in the bedroom with the door closed," Maggie said, her eyes and nose turning pink. "He thought I'd do what he said, because he knew I didn't want you to see me, that I was self-conscious about how much I'd changed. But I had to find out what you wanted after all these years."

"So you eavesdropped?" Kiki asked. Her intonation made it sound like she didn't approve of such behavior, which Hannah found amusing, even in their current grim predicament.

"I stood in the hallway where he couldn't see me," Maggie continued, sounding relieved to tell the story, even to an enemy. "And I heard the horrible things he said. After everything I'd done for him, all the love I'd shown him. Even when he brought women home, I didn't mind, because I knew he and I had this spiritual relationship."

"Yeah, so spiritual you decided to send him straight to heaven with no pit stops," Lorna said. "You're the one who killed him. It had to be you. You poisoned him and then sat by and did nothing while the cops tried to pin it on Oxie."

"Alex deserved it," Maggie said, her heat rising. "You would have killed him yourself back then when he left you, if you'd had the chance. I forgave him for what he did to me twenty years ago, at least I thought I had. But for him to take advantage of me again, then laugh at me behind my back. That filthy bastard."

"At some level I can understand what you did to Alex," Hannah said. "But why poor Charlie?"

"Charlie should have minded his own business," Maggie said with a callousness that shook Hannah.

"He wanted to help you," Hannah said to her.

"He wanted me to turn myself in. I see that look on your face, Hannah, but don't you judge me," Maggie said. "You people know nothing, living your safe little lives in this highbrow town. Driving your fancy cars, spending more on cappuccinos than I

spend on a meal. I wasn't going back to prison because of any
of you."

"Oh, boo hoo. Let's hear some violins," Lorna said with mock
pity. "I've never paid more than fifty cents for a cup of java in
my life, and my Ox almost went to the slammer for the crime
you committed. That would be the second man you took from
me."

"There's no man on earth worth crossing the street for," Maggie said.

Lorna pointed a finger at her. "Hold it right there, babe. You
watch what you say about Ox." Her lips curled up. "But I guess
it doesn't matter what you say any more. You're going back to
jail, Moonbeam, and we're not talking any country club prison
for dopeheads. We're talking hard time. Little miss hippie bitch,
back where she belongs. Maybe they'll let you clean the latrines
so you'll feel at home."

Before Hannah knew what had happened, Maggie hurled herself at Lorna. Lorna jumped right, and Maggie fell clumsily to
the ground. Hannah ran over to her.

"Please, ladies, let's calm down!" Hannah said with an ironic
fluster, taking Maggie's arm and helping her up. She saw a
flashing light and noticed Kiki a few feet away, holding the
camera to her face. "Kiki, put down that camera and go call the
police!"

Maggie shoved Hannah away. "No one's calling the police!"
With one quick grab, Maggie took hold of Kiki. Dropping the
camera, Kiki let out a yowl and jerked free, but the cursed metal
tip on her boot caught on the power hedger lying on the ground,
and she sprawled flat on her face on the lawn, her purse falling
from her shoulder. Before Hannah could get to her, Maggie
jammed one foot onto the small of Kiki's back, then leaned
down and picked up the power hedger. She switched it on and
the machine came to life with an earsplitting roar.

"Don't you touch her!" Hannah screamed at Maggie, but
nothing could be heard over the hedger's noise.

Hannah saw the fear on Maggie's face, could see her running
over her options in her head. The process wouldn't take long.
There weren't many options available. Only a moment earlier,
Hannah had felt some sympathy for Maggie, in spite of her
crimes, the way one woman can look into another woman's
eyes, and, no matter what she's done, see herself there. But with

her sister at risk, all sympathy was gone and Hannah was ready to drop kick Maggie into Nevada. The problem was the hedger. Maggie had its deadly vibrating blade aimed straight at Kiki's head.

Hannah picked up a shovel, poised to strike at Maggie. Maggie thrust the hedger's blade at her. While Maggie focused on Hannah, Kiki reached for her handbag strap and inched it toward her, then slid her hand inside and pulled out the meat tenderizer. With Maggie's foot still pressed on her back, Kiki had limited movement, but she managed to raise herself on one elbow, and with her other hand, she brought the meat tenderizer sharply against Maggie's ankle. Maggie cried out and jumped back just long enough for Kiki to scramble away.

Hannah swung the shovel and whacked Maggie hard on the side of the head, the shovel's blade making a cracking sound as it hit her skull. The hedger dropped from Maggie's hands and the motor cut off as it hit the ground. Stunned, Maggie sank to her knees. When she saw Lorna coming at her, she stood halfway up, her legs wobbly, but still ready to fight.

Lorna cocked her fist and threw a blow that landed square on Maggie's jaw. Maggie collapsed.

Shaking her hand, Lorna glared at Maggie, who lay moaning on the ground. "That's for trying to frame my Oxie." She looked at Hannah. "Nice work with the shovel. I always knew you had some fire in you. I guess the only thing left to do is to call the cops."

"First we have to call an ambulance," Hannah said, kneeling down by Maggie. "She's hurt."

"Be a bleeding heart," Lorna said. "I don't see why we have to call an ambulance for a killer."

Maggie was lying on her back, a rivulet of blood streaming out her nose. Hannah propped up her head with one hand, then looked up at Lorna. "You realize we can't prove anything."

"The bitch just admitted she killed Al and that other guy," Lorna said. "What else do you want?"

"It's her word against ours," Hannah said.

Lorna's mouth gaped open. "You're joking, right?"

"I wish I were."

Kiki had just managed to pull herself to a standing position. She walked over to Maggie. "You'll be getting no Kiki Beauty Blitz." Maggie didn't seem to hear. Kiki turned her attention to her sister. "What if we had everything Maggie said on tape?" Kiki asked as she brushed off her clothes.

Hannah looked at her sister with bafflement. "That would be a help, obviously."

Kiki pulled Hannah's small tape recorder from her shoulderbag.

"It's still running. I turned it on as soon as soon as the conversation got so darn interesting," Kiki said. "I wanted to get all those good quotes while you girls were yelling at each other. I thought even if I couldn't use them in a newspaper article, I could play it for everybody at Lady Nails, and Wanda would be pea green with envy that she'd missed it."

TWENTY-SIX

⁂

*I*T ONLY VAGUELY RESEMBLED THE Hill Creek town hall and looked even less like a small town inauguration ceremony. With the bright banners and marching music, the clumps of red and blue balloons drifting down from the ceiling, the photos of Wanda pinned to the walls, it looked more like some small South American dictatorship after a military coup. The Wandanistas had seized power, and now they were throwing a party.

A couple of hundred Hill Creekers milled around with Wanda's face grinning from buttons pinned to their chests, all of them dressed to the hilt in chic funereal black. In a way it was a funeral. It was Alex's and Charlie's, the inauguration a farewell to them both. Yet at the same time it was an embracing of something new, a fresh era for Hill Creek. The truth was, the townspeople had grown a bit weary of Alex Portman's communal oneness. After all that talk of uplifting spirituality they found themselves licking their chops for some self-gratifying shallowness. And if it was shallowness you wanted, Wanda Backus could deliver it by the truckload.

Wanda had paid for the inauguration hoopla out of her own velvet-lined pocket, including her colossal color photograph hanging behind the podium, just in front of the glass wall that looked out on the trees. As Hannah observed the six-foot photo, she found Wanda's smiling visage much like Wanda's campaign platform—too vague and blurred to be believable. But then, Hill Creek had never much liked harsh realities.

"She had that photo shot with one of those fuzzy lenses like they use on half-dead actresses," Kiki said, fixing a steely eye on Wanda's photo. "She had them airbrush out every bump and wrinkle."

"You can't blame her," Hannah replied. "The photo's so big

you can practically see up her nostrils. Enlarged to that size, my face would look like a geological survey map."

"I don't understand why you're being so darn gracious," Kiki complained, tugging at her skin-tight spandex purple dress. After her signature boots had almost gotten her killed, she retired them to the depths of her closet, and was back to her favorite high-heeled gold sandals. "Wanda stole the election from you, with all her radio ads and that double-decker bus parading through town with the loudspeakers blaring out her name. Your little 'Vote for Hannah' flyers never had a chance. All that razzmatazz made the whole town forget that you solved the murders."

"It's natural for people to put away bad memories and move on. To be honest, losing the election was a relief. Perez was right. I didn't really want to be mayor."

Hannah scanned the crowd to see who was there, the answer being everybody. The official ceremony only moments away, people merrily circulated, waving "Wanda" banners and swapping gossip, the mood festive. The swearing in of a new mayor was usually a dull affair witnessed only by the council members, but Wanda considered this more than an inauguration. It was her crowning as the official queen of Hill Creek.

Hannah and Kiki had just started off to find their seats when they heard a "pssst" followed by their names, and they saw Wanda's head, the real one, sticking out from a side door. She waved them over. "Darlings, can I speak to you just a moment?"

When the sisters got close, Wanda pulled them into a dim hallway. With the election safely won, Wanda had dumped the drab suits and gone back to chic designer wear. Tonight she wore an elegant floor-length gown topped with a triple strand of pearls, her hair fluffed and curled into a style suspiciously similar to Queen Elizabeth's. Hannah wondered if they would all have to curtsy. Wanda already made Walter walk a few paces behind her.

"In the spirit of communal harmony," Wanda began, "I want you to know, Kiki, dear, that I consider our little election bet to be officially null and void." Her hand swept up in front of her face, then sideways in a Pope-like, absolving gesture. "I wouldn't want you to embarrass yourself."

Hannah held back a laugh, but Kiki fumed. "Oh, piddle, it's you who doesn't want to be embarrassed," Kiki said, steam practically blowing out her ears. "When it was going to be someone else's inauguration, a little mooning was A-OK."

Wanda's lips pinched. "There's some truth to that," she admitted. "But you see, dear, I'm going to be bringing a certain sophistication to our little town, a savoir faire that's been sorely missing, and I want my first official appearance as mayor to have that grace and elegance that I'll soon be known for throughout the state. I'm so glad you understand," she said, not caring a bit whether Kiki understood or not. "By the way, I've always thought a woman your age should only be caught in spandex if she's sprained something. And Hannah, why are you clomping around in those silly boots?"

Hannah looked down at her feet. "I thought this long skirt hid them. They're my new hiking boots. Perez said I have to break them in before the trip so I don't get blisters."

"Well, they make you look like Ma Kettle, and please don't take this wrong, but if both of you could stay near the back so you don't get in any photographs. Well, I'm off." With the verbal feces tossed, Wanda whisked down the hallway, disappearing through a door before either of the sisters could retaliate.

"Granny sucking eggs," Kiki muttered with contempt as she and Hannah walked back into the noise and lights of the assembly room. "The next few weeks will be holy hell with Wanda strutting around like the queen of Sheba. Lucky you, you'll be in Colorado."

"I'll admit, not having to endure Wanda will make up for any snakes or mosquitoes," Hannah replied good-naturedly. "But let's not begrudge Wanda winning the election. The voters wanted her. I just wish she wouldn't rub it in our hair."

"It's going to get worse. Ellie said she asked for a special chair at Lady Nails with 'Mayor' printed on it, and she wants her own ladies room. And Bertha said that Wanda's buying a limo and putting little flags on the front fenders. Can you stand it? If only there was a way to bring her down a few notches, it would make this all more bearable," Kiki said, scowling, then suddenly she brightened. "I see Naomi in the back, and I need to talk to her. It's urgent."

"Why are you so anxious to talk to her now?" Hannah asked. "You just spoke to her on the phone before we left."

"She wants to hear more about your trip. She's dying for every detail," Kiki said before hurrying off.

A few days earlier Hannah had finally agreed to Perez's hiking trip, although with some reluctance, but she was now excited about the chance to be alone with him for two whole weeks. They were taking off the next day, and he was currently home getting the rest of their things stuffed into a backpack the size of a deep freezer that supposedly he was going to carry. She was trying not to be disturbed by his packing list, which included all sorts of emergency freeze-dried food and snakebite antidote.

Hannah looked around the room for Lauren and Detective Morgan, and found them deep in conversation by the entrance. In the past weeks their romance had progressed, with Morgan eagerly helping Lauren rehearse for *Irma la Douce*. It turned out that he harbored a secret desire to be a cabaret singer and spent Tuesday nights at a karaoke bar in Sausalito. Hannah didn't know how Lauren was going to break it to him that there wasn't a play, but Hannah would think of something.

The crowd grew thicker and noisier. After being jostled one too many times, Hannah moved to a spot near the wall where she could watch things outside the fray. She tried to feel as festive as everyone else but couldn't. Not that she didn't have plenty of reasons to celebrate. The police had found Charlie's blood and some algae traces in Maggie's car, and they now had a good case against Maggie for both murders. And Hannah had found a man in Petaluma who adopted Charlie's goldfish, which she knew would have made Charlie happy. It was her failure in keeping Signatech from moving to town that weighed on her. Murders solved, goldfish saved, town ruined. She didn't much like that lineup. She had tried talking to Wanda, but Signatech had offered to put Wanda's picture on a plaque in front of their parking lot. Now Wanda was all for Signatech and refused to listen to reason. But Hannah wasn't about to give up. There had to be some way to change her mind.

As Hannah searched for Kiki so they could find seats, she caught sight of Ox's head above the throng. Hannah waved at him and a few seconds later he and Lorna emerged holding hands. They looked out of place in the elegantly dressed crowd, both wearing T-shirts and old blue jeans, with Lorna's tucked into her white boots.

"I thought you two left to get married," Hannah said. Bertha's voice blared from the loudspeaker announcing that the ceremony was about to start and for everybody to find seats.

"We got hitched in Carmel two days ago," Lorna replied, having to shout over the noise. She held out her left hand to show off her shiny gold wedding band.

"Congratulations," Hannah said, sincerely happy for them.

Lorna tucked herself in Ox's arm and he beamed at his new wife with pride. "After we got married we did some sightseeing along the coast," he said.

Hannah smiled. "Sounds romantic."

"It was until the Buick lost a fan belt at Hearst Castle," Lorna said. "But we got it fixed. We're starting back for Big Spring tonight, but we wanted to see you before we left. We wanted to apologize."

"What for?" Hannah had to shout, the music and chatter getting louder. Gesturing for Lorna and Ox to follow, she moved down the side aisle, through the door, and into the hallway where she had spoken to Wanda. With the heavy door closed behind them, it was quiet there. "That's better," Hannah said, grateful for the tranquility, however brief. "Now what were you saying?"

"That we wanted to apologize for all those terrible things I said about you when you were really just trying to help Ox," Lorna said. She kicked at the floor with her boot, the apology coming hard.

"It's all forgotten," Hannah told her.

"Yeah, well, Ox wanted us to do something for you, so we got you a little gift. I think you'll like it," Lorna said, her expression turning sly. "I know how upset you were about that big company moving to town, and we heard that Wanda, now that she's mayor, is all for it."

"So we did a background check on her," Ox chimed in.

"In my old business," Lorna said. "You learn how to do these things."

"But why?" Hannah asked. "What could you possibly find out about Wanda?"

"Nothing too interesting at first, other than a string of husbands and some juicy divorces," Lorna replied. "Then we came across a police report in Sedona, Arizona, from two years back."

Hannah nodded, still confused. "I remember that she and her husband Walter went there for the Aqua-Tantric Love workshop."

"That was in the report." Lorna rolled her eyes. "They were trying to fix their sex life by doing weirdo exercises naked in the pool with some Zen master bozo. You California weirdos just kill me."

"The police report?" Hannah pressed politely.

"Oh, yeah, well this yogi Zen guru guy had to call the cops because they were all in the pool doing some sex thing, when all of a sudden old Wanda started spitting water and yelling her head off that her husband Walter had tried to drown her. She got so hysterical the yogi guy had to call the cops. Walter told them he just got the instructions wrong and didn't mean to get her in that underwater chokehold for so long. One of the cops said he didn't much blame Walter anyway when he heard from a couple of other people in the class how Wanda was barking sex orders at him like some kind of drill sergeant. But even though the next day Wanda dropped the assault charges, I figured she wouldn't want something like that broadcasted. When I told her about it she almost fainted. But I said as long as Signatech didn't move here, it would all stay quiet. She saw things my way." Lorna stuck out her hand. "So we're even, right?"

Hannah burst out laughing. "We're even. Thank you. You couldn't have gotten me a better present, on several levels." She hugged Ox, then Lorna. Lorna pulled quickly away, embarrassed.

"Listen, I've got to go to the little girls' room, since we don't want to be taking too many pee breaks once we hit the road," Lorna said. "Could you take care of Oxie until I get back?"

As soon as Lorna was gone, Ox stared at his hands, being unusually silent. Hannah wondered what was bothering him.

"Thanks for helping with Signatech," she said, trying to put him at ease. "I know it was your idea."

His soft, serious brown eyes met hers. "I owed you."

The vibrations between them subtly changed, Hannah knowing Ox had moved on to a new subject.

"Why do you owe me?"

"Because it was me who locked you in that shed and set fire to it."

Hannah felt the blood drain from her face. She had assumed that Maggie had done it even though Maggie had sworn to the police that she hadn't. But as long as Maggie went to prison for

Charlie's murder, that was enough for Hannah. In her mind, she had filed the shed incident neatly away in the category of justice served. This new information floored her.

"I know you're upset, Mrs. Malloy."

"Upset doesn't . . . it doesn't describe it."

"I've got to explain quick before Lornie comes back. She doesn't know. You see, I thought she'd killed Al, that her asking you to help us was just her trying to convince me she hadn't done it. That's why I confessed to killing him. I didn't want her to go to jail. I was following you around, looking for a way to scare you, that's all. I knew you were smarter than Lornie gave you credit for, and that if Lornie killed Al, you'd find out. I had to stop you. But I only wanted to scare you. That's all it was." He edged closer. "I'm asking you to forgive me for what happened in that shed."

Hannah jerked backward. "Forgive you? You put us in a situation where we might have been identified by dental records."

"You're wrong, I swear," he pleaded. "I was watching from the bushes the whole time. Those bags of dirt were piled inside, so I knew if I set fire to that part of the shed you'd have plenty of time to get out."

"How did you even know the bags were there?"

"I'd looked inside the shed when I was poking around Al's house the day he died. I couldn't resist checking out his gardening tools. And I remembered that there was a little spike there on the counter. I thought you'd use it to lift up the latch from the inside and open the door."

"Where did you get the gasoline?"

"Al's garage. I saw that too when I was looking around. I got scared when you didn't come out right away. I still don't get it. With that spike you should have been out of there in two seconds."

Hannah thought back on that terrible day and remembered Kiki breaking the spike on her boot. There was no way Ox could have predicted that. No one could predict Kiki.

"And you finally opened the door latch yourself?"

He nodded. "I'm sorry I scared you so bad. It was a crazy thing to do, but I wasn't thinking straight. I was so worried about Lornie."

His tone was beseeching, that of a child making excuses and begging forgiveness. In a way, Ox was like a child, Hannah thought. Naïve, vulnerable, unaware of the harm he could cause.

"Here's what I don't understand. Kiki saw that red mark through the gap in the wall, and she checked your ankles."

Ox rolled up his sleeve and showed Hannah two curved red lines tattooed on either side of his inner elbow. He bent his arm and the two curves came together to form a set of pouty lips. "I got it when I was in the army."

The door opened, letting in a short burst of music as Lorna strutted in. She looked at Ox, then at Hannah. "What's going on here? You both look funny."

Ox's cheeks turned pink.

"He's telling me about Hearst Castle," Hannah said. Ox's shoulders slumped with relief.

"Great, well, come on babe, we've got to skedaddle if we're going to cover any ground tonight." She gave Hannah's arm a small punch. "We want to start checking out properties right away for our new chocolate shop. You'll be getting a box from our grand opening." Lorna winked. "And I know deep down you want the sexy stuff."

Ox bent down and kissed Hannah on the cheek, then Lorna pulled him away, Hannah following them into the assembly room. They disappeared into the crowd, Ox's head bobbing above the sea of people. He looked back at her, and as he did, she realized he never would have risked telling her about what happened at the shed if he had meant any harm to her or her sister. He was so big, dumb, and sweet. Not exactly the son she wished she could have had, but still. She smiled her forgiveness and Ox grinned.

Bertha Malone, dressed in a denim dress and enough silver jewelry to fill a boutique, tapped the microphone. "We'd like to get started," she bellowed, her voice bouncing against the walls. Hannah found a seat in the fifth row, Kiki nowhere to be found. Once the crowd was seated, the music stopped, and Bertha welcomed everyone, then introduced Wanda. There was enthusiastic applause as Wanda glided out, her arms raised in triumph. She kept blowing kisses and taking bows for a good thirty seconds after the applause ended. Her speech was the same growth and Gucci pabulum she had been dishing out for weeks, but now there was a new and interesting angle. She spoke of how the town needed to maintain its villagy atmosphere and control rampant growth, giving the first hint that Signatech was out of the picture. Change did not always mean progress, Wanda said, stealing Hannah's campaign words, but Hannah didn't mind.

During Wanda's speech, Hannah looked around for Kiki, but didn't see her. She did see Naomi standing by the back door near the wall. Wanda was talking about town-funded inner selfness seminars when suddenly the lights went out. A disturbed rumble ran through the crowd, and then the lights popped on again, followed by a collective gasp. Hannah looked at the stage and saw a set of rotund, pinkish buttocks pressed against the large picture window behind Wanda, just to her right. Wanda continued on about the town's future, her brow corrugating at the audience's laughter and the especially loud and disruptive guffaw coming from Walter in the first row.

Wanda glanced worriedly at Bertha and saw her friend staring with a shocked frown at the window, but as soon as Wanda turned around to check it out for herself the room again went dark. After a couple of seconds the lights came back on. Wanda looked again, but the buttocks were gone, and along with them any semblance of dignity for the inauguration. She stumbled through the rest of her speech as best she could, mystified by the continuing snickers. She remained unaware of the large, roundish smudge on the glass behind her that kept the previous display of plump derriere fresh in the audience's memory, their thoughts buzzing over who in town had the bravado and the breadth of hip to commit such an audacious act.

Hannah looked back at Naomi, who had sidled safely away from the light switches. They caught each other's eyes, both of them stifling their laughter, well aware that those buttocks had been a size fourteen petite.